"You make it sound like I'm your cheating wife."

She sighed. "I didn't leave you. I left my job."

But she *had* left him, Mac thought. It hadn't felt like an employee walking out, but a betrayal.

"Same thing." His gaze fixed on her and for the first time, he noticed that she wore a tiny tank top and a silky pair of drawstring pants. Her feet were bare and her toenails were painted a soft blush pink. Her hair was long and loose over her shoulders, just skimming the tops of her breasts.

Mac took a breath and wondered where that flash of heat swamping him had come from. He'd been with Andi nearly every day for the past six years and he'd never reacted to her like this before. Sure, she was pretty, but she was his assistant. The one stable, organized, efficient woman in his life, and he'd never taken the time to notice that she was so much more than that.

Now it was all he could notice.

Cardiff Libraries
www.cardiff.gov.uk/libraries

Llyfrgelloedd Caerdyd
CARDIFF
CAERDYDD www.caerdydd.gov.uk/llyfrgelloe

A Bride for the Boss is part of the series: Texas Cattlemen's Club:

D0544394

A BRIDE FOR THE BOSS

BY
MAUREEN CHILD

MILLS & BOON

All rights reserved including the right of reproduction in whole or in part in any form. This edition is published by arrangement with Harlequin Books S.A.

This is a work of fiction. Names, characters, places, locations and incidents are purely fictional and bear no relationship to any real life individuals, living or dead, or to any actual places, business establishments, locations, events or incidents. Any resemblance is entirely coincidental.

This book is sold subject to the condition that it shall not, by way of trade or otherwise, be lent, resold, hired out or otherwise circulated without the prior consent of the publisher in any form of binding or cover other than that in which it is published and without a similar condition including this condition being imposed on the subsequent purchaser.

® and ™ are trademarks owned and used by the trademark owner and/or its licensee. Trademarks marked with ® are registered with the United Kingdom Patent Office and/or the Office for Harmonisation in the Internal Market and in other countries.

First Published in Great Britain 2016
By Mills & Boon, an imprint of HarperCollins*Publishers*
1 London Bridge Street, London, SE1 9GF

© 2016 Harlequin Books S.A.

Special thanks and acknowledgement are given to Maureen Child for her contribution to the Texas Cattleman's Club: Lies and Lullabies series.

ISBN: 978-0-263-91864-9

51-0616

Our policy is to use papers that are natural, renewable and recyclable products and made from wood grown in sustainable forests. The logging and manufacturing processes conform to the legal environmental regulations of the country of origin.

Printed and bound in Spain
by CPI, Barcelona

Maureen Child writes for the Mills & Boon Desire line and can't imagine a better job.

A seven-time finalist for a prestigious Romance Writers of America RITA® Award, Maureen is an author of more than one hundred romance novels. Her books regularly appear on bestseller lists and have won several awards, including a Prism Award, a National Readers' Choice Award, a Colorado Romance Writers Award of Excellence and a Golden Quill Award. She is a native Californian but has recently moved to the mountains of Utah.

To all of the wonderful writers in this fabulous continuity series—it's been an honour working with all of you.

And to Charles Griemsman, thanks for being such a great editor and for not tearing your hair out during this process!

One

"What do you mean, *you quit*?" David "Mac" McCallum stared at his assistant and shook his head. "If this is a joke, it's not funny."

Andrea Beaumont took a deep breath, then said sharply, "Not a joke, Mac. I'm dead serious."

He could see that, and he didn't much care for it. Usually when Andi stepped into his office, it was to remind him of a meeting or a phone call, or to tell him she'd come up with some new way to organize his life and business.

But at the moment, she had angry glints firing in her normally placid gray eyes, and he'd do well to pay attention. Having a younger sister had taught him early to watch his step around women. Violet had a temper that could peel paint, and Mac knew that a wise man stayed out of range when a woman got a certain look about her.

Right now, Andi—his calm, cool, organized executive assistant—appeared to be ready for battle.

Andi looked the same as always, even though she was in the middle of tossing his well-ordered world upside down. June sunlight slipped through the wide windows at Mac's back and poured over her like molten gold. Her long, straight, dark brown hair hung past the shoulders of the pale blue blazer she wore over a white dress shirt and dark blue jeans. Black boots, shined to a mirror gleam, finished off the outfit. Her storm-gray eyes were fixed on him unblinkingly and her full, generous mouth was pinched into a grim slash of determination.

Looked like they were about to have a "discussion."

Mac braced himself. Whatever she had in mind just wasn't going to fly. He couldn't afford to lose her. Hell, running McCallum Enterprises was a full-time job for ten men and damned if he'd let the woman who knew his business as well as he did simply walk away.

She'd been his right-hand man—woman—*person*— for the last six years and Mac couldn't imagine being without her. When something needed doing, Andi got it done. Mac didn't have to look over her shoulder, making sure things were handled. He could tell her what he needed and not worry about it. Andi had a knack for seeing a problem and figuring out the best way to take care of it.

She could smooth talk anyone, and if that didn't work, he'd seen her give an opponent a cool-eyed glare that could turn their blood cold. There'd been plenty of times when Mac had actually enjoyed watching her stare down an adversary. But he had to say, being on the receiving end of that icy look wasn't nearly as enjoyable.

What had brought this on?

"Why don't you take a seat and tell me what's got you so angry."

"I don't want a seat," she said. "And I don't want to be soothed like you do those horses you love so much..."

He frowned. "Then what exactly do you want?"

"I already told you. I want to quit."

"Why the hell would you want to do that?"

Her gray eyes went wide, as if she couldn't believe he even had to ask that question. But as far as Mac knew, everything was just as it should be. They'd closed the Donaldson deal the day before and now McCallum Enterprises could add Double D Energy Services to its ledgers. And Andi'd had a lot to do with getting David Donaldson to sign on the dotted line.

"I just gave you a raise last night for your work on the energy project."

"I know," she said. "And I earned it. That deal was not pretty."

"So what's the problem?"

"You told me to take over the planning for Violet's baby shower."

He drew his head back and narrowed his eyes on her in shocked surprise. With her talent for list making and organization, Andi should be able to handle that shower in a finger snap. "That's a problem? I thought you and Vi were friends."

"We *are*," she countered, throwing both hands high. "Of course we are. That's not the point."

"What *is* the point, then?" Mac dropped into his chair and, lifting his booted feet, crossed them at the ankle on the edge of the desk. "Spit it out already and let's get back to work."

"For one, *you* don't decide on Vi's baby shower. For heaven's sake, you stick your nose into everything."

"Excuse me?"

"But my main point is," she said, setting both hands at her hips, "I'm tired of being taken for granted."

"Who does that?" he asked, sincerely confused.

"*You* do!"

"Now, that's just not so," he argued. "Let's remember that raise yesterday and—"

"In the last day or so, you had me arrange for the new horse trailer to be dropped off at the ranch. I called Big Mike at the garage to get him to give your car a tune-up before the weekend, then I saw to it that the new horses you bought will be delivered to the ranch tomorrow afternoon."

Scowling now, Mac bit back on what he wanted to say and simply let her get it all out.

"I drew up the plans for the kitchen garden your cook wants for behind the house and I made sure the new baby furniture you're giving Vi was delivered on time." Andi paused only long enough to take a breath. Her eyes flashed, her mouth tightened as she continued. "Then I called Sheriff Battle to make sure he cleared the road for the delivery of the last of the cattle water tanks."

"Had to clear the road—"

"Not finished," she said, holding up one hand to keep him quiet. "After that, I bought and had delivered the standard half-carat diamond bracelet and the it's-not-you-it's-me farewell note to the model who can't string ten words together without hyperventilating…"

Mac snorted. All right, she had a point about Jezebel Fontaine. Still, in his defense, Jez was seriously built enough that he'd overlooked her lack of brain cells for the past month. But even he had his limits.

"You're my assistant, aren't you?"

"I am and a darn good one," she countered. "I've kept your life running on schedule for the last six years, Mac. No matter what you throw at me, I handle it and add it into the mix I'm already juggling."

"You're a damn fine juggler, too," he said.

She kept talking as if he hadn't said a thing.

"Then when I asked you for this afternoon off so I could go see my nephew's baseball game, you said you had to *think* about it. *Think about it?*"

"I appreciate a good Little League game as much as the next man," Mac said slowly, keeping his gaze fixed on hers, "but we've still got some details to be ironed out on the Double D deal and—"

"That's my point, Mac." His eyes widened when she interrupted him. "There's always *something* that needs to be handled and I'm so busy taking care of those things I haven't had time to find a *life*."

"You've got a pretty good life from where I'm standing," he argued, pushing up from his desk. "Great job, terrific boss—" He paused, waiting for a smile that didn't come, then tried to continue, but he couldn't come up with a third thing.

"Uh-huh. Job. Boss. No life." She took a deep breath. "And that stops today."

"Okay," he said flatly. "If it's that important to you, go. See your nephew's game. Have some popcorn. Hell, have a beer. We'll talk more tomorrow morning when you come in."

"I won't be in," she said, shaking her head. "It's time for a change, Mac. For both of us. I've gotten too comfortable here and so have you."

He laughed abruptly. "You call dealing with what all that's been going on around here *comfortable*?"

She nodded. "There've been problems, sure, but we handled them and things are slowly getting back to normal. Or, as normal as life gets around here."

Mac sure as hell hoped so. It had been a wild time in Royal, Texas, over the past couple of years. A lot of turmoil, more than their share of trouble. There was the tornado, of course, then the drought that held most of Texas in a tight, sweaty fist and then a man he used to think of as one of his oldest friends, Rafiq "Rafe" bin Saleed, had come to town with the express purpose of ruining Mac's reputation, his business and his family. And he'd come damn close to pulling it off.

Remembering that was still enough to leave Mac a little shaken. Hell, he'd trusted Rafe and had almost lost everything because of it. Sure, they'd worked everything out, and now Rafe was even his brother-in-law, since he and Mac's sister, Violet, were married and having a baby.

But there were still moments when Mac wondered how he could have missed the fact that Rafe was on a misguided quest for revenge.

Without Andi to help him through and talk him down when he was so damned angry he could hardly see straight, Mac didn't know if the situation would have resolved itself so quickly.

So why, when life was settling down again, had she chosen *now* to talk about quitting? Mac had no idea what had brought this nonsense on, but he'd nip it in the bud, fast. Now that things were calming down in Royal, Mac had plans to spend more time actually working and even expanding the family ranch, which Violet used to handle. With his sister focusing on the place Rafe had bought for them, Mac wanted to get back to his roots: being on a horse, overseeing the day-to-day decisions of ranch life and working out of a home office to keep his wildly divergent business interests growing.

Life was damn busy and Andi was just going to have to stay right where she was to help him run things—the way she always had.

"Where's this coming from, Andi?" he asked, leaning one hip against the corner of his desk.

"The fact that you can even ask me that is astonishing," she replied.

He gave her a slow grin, the very same smile that worked to sway women across Texas into agreeing with anything he said. Of course, Andrea Beaumont had always been a tougher sell, but he'd use whatever weapons he had to hand. "Now, Andi," he said, "we've worked together too long for you to get snippy so easily."

"Snippy?" Her eyes fired up again and Mac thought for a second or two that she might reach up and yank at her hair. "That is the most insulting thing…"

She took another deep breath and Mac idly noticed how those heavy breaths she kept taking made her small, perfect breasts rise and fall rhythmically. For such a tiny woman, she had curves in all the right places. Funny he'd really not taken the time to notice that before.

Andi was simply *there*. She kept on top of everything. Nothing ever slipped past her. But apparently *this* had slipped past *him*.

"This is coming out of the blue and I think you owe me some sort of explanation."

"It's *not* out of the blue, Mac," she said, throwing both hands high. "That's the point. I've worked for you for six years."

"I know that."

"Uh-huh. And did you notice I didn't even take a va-cation the last two years?"

His frown deepened. No, he hadn't noticed. Proba-bly should have, though, since every damn time she *did* take some time off, he ended up hunting her down, get-ting her to solve some damn problem or other. The fact that she'd stayed here, working, had only made his life continue on its smooth, well-planned path, so he hadn't had to think about it.

"Is that what this is about?" He pushed off the desk, braced his feet wide apart and folded his arms across his chest. "You want a vacation?"

Her mouth flattened into a straight, grim line. "No. I want a life. To get that life, I have to quit. So, I'm giv-ing you my two weeks' notice."

"I don't accept that."

"You don't get a vote, Mac."

"See," he said tightly, "that doesn't fly with me, either."

It was like talking to two brick walls, Andrea thought, staring up at the man who had been her focus for the past six years. About six foot one, he had short, dark blond hair that in another month or so would be shot through with sun streaks. His summer-green eyes were cool, clear and always held a sort of calculating gleam his competi-tors usually took for affability. He was lean but strong, his build almost deceptively lanky.

Mac McCallum was the stuff women's dreams were made of. Sadly, that was true of Andi's dreams, too.

Six years she'd worked for him. She wasn't sure ex-actly when she'd made the supreme mistake of falling in love with her boss, but it seemed as if those feelings had always been with her. A part of her had always hoped that one day he might open his eyes and really *see* her—but the more rational, reasonable part of Andi knew that was never going to happen.

To Mac, she would always be good ol' Andi. She knew he saw her as he did the new laser printer in the office. Efficient, able to get the job done and nearly invisible. The raise he'd given her notwithstanding, he didn't really appreciate just how hard she worked to keep McCallum Enterprises running smoothly—he just expected it. Well, it had taken her a long time to reach this point, but she really wanted a life. And as long as she was here, mooning after a man she couldn't have, that wouldn't happen. Andi had been working up to quitting for a long while now, and today had finally given her the last little nudge she'd needed.

It was liberation day.

"Go on, Andi. Go to your nephew's game. Enjoy the rest of the day and we'll talk about this again when you calm down."

He still didn't get it, and she knew that she had to make herself clear. "I'm completely calm, Mac. I'm just done."

A slow, disbelieving smile curved his mouth, and Andi told herself to stay strong. Stay resolved. There was no future for her here. But watching him, she realized that he would spend her two weeks'-notice time doing everything he could to change her mind. Knowing just how charming he could be was enough to convince her to say, "I haven't had a vacation in two years. So I'm going to take my vacation time for the next two weeks."

"You're just going to leave the office flat?" Stunned now, he stared at her as if she had two heads. "What about the contracts for the Stevenson deal? Or the negotiations on the Franklin Heating project?"

"Laura's up-to-date on all of it and if she needs me," Andi said firmly, "she can call and I'll be happy to walk her through whatever problem she's having."

"Laura's the office manager."

True, Andi thought, and though the woman had been with the company for only a couple of years, she was bright, ambitious and a hard worker. And as a newly-wed, she wouldn't be spinning romantic fantasies about her boss.

"You're serious?" he asked, dumbfounded. *"Now?"*

"Right now," Andi told him and felt a faint flutter of excitement tangled with just a touch of fear.

She was really going to do it. Going to quit the job she'd dedicated herself to for years. Going to walk away from the man who had a hold on her heart whether he knew it or not. She was going out into the world to find herself a life.

With that thought firmly in mind, she turned and headed for the door before Mac could talk her out of leaving.

"I don't believe this," he muttered.

Can't really blame him, she thought. This was the first time since she'd met Mac that she was doing something for herself.

Andi paused in the doorway and glanced back over her shoulder for one last look at him. He was everything she'd ever wanted and she'd finally accepted that she would never have him. "Goodbye, Mac."

Outside, the June sunlight streamed down from a brassy blue sky. Summer was coming and it seemed in a hurry to get here. Andi's footsteps crunched on the gravel of the employee parking area behind the office.

With every step, she felt a little more certain that what she was doing was right. Sure, it was hard, and likely to get harder because Andi would miss seeing Mac every day. But hadn't she spent enough time mooning over him? How would she ever find a man to spend her life with if she spent all her time around the one man she couldn't have?

"Just keep walking, Andi. You'll be glad of it later." Much later, of course. Because at the moment, she felt as if she couldn't breathe.

What she needed was affirmation and she knew just where to find it. When she got to her car, Andi opened the door and slid into the dark blue compact. Then she pulled her cell phone from her purse, hit the speed dial and waited through five rings before a familiar voice answered.

"Thank God you called," her sister, Jolene, said. "Tom's shift ended two hours ago and now that he's home, he says he needs to unwind…"

Andi laughed and it felt good. "So which wall is he tearing down?"

Jolene sighed. "The one between the living room and the kitchen."

While her sister talked, Andi could picture exactly what was happening in the old Victorian on the far side of Royal. Her brother-in-law, Tom, was a fireman who relaxed by working on his house. Last year, after a brushfire that had kept him working for more than a week, he built a new powder room on the first floor.

"It's a good thing you bought a fixer-upper," Andi said when her older sister had wound down.

"I know." Laughing, Jolene added, "I swear the man's crazy. But he's all mine."

Andi smiled sadly, caught her expression in the rearview mirror and silently chastised herself for feeling even the slightest twinge of envy. Jolene and Tom had been married for ten years and had three kids, with another on the way. Their family was a sort of talisman for Andi. Seeing her sister happy and settled with her family made Andi want the same for herself.

Which was just one of the reasons she'd had to quit her job. Before it was too late for her to find what her heart craved. Love. Family.

"And," Jolene was saying, "I love that my kitchen's about to get a lot bigger. But oh, Lord, the noise. Hang on, I'm headed out to the front porch so I can hear you."

Andi listened to the crashing and banging in the background fade as her sister walked farther away from the demolition zone.

"Okay, backyard. That's better," Jolene said. "So, what's going on, little sister?"

"I did it." Andi blew out a breath and rolled her car windows down to let the warm Texas wind slide past her. "I quit."

"Holy…" Jolene paused and Andi imagined her sister's shocked expression. "Really? You quit your job?"

"I did." Andi slapped one hand to her chest to keep her pounding heart from leaping out. "Walked right out before I could change my mind."

"I can't believe it."

"You and me both," Andi said. "Oh, God. I'm *unemployed*."

Jolene laughed. "It's not like you're living on the streets, Andi. You've got a house you hardly ever see, a vacation fund that you've never used and a rainy-day savings account that has enough in it to keep you safe through the next biblical flood."

"You're right, you're right." Nodding, Andi took a few deep breaths and told herself to calm down. "It's just, I haven't been unemployed since I was sixteen."

The reality of the situation was hitting home and it came like a fist to the solar plexus. If this kept up, she might faint and wouldn't that be embarrassing, having Mac come out to the parking lot and find her stretched out across her car seats?

She'd quit her job.

What would she do every day? How would she live? Sure, she'd had a few ideas over the past few months about what she might want to do, but none of it was carved in stone. She hadn't looked into the logistics of anything, she hadn't made even the first list of what she'd need do before moving on one of her ideas, so it was all too nebulous to even think about.

She had time. Plenty of time to consider her future, to look at her ideas objectively. She would need plans. Purpose. Goals. But she wasn't going to have those right away, so it was time to take a breath. No point in making herself totally insane. Jolene was right. Andi had a big savings account—Mac was a generous employer if nothing else—and it wasn't as if she'd had time to spend that generous salary. Now she did.

"This is so great, Andi."

"Easy for you to say."

Jolene laughed again, then shouted, "Jilly, don't push your sister into the pool."

Anyone else hearing that would immediately think built-in, very deep pool. In reality, Andi knew the kids were jumping in and out of a two-foot-deep wading pool. Shallow enough to be safe and wet enough to give relief from the early Texas heat.

"Jacob's game still at five today?" Andi asked abruptly.

"Sure. You're coming?"

Of course she was going to the game. She'd quit her job so she'd be able to see her family. She smiled at her reflection as she imagined the look on Jacob's little face when she showed up at the town baseball field. "You couldn't keep me away."

"Look at that—only been unemployed like a second and already you're getting a life."

Andi rolled her eyes. Jolene had been on her to quit for the past few years, insisting that standing still meant stagnating. As it turned out, she had a point. Andi had given Mac all she could give. If she stayed, she'd only end up resenting him and infuriated with herself. So it was no doubt past time to go. Move on.

And on her first official day of freedom, she was going to the Royal Little League field to watch her nephew's game. "I'm just going home to change and I'll meet you at the field in an hour or so."

"We'll be there. Jacob will be so excited. And after the game, you'll come back here. Tom will grill us all some steaks to go with the bottle of champagne I'm making a point of picking up. You can drink my share."

Andi forced a smile into her voice. "Champagne and steaks. Sounds like a plan."

But after she hung up with her sister, Andi had to ask herself why, instead of celebrating, she felt more like going home for a good cry.

Two

Andi went to the baseball game. Jolene had been right: eight-year-old Jacob was thrilled that his aunt was there, cheering for him alongside his parents. Of course, six-year-old Jilly and three-year-old Jenna were delighted to share their bag of gummy bears with Andi, and made plans for a tea party later in the week.

It had felt odd to be there, in the bleachers with family and friends, when normally she would have been at work. But it was good, too, she kept telling herself.

After the game, she had dinner with her family and every time her mind drifted to thoughts of Mac, Andi forced it away again. Instead, she focused on the kids, her sister and the booming laugh of her brother-in-law as he flipped steaks on a smoking grill.

By the following morning, she told herself that if she'd stayed with Mac and kept the job that had consumed her life, she wouldn't have had that lazy, easy afternoon and evening. But still she had doubts. Even though she'd enjoyed herself, the whole thing had been so far out of her comfort zone, Andi knew she'd have to do some fine-tuning of her relaxation skills. But at least now she had the time to try.

Sitting on her front porch swing, cradling a cup of coffee in her hands, Andi looked up at the early-morning sky and saw her own nebulous future staring back at her. Normally by this time she was already at the office, brewing the first of many pots of coffee, going over her and Mac's calendars and setting up conference calls and meetings. There would already be the kind of tension she used to live for as she worked to keep one step ahead of everything.

Now? She took another sip of coffee and sighed. The quiet crowded in on her until it felt as though she could hear her own heartbeat in the silence. Relaxation turned to tension in a finger snap. She was unemployed and, for the first time since she was a kid, had nowhere in particular to be.

It was both liberating and a little terrifying. She was a woman who thrived on schedules, preferred order and generally needed a plan for anything she was going to do. Even as a kid, she'd had her closet tidy, her homework done early and her bookcases in her room alphabetized for easy reference.

While Jolene's bedroom had been chaotic, Andi's was an island of peace and calm. A place for everything, everything in its place. Some might call that compulsive. She called it organized. And maybe that was just what she needed to do now. Organize her new world. Channel energies she would normally be using for Mac and his business into her own life. She was smart, capable and tenacious. There was nothing she couldn't do.

"So." After that inner pep talk, she drew her feet up under her on the thick, deep blue cushion. "I'll make a plan. Starting," she said, needing the sound of her own voice in the otherwise still air, "with finally getting my house in shape."

She'd bought the run-down farmhouse a year ago and hadn't even had the time to unpack most of the boxes stacked in the second bedroom. The walls hadn't been painted, there were no pictures hung, no rugs scattered across the worn, scarred floor. It pretty much looked as lonely and abandoned as it had when she first bought it. And wasn't that all kinds of sad and depressing?

Until a year ago, Andi had lived in a tiny condo that was, in its own way, as impersonal and unfinished as this house. She'd rented it furnished and had never had the time—or the inclination—to put her own stamp on the place. Working for Mac had meant that she was on duty practically twenty-four hours a day. So when was she supposed to be able to carve out time for herself? But in spite of everything, Andi had wanted a home of her own. And in the back of her mind, maybe she'd been planning even then on leaving McCallum Enterprises.

Leaving Mac.

It was the only explanation for her buying a house that she had known going in would need a lot of renovation. Sure, she could have hired a crew to come in and fix it all up. And she had had a new roof put on, the plumbing upgraded and the electrical brought up to code. But there were still the yards to take care of, the floors to be sanded, the walls to be painted and furniture to be bought.

"And that starts today," she said, pushing off the swing. With one more look around the wide front yard, she turned and opened the screen door, smiling as it screeched in protest. Inside, she took another long glance at her home before heading into the kitchen to do what she did best. Make a list.

She knew where she'd start. The walls should be painted before she brought in sanders for the floors, and they'd probably need a couple of coats of paint to cover the shadow images of long-missing paintings.

In the kitchen she sat at a tiny table and started making notes. She'd go at her home exactly as she would have a new project at McCallum. Priorities. It was all about priorities.

An hour later, she had several lists and the beginnings of a plan.

"There's a lot to do," she said, her voice echoing in the old, empty house. "Might as well get started."

She worked for hours, sweeping, dusting, mopping, before heading into Royal to buy several gallons of paint. Of course, shopping in town was never as easy as entering a store, getting what you wanted and then leaving again. There were people to chat with, gossip to listen to and, as long as she was there, she stopped in at the diner for some tea and a salad she didn't have to make herself.

The air conditioning felt wonderful against her skin, and Andi knew if it was this hot in early June, summer was going to be a misery. She made a mental note to put in a call to Joe Bennet at Bennet Heating and Cooling. If she was going to survive a Texas summer, she was going to need her own air conditioning. Fast.

"So," Amanda Battle said as she gave Andi a refill on

her iced tea. "I hear you quit your job and you're running off to Jamaica with your secret lover."

Andi choked on a cherry tomato and, when she got her breath back, reached for her tea and took a long drink. Looking up at Amanda, wife of Sheriff Nathan Battle and owner of the diner, she saw humor shining in her friend's eyes.

"Jamaica?"

Amanda grinned. "Sally Hartsfield told me, swears that Margie Fontenot got the story direct from Laura, who used to work with you at Mac's. Well, Laura's cousin's husband's sister got the story started and that is good enough to keep the grapevine humming for a while."

Direct was probably not the right word to describe that line of communication, but Andi knew all too well how the gossip chain worked in town. It was only mildly irritating to find out that she was now the most interesting link in that chain. For the moment.

But Jamaica? How did people come up with this stuff? she wondered, and only briefly considered taking her first vacation in years, if only to make that rumor true. Still, if she went to Jamaica, it would be a lot more fun if she could make the secret-lover part of the gossip true, too.

"Secret lover?" If only, she thought wistfully as an image of Mac rose up in her mind.

"Oooh. I like how your eyes got all shiny there for a second. Tells me there might be something to this particular rumor. Something you'd like to share with a pal? Wait." Amanda held up one finger. "Gotta fill some coffee cups. Don't go anywhere until I get back."

While she was gone, Andi concentrated on the sounds and scents of the Royal Diner. Everything was so familiar; sitting there was like being wrapped up in a cozy blanket. Even when you knew that everyone in town was now talking about *you*. Royal had had plenty of things to chew over the past couple years. From the tornado to an actual *sheikh* working a revenge plot against Mac, local tongues had been kept wagging.

And the diner was gossip central—well, here and the Texas Cattleman's Club. But since the club was limited to members only, Andi figured the diner was the big winner in the grapevine contest.

She looked around and pretended not to notice when other customers quickly shifted their gazes. The black-and-white-tile floor was spotless, the red vinyl booths and counter stools were shiny and clean, and the place, as always, was packed.

God, she hated knowing that mostly everyone in there was now talking and speculating about her. But short of burying her head in the sand or locking herself in her own house, there was no way to avoid any of it.

Amanda worked the counter while her sister, Pamela, and Ruby Fowler worked the tables. Conversations rose and fell like the tides, and the accompanying sounds of silverware against plates and the clink of glasses added a sort of background music to the pulse of life.

When Amanda finally came back, Andi mused, "Where did Laura come up with Jamaica, I wonder?"

"Nothing on the secret lover then?" Amanda asked.

Andi snorted. "Who has time for a lover?"

Amanda gave her a sympathetic look, reached out and patted her hand. "Honey, that's so sad. You've got to make time."

She would if she had the option of the lover she wanted. But since she didn't, why bother with anyone else? "How can I when I'm going to Jamaica? But again, why Jamaica?"

"Maybe wishful thinking," Amanda said with a shrug, leaning down to brace folded arms on the counter. "Heaven knows, lying on a beach having somebody bring me lovely alcoholic drinks while I cuddle with my honey sounds pretty good to me most days."

"Okay, sounds pretty good to me, too," Andi said. If she *had* a honey. "Instead, I'm headed home to start painting."

Amanda straightened up. "You're planning on painting your place on your own? It'll take you weeks."

"As the gossip chain informed you already," she said wryly, "I'm unemployed, so I've got some time."

"Well," Amanda said, walking to the register to ring up Andi's bill, "using that time to paint rather than find yourself that secret lover seems a waste to me. And, if you change your mind, there's any number of kids around town who would paint for you. Summer jobs are hard to come by in a small town."

"I'll keep it in mind. Thanks." Andi paid, slung her purse over her shoulder and said, "Say hi to Nathan for me."

"I'll do that. And say hi to Jamaica for me." Amanda gave her a wink, then went off to check on her customers again.

Several hours later, Andi knew she should have been tired. Instead, she was energized, and by the end of her first day as a free woman, the living room was painted a cool, rich green the color of the Texas hills in springtime. It would need another coat, but even now she saw the potential and loved it. She had a sense of accomplish-

ment, of simple satisfaction, which she hadn't felt in far
too long. Yes, she'd been successful in her career, but
that was Mac's business. His empire. This little farmhouse, abandoned for years, was all *hers*. And she was
going to bring it back to life. Make it shine as it had to
some long-gone family.

"And maybe by the time it's whole and happy again,
I will be, too," she said.

"Talking to yourself?" a female voice said from the
front porch. "Not a good sign."

Andi spun around and grinned. "Violet! Come on in."

Mac's sister opened the screen door and let it slap
closed behind her. Being nearly seven months pregnant
hadn't stopped Vi from dressing like the rancher she
was. She wore a pale yellow T-shirt that clung to her
rounded belly, a pair of faded blue jeans and the dusty
brown boots she preferred to anything else.

Her auburn hair was pulled into a high ponytail at
the back of her head and her clear green eyes swept the
freshly painted walls in approval. When she looked back
at Andi, she nodded. "Nice job. Really. Love the darker
green as trim, too. Makes the whole thing pop."

"Thanks." Andi took another long look and sighed.
"I'll go over it again tomorrow. But I love it. This color
makes the room feel cool, you know? And with summer coming…"

"It's already hot," Vi said. "You are getting air conditioning put in, right?"

"Oh, yeah. Called them at about eight this morning,
as soon as the sun came up and started sizzling. They're
backed up, though, so it'll be a week or two before they
can come out here."

"Well," Vi said, walking into the kitchen as comfortably as she would at her own house. "If you start melting before then, you can come and stay with Rafe and me at the ranch."

"Ah, yes," Andi said, following her friend into her kitchen—which was comfortably stuck in the 1950s. "What a good time. I can be the third wheel with the newlyweds."

"We don't have sex in front of people, you know," Vi told her with a laugh. "We tried, but the housekeeper Rafe hired disapproved."

She stuck her head in the refrigerator, pulled out a pitcher of tea and sighed with pleasure. "Knew I could count on you to have tea all ready to go. You get glasses. Do you have any cookies?"

"Some Oreos." They'd been friends for so long, they worked in tandem. "In the pantry."

"Thank God."

Laughing, Andi filled two glasses with ice, then poured each of them some tea as Vi hurried into the walk-in pantry and came back out already eating a cookie. She sighed, rolled her eyes and moaned, "God, these are so good."

Still chuckling, Andi took a seat at the tiny table and watched her friend dig into the cookie bag for another. "Rafe still watching what you eat?"

Vi dropped into the chair opposite her, picked up her tea and took a long drink. "Like a hawk. He found my stash of Hershey's bars, so they're gone." She ate the next cookie with as much relish as she had the first. "I love the man like crazy but he's making me a little nuts. Although, one thing I'll say for him, he does keep ice cream stocked for me."

"Well, that's something," Andi agreed, taking a seat opposite her.

"But, wow, I miss cookies. And cake. And brownies. The only bad part about moving to the Wild Aces when I married Rafe? Leaving the Double M and our housekeeper Teresa's brownies. I swear they're magic." Vi sighed and reached for another cookie. "You want to make a batch of brownies?"

Andi really hated to quash the hopeful look on her friend's face, but said, "Oven doesn't work." Andi turned to look at the pastel pink gas stove. The burners worked fine, but the oven had been dead for years, she was willing to bet. "And it's too hot in here to bake anything."

"True." Vi turned her tea glass on the narrow kitchen table, studying the water ring it left behind. "And I didn't really come here to raid your pantry, either, in spite of the fact that I'm eating all of your Oreos."

"Okay, then why are you here?"

"I'm a spy," Violet said, laughing. "And I'm here to report that Mac is really twisted up about you quitting."

"Is he?" Well, that felt good, didn't it? She had long known that she was indispensable in the office. Now he knew it, too, and that thought brought her an immense wave of satisfaction. Instantly, a ping of guilt began to echo inside her, but Andi shut it down quickly. After all, it wasn't as if she *wanted* Mac to have a hard time. She was only taking the opportunity to enjoy the fact that he was. "How do you know?"

"Well, spy work isn't easy," Violet admitted. "We pregnant operatives must rely on information from reliable sources."

Andi laughed shortly. "You mean gossip."

"I resent that term," Violet said with an indignant

sniff. Then she shrugged and took another cookie. "Although, it's accurate. Mac hasn't actually said anything to me directly. *Yet*. But Laura called a couple hours ago practically in tears."

"What happened?" Andi asked. "Mac's not the kind of man to bring a woman to tears."

"I don't know," Violet said, smiling. "He's made me cry a few times."

"Angry tears don't count."

"Then Laura's tears don't count, either," Vi told her. "She was really mad—at *you* for leaving her alone in the office."

"Probably why she made up the Jamaica story," Andi muttered.

"Jamaica?"

"Never mind." She waved one hand to brush that away. "What did Mac do?"

"Nothing new. Just the same old crabby attitude you've been dealing with for years. Laura just doesn't know how to deal with it yet."

Okay, now she felt a little guilty. Mac could be…difficult. And maybe she should have used her two weeks' notice to prepare Laura for handling him. But damn it, *she'd* learned on her own, hadn't she? Laura was just going to have to suck it up and deal.

"Anyway," Vi continued, "I told her the best thing to do was stay out of his way when he starts grumbling under his breath. She said that's exactly what he was doing already and that the office was too small for her to effectively disappear."

Andi chuckled because she could imagine the woman trying to hunch into invisibility behind her desk. "Poor Laura. I really shouldn't laugh, though, should I? I sort of left her holding the bag, so to speak, and now she's having to put up with not only Mac's demands but the fact that I'm not there to take the heat off."

"Laura's tough. She can take it." Vi picked up a fourth cookie and sighed a little as she bit in. "Or she won't. Either way, her choice. And if she walks out, too? An even better lesson for Mac."

"You think?"

"Absolutely," his sister said, waving her cookie for emphasis before popping it into her mouth and talking around it while she chewed. "The man thinks he's the center of the universe and all the rest of us are just moons orbiting him.

"Maybe it really started when our parents died and he had to step up. You know, he's only six years older than me, but he went from big brother to overbearing father figure in a finger snap." She frowned a little, remembering. "We butted heads a lot, but in the end, Mac always found a way to win."

Andi knew most of this family history. Over the years, Mac had talked to her about the private plane crash that had claimed his parents and how he'd worked to make sure that Violet felt safe and secure despite the tragedy that had rocked their family. He'd done it, too. Violet was not only a successful, happy adult, she was married and about to become a mother.

Maybe he had been overbearing—and knowing Mac, she really had no doubt of that—but he'd protected his sister, kept the family ranch and even managed to build on the business his parents had left behind until McCallum Enterprises was one of the biggest, most diversified companies in the country.

In all fairness to him, Andi had to say, "Looks to me like he did a good job."

Violet shrugged and nodded. "Yeah, he did. But the thing is, he's so used to people snapping to attention whenever he walks into a room, I think it's good for him that you quit. That he's finding out he can't *always* win. It'll be a growth moment for him."

But Andi knew that growth wasn't always easy. She also knew she should feel bad about being glad that Mac would have a hard time without her.

Apparently, though, she wasn't that good a person.

She still wasn't there.

From the moment Mac walked into the office that morning, a part of him had fully expected to find Andi right where she belonged, at her desk. But she hadn't been.

Except for a few times when he'd had no other choice, Mac had spent most of the day ignoring Laura as she hunched behind her computer, pretending to be invisible. No doubt she'd been worried how the day would go without Andi there to take care of things.

Well, hell, he had been, too.

As it turned out, with reason.

"This day just couldn't get worse."

Mac left his office and fired a hard look at Laura. "I need the Franklin contracts. I tried to pull up the pdf and it's not where it's supposed to be. Bob Franklin just called, he's got some questions and—" He noticed the wide-eyed expression on Laura's face and told himself it was pointless to hammer at her.

This was Andi's territory. Turning, he stomped into the back of the building where Andi had stored hard copies of each of their in-progress deals in old-fashioned file cabinets. Of course, their records were mostly digitized and stored in the cloud, with several redundant backup sites so nothing could be lost. But there was something to say for holding a hard copy of a contract in your hands. It was immediate and more convenient, in his mind, than scrolling up and down a computer screen looking for a particular clause. Especially when you couldn't find the damn digital copy.

"And now I have to hunt down the stupid contract the hard way." He yanked open the top file drawer and started flipping through the manila separators. He made it through the *F*s and didn't find the Franklin takeover.

Shaking his head, he told himself that he was the damn *boss*. It wasn't up to him to find a damn contract on a damn deal they'd done only three weeks ago. The problem was it was *Andi's* job and she wasn't here to do it.

Laura was good at what she did and he had no doubt that in time she might grow to be even a third as good as Andi at the job. But for now, the woman was an office manager suddenly tossed into the deep end. There were a couple of part-time interns, too, but neither of them could find their way out of a paper bag without a flashlight and a map.

"So bottom line?" he muttered, slamming the drawer and then opening another one. "I'm screwed."

Normally, this late in the afternoon, he and Andi were huddled around his desk, talking about the day's work and what was coming up on the schedule. He really didn't want to admit how much he missed just talking to her. Having her there to bounce ideas off of. To help him strategize upcoming jobs.

"Plus, she would know exactly where the stupid contract is," he muttered.

Mac hated this. Hated having his life disrupted, his business interfered with—hell, his *world* set off balance. Worse, Andi had to have known this would happen when she walked out and, no doubt, she was sitting on a beach in Bimini right now, smiling at the thought of him trying to set things right again on his own.

"Take a vacation. Who the hell has time for a vacation?" he asked the empty file room. "If you love what you do, *work* is vacation enough, isn't it?" He slammed the second drawer shut and yanked the third open. What the hell kind of filing system was she using, anyway?

"She loved her work, too," he muttered. "Can't tell me otherwise. In charge of every damn thing here, wasn't she? Even setting up the damn filing system in some weird way that I can't figure out now. If she thinks I'm going to let this damn office crumble to the ground then she's got another damn think or two coming to her because damned if I will, damn it!"

Temper spiking, he slammed the third drawer shut and then just stood there, hands on his hips, and did a slow turn, taking in the eight filing cabinets and the dust-free work table and chairs in the center of the room.

"Why the hell is she on a beach when I need her help?"

His brain dredged up a dreamlike image of Andi, lying back on some lounge, beneath a wide umbrella. She sipped at a frothy drink and behind huge sunglasses, her eyes smiled. Some cabana boy hovered nearby enjoying the view of Andi in a tiny yellow bikini that Mac's mind assured him was filled out perfectly.

Mac scowled and shut down that mental image because he sure as hell didn't need it. "Why is she off enjoying herself when I'm here trying to figure out what she did?"

But even as he complained, he knew it wasn't the filing that bothered him. Given enough time, he'd find whatever he needed to find. It was being here. In the office. Without Andi.

All day he'd felt slightly off balance. One step out of rhythm. It had started when he got there early as usual and didn't smell coffee. Andi had always beat him to work and had the coffee going for both of them. Then she'd carry two cups into his office and they'd go over the day's schedule and the plans that were constantly in motion.

Not today, though. He'd made his own damn coffee— he wasn't a moron after all—then had carried it to his desk and sat there alone, going over schedules that *she* had set up. She wasn't there to talk to. She wasn't there to remind him to keep on track and not to go spinning off into tangents—so his brain had taken one of those side roads and he'd lost two hours of time while researching an idea on the internet. So the rest of the day he was behind schedule and that was her fault, too.

"What the hell is she doing in Bimini? Or Tahiti or wherever it is she went looking to relax?" Shaking his head, he walked to the window and stared out as the twilight sky deepened into lavender and the first stars winked into existence.

In the distance, he could see the fields of his home ranch, the Double M, freshly planted and only waiting for summer heat to grow and thrive and become a sea of waving, deep, rich green alfalfa. Beyond those fields lay miles of open prairie, where his cattle wandered freely and the horses he wanted to focus on raising and breeding raced across open ground, tails and manes flying.

This was his place. His home. His empire.

He'd taken over from his father when his parents died and Mac liked to think they'd have been proud of what he'd done with their legacy. He'd improved it, built on it and had plans that would continue to make it grow and thrive.

"And it would be a helluva lot easier to do if Andi hadn't chucked it all for the beach and a margarita."

When his phone rang, he reached for it, digging it out of his pocket. Seeing his sister's name pop up didn't put a smile on his face. "What is it, Vi?"

"Well, hello to you, too," she said, laughing in his ear. "Nothing like family to give you that warm, fuzzy feeling."

He sighed, scraped one hand across his face and searched for patience. He and Vi had been at odds most of their lives, especially since he had been in charge of her and Vi didn't take kindly to anyone giving her orders. Through it all, though, they'd remained close, which he was grateful for.

Usually.

Already annoyed, he didn't need much of a push to pass right into irritated. "What is it, Vi? I'm busy."

"Wow, I'm just choking up with all this sentiment. Must be all these hormones from being pregnant with your first niece or nephew."

Reluctantly, Mac smiled. Shaking his head, he leaned back against the nearest cabinet and said, "Point made. Okay then, what's going on, little sister?"

"Oh, nothing much. Just wanted to see how you were

holding up—you know," she added in a sly tone, "with Andi gone and all."

"Heard about that, did you?" Hadn't taken long, Mac thought. But then the only thing that moved faster than a Texas tornado was gossip in Royal. He hated knowing that the whole town was talking about him.

Again. During that mess with Rafe, the McCallum family had been pretty much front and center on everyone's radar. With that settled, he'd expected life to go back to normal. Which it would have if Andi hadn't gotten a wild hair up her—

"Of course I heard," Vi was saying, and he could tell by her voice she was enjoying herself. "People all over town are talking about it and I figured Laura could use some advice on how to defuse your temper."

"Temper?" He scowled and shifted his gaze back to the view out the window. He realized it was later than he thought, as he watched Laura hurrying across the parking lot to her car. He sighed when she glanced back at the building uneasily. Hell, he'd be lucky if Laura didn't desert him, too. Still, he felt as though he had to defend himself. "I don't have a temper—"

Violet laughed and the sound rolled on and on until she was nearly gasping for breath. "Oh my, Mac. That was a good one."

He scowled a little as Laura drove out of the lot, then he shifted his gaze to the twilight just creeping across the sky. "Glad you're having a fine time."

"Well, come on," she said, laughter still evident in her tone. "Don't you remember the roof-raising shouting you used to do at me when I was a kid?"

"Shouting's not temper," he argued, "that's communication."

"Okay, sure," she said, chuckling. "Anyway, how's it going in the office without Andi there riding herd on everything?"

"It's *my* business, Vi," he reminded her. "I think I can take care of it on my own."

"That bad, huh?"

His back teeth ground together and he took a tight grip on the shout that wanted to erupt from his throat. It would only prove his sister right about his temper. And yeah, she was right about Andi being gone, too. It wasn't easy. Harder, frankly, than he'd thought it would be. But he wouldn't admit it. Wouldn't say so to Vi and for damn sure wouldn't be calling Andi to ask for help while she sat on some beach sipping cocktails. She'd made her choice, he told himself. Walked away from her responsibilities—from *him*—without a backward glance.

"Well, when I saw Andi earlier, she was doing just fine, in case you were interested…"

He came to attention. "You *saw* her? Where?"

"Her house."

Mac frowned out the window at the darkening sky. "She said she was taking her vacation time."

"And she's using it to fix up the house she's barely seen since she bought it."

He heard the dig in there and he wouldn't apologize for working so much. And as his assistant, Andi had been expected to spend as much time as he did at the job—and she'd never complained until now.

"With what I pay her as my executive assistant," he argued, "Andi could have hired crews of men to pull that house together at any point in the last year."

"Speaking of points," his sister said, "you're missing

Andi's entirely. She wants a *life*, Mac. Something you should think about, too."

"My life is just fine."

"Right. It's why you're living in the big ranch house all by yourself and the last date you had was with that airhead model who had trouble spelling her own name."

Mac snorted. She had a point about Jez. But when a man dated a woman like that, he wasn't worrying about her IQ.

"You realize you're supposed to be on *my* side in this?"

"Strangely enough, I am on your side, Mac. You're the most hardheaded man I've ever known—and that includes my darling husband, Rafe."

"Thanks very much," he muttered.

"I'm just saying," Vi went on, "maybe you could learn something from Andi on this."

"You want me to quit, too? You ready to take over?"

She laughed and he could almost see her rolling her eyes. "A vacation isn't the end of the world, Mac. Even for you."

While Vi talked, telling him all about the new nursery she and Rafe were having designed, Mac's mind once again focused on Andi.

Why in hell she'd all of a sudden gone off the rails, he still didn't understand. But if she was here in Texas and not being waited on by hot-and-cold-running cabana boys, maybe he could find out.

He smiled to himself. And maybe, he could convince her that quitting this job was the biggest mistake she'd ever made.

Three

It had been a long day, but a good one.

Andi was feeling pretty smug about her decision to quit and was deliberately ignoring the occasional twinges of regret. She'd done the right thing, leaving her job and—though it pained her—Mac behind. In fact, she should have done it three years ago. As soon as she realized that she was in love with a man who would never see her as more than a piece of office equipment.

Her heart ached a little, but she took another sip of wine and deliberately drowned that pain. Once she was free of her idle daydreams of Mac, she'd be able to look around, find a man to be with. To help her build the life she wanted so badly. A house. Children. A job that didn't eat up every moment of her time until it was all she could do to squeeze out a few minutes for a shower every day.

Shaking her head clear of any thoughts at all, she

sipped her wine and focused on the TV. The old movie playing was one of her favorites. And *The Money Pit* seemed particularly apt at this moment. The house needed a lot of work, but now she had the time and the money to put into it. It occurred to her that she was actually nesting and she liked it. The smell of fresh paint wafted through the room, even with the windows open to catch whatever the early-summer breeze might stir up. It was a warm night, but Andi was too tired to care. Her arms ached from wielding a roller all day, but it felt good. So good, in fact, she didn't even grumble when someone knocked on the front door, disturbing her relaxation period.

Wineglass in hand, she answered the door and jolted when she saw Mac smiling at her from across the threshold. He was absolutely the last person she would have expected to find on her porch.

"Mac? What're you doing here?"

"Hello to you, too," he said and stepped past her, unasked, into the house.

All she could do was close the door and follow him into the living room.

He turned a slow circle, taking in the room, and she looked at her house through his eyes. The living room had scarred wooden floors, a couch and coffee table and a small end table with a lamp, turned on now against the twilight gloom. The attached dining room was empty but for the old built-in china cabinet, and the open doorway into the kitchen showed off that room's flaws to perfection.

The whole house looked like a badly furnished rental, not like someone's home. But then, in her defense, she hadn't had the opportunity before now to really make a difference in the old house. Still, her newly painted soft green walls looked great.

He sniffed. "Been painting."

"Good guess."

He turned around, gave her a quick smile that had her stomach jittering before she could quash her automatic response. "I can smell it. The color's good."

"Thanks. Mac, why are you here?"

"First off," he said, "where the hell did you file the Franklin contracts?"

She hadn't been expecting that. "Alphabetically in the cabinet marked *T* for *takeovers*. There's also a *B* for *buyouts* and *M* for *mergers*."

He whipped his hat off and ran his fingers through his hair. "Of course there is."

"Laura could have told you this."

"Laura's not speaking to me."

"You scared her, didn't you," Andi said, shaking her head.

"I'm not scary."

"You don't scare *me*."

"Maybe I should," he muttered, then shrugged. "I'm also here because I wanted to get a look at what you left me for."

"You make it sound like I'm your cheating wife." She sighed. "I didn't leave you. I left my job."

But she *had* left him, Mac thought. It didn't feel like an employee walking out, but a betrayal. Damn it, she'd taught him over the years to count on her. To depend on her for too many things—and then she was gone. How the hell else was he supposed to feel?

"Same thing." His gaze fixed on her and for the first time he noticed that she wore a tiny tank top and a silky pair of drawstring pants. Her feet were bare and her toe-nails were painted a soft, blush pink. Her hair was long and loose over her shoulders, just skimming the tops of her breasts.

Mac took a breath and wondered where that flash of heat swamping him had come from. He'd been with Andi nearly every day for the past six years and he'd never reacted to her like this before. Sure, she was pretty, but she was his assistant. The one stable, organized, efficient woman in his life and he'd never taken the time to notice that she was so much more than that.

Now it was all he could notice.

Dragging his gaze from her, he took a deep breath and looked down the short hall toward the back of the house. "Do I get a tour?"

"No." She really wanted him out of there. He had to wonder why. "I painted all day. I'm tired. So—"

He looked back at her and thought she didn't look tired to him. She looked downright edible. "You don't have to do it all yourself, Andi. I could have a crew out here tomorrow and they'd be done with the whole place by the end of the week."

"I enjoy painting."

He shot her a speculative look. "You enjoy hacking your way through jungles, too? A team of gardeners could tear out those briars growing wild by the front porch."

"I don't want to hire someone—"

"I said I would hire them."

"No."

"Why the hell not?" He could understand stub-bornness. Hell, he sort of admired it. But this was pure mule-headedness. There was no reason for her to work herself into the ground trying to prove a point. "People who own houses hire people to work on them all the time."

"You don't get it, Mac," she said. "I want to do the work."

"You obviously need the help." He gave another quick look around. He could see what his sister had meant. The house did seem to be practically void of any kind of personal decoration or warmth. "You've been here—what? A year? As organized as you are, it shouldn't have taken you nearly that long to whip this place into shape. But it looks like you've hardly touched it."

Insult shot through her tone. "Seriously? When was I supposed to do any of that? I spend—spent—all of my time at the office. And on those extremely rare—I'm talking bigfoot-sighting rare—occasions when I did get an entire weekend off, I tried to squeeze in a little family time. See people. Go outside."

Mac rubbed one hand across the back of his neck and wished he could argue with her, but he knew she was right. He had pretty much monopolized her every waking moment for the past six years. But it wasn't as if he'd held her hostage. She'd made a hell of a lot of money thanks to the job she'd walked away from so easily.

"You don't have to make it sound like you were in prison," he pointed out in his own defense. "You love the work as much as I do."

"I do enjoy the work, and I'm good at it," she added as if he needed reminding. "But I want more out of life than closeting myself up in an office."

"And painting your house yourself, digging out briars and a mountain of weeds like I've never seen before, is 'more'?"

She frowned and he felt her irritation coming at him in thick waves. "For now, yes."

"You really must be desperate if you call painting and gardening a vacation," he said, watching her. "I really expected the rumor about you and Jamaica was true and you were off having silly drinks in coconut shells."

That mental image of Andi in a bathing suit rose up in his mind again, and now, thanks to seeing her out of her normal buttoned-down attire, his imagination was doing a much better job of filling out that dream bikini.

She huffed out a breath, folded her arms over her middle, unconsciously lifting her breasts high enough that he got a peek at the tops of them thanks to the scoop-necked tank she wore. A buzz of electricity zapped Mac and he had to work to keep his own hormones in line. How had he spent six years with this woman and *not* noticed how nicely she was put together?

She'd always worn her long, straight brown hair pulled back in a businesslike knot or ponytail, so until tonight he never would have guessed that it was wavy when she let it down around her shoulders—or that lamp-light brought out hidden golden streaks among the dark brown. Andi had always worn sensible, straitlaced clothing on the job, so seeing her in that sleeveless tank and loose, silky sleep pants was a jolt to his system. Not to mention the fact that her upper arms were sleekly muscled and tanned. Where did she get that tan?

"Do I really strike you as the kind of woman who would enjoy lounging on a beach for two weeks?"

"Yesterday," he told her, "I would have said no way. But today—" he paused and let his gaze sweep up and down the length of her in an appreciative glance "—maybe."

She seemed to realize what she was wearing and he thought he actually caught a flush of color fill her cheeks briefly. *Andi blushing?* How many more surprises could a man take?

"You should go," she said simply.

Yeah, he probably should. But not yet. He could see that she was nesting or some damn thing here and until she'd gotten it out of her system, nothing would budge her out of this tiny, unfinished house. So the quickest way to get things back to normal would be for him to help her. Besides, if he really had kept her so busy she couldn't even unpack over the past year, maybe he owed it to her.

Whether Andi knew it or not, she was going to be bored senseless with nothing more to do than paint and mow the yard and whatever the hell else needed doing around here. Her mind was too sharp, her organizational skills too well honed for her to be happy puttering around the house. The sooner she realized that, the better for all of them.

"Tell you what," he announced. "I'll take the next two weeks off, too."

"What? Why? What?" She shook her head as if she hadn't heard him clearly, and who could blame her?

Mac couldn't remember when he'd last taken time off. He'd always been reluctant to leave the business in anyone's hands but his own. Not even his vice president's, and there weren't many people Mac trusted more than Tim Flanagan.

Now, with both Mac and Andi out of the office, and Tim off investigating another possible business move, there'd be no one there but Laura and a couple of interns. But it wasn't as though he was leaving the country, he told himself. He was right here in Royal, so if Laura ran into problems, he was completely reachable. Besides, two weeks would be over in a blink and everything would get back to normal.

"You quit your job so you'd have time to do stuff like this, right?"

Andi's lips pursed for a second before she nodded. "In a nutshell, yes."

"Fine. Then I'll be here for the next two weeks, helping you slap this place into shape." He curled his fingers over the brim of his hat. "Once we're done, if you still want to quit, fine."

"I will," she told him. "In fact, I already *have* quit."

He shrugged. "You can always change your mind."

"Not going to happen."

"We'll just think of these next two weeks as a sort of trial period," he said as if she hadn't spoken at all. "You can see what it's like to be out of the office and still have a chance to call off your resignation."

"Mac, you're making this harder than it has to be."

Yeah, he thought, recognizing the stubborn set to her chin, the flash in her eyes. Her mind was set. But then, he reassured himself, so was his. And when Mac McCallum made a decision, it was set in stone. In short order, he was going to prove to Andi that she wasn't the kind of woman to walk away from a high-powered job. She liked the responsibility. Thrived on it.

He had no doubt at all who was going to come out the winner in their little contest of wills. And by the time Andi had spent two weeks doing nothing but nesting, she'd be yearning to get back to the office and dive right in.

Giving her a slow smile, he said, "Tomorrow morning, I'll go in, take care of a couple things, tie up some loose ends and then I'm all yours."

"Mine?"

His smile deepened. Maybe it was small of Mac, but he enjoyed seeing her confused and just a little flustered. That almost never happened. Andi was too controlled. Too organized. Too on top of every damn thing that entered her universe. Being able to throw her for a loop, he decided, was fun.

"Yeah," he said, hooking his thumbs in the front pockets of his jeans. "Like I said, I'll be here, helping you. So for the next two weeks, you're the boss and I'm the employee."

"I'm the boss?"

He winked. "Like the sound of that, don't you?"

While she stared at him, he shifted his gaze around the room, checking out the freshly painted walls. "You did a nice job in here—"

"Gee, thanks."

"—*but*," he added as if she hadn't spoken, "the ceiling could use another coat. Hard for you to reach it I guess, since you're not all that tall."

"I used a ladder—"

"I won't need one to go over it tomorrow. Then we'll do the trim."

"I don't want your help."

His gaze immediately locked on hers. "Maybe not. But you need it."

She opened her mouth, then shut it again and took a breath before speaking. "Mac, I appreciate the offer…"

"No, you don't." In fact, her storm-gray eyes were smoldering. Typical Andi—she'd never admit there was something she couldn't do on her own.

Her lips twitched. "Okay, no, I don't. But then, you don't really want to take time away from the office to paint my house, either."

Mac thought about it for a minute. Ordinarily no, he wouldn't. His company had been his life for so many years now, he couldn't really imagine taking two weeks away from it. But if he wanted to keep Andi working for him—and he did—then he'd have to invest the time to convince her to stay. So he shrugged off her comment as if it meant nothing. "When I was a kid, my dad had me out on the ranch painting the barn, the stables, the fence around my mother's garden. I'm damn good with a paintbrush. And at woodworking. The ranch carpenter taught me a lot back then. I've got a fair hand at plumbing, too, though that can be iffy."

"Why would you want to use your no doubt impressive skills on my house?"

Here he gave her a grin and a wink. "What kind of Texan would I be if I didn't ride to the rescue?"

Her head snapped back. "*Rescue?* I don't need to be rescued, Mac. And now's a good time to remind you that for the last six years, I'm the one who's done most of the rescuing."

He laughed. Her outrage put fire in her eyes and a rush of color in her cheeks. Her breath was coming fast and furious and her breasts hitched even higher beneath that skimpy tank top. He'd have to remember to make her furious more often.

"Okay," he said, "I'll give you that. You've been riding herd on the business and keeping things moving for six years. So now it's time I paid that back."

She shook her head. "I don't need you to pay me back for doing my job."

"Maybe it's not about what you need," he said, and felt tension crawl through him as he stared into her gray eyes, where the fire was now banked, simmering low. This woman had been a central part of his life for years and he wasn't ready for that to end yet. Now that he was here, with her, in this nearly empty house with the dark settling around them, he wanted that even less than when he'd first come here.

"We'll work together and at the end of two weeks, if you still want to walk away, so be it." Sounded reasonable, though Mac had no intention of letting her go. "This is my decision, Andi. And you should know better than anyone else, once I make a call, I stick to it."

A second or two passed before she blew out a breath. "You're impossible."

"You set this in motion, Andi," he told her, shaking his head. "I'm just riding your wave."

Until, he told himself, he could get her back to the office, where she belonged. In the end, he would have his way and his life and the office would get back to normal. He and Andi would be working together again. Because Mac McCallum never accepted less than exactly what he wanted.

She shouldn't have been nervous, but she was.

Andi got up the next morning and her stomach was a twist of knots in anticipation of Mac's arrival. Why was he making this so hard? Why couldn't he just accept her resignation and let her go? For six years he'd treated her as if she were nothing more than an efficient, invisible worker bee.

Why was he noticing her now?

Andi poured herself a cup of coffee and carried it out

to the front porch. She sat down on the top step, cradled her cup between her palms and stared out at the gnarled oaks and the fields that surrounded her small house. But her mind wasn't on the view. Instead, every thought she had was for Mac. He might think she'd change her mind and go back to work, but she wouldn't.

Yes, dealing with Mac when he was determined to do something was a little like being a wave pounding away at a boulder. But over time, she assured herself, water won. It wore the rock away until only the water remained.

So she would be a wave. Relentless. Taking a deep breath, she looked up at the wide sweep of deep blue sky and told herself that it was a good thing Mac was coming over. When he realized she wouldn't change her mind, they could both move on.

And, she didn't believe for a minute that he'd last the entire two weeks. But maybe while he *was* here, she could help him discover how to relax. Turn off his big brain and think about something other than McCallum Enterprises. The man had been working nonstop since he was a teenager and needed a break even more than she did. If she could help him find it while getting her house in shape, then she'd do it. It was one last thing she could do for him. She just hoped she'd survive having him so close and so out of reach all at the same time.

He showed up an hour later, dressed in battered jeans, a stained University of Texas T-shirt and the scarred, worn boots she knew he wore for working on the ranch. His dark blond hair ruffled in a hot breeze when he yanked his hat off and grinned at her. "Ready to work?"

What was it about the man's smile that could tangle

her stomach up into twisted threads of desire? Just that simple curve of his mouth was enough, though when it was matched with his deep voice and lazy way of speaking, he was her kryptonite.

"Ready?" she asked, lifting her coffee cup. "I'm on a break. Already started."

He winked and walked past her. "Then I'd best start catching up."

She followed him into the house, her gaze dropping unerringly to his butt, covered with soft, faded denim. Oh, this was such a bad idea.

"The living room needed another coat," she said, clearing her throat, "so I started in there."

"Yeah, I can see that." He tipped his head back, studied what she'd done so far and what still needed doing. Tossing his hat to the couch, he turned and asked, "Where's your roller? I'll get the ceiling and the walls while you cut in against the trim."

"Who put you in charge?"

He winked. "Honey, when a McCallum's around, they're just naturally in charge."

"Oh, for—" Irritating, yes, she admitted silently, but he made her laugh, too. He always had. She watched him pick up the roller with the extension pole and swipe it through a tray of paint. As much as it pained her to admit it, she really could use his help on the stupid ceiling. Her neck had hurt all night from straining and looking up for hours the day before.

He glanced over his shoulder at her and there was a knowing smile in his eyes. "So, you gonna start painting again or are you just going to stare at me?"

"Paint. I'm going to paint," she said firmly, not sure

if she was convincing him or herself. "Just go. Be in charge."

"Always easier when they acquiesce so quickly."

Andi snorted and deliberately ignored him as she started painting. It wasn't easy. She could *feel* him in the room. *Hear* him breathing her air. If she looked over her shoulder, would he be looking at her, too? Wow, she was way too old for these junior high school thoughts.

"It's a good color," he said, that deep voice of his reverberating in the room before rumbling up her spine.

She shrugged the sensation off and concentrated on laying down a wide path of paint. "Yeah, it feels cool and in summer, that'll help."

"You've got air conditioning, right?"

"Not yet," she admitted and sighed a little. It was already hot and she knew it was going to get ugly by afternoon. Last night had been a long, private misery. She'd kept her bedroom windows open, hoping a breeze would find its way in, but it hadn't helped.

"Bet it's number one on your list," he said.

"My list?" She turned to look at him.

He was grinning and his gaze fixed on her briefly as he said, "Andi, you make so many lists, you have a master list to keep track of them all."

Did he really know her that well? He turned back to work and probably didn't see evidence of the surprise that flickered inside her, then changed to something else the longer she watched him. Heat that had nothing to do with the weather pumped through her as she watched the play of muscles across his back and shoulders. Mac moved the roller smoothly, applying even swaths of paint with much more ease than she had the day before.

But it wasn't paint that interested her at the moment.

It was the man standing so close, so tall, so...*there*. Mesmerizing really, she thought, the ripple and flow of those muscles was just—

"Andi? Hey, you all right?"

She shook her head, forcing herself out of the hormonal stupor she'd slipped into. "What? Yes. Fine. What?"

He grinned and dipped the roller into the tray for more paint. "Daydreaming won't get the work done."

"*Right.*" *Idiot.* Six years she'd worked with him and hadn't once betrayed anything she felt for him. Darned if she'd start now. She went to work, determined to concentrate on the task at hand.

"I asked if it was Bennet Heating and Cooling you called about the AC."

"Yes," she said, not bothering to turn around to look at him. "But they're backed up. It seems everyone in the county is getting their air worked on or installing new units. Won't get out here for another week or two."

He didn't answer, so she figured the conversation was over. Easier to keep her mind on painting when she could pretend he wasn't in the room with her, anyway. Then he started talking again—but not to her. Andi turned around to face him.

"Hey, Joe, it's Mac McCallum." He smiled at her and kept talking into his cell phone. "Yeah, I'm over at Andi Beaumont's place and she tells me you can't get out to install air conditioning for a week or two. That right?"

It was that whole "take charge" thing again. He couldn't seem to help himself. She started to tell him to butt out, but he actually held one finger up in the air in a sign for quiet. So Andi did a slow, silent burn.

"Yeah, that's not going to work for me. How about

you get your boys out here tomorrow? Damn hot in here and we're painting and fixing the place up." He winked at Andi then said more softly, "Now, Joe, I don't want to wait for this, understand me? I'd consider it a personal favor if you could handle this tomorrow."

Personal favor. Everyone in town was eager to do favors for Mac because he never forgot, and if Joe Bennet ever needed help down the line, Mac would be there to return the "favor."

Nodding, he said, "That's good news. I'll tell Andi you'll be here tomorrow then. Oh, and how about installing some of those new units where you don't need to put in all the duct work? Like you installed at my office? That way we get that puppy up and running soon as we can. Hotter than the halls of hell in here, Joe." Mac laughed, then nodded. "Good. Good, we'll see you then. Appreciate it."

He shut his phone off, stuck it in his pocket and said cheerfully, "There I go, rescuing you again."

"I didn't ask to be rescued," she reminded him.

"A good rescuer doesn't wait to be asked."

"You shouldn't have done that, Mac." He was rich, powerful and so damn likable with it, most people went along just because he'd charmed them. It was well-known in Royal that Mac McCallum got what he wanted when he wanted it, and as far as she knew, no one had ever told him no. At least, not for long.

His eyebrows lifted. "Want me to call him back, then? Tell him there's no hurry? You're fine with the heat?"

She bit down on her bottom lip. He had her and he knew it. No, she didn't need rescuing, but she'd be spiting herself if she turned down help when it was offered. What would she prove by doing that?

"No."

"Good."

"You still shouldn't have."

"You're welcome."

"I didn't say thank-you."

"I'm willing to look past that shameful lack of gratitude." He winked again. "And if I get a sandwich and some cold tea out of this deal I'll forgive you completely."

"You'll forgive *me*?" She choked out a laugh. "You're impossible."

"Can't be impossible," he said as he worked the paint roller smoothly. "Here I stand."

"The question is, why are you standing *here*?"

He lowered the roller, turned to look at her and said, "Because we're not done, Andi. I'm not willing to let you go, and I think over the next couple weeks we're both going to learn a thing or two."

Her stomach shivered and her mouth went dry. "If you really want to take time off—which is hard to believe—why not Paris? London? Jamaica?"

His eyes burned into hers. "You're not there, are you? Besides," he added, "why would I want to leave Texas?"

"You're making me a little crazy," she admitted, shaking her head.

"Nothing wrong with being a little crazy," he said. "It's the *lot* of crazy you have to watch out for."

He started painting again and Andi could only stare at him. He'd pretty much been the center of her business life for six years and now he was steamrolling his way through her personal life. Andi had deliberately taken these two weeks so she could get some space between herself and Mac.

How could she get over him if she was *with* him? But

she was forced to admit that she was glad she'd have two more weeks with him. It was probably foolish, but maybe while he was here, she really could help him find a way to relax. To turn off that sharp, brilliant mind long enough to enjoy his life a little. Except for the rare times when he went out on a date or two with some gorgeous yet dim model, actress or flight attendant, Mac was as relaxation-deprived as she was.

Then she remembered what Amanda had said only yesterday about *making* the time to have a secret lover in her life. She shot Mac a sidelong look and let her gaze sweep over him.

And suddenly, the next two weeks looked a lot more interesting.

Four

"Where have you been hiding the last few days?"

Mac looked across the table at one of his oldest friends. Rafiq "Rafe" bin Saleed no longer looked the part of a Harvard-educated sheikh. Between moving here to Royal and marrying Mac's sister, Vi, Rafe had been transformed into an honorary Texan.

Since he'd had to go by the office and take care of a couple of things—how did people go on vacations?—Mac had called Rafe to meet him at the Royal Diner. They were sharing a booth in the back, and Mac caught a couple of the other customers shooting them curious glances. He ignored them and lifted his coffee cup for a sip of the dark, hot brew.

"Thought for sure Vi would have told you. I've been at Andi's house, helping her put it together." He shrugged. "It's really why I called. I've spent most of my time here lately talking to no one but women. Andi. Laura. Your wife."

"Your sister," Rafe reminded him. "And why are you helping Andi fix up that old house?"

In that clipped, well-bred accent, the question sounded more demanding than inquisitory. Mac chuckled. "You may not be a sheikh anymore, but you've still got that do-as-I-say thing in your voice."

Rafe smiled and sipped at his own coffee. "I believe the correct phrase here would be 'it takes one to know one.'"

"Okay. Touché." Easing back in the booth, Mac glanced out the windows at Main Street. Shoppers hurried up and down the sidewalks, carrying bags and herding toddlers. Cars crawled along the street, mindful of the speed limit. Rivers of colorful flowers spilled from baskets hanging from the streetlights. It was Main Street, USA, out there—just the way Mac liked it.

"Did Vi tell you about Andi quitting her job?"

"She did." Rafe, too, looked out the window briefly before shifting his gaze back to his friend. "And that you're trying to change her mind. My friend, you should know that a woman is difficult to manage."

He snorted. "Manage? Nobody manages Andi." He admired that about her even as that personality trait was working against him at the moment. Grinning at Rafe, he said, "And I'd truly love to be there when Vi finds out you think you're *managing* her."

Rafe shivered. "A wise man never lets that information slip."

"True." While the diner filled with customers who went about their business, Mac looked at his old friend and took a moment to realize how glad he was that they had managed to put their friendship back together. "Off the fascinating subject of women for a minute," he said abruptly, "have you given any more thought to officially joining the Texas Cattleman's Club?"

"I have," Rafe said softly. "And I actually wanted to ask if you would be the one to support my application."

A wide, satisfied smile stretched across Mac's face as he held one hand out across the table. When Rafe took it in a hard, firm shake, Mac said, "My pleasure. Really."

"I appreciate that. It's good to be here with you like this, Mac." Rafe took a breath and let it out. "When I let myself think about what I almost lost, almost threw away, by refusing to see the truth—"

"Almost doesn't mean a damn, Rafe. What matters is that you did see it. Finally," he added, and laughed when his friend winced at the reminder. "I'm glad to have you back, too. Plus, you married my sister, you poor dumb fool…"

"She's wonderful and you know it."

"Yeah," Mac allowed. "But don't tell her I said so." Shaking his head again, he said, "Wish to hell Andi was as easy to read as Violet."

"I wouldn't say your sister is 'easy' to understand."

Mac brushed that comment aside. "But Andi's always been easy to be around. She's a hell of a taskmaster. Kept the business running without a bump for years. Hell, Rafe, I thought I *knew* her. And all of a sudden, she's turned everything around on me. I feel like this is a woman I don't know at all."

"Maybe you don't," Rafe mused. "A work relationship is entirely different from life on the outside."

"Yeah, but people are who they are."

"Not always. When you're not wheeling and dealing,

you like being on a horse and speaking as if you're in an old Western movie."

Mac snorted. "Why was I glad to see you again?"

"Because everyone needs an honest friend." Rafe lifted his coffee cup in a salute.

"Maybe. And maybe you're right, too, about the work thing. Andi's determined to quit, damn it, and I can't let that happen."

"It may be that you won't be able to stop it."

Mac shot him a hard look. "Whose side are you on?"

Rafe held up both hands in mock surrender. "Yours, my friend. Of course. But as I have learned in dealing with your sister, I can say that a woman's mind is a tricky, always evolving thing."

"So I've noticed." He took another drink of coffee.

"And I've noticed," Rafe said with a cautious glance around, "that some in Royal are still unsure about me."

Mac sighed a little. "Well, this is one of the reasons I wanted you to meet me here. The more people see us together, as friends, the more they'll move on from what happened before. They'll all figure out that the hatchet's been buried and there's no hard feelings. Folks in Royal aren't the type to hold grudges, Rafe. They'll get past it—just like I did."

Rafe smiled. "Thank you for that, my friend. With you and Violet on my side, I'm sure all will be well."

"Wish I was as sure of my own situation as I am of yours," Mac said.

"How are my two most handsome customers doing?" Amanda Battle walked up to their table and gave each of them a wide smile.

"Coffee's good and so's the ambience," Mac said, smiling back.

"It's what I like to hear," Amanda said. "Now, Rafe, you tell Violet I expect her to come around soon. I want to keep an eye on that baby bump of hers."

"I will do it," he agreed, pleasure shining in his dark eyes.

"As for you," Amanda said, giving Mac a wink, "you tell Andi I said to remember that 'secret' we were talking about."

"Okay," Mac said warily.

She gave them their check, told them to hurry back, then walked away to say hello to more of her customers.

"Now, what do you suppose that was about?" Mac asked. "What 'secret'?"

"I have already said, my friend," Rafe told him as he picked up the check and headed for the cash register. "A woman's mind is a tricky and evolving thing."

"Yeah," Mac muttered as he followed his friend. "Just what I need. Tricky women with secrets."

For the next couple of days, Mac and Andi worked together on the old house. The amount of renovation that still needed to be done was staggering, though, and Mac had a twinge or two of guilt a couple times. It was because of him and his business that Andi hadn't had time to take care of her house before. But he didn't let regret take too big a chunk out of him because damned if he'd feel bad for hiring her, handing over responsibilities and coming to count on her for too damn much.

If she hadn't wanted to become irreplaceable, then she shouldn't have been so good at her job.

"She's not walking away. Not from the office. Not from *me*," he swore quietly. He'd figure out a way past all of this. It was what he did.

He'd still like to know what "secret" Amanda Battle had been talking about. Especially because when he'd mentioned it to Andi, she'd blushed a fiery red and smiled to herself. And if that wasn't enough to make a man wonder, he didn't know what would. But she'd refused to tell him, and just got to work stripping old wallpaper off the dining room walls so they, too, could be painted.

Now while she was in there, here he was, head and shoulders under her first-floor powder room sink. When Mac had arrived, she was about to call a plumber to fix a leaking pipe and he'd insisted on doing it himself. If she needed help then he'd damn well provide it. He was going to make himself as irreplaceable to her as she was to him.

Mac wielded a pipe wrench on the joist that was tight enough to have been welded on, and when the damn wrench slipped free, he scraped his knuckles on the old copper pipes. He hissed in a breath and let it go on a string of muffled curses. Then he jolted when his cell phone rang and rapped his head on the underside of the sink and briefly saw stars. Cursing a bit louder now, he wiggled out, reached for the phone and muttered, "What?"

"Hey, boss, good talking to you, too."

Reaching up, Mac rubbed the growing knot on top of his head then glared at the raw scrape on his knuckles. "Tim. What's going on?"

Tim Flanagan, a friend since college, was now Mac's vice president. He was currently in Montana going over the details of a ranch takeover. The Gilroy ranch was being swallowed by McCallum Enterprises and would soon be stocked with prime cattle.

"I called the office looking for you," Tim said. "Laura

told me you haven't been in for a few days." He paused. "Somebody die?"

Snorting, Mac shook his head, drew one knee up and rested his forearm on it. His gaze shot around the incredibly tiny first-floor powder room. Whoever the last owner had been, they'd painted it a dark brick red, making the room seem even smaller than it actually was. And to top it off, they'd used gold paint for the trim. It looked as if it belonged in a bordello. Not a particularly exclusive one, either. Naturally, Andi had plans for it, but first thing was getting the plumbing working right—such as making it so the sink would drain.

"Yeah, nobody's dead. I'm taking a few days is all." He rested his head against the bottom of the old sink and let the cool of the porcelain seep into his body. Thanks to the newly installed air conditioning, he wasn't dying of heat, but a man could still work up a sweat when wrestling with stubborn pipes.

"I heard Andi quit," Tim said. "What's up with that?"

Mac shot a glance out the door to make sure the woman in question wasn't in earshot. Then he said, "I'm working on it."

"Good," Tim told him with a slight laugh. "Because without her as a buffer I probably would have killed you five, six years ago."

Mac's mouth twitched in a smile. "You would have tried. So, is there some reason in particular you're calling or was it just to harass me?"

"There's a reason. Harassment's just a bonus. Old man Gilroy's wanting to hold back ten acres, claiming it's in the contract for him to get the allowance for a hay field."

Frowning now, Mac said, "I don't remember it that way." They'd made allowances for the Gilroy ranch house and the surrounding five acres to remain in their name, as a courtesy since the Gilroys had been on the land more than a hundred years.

But the truth was, the old man couldn't run the ranch on his own anymore and his kids weren't interested in being ranchers. They loved the land and wanted at least some of it to remain in the family, but the younger Gilroys all had jobs that took them off the ranch. McCallum Enterprises was paying fair market value for the land and Mac wasn't about to hand out favors. That just wasn't how you ran a business.

"Call the office, have Laura pull up the contract and get the details," Mac said. "We want to be sure of our standing here and—"

"What's going on?" Andi stepped into the doorway and leaned one shoulder against the jamb.

Mac looked up at her and damn, she looked good. No woman should look as fine as when she'd been ripping away at dirty old wallpaper. He gave his head a shake, reminding himself to focus, then told Tim to hang on and explained, "Tim says Mr. Gilroy in Montana is insisting that we agreed to an extra ten acres set aside for him in the contract and I don't—"

"You did," she said, then reached down and plucked the phone from his hand. "Hi, Tim, it's Andi. The original contract called for just the house and the surrounding five acres to remain in Gilroy hands. But we renegotiated several points about two weeks into the deal and Mac agreed to a ten-acre plot behind the main ranch house. Mr. Gilroy wants his daughter and her husband to be able to build near the main house. And they want to grow enough hay for the animals they're keeping."

Mac watched her. She had pulled that information out

of her computerlike brain, and damned if he didn't find that sexy as hell. A woman with a mind like that didn't waste herself. She needed challenge. Needed the kind of work she'd been doing for six years. Why the hell did she think she could be happy without it?

"Sure," Andi said and grinned. "It's no problem, Tim. Happy to help. Okay, here's Mac again."

She handed him back the phone. "Problem solved."

"Yeah," he said, still watching her. "I see that. You always were impressive."

"Thanks." She left a second later but he continued to look after her. Then he spoke into the phone. "Everything straightened out now?"

"Yeah," Tim said. "She is *good.* With all the things we have going on concurrently, it amazes me that she could just remember details like that. What the hell are we going to do without her?"

Mac shifted his gaze to the ceiling when he heard her footsteps pass overhead. He wondered briefly what she was doing up there. Then he realized that if she left, he'd spend the rest of his life wondering what she was up to. That was unacceptable. "We're never gonna have to find out."

Two hours later, Andi set two sandwiches on her tiny kitchen table and poured two tall glasses of iced tea. If it felt odd serving Mac lunch, she brushed it off, knowing that with all the work he'd done around there the past few days, the least she owed him was a meal.

He walked into the kitchen and grinned at her. "I didn't even know you could cook."

"A ham and cheese sandwich is not cooking," she said, and took a seat. Picking up a potato chip, she bit in and chewed. "However, I'm a darn good cook—when I have the time."

He winced and sat down opposite her at the table. "Time again. Point made."

She shrugged and smiled. "It's not all you and the job," she admitted as she looked around the room. "This kitchen is not exactly conducive to creative cookery. Plus, the oven doesn't work."

He looked behind him and laughed. "A pink stove?"

"It might come back in style," she said, not sure why she was bothering to defend the appliance she had every intention of replacing. When he just gave her a you've-got-to-be-kidding look, she said, "Fine. It's terrible. But getting a new one is low on my list right now. Anyway, you bought pizza yesterday, so it's only fair I take care of lunch today."

"Always about what's fair, aren't you?"

"Something wrong with that?"

"Not a thing," he assured her and picked up half his sandwich. "But if you're so fired up about being 'fair' you might want to rethink walking out on a business that needs you."

Andi watched him, and though she felt that rush of knowing he didn't want to lose her, she knew it was still the only answer for her. Being around him so much the past few days had been so hard. Her heart ached for what she couldn't have, and if she stayed working for him, that ache would eventually swallow her whole.

"You were doing fine before me and you'll do fine without me," she said, taking a bite herself.

"Fine's one thing," he said, waving his sandwich at her. "Great's another. And you know damn well that together, we were doing great."

"There's more to life than work, Mac." At least she hoped there was. And she fully intended to find out.

"If you love what you do, you'll never work a day in your life. My dad told me that when I was a kid," Mac said. "Someone famous said it, I think. Anyway, turns out Dad was right. Work is *fun*, Andi, and you know it."

She had enjoyed her job, keeping on top of problems, working out strategies and plans for the future. It was exciting and fulfilling and everything a good career should be. But to be honest, doing all of that *with Mac* was what had really been the best part for her.

With his free hand, he pulled his phone out of his shirt pocket and scrolled through, checking email. Andi shook her head. Even during lunch, he couldn't stop working. "This is exactly what I'm talking about."

"Huh? What?" He didn't look at her. Instead, he tapped out an answer, hit Send, then checked for incoming texts and missed calls.

"Look at you. You can't even stop working long enough to eat a sandwich."

"Multitasking," he argued, shooting her a quick look. "Contrary to what women believe, men are capable of doing more than one thing at once. Besides, I'm just—"

Before he could finish, she interrupted. "Twenty dollars says you can't go an hour without checking your phone."

"What?" His cool green eyes shone with bemusement.

"It's a bet, Mac." She braced her forearms on the table and gave him a rueful smile.

"Yeah, I know that," he said, setting the phone at his elbow. "But I don't feel right about taking your money."

His phone vibrated and he glanced at the readout. When he looked back at her, her eyebrows were arched and there was a definite smirk on her mouth. "Oh, I think my money's safe enough. Especially since I don't think you'll take the bet, because you know you'd lose."

Frowning, he picked up the phone and tapped out an answer to the text from Laura. "I've got a business to run, you know."

"That's *all* you've got, Mac," she said as he set the phone aside again. "It's all I had until I quit."

His mouth tightened and she watched a muscle in his jaw twitch as if he had plenty to say but was holding the words back.

It took a couple of seconds, but he finally put his sandwich down, tipped his head to one side and asked, "And you really believe you had to walk out to find more?"

"Yeah." She took a sip of her tea because her throat was suddenly dry and tight. "Look at you. You said you were going to be here, working on the house for two weeks. But you haven't really left the office at all."

He grabbed a chip, tossed it into his mouth and crunched viciously. "What's that supposed to mean?"

"It means that you can take the boy out of the office, but you can't take the office out of the boy." She shook her head, sad to realize that she'd been right to leave. Mac didn't need a woman in his life. He had his *work*. "All the while you're painting or fixing the broken tiles or unclogging a sink, you're checking your phone. Answering emails. Texts. Checking with Laura about the situation at the office."

"What's wrong with that?"

"Nothing if it's all you want. Heck, until I quit, I was doing the same thing." Andi looked down at her own empty hands and said, "I was almost convinced my phone was an extension of my hand. Every waking moment revolved around the business and all of the minutiae involved with keeping it running. It was getting crazy, Mac. I was practically *showering* with my phone. That's when it hit me that not only did I want more, but I *deserved* more. And you do, too."

"This is all because I check my phone?"

"Because you can't *stop* checking your phone."

It vibrated on the table again and instinctively he started to reach for it—then stopped, curling his fingers into his palm. He locked his gaze with hers. "Twenty bucks?"

"Only if you can go an entire hour without checking your phone—or responding to a call." He'd never be able to do it, Andi told herself. Right now, she could see it was *killing* him to not answer whoever had called or texted.

He thought about it for a long moment, then seemed to come to a decision. "You're on, but first—" he hedged as he picked up his phone "—I send one text to Laura telling her to go to Tim with any questions."

Andi met his gaze and nodded. "Agreed. But after that, it's one hour. No phone."

Mac texted Laura at the office, put the phone in his pocket and held out one hand to her. "Deal."

The instant his hand closed around hers, Andi felt a rush of heat that raced up her arm to settle in the middle of her chest. As if he, too, felt that zip of something wicked, he held on to her hand a little longer than necessary. She couldn't look away from his eyes. The sharp, cool green of them drew her in even when she knew she should resist the fall. With the touch of his hand against hers, though, it was so hard to think about caution.

When he finally let her go, Andi could still feel the

warmth of his skin, and clasped her hands together in her lap to hang on to that feeling as long as she could.

"What do I get when I win?" he asked.

Was it her imagination or was his voice deeper, more intimate than it had been only a moment ago? Quickly, she picked up her glass of tea and took a long drink before answering.

"The prize is twenty dollars. But you won't win."

"Uh-huh." One corner of his mouth curved up and Andi tightened her grip on the tea glass in response.

"When I win," he said, "I'm going to need a little more than a paltry twenty dollars."

She swallowed hard. "Is that right?"

"Oh, yeah." He picked up his sandwich again and gave her a teasing smile over it.

Well, when Mac's eyes gleamed like that, Andi knew he had something up his sleeve. Over the years, she'd watched him back opponents into corners or wheedle exactly what he wanted out of a deal in spite of the odds being against him. And it was always heralded by that smile.

So warily, she asked, "What did you have in mind?"

"Well, now," he mused, taking another bite, "I believe that after this amazing sandwich, we're going to be needing dinner."

"And?" she prompted.

"And, the two of us. Dinner. The club."

"The TCC?" she asked, surprised.

Mac, like his father before him, was a member of the Texas Cattleman's Club, a members-only private organization that had only recently begun to welcome women as full members. The club was legendary in Royal, with most people going their whole lives and never seeing the inside of the place. "Why would you want to do that?"

"They serve a great steak," he said with a careless shrug that she didn't believe for a minute.

Whatever his reasons for suggesting they go out on a real dinner date—he was suggesting a *date*, wasn't he? Oh, God, why was he asking her on a date? Because he knew he'd never have to go through with it, that's why, she thought an instant later. He couldn't win this bet and he knew it.

"Okay," she said, agreeing in the same spirit he'd asked. "Deal. Dinner at the TCC if you win. Which you won't."

"Seem awful sure of yourself," he mused.

"You'll never be able to go without answering your phone," she said, taking a bite of her sandwich.

"Never say never, darlin'."

Five

The first half hour just about drove him out of his mind. He couldn't count how often he actually went to reach for his phone before stopping himself just in time. Whenever his phone rang, Andi watched him, one eyebrow lifted high as she waited for him to surrender to the inevitable. But he didn't do it. Mostly because she was so sure he would and that just annoyed the hell out of him. So he held out and poured his concentration into painting, and humming along with the country tunes on the radio.

He and Andi talked and worked together as well as they always had, and before Mac knew it, three hours had gone by. He hadn't checked his phone once, he realized, and the world hadn't ended. His business was still up and running and there were no signs of a coming apocalypse. Even more than that—after the first agonizing half hour, he'd actually enjoyed not grabbing for the phone whenever it beeped or vibrated.

"You did it," Andi said, with just a hint of surprised admiration in her voice. "I didn't think you'd make it, but you did."

"You should have learned by now not to doubt me," he said, taking a step back to survey the job they'd done. "Looks good, Andi."

"It does," she said, turning in a circle to admire the room now that it was finished. "We make a good team."

"Always did," he agreed, then kept talking before she could back away from that one simple truth. "So, if it's okay with you, think I'll use my phone now and make us a reservation at the TCC. Then I'll use that twenty bucks you owe me to put gas in my truck."

Her head tipped to one side. "You want to have dinner with me?"

"I guess I do." He wanted a lot more than dinner, too. But a man had to start somewhere. He pulled his phone from his pocket and hit the speed dial. When she started to speak again, he held up one finger for quiet and watched her quietly steam. It was probably wrong how much he enjoyed doing that.

"Afternoon, James. This is Mac McCallum. I'll be bringing a guest in for dinner tonight. Around eight. Thanks. Appreciate it." He hung up and looked at her. "They're holding my favorite table."

"Of course they are."

"Problem?" he asked.

"You always get what you want, don't you?"

"Damn straight."

"I shouldn't even be surprised when people snap to attention when you speak, should I?"

"I've never seen you jump when I speak," he said.

Her mouth curved. "True."

"Always liked that about you," he admitted. That stiffness in her spine, the determined gleam in her eyes and the defiant tilt to her chin all rolled together to make her one amazing woman. "From that first day you came in to interview for the job. You let me know from the start that you'd work your butt off, but you wouldn't be a yes woman."

"You didn't need one more person kowtowing to you."

Amusement filled him. "Kowtow?"

"It's an appropriate word."

His eyebrows lifted as he considered it. He supposed she had a point, in spite of that snotty tone. However everyone else treated him, Andi had always given him an honest opinion. No matter what. He had always known that she'd tell him straight and wouldn't hold back. And he was only now seeing how much he'd come to rely on that trait over the years.

He could still see her as she had been that first day. He'd interviewed three people for the job before her, but the moment she walked into the office, all starch and precision, he'd known she would be the one. She'd had a great résumé, a firm demeanor and he liked how she had stood right up to him.

Now she wanted to leave. Was it any wonder he was trying so hard to keep her?

He studied her for a second or two, and in her eyes he saw more than his trusted assistant. More than the woman who'd made his work life run like a Swiss watch. He saw a woman he enjoyed being around. A woman who made his skin sizzle with a touch and irritated him and intrigued him all at once. Why had he never opened his eyes to the possibilities before this?

Looked as though he was just going to have to make up for lost time.

"So," he said, cutting his own thoughts off. "Dinner tonight. I'll pick you up at eight."

He looked at her steadily, silently daring her to say no. Just when it seemed she might, she said, "Fine. Eight."

Nodding, Mac started talking again before she could change her mind. "I'll finish with this sink, then head home to clean up, take care of some things."

She was standing close. So close he could smell her shampoo. Why had he never noticed that soft, flowery scent before? Her T-shirt was tight, clinging to her breasts and her narrow waist. Her cutoff denim shorts were cuffed high on her thighs and those pale pink toes looked too damn sexy.

His breath labored in his lungs, and every square inch of his body tightened until he felt as if a giant fist was wrapped around him, squeezing. They stared at each other for several long seconds, and then Andi broke away, shattering whatever thread had been stretched between them. Mac took a deep breath, thinking to settle himself, but all it did was make him appreciate her scent that much more.

"Um, okay then. I'll get back to the hideous cabbage rose wallpaper and—" She half turned and he stopped her.

"Wait," he said tightly. She tensed up. He could see it and he enjoyed knowing that she was feeling as twisted up as he was. Reaching out, he pulled flakes of wallpaper out of her hair, then held them out to her with a smile.

"Isn't that perfect?" she muttered. Taking them, her fingers brushed against his and sent another quick snap of sensation between them. "Thanks. I'll be sure to wash my hair before dinner."

Well, now he was imagining her in the shower, soap suds and water running over her bare skin, hair slicked back from her flushed face to hang down her back in heavy, wet strands... Oh, man. He rubbed one hand across his mouth, hoping he wasn't drooling.

She gave him a long look out of those storm-gray eyes that had his insides fisting. He fought down an urge to grab her, pull her close and hold on to her. Because if he held her, he'd have to kiss her. Taste the mouth that was suddenly more tempting to him than anything he'd ever seen before. But if he did that, it would change their relationship completely and, knowing her, Andi would only use that shift between them as another reason to leave her job. So he wouldn't risk it. Not yet, anyway.

When she turned to the hall, this time he let her go.

"A date? Seriously? You're going on a date with Mac?"

Jolene and the kids had stopped by on their way home from baseball practice and now Andi and her sister were sitting in the kitchen, keeping an eye on Jacob, Jilly and Jenna playing in the backyard. She had less than two hours before Mac picked her up for their not-a-date.

"It's not a date," Andi insisted, as she had been telling herself all afternoon.

"Really?" Jolene reached out and tapped her fingernail against the window until her son looked up. She wagged her finger at him and Jacob got the message, immediately letting go of his baby sister's doll. The little girl's shrieks broke off instantly. Satisfied, Jolene turned back to Andi.

"If it's not a date, what's the word they use to describe it these days?"

"Funny," Andi told her. She sliced a couple of apples into wedges, then added squares of cheese to a plate before carrying it all to the table and sitting down opposite her sister. "Really, I don't know what it is. But he's never thought about me *that* way, so I know it's not a date."

"Uh-huh." Jolene took a sip of her tea and flicked another glance out the window to make sure no one was killing anybody. "Sounds to me like he's thinking of you 'that' way now."

"No, he's not. Is he?" She worried her bottom lip as she considered, then rejected the whole idea. "No, he's not."

"Things change," Jolene said, snatching a slice of apple and crunching into it. "Let us pause to remember that after my first date with my beloved Tom I told him I never wanted to see him again."

"That's because he took you fly-fishing."

"He really was an idiot," Jolene murmured with a smile. Rubbing one hand over her belly, she said, "But look at us now."

"Okay, you have a point. Things have already changed." In the past few days, there had been a kind of *shift* in her relationship with Mac. Always before, they'd been friendly, but she'd been determined to maintain that cool separation of boss and assistant. But here, away from the office, that barrier had dropped and they'd both reached across it.

What that meant, she had no idea.

"What're you going to wear?" Jolene asked.

"Oh, God." She dropped her head to the table and only groaned when her sister laughed.

* * *

Andi swiveled her head from side to side and didn't even care that she must look like a tourist on their first visit to New York City. It was how she felt. She'd never been inside the Texas Cattleman's Club before, so this was a real moment for her. She didn't want to miss a thing—and not only because Jolene had demanded a full description.

The building itself was stone and wood and boasted a tall slate roof that afforded the rooms in the club with nearly-cathedral ceilings. The paneled walls were dotted with hunting trophies and pieces of the history of Royal, Texas. Old photos of stern-looking men glaring at the camera were interspersed with other Texas memorabilia. Andi took it all in as Mac led her toward the dining room.

"I feel like we should have had to use a secret password to get in here," she said, keeping her voice low as if she were in a library.

"Ah, we use code signals. Much more stealthy." He leaned his head toward hers. "Did you see how I tipped my hat to the right when I took it off? There you go."

Her lips twitched. A playful Mac was a dangerous Mac. At least to her heart. "This is exciting. To finally see it all."

Mac tucked her arm through his. "Well, the dancing girls are only here Tuesdays and Thursdays, and the harem's closed to female guests, so you'll have to make do with the dining room."

She tipped her head up to give him a sardonic look. "Aren't you the funny one?"

"Charm, Andi. It's called charm."

"There's a less attractive name for it, as well," she told him.

He laughed. "You're quick. I like it. Always did. So what do you think of the place?"

"I feel like we should be whispering," she confessed, lowering her voice again as she looked at the old framed letters on her left and nearly gasped when she saw one signed by Sam Houston himself.

"The place has got plenty of history," he said, "but it's moving with the times, too."

She raised an eyebrow at that.

"Okay, turtle speed," he allowed. "But we are moving. We even have a day care center here now and I thought that was going to send a couple of the older members into heart attacks."

She chuckled, but realized he was probably right. The arguments over the day care center had kept the town talking for weeks. But oh, she remembered well how infuriated the old guard of the club had been to grudgingly accept female members.

In a way, she felt sort of sorry for the poor old dinosaurs. Their world was changing and they couldn't stop it.

"Of course," Mac was saying as he shifted his gaze to the ceiling, "the building suffered some damage during the tornado. But I like what they did when they repaired it. There's a little more light in here—makes it seem less like a paneled cave when you walk through."

"I love it." She tipped her head back to look up at him. "I've always had a mental image of what the inside of this place might look like and, surprisingly enough, I was pretty close. But you've fulfilled a childhood dream by bringing me here. So thank you."

"Absolutely my pleasure," he assured her. Then he covered her hand on his arm with his own. The closeness to him was exhilarating and made her head swim. She liked it.

He looked wonderful, though she had to admit that he always looked far too good. Tonight, he wore black slacks, black boots, a white collared shirt and a black jacket. He carried his black dress Stetson in his free hand and his sharp green eyes surveyed every inch of his surroundings.

He *fit* in this building that was so much a combination of past and present. She could completely see Mac McCallum a hundred and fifty years ago, still having that steely gaze, carving out an empire in the Old West.

As if he felt her watching him, he turned his head, looked down into her eyes and asked, "What's going on in your mind right now?"

"Too many things I don't want to talk about."

"Intriguing."

She sighed a little. "I'm not trying to be intriguing."

"Maybe that's why you are," he said, voice low, a caress of sound in the hushed atmosphere. Well, that should keep her system humming for a while, she thought as he led her into the main dining room.

Here, the tables were square, covered in white linen then draped with deep red cloths. There were candles and tall, fragile vases, each holding a single yellow rose. It made her smile.

Leaning toward him, she whispered, "The yellow rose of Texas?"

He grinned, as if pleased she'd caught it. "Nobody has traditions like Texas."

She'd been so nervous about coming here with him,

worried about what it might mean, what would happen. And now she was enjoying herself too much. It wasn't good, she thought. She couldn't allow her feelings for him to keep growing. If she did, walking away would be even harder than it had to be.

"Stop thinking."

Andi blinked and shook her head as if coming up out of a trance. "What?"

"I can see you're starting to second-guess tonight." Mac dropped one hand to the small of her back. "Why not just let it roll on and see where it takes us instead?"

Ignoring the burst of warmth that bloomed from his touch, she sat down and kept her gaze on his as he took the seat beside her at the table for four. "You hired me for my organizational skills, for my ability to think everything through from every angle."

"As you're continually reminding me," he said with a quick smile, "we're not at work."

If they were, Andi would know where she stood. As it was now, she felt a little off balance—a not altogether uncomfortable feeling.

"Right. Okay. Just enjoy." She looked around the dining room. There were several other people at the tables scattered across the gleaming wood floor. She recognized most of them and nodded to Joe Bennet, who excused himself to his wife and headed across the room toward them.

He and Mac shook hands, then Joe turned to Andi and asked, "How's that new air conditioning system I installed working out for you?"

Here she had no trouble knowing exactly what to say. Giving him a wide smile, she said, "It's wonderful, Joe.

I can't thank you enough. It's lovely being able to sleep at night without gasping for air."

His wide, plain face beamed with pleasure. "Happy to hear it. Now, if you have any problems at all, you let me know, all right?"

"I will."

"You enjoy your night, you two." He gave Mac a conspiratorial wink, then walked back to his own table.

"Oh, boy." That man-to-man wink was a sure sign that she and Mac were about to be the hot topic of conversation tomorrow in Royal.

"Yeah," Mac said, nodding. "I know what you mean. Joe's a good guy, but the man gossips like an old woman. Did you know he spent a half hour telling me how the Grainger boy's scholarship to UT came at the right time. His dad was so proud he forgot all about the boy crashing the family car."

"Did he?" Amused, Andi listened.

"And when he'd finished with that tale, he moved right on to Sylvia Cooper and how her husband, Buck, bought her a shiny new cast-iron skillet for their twenty-fifth anniversary—and she promptly bounced it off his forehead."

She cringed. "Oh!"

"Yeah," he said with a wince. "Have to say, though, I think Buck had that one coming. Anyway, twenty stitches and a mild concussion later, Buck saw the light, bought two tickets to Paris and the lovebirds leave next week."

Andi laughed, enjoying herself as Mac continued.

"Then Joe went on a rant about Pastor Stevens and how he preaches against gambling but made a bet on a horse race last Friday night and won—without telling his old friend Joe about the tip he got before the race."

She was having fun. Andi hadn't expected to, not really. There was too much tension between them.

The quiet of the restaurant, the efficient smoothness of the waiters moving from table to table and the intimacy of the candlelight flickering in his eyes made her want to hug this moment close. Watching his easy smile slide across his face had her returning it and saying, "So Joe's a big gossip, is he?"

Mac laughed, then shrugged off the obvious dig. "Must be contagious."

"I think it is," she agreed and looked around at the people shooting them interested glances. "And by tomorrow afternoon, everyone in town will know we were out to dinner together."

"That bothers you?"

Her shoulder blades itched as though people were staring. "I don't like being talked about."

He laughed again and the sound was low and deep. "Don't know how you could avoid it around here. You know how it is in small towns. You've lived in Royal all your life just like me."

True, they had grown up just a few miles apart, but their lives were so different they could have been on separate planets. Mac had been the golden boy. Football team captain, star baseball player. His parents were wealthy, he lived on one of the biggest ranches in the state and everything he touched turned to gold. Until his parents died, leaving him to care for Violet and find his own way alone.

Andi and Jolene had grown up in town, in a nice middle-class home with two parents who doted on them and loved each other. She and her sister had worked hard at after-school jobs, not leaving much time for activities like cheerleading or drill team or band.

So, though they had both grown up here, and she had of course known who Mac was, Andi had never met him until the day she applied for a job with his company. She'd thought she'd come to know him very well over the years, but the past few days had shown her a new side of him, and it was fascinating to discover there was still so much more of him to know.

He was staring at her as if he could delve into her mind and read her every thought. Just in case he could, she spoke up quickly. "Vi seems really happy."

Mac nodded as if accepting her change of subject. "She is. Rafe loves her, which I'm grateful for, as I'd hate to have to pound on one of my best friends. And right now, she's driving the poor guy nuts with trying to get the nursery ready for the baby."

"He's loving it and you know it," Andi said.

"Okay, he is. It's only me she's driving nuts."

The waiter arrived, took their order and Andi listened as once again Mac took charge. She gave him this one, since, being a Texan, she liked a good steak now and then. The wine he ordered was served a few minutes later and, after being sampled, was poured. Then the two of them were alone again and she took a long sip of that wonderful red, just to ease the twisting knots in her stomach.

"Do you spend a lot of time here at the club?" she asked.

Mac winked. "Lately, it's been pointed out to me repeatedly that the only place I spend a *lot* of time is at work…"

She nodded at his implication.

"But yes," he said, glancing around the dark, intimate dining room. With a shrug, he added, "Food's good. If I want company, it's here, if I don't, I get left alone. Not much point in making Teresa dirty up the kitchen at home cooking just for me."

His housekeeper, Teresa Mooney, was a fifty-year-old widow who, Andi guessed, would love to be allowed to fuss over her employer. But typically enough, Mac made that call for her, not bothering to find out how she felt about it.

"You do that a lot, you know?" she said.

"What's that?"

"Make decisions for people."

"What're you talking about?"

"I ran into Teresa at the grocery store a few weeks ago. She was looking at a huge pot roast and bemoaning the fact that you don't want her to cook for you."

"Really?" He frowned a little, took a sip of wine.

"Yes, really." Andi sighed. "People like to feel needed. Useful. You're taking that away from her."

"Bad analogy," he said, shaking his head. "*You* felt needed and useful at the office and yet you walked away."

She shifted uneasily in her chair. "That's different."

"Not so much," he said, drinking his wine, then thoughtfully staring at her over the rim of the glass. "You're leaving *because* you were needed."

"It's not only that."

"Then what else?"

Okay, she wasn't about to admit that she'd left because she loved him and knew her dreams were doomed to die. "It doesn't matter," she said, evading the question she couldn't answer.

"Well," he said, setting his glass down as their meal arrived, "once you're back in the office where you belong, I'll have plenty of time to find out what's really bothering you."

She glanced up at the waiter and smiled as he served her dinner, waiting until the man was gone again to speak. When she did, she leaned in close enough that Mac could hear her whisper, "You're not going to convince me to come back."

"You didn't think I'd win our bet today either, but here we are." Smiling to himself, he cut into his steak.

Andi sat there quietly simmering, wondering just when it was she'd lost control of the situation. She'd quit her job, yet now she was half convinced that Mac was right. He would find a way to get her back.

Six

$\mathbf{M}$ac didn't want the night to end yet—though he wasn't interested in asking himself why. It was enough to keep her with him awhile longer. After dinner, he coaxed her into taking a walk down Main Street. With the summer just getting started, the night was warm, but the breeze was cool and just strong enough to lift the hem of the dark red dress she wore and flutter it above her knees.

He was forced to admit that he'd felt staggered from the moment he picked her up at her house tonight. Over the past few days, Mac had been seeing Andi in a whole new light and it was just a little disconcerting. And tonight, she'd kicked it up several notches.

She had her hair pulled back at the sides so that it tumbled down her back in a waving mass that tempted a man to sink his hands into it. Her red dress had thin, narrow straps and a bodice that dipped low enough that he got another peek at the breasts she had apparently been hiding from him for six years. The fabric then nipped in at a waist so narrow he was willing to bet he could encircle it with his hands, then sloped down over rounded hips and clung there, just to torment him further. Not to mention, he thought with an inner groan, the heels. Black, shiny, four inches at least, with a cut-out toe that showed off the dark red polish on her nails.

She'd practically killed him right there on her front porch.

Every man at the club had watched her pass by and for the first time ever jealousy stirred through Mac. He'd never been possessive about a woman. Never cared if other men looked at her or even if she looked back. Until now. Admitting that to himself was damned unsettling.

At work, she had always been the personification of professionalism. Tidy, businesslike, she'd never once hinted at the woman beneath the veneer, and right now he figured that was a good thing. If she had, he might have fired her so he could date her and would never have been able to appreciate what she could bring to the business. And now, he thought, work was the furthest thing from his mind.

Her scent wafted to him on a sigh of wind and he inhaled it deeply, drawing it into him until he could practically taste her. Which was just what he wanted to do.

"It's a pretty little town, isn't it?" she asked when they got back to the car. She'd turned to look back down Main, and the expression on her face was soft and dreamy.

He turned to face the town he'd grown up in and saw it as she did. Street lamps formed globes of yellow light that were reflected in puddles on the sidewalk. Tubs and hanging baskets of flowers brightened the scene and the

shop windows were ablaze with light, welcoming customers to come in and browse.

Mac had lived in Houston for a while, but he hadn't
lasted long. Big cities were fun to go to for a few days,
but his heart would always draw him back here. He liked
the slower pace, the familiar faces and the views out his
own windows. He liked knowing every inch of his surroundings and he enjoyed being in a place where everyone and their uncles and cousins made it their business
to know yours.

"It's changed a lot from when we were kids," Andi
mused, "but somehow it stays the same, too." She turned
her head to look up at him. "You know what I mean? The
heart of Royal is still small-town beautiful."

"Yeah, it is," he finally said, shifting his gaze to hers.
Those gray eyes shone a little brighter with the gleam
of lamplight reflected in their depths. It was enough to
stop a man's heart if he wasn't careful. Which Mac generally was.

"You know," he said abruptly, "it's early yet. How
about you come with me to the ranch? I can show you
that mare you had to make all the travel arrangements
for."

She bit down on her bottom lip as she considered it,
and he tried not to watch. "I don't know. I've got a lot of
things to do tomorrow and—"

"Being alone with me scare you a little?" he asked in
a whispered hush.

Her gaze snapped to his. "I told you before, you don't
scare me."

But she was nervous. He could see it. And that gave
him the nudge to push her into coming out to his place.
Maybe it wasn't a smart move, but right now he wasn't

interested in being "smart." "Then there's no problem, is there?"

He'd delivered her a direct challenge, one she wouldn't be able to resist. He knew her as well as she did him, so Mac realized that she'd never say no. Because she wouldn't want him to think she was as uneasy as she obviously was.

Damn. His thoughts were starting to circle like a merry-go-round in a tornado. What was the woman doing to him?

"All right," she said, shaking him out of his own head, for which he was grateful. "But after you show me the mare, you take me home. Deal?"

He took her hand but instead of shaking it, lifted it to his mouth. Keeping his eyes on hers, he kissed her knuckles and saw the flare of heat flash across that cool, gray surface. Her skin was soft, smooth, and the scent of her pooled in his gut and began to burn. "We're making a lot of deals here lately, Andi."

She pulled her hand from his, and damned if he didn't miss the feel of her. "Just remember this one, okay? Horse, then home."

"Oh, I'll remember."

He opened the car door for her, then closed it firmly and smiled to himself. He didn't say how *long* it would be after she saw the horse that he would take her home. For a woman as organized and detail-oriented as she was, she'd really overlooked that particular loophole.

He smiled all the way to the ranch.

The twenty minute drive from town to the Double M ranch seemed to pass in seconds. Andi couldn't even enjoy the scenery they passed, with the moonlight washing over it all in a pale, cool light. She was way too tense to appreciate the view, for heaven's sake.

The ride in Mac's Range Rover was smooth, and quiet but for the Southern blues pumping from the stereo. She hardly spoke because she had too many thoughts racing through her mind. Mac didn't have much to say, she was guessing by his smug smile, because he'd already gotten his way by getting her to go to his ranch with him.

Why was she going with him?

He had kissed her hand.

That one small, sexy action had pulled her in and made it impossible for her to say no. Darn it, Mac was being sweet and seductive and she felt herself weakening. She'd loved him for years, wanted him for years, and now, for whatever reason, he'd turned his charm onto her and she was slipping. Slipping down a slope that was going to be so hard to climb back up.

At the edge of the McCallum ranch land, they passed the office where she'd worked for six years. There were low lights burning in the windows and the gravel parking lot was empty in the moonlight. A huge chunk of her life had been spent there and a part of her was sorry to see it go—the part that wanted to be with Mac, no matter what.

Andi's stomach pitched and she shot him a careful look from the corner of her eyes. He was smiling to himself and that only increased the anxiety already pumping through her. What was he thinking? Heck, what was he planning?

How strange. She had believed she knew Mac better than anyone in the world. For years, she had anticipated his every professional need and rushed to meet it. But the Mac who kissed her hand and gave her wicked smiles over a shared bottle of wine while firelight shone in his eyes was a whole new ball game. She wasn't sure of her next move.

Frankly, she wasn't sure of much at the moment. But Amanda's words kept whispering through her mind. *Make time for a secret lover.* Is that what she was doing?

Heat zipped through her, head-to-toe, at the thought, leaving a lingering burn that sizzled somewhere in the middle. Going to bed with Mac was a bad idea and yet…

They turned off the main road and drove beneath the Double M gates, which swung open, then closed with a touch of a remote button. The land seemed to stretch out for miles, while the long drive to the ranch house was lined with oaks, their gnarled, twisting branches reaching for each other across the graveled drive. In full summer, this drive would be a shaded lane. Right now, there were still some bare branches that allowed moonlight to slip through and lie in silvered patches on the ground in front of them. At the end of the drive, the house waited.

A sprawling affair, it was two stories, built of stone and wood with wings that spread out from the center. More oaks stood sentinel at the corners of the house and the flower beds were a riot of color that even in the moonlit darkness looked cheerful and welcoming. The windows were lit, creating squares of gold across the front of the house, and the yard lights blinked on as Mac pulled up and parked.

Now what?

He hopped out of the car, came around to her side and opened the door, giving her a hand down. She appreciated it, since the heels she was currently teetering on weren't made for climbing. Or walking, when it came

to it, which was why she winced when he took her hand
and led her toward the stables.

"You know, I'm not really dressed for a barn visit—"

Mac glanced at her and one corner of his mouth tipped
up. "It's okay. Next time you can dress up."

"What? Oh, for—"

He winked at her and kept walking.

That charm of his kept tugging at her and she was
pretty sure he knew it. Andi huffed out a breath because
clearly the man was not going to be dissuaded. Hurrying her steps to keep up with his much longer strides,
she asked, "Is this a race?"

"Sorry," he said, and slowed down, never letting go
of her hand. Not that she wanted him to. She liked the
feel of his hard, calloused palm pressed close to hers.

That was the problem.

Every step they took crunched out into the country
quiet. The soft breeze was still blowing and felt cool
against her skin. Mac was a tall, solid presence at her
side, and as they walked together in the moonlight, she
had a hard time holding her all-too-eager heart back
from taking a tumble to land at his feet.

"Soon enough, it'll be steaming hot here, but for now,
it's a nice night for a walk."

She looked up at him. "It is. If you're wearing the
right shoes."

"If you can't walk in them," he said, giving her heels
a quick glance, "why wear them?"

"They're not for walking," she said. "They're for making my legs look great."

He took another look, a slow, lengthy one this time,
then met her eyes with a smile. "Mission accomplished."

"Thanks." Her heart started that tumble again and she

steeled herself against giving in. She already loved the man. And the Mac she knew would run like a scalded cat if he knew it. In the past, any woman who'd started getting what he called the "white-fences gleam" in her eye had been set aside so fast their heads were probably still spinning.

If Andi didn't keep a grip on her feelings, she really would wind up lying alone in a dark room with nothing but her pain for company. So instead of concentrating on the man at her side, she looked around as they neared the stable.

The corral fences were painted white and stood out against the darkness like ghostly barricades. The stable itself was moon-washed and looked like a deeper shadow against the night. The barn farther off to the right was bigger, wider, to accommodate all of the equipment needed to keep a ranch of this size running. There were other outbuildings, too. A house for the ranch manager and his wife, a barracks of sorts where unmarried employees lived and a separate storage building where winter feed could be kept until it was needed.

Mac McCallum might be a wildly successful businessman, but at the core of him, Mac was a rancher. He would always love this land, this place, the horses and cattle he ran and the wide-open stretch of sky that seemed as if it went on forever. This ranch was in his blood, it was bred in his bones, and whether he acknowledged it or not, this place was the beating of his heart.

"You went quiet all of a sudden," he said. "A sure sign you're thinking too much again."

She laughed and shook her head. "Since when do you notice what I'm doing?"

"I always noticed, Andi," he said softly, and his voice

slipped inside her to caress every last nerve ending. "Though I'll admit, I just took you for granted before."

"Really?"

He glanced at her and smiled. "Don't be so surprised. Even I can grow some."

How was she supposed to fall *out* of love with a man who could say something like that?

"I figured," he continued, "that you'd always be there when I needed you. In my own defense, though, you're the one who caused me to believe it."

Wryly, she shook her head and smiled. "So it's my fault."

"Absolutely."

She laughed again. "Well, then, I'm so very sorry."

"Don't be," he said and drew them to a stop. Hands on her arms, he turned her to face him. "I wouldn't change a damn thing, except for the idea of you quitting."

"It's not an idea. It's fact. You can't change it, Mac. It already happened."

"Don't count me out just yet," he warned, one corner of his mouth lifting into that half smile that did amazing things to the pit of her stomach.

It was a scene built for romance. If she wasn't living it, Andi would have thought it was like being in the pages of a romance novel. Moonlight, soft breezes, stars glittering overhead and a tall, gorgeous man looking down at her as if she were the center of the universe.

Just for a moment, for the length of a single heartbeat, Andi wished it were true. Wished she and Mac were a couple. That they were here on *their* home ranch, taking a walk in the moonlight before going upstairs together.

Then the moment passed and reality came crashing

back down on her. "Um, you going to show me that mare?"

"You bet," he said, then in one smooth move bent down, scooped one arm under her legs and swung her up against him.

So surprised she could hardly speak, Andi just gaped at him. Whether he knew it or not, he was really filling in the blanks on her romantic fantasy.

"Mac!" She pushed ineffectually at his chest and wasn't surprised at all when she didn't make a dent. "What are you doing?"

"Look there," he said, jerking his head to a spot just ahead of them.

She did, and saw a mud puddle that stretched from the stable fence to nearly the back of the ranch house. "Oh."

"That's right." He looked down at her. "Those pretty shoes of yours would never make it through the mud. A shame to ruin them."

"Or," she said, squirming a little in his hard, tight grasp, "I just won't go see the horse tonight. Put me down."

"Nope, we had a deal. I'll carry you to the stable." He started walking and then added, "Guess I just have to rescue you again. How many does that make now?" he wondered aloud. "Are you keeping count?"

"This isn't a rescue," she said, not completely able to hide the exasperated laughter bubbling from her throat as she wrapped her arms around his neck. "This is a kidnapping."

"Is that right?" He shrugged and hefted her just a little higher in his arms. "Well, it's my first."

"Congratulations."

"Thanks." He looked at her again. "I'm having a hell of a good time."

"Strangely enough," she said wistfully, "so am I."

He stopped, stared down into her eyes. "Good to know."

A couple of humming, electrical seconds passed while they stared at each other and the soft, early summer breeze wrapped itself around them. She was in so much trouble, Andi told herself.

Finally, he went on, carrying her across the muddy water and into the stable, where the scents of fresh hay and horses greeted them. It was quiet but for the occasional stamp of a hoof against the floor. Slowly, Mac set her on her feet, but caught her hand in his and held tight.

"Come on," he said, "I'll show you the mare."

They walked the length of the freshly swept aisle between stalls and as they passed horses poked their heads out as if to say hello. Mac had a moment with each of them, stroking noses, murmuring soft words to the animals until Andi was half convinced they were actually communicating.

At the last stall, he stopped and smiled at a gray horse with a blond mane as the animal reached out her nose toward him. "Andi, this is Moonlight."

"She's beautiful." She stroked the horse's neck and jaw, loving the soft, sturdy feel of the friendly mare.

"Yeah," Mac said, shifting his gaze from the mare to her. "She is. And this pretty girl's going to produce some beautiful children over the next few years."

"Who's the proud father-to-be?"

"Ah," he said, giving the mare one last pat before turning and pointing to a stall twice as big as the other animals had. "That would be Apollo."

The stallion was a dark, sleek brown with a black mane and tail, and he held his head high and aloof as if he knew just how important he was.

"He looks as if he thinks of himself as a god, so, appropriate name," Andi said.

"For a stallion, he's got a great temperament, too." They walked closer and the big horse shook his head and snorted.

"Yeah, I can see he's really friendly," Andi said, laughing nervously.

"He just doesn't like being tied down. He'd rather be out in the corral kicking up his heels than shut down for the night."

"So he's definitely male."

One eyebrow lifted. "Is that a slur against my gender?"

"Not a slur. An observation," she said, walking back up the aisle, pausing now and again to say hello to one of the horses or to stroke or pat.

"Based on your vast experience?" he teased from just a step behind her.

She looked over her shoulder at him. "I've known a few who've taken off for the hills as soon as anything remotely serious pops up. Take you, for example."

"Me?" He slapped one hand to his chest as if deeply wounded.

She laughed again, enjoying herself in the quiet, dimly lit stable. "Please. How many times have I purchased the see-you-later-thanks-for-the-memories bracelets?"

He winced and that only made her laugh harder. "Admit it, Mac. It's not only when you get bored with a woman that you move on. It's also when she starts getting stars in her eyes over you. Much like your stallion over there, you prefer running free. The only real commitment you've ever made was to the business."

"Maybe," he said, taking her arm and pulling her around to face him, "it's because I haven't met the right woman yet."

"Not for lack of trying," she said wryly.

He grinned and shrugged that off. "I'm no quitter."

He slid his hands up her arms to cup her face between his work-roughened palms. His thumbs stroked her cheekbones as his gaze met hers and held, warming the longer he looked at her. "You're confusing me, Andi," he said so softly she wasn't sure she'd heard him correctly.

Andi felt that rush of heat she'd come to expect from his touch, then her breath caught when the heat exploded into an inferno as he leaned down, bringing his mouth just inches from hers. If she had a single working brain cell, she would move back, keep a distance between them. A kiss from Mac was going to lead to places she really shouldn't consider going.

But she couldn't think. What woman could under the same circumstances? Her heartbeat sounded like a bass drum in her own ears. Breathe, she reminded herself. *Breathe.*

He smiled, a slow, slight curve of his mouth. "What's the matter, Andi? Feeling a little nervous after all?"

"No." *Liar.* Nerves, yes. Excitement, oh yes. Worry? She should be worried. Instead there was a tiny, faint voice crying out for caution, trying to be heard over the clamor of need screaming in her head.

She licked her lips and watched his eyes flare at the motion.

"Seduction in a stable, Mac?"

"The horses won't mind," he assured her.

"Maybe not," she whispered, her gaze dropping briefly to his mouth before meeting his again. "But I should."

His hands stilled as he stared into her eyes. "Do you?"

"No."

"Thank God."

She leaned into him and he moved quickly, laying his mouth over hers. Andi thought she heard herself groan, but that was the last thought she had. It was impossible to think when so many sensations were awakening, demanding to be relished, explored.

He pulled her tight against him, his arms coming around her like a vise, squeezing as though he thought she might try to escape his hold. But that was the last thing Andi wanted. This was probably a mistake and no doubt she'd come to regret it at some point, but at the moment, all she could think was *yes. Touch me. Hold me. Be with me.*

For six years, she'd loved him. For six years, she'd hidden everything she felt. Now finally, if only for this one night, she would be with the man she loved. Know what it was like to hold his body close to hers. To take him inside. And she wouldn't give up that chance for any amount of logic and reason.

He drew his head back and looked down at her, eyes wide, flashing with emotions that changed too quickly for her to read. But maybe that was for the best.

"Man," he whispered. "Should have done that a long time ago."

"Now is good, too," she said, though her voice sounded breathy and so unlike her she hardly recognized it. Her whole body was humming with impatience, with need. She was practically vibrating with the tension coiled tight in the pit of her stomach.

"Now is *great*," he amended, then swept her up into his arms again.

"What are you doing?"

"Just another rescue," he said, and headed out of the stable. But instead of going toward his car, Mac made a right turn and started for the ranch house. "This time, though," he told her, "I'm saving us both."

Seven

Andi held on, then leaned up and kissed the side of his neck. Her decision was made. There would be no turning back now. Tonight, she would make memories that years from now she'd relive and remember. "Hurry."

A low, throaty growl rolled from his throat, but he did exactly as she ordered, his long legs eating up the distance to the house in a few minutes. Overhead, the sky was black with a wide sweep of stars impossible to see unless you were outside a city, away from the lights. A nearly full moon glowed against the blackness and sent that wash of light over everything like a blessing. The warm June wind wrapped itself around them and swept them on toward the lamplit house ahead of them.

He opened the door, stepped through and kicked it shut behind him. The kitchen lay empty and still in the glow of a stove light, but Mac didn't stop to admire the elegantly remodeled space.

Andi barely had a chance to admire it, even if she'd been interested, before he was across the room and striding down a long hallway. They passed a dining room, Mac's study and the great room at the front of the house before he came to the wide oak staircase, where he suddenly stopped.

Surprised, Andi tore her gaze away from the massive iron and wood chandelier hanging from the cathedral ceiling over the foyer to look into his eyes. A view she preferred.

"What is it? What's wrong?" Her heart galloped in her chest as his hands held her in a proprietary grasp.

Keeping her pressed tightly against him, Mac said, "Nothing's wrong as far as I'm concerned. I'm just checking one last time."

She smiled and trailed the tips of her fingers along his jaw and throat. He shivered, then sucked in a gulp of air like a drowning man tasting hope.

She smiled, loving his response. And she knew exactly what he was doing now. Mac being Mac, he was giving her one last chance to change her mind about what was about to happen. He was charming, gorgeous and had a sense of honor that not enough men these days possessed. How could she resist him?

But still she asked innocently, "Checking what?"

"God help me," Mac said, letting his head fall back helplessly. "Yes or no, Andi. Don't make me beg."

"It's a big step," she teased. "I just don't know…"

He narrowed his eyes on her and gave her a hard squeeze. "Woman, you're treading on thin ice here."

She smiled and asked, "How fast can you take these stairs?"

His grin flashed bright. "We're about to find out."

Probably silly, Andi thought as her heart raced, to feel such a wild rush of pleasure at the man she loved holding her close and sprinting up a staircase.

She'd been in the house before, to see Vi when she'd lived in the west wing. But Andi now caught glimpses of Mac's side of the house when he made a sharp right at the top of the stairs. She couldn't have been less interested in the decor, but noted the Western paintings on the cream-colored walls as he passed. She saw the heavy, dark beams on the ceiling and heard every muffled boot step on the carpet runner along the hall. Then he turned into his bedroom and Andi focused only on him.

He swung her to her feet, but didn't let her go. Instead, he cradled her close to his chest, lowered his head to hers and kissed her breathless.

There was no slow slide into delight here; this was like a fall on a roller coaster. A whoosh of sensation that rushed through the blood and then gave you just enough time to breathe before starting all over again.

His hands, those big, strong hands, were everywhere at once—sliding up and down her spine, around to cup her breasts and then up to touch her face, fingers spearing through her hair, tipping her head first one way then the other as he deepened a kiss that was already searing her soul.

"I've been wanting my hands on you," he murmured when he tore his mouth from hers.

"I've been wanting that, too." *For so long.*

"Glad to hear it," he said, giving her the wicked half smile that never failed to send jolts of anticipation rocketing through her. And now, that sensation was going to have a payoff. At last.

He turned her around, her back to his front, and

tugged her zipper down slowly. She sighed, air sliding from her lungs on a half moan at the touch of his fingers against her back.

The bed in front of her was huge. Like an adult playground, with a midnight-blue duvet and a dozen pillows propped at the headboard. Across the room, there were French doors that led out onto the second-story balcony and a door on the right of the room that no doubt led to a bathroom suite. A cold hearth stood on one side of the room and there were two matching leather comfy chairs in front of it.

She wasn't feeling comfy at the moment, though; she was on edge, every nerve in her body tingling with expectation. Mac slid the shoulder straps of her dress down her arms and followed the motion with his mouth. Lips, teeth, tongue trailed over her skin and made her shiver. She couldn't believe this was happening. After six long years of loving, she was finally *being* loved by the man she'd thought she could never have.

And even if this was only one night, it was one she would always remember. She would etch it into her memory so she could replay it over and over again. Relish every touch, every breath, every sigh—and regret that it hadn't lasted longer than one night.

"I wanted slow and seductive," he admitted as he turned her to face him and watched as the bodice of her dress dropped to her waist, displaying a strapless black lace bra. His eyes went wide and hot as he lifted his gaze to hers. "But I find I'm too hungry for you to take my time."

"Me, too, Mac." She'd wanted for so long, needed so much; this was no time for lazy caresses and tenderness.

This was a rush to fulfillment. To ease the aches they both felt. And she was ready.

Andi reached for the buttons on his shirt even as he shrugged off his jacket and let it fall. When the shirt lay open, she splayed her hands on his hard, muscled chest and felt his heart pound in time with her own. His eyes caught hers and locked, passion glittering bright and sharp in those green depths. He kissed her again, long and deep, eliciting another groan from her as he tumbled her back onto the bed and followed her down. He tore his own shirt off, then came back to her, sliding her dress down her hips and taking her black lace panties with it. He pushed them off and onto the floor.

The duvet felt silky and cool against her back, adding contrasting layers to the sizzling warmth pumping through her. Andi unhooked her bra and watched his eyes as her breasts were bared to him. Heat flashed in his gaze just before he lowered his head to take, first, one rigid nipple, then the other into his mouth. His tongue lapped at her, his lips and teeth tugged and suckled at her, and in seconds, Andi was writhing beneath him, moving with the need erupting like lava in her blood. She held his head to her and watched him, and her mind spun out into sparkle-splashed darkness. There was nothing in the world but the two of them. This moment. This bed. This…wonder.

Then he moved up her body and took her mouth again, their tongues tangling together in a frenzied dance of passion that fed the fires already burning inside them both.

His right hand swept down her length and into the heat of her. She was wound so tight, had waited so long, that that first intimate touch was enough to make her shatter in tiny, helpless waves of pleasure that flickered and shone like lit sparklers just beneath her skin. "Mac…"

"Just getting started, darlin'," he promised, and delved deep, his fingers stroking, caressing already sensitive skin until she lifted her hips into his hand, hoping to ease the sudden burst of need that continued to build.

"I can't do this again so soon." Proud of herself for getting the words out, she clutched at his shoulders and held on as her body did things she hadn't expected it could.

Always before, sex had been a soft, almost sweet release of tension. A gentle ripple that drifted through her body on a tender sigh of completion.

This was different. That soft ripple had already washed away in a rising tide of fresh need that swamped everything that had come before.

He kissed her mouth, her shoulders, her breasts; he touched her deeply, intimately, and watched her every reaction. She gave him everything she had. She showed him everything she felt. Andi held nothing back because she'd waited too long to feel it all.

His touch was fire. His eyes were magic. She felt her own body jumping out of her control and she let it go.

Another climax hit her, stronger than the last, and she cried out his name as her body trembled and shook beneath his hands. But he wasn't finished, she realized as she lay there, struggling for air, trying to make her mind clear enough to appreciate just where she was.

She opened her eyes and saw him slide off the bed, strip off the rest of his clothes. Her eyes went wide as she looked at his amazing body, so lean and strong and sculpted. And for tonight at least…hers.

He joined her on the bed again, this time covering her

body with his, sliding up the length of her. Andi's hands and nails scraped up and down his back. Her legs parted, lifted, welcoming him to her, and when he entered her, she gasped and arched at the swift invasion. He felt so good. So right. So big. He filled her until it seemed as though they'd joined on much more than a physical level.

In this moment, they were one unit, and as she moved with him, she stared up into his eyes and lost herself in the wild gleam she saw there. He plunged into her heat, and unbelievably, she responded by tightening into another fiercer ball of tension deep inside. She felt the now familiar buildup and knew that this time, when he pushed her over the edge, it would be shattering. She couldn't wait.

So when he pulled away from her, Andi nearly whimpered with the boiling need clawing at her. But he paused only long enough to dig into the bedside table drawer and grab a condom.

"Damn," he said, glancing at her. "I was so caught up in you I almost forgot protection."

"You're not alone in that. I can't believe it, but I wasn't thinking—"

"Who needs to think?" he asked, and in a second he was back, buried inside her, and the two of them raced toward the finish line.

She held him, hooked her legs around his waist even as he reached under her with one hand and lifted her hips. Andi struggled to breathe, gave up any attempt to hang on to sanity and threw herself into the moment with an abandon she'd never experienced before.

Here was the difference, she thought wildly, between sparklers and skyrockets. Pleasure slammed into her with a crash, making it hard to breathe and harder to care. As the first incredible eruptions exploded inside her, she cupped his face between her hands and looked deeply into the green of his eyes as she jumped into the void.

She was still holding him when his eyes glazed over, his hips pumped against her and he tumbled into the same starlit darkness with her.

Minutes, hours, heck, maybe *weeks* later, Andi's brain started working again. She simply lay there, completely spent. She loved the feel of Mac lying on top of her and would have been perfectly content to stay in just that position from now until whenever. But even as that thought slipped through her mind, he was rolling to one side of her. He kept one arm wrapped around her, though, and pulled her in close, nestling her head on his chest. She heard the frantic pounding of his heart and knew her own was racing, as well.

God, she'd never been through anything like that before. Every other sexual experience she'd had in her life paled alongside what she'd just lived through. The man was…gifted.

"That was," he whispered into the darkness, "well, I don't think I can find a word for it."

"Yeah," she agreed. "Me, either."

He rolled her over onto her back and levered himself up until he was looking down into her eyes. "Can't believe it took us six years to do that."

"It was worth the wait," she told him.

"And then some," he agreed, pushing her hair off her shoulder, dipping his head to kiss that warm curve at the base of her throat.

Andi shivered again. Oh, she was in so much trouble. When she'd first decided that going to bed with Mac was a good idea, there'd been a small part of her convinced that if she did, it might help her get over him. Get past the feelings she had for him so she could move on with her own life. Instead, she was in even deeper trouble than she had been before.

He hadn't made love only to her body, but to her heart, too. Love welled up and spilled over. She wasn't going to get over him. Ever. And that was a thought designed for misery. Because he didn't love her back. And there was just no lonelier feeling in the world than loving someone who didn't love you.

He lifted his head, smiled down at her and said, "Hope you're up for a repeat performance, because I don't think I'm done with you yet."

She loved hearing that, and there was nothing she'd like more. The idea of staying right there in that big bed with Mac was more appealing than she could admit. She wanted to watch the sunrise with him. Wanted to be here again in the evening and spend her nights wrapped around him.

But none of that was going to happen.

Andi had already indulged herself; now it was time to start protecting herself. For her own good.

"That's probably not a good idea," she said.

"Why the hell not?" he demanded, tightening his hold on her as if she might try to get out of bed.

Which she really should.

"Because this—between us—it's not going anywhere, Mac, so what's the point?"

He laughed. "You can ask me that after what we just shared? Andi, that was incredible."

"It was," she said, starting to feel the chill of the room on her skin. "And now we're done."

"Don't have to be," he told her, bending down to kiss her once, twice, just a brush of her lips with his. "Andi, this just proves what I've been saying all along. We make a great team."

"A team?" The chill she felt deepened as she waited for him to continue.

"Yeah." Idly, he ran one hand over her skin until he finally cupped one of her breasts. As he talked, his fingertips caressed her.

A new wash of heat swept over her, but was lost in the chill when he continued.

"We're a team, Andi. At the office. Clearly, in bed." He dropped his head, kissed her briefly, then looked at her, satisfaction shining in his eyes. "You've got to come back to work now. Can't you see what a mistake it would be to walk away from everything we have together?"

Okay. The chill was now icy. Her heart was full of love and all he could think about was using sex to get her back to the office? She brushed his hand aside and scooted back from him. Her own nudity didn't bother her; she was much too consumed by a temper that bubbled and frothed in the pit of her stomach to worry about being naked.

She knew he'd felt what she had when they came together. He couldn't have been immune to the incredible sense of "rightness" that had lit up between them. Could he? Could he have experienced just what she had and explain it all away as *teamwork*?

Sad, that's what it was. Just sad. But anger was better than sorrow, so she gave herself over to it.

"Seriously?" she asked, shaking her hair back from her face. "You think promising me more sex will keep me as your assistant?"

"Why not?" He grinned again, clearly not picking up on the ice in her tone. "Honey, we just made the world tremble. I don't know about you, but I've never experienced anything even remotely like it before. Why the hell wouldn't we do that again? As often as possible?"

He couldn't see why and she couldn't tell him. So they were at an impasse. One that wasn't going to be maneuvered around. Before she could say anything, he started talking again, clearly enthused with his idea.

"As long as no one at the office knows what's going on between us, we can go on being lovers and work together just like we did before."

He reached for her, but she shook her head. "Just like before."

"Yeah." His smile slipped a little as if he were beginning to pick up on the fact that she wasn't all that enthused with his "plan." But still, he kept going. "We work together, each have our own homes and we share amazing sex."

"So we're boss and assistant at the office and bed buddies once that door's closed."

He frowned. "Bed buddies seems a little—"

"Accurate?"

"Okay, something's bothering you."

She laughed shortly and the sound of it scraped across her throat. "Yeah. Something."

God, she was an idiot. Yes, she had the memory of this night to cling to, but now, she'd also have the memory of this conversation to color it. How could he be so smart and so stupid all at once? And how could she have walked right into this situation, a smile on her face and eagerness in her heart?

"It's the best of all possible worlds, Andi," he said, voice deep, low. "What could be better?"

So many things, she thought. Love. Commitment. Marriage. Family. The offer he'd just made her paled in comparison. She couldn't say any of that, of course. For him, love had never entered the picture and damned if she'd shove it through the door now.

"No." Shaking her head, she scooted off the bed and grabbed her dress off the floor.

"No?" he echoed, sitting up to stare at her. "That's all you've got to say? Just…no?"

"Just no." Stepping into the dress, she pulled it up, then fought with the zipper. Andi was so done. She needed to get out of there. Fast. Before she said too much of what she was thinking. Problem? She didn't have her car. She'd be trapped in his all the way back to town. Nearly groaning in frustration now, she tugged again at the *stupid* zipper, which remained stuck.

Still, psychologically, she felt much more able to have a fight if she at least wasn't naked.

"Why no, Andi?" He came off the bed, too, and went to grab her shoulders before she slipped away. His eyes fired. "Is there someone else? Some guy I don't know about? Is that what this is?"

She looked at him in disbelief. "Are you kidding? *When* could I possibly have found a guy, Mac?" She whipped her hair behind her shoulders, tugged at the damned zipper again and knew she'd snagged it in the fabric. Letting her arms fall to her sides, she glared at him as if even the zipper was his fault. "Until several days ago I was pretty much an indentured servant. I had no life outside that office."

"Servant?" His eyes flashed and this time it was anger

pumping from him, not sexual energy. "A damn well-paid servant if you're asking me."

"I'm not," she countered.

"Well, you should." He shoved one hand through his hair and gritted his teeth.

"Sure, I made a great salary—and had zero chance to spend any of it." Andi met his anger with her own and stood her ground, just as she always had. "How do you think I can afford to quit? I've got everything you ever paid me sitting in a bank account."

"That's great." He threw his hands up and let them fall again. "So I'm *paying* you to leave me."

"In a nutshell." She looked around wildly, searching for her shoes. He'd carried her in here, and right now that little romantic moment felt light-years away. Had she kicked them off? Had he pulled them off? Did it matter?

"There!" She spotted one of her heels under a chair near the fireplace. Surely the other one would be close.

"What're you doing?"

"It should be obvious." She picked up one shoe and continued the search for the other. "I'm getting dressed. I need to go home."

"You can't leave in the middle of a fight."

She saw the other shoe and snatched it. "Watch me."

"How?"

God, she was so done. Andi couldn't believe that what had started out as an amazing evening had devolved into a battle. And what was she fighting for? He didn't want to be won. He wanted his assistant back—with fringe benefits. How humiliating was that?

"How what?" She pulled her shoes on, straightened up and glanced at Mac.

"How are you going to leave?" He was still blissfully

naked and it was a struggle to keep her hormones from jumping up and down just from looking at him. His arms were folded across his chest, his green eyes were narrowed. "It's a hell of a long hike from the ranch to town. Especially in those heels."

Here was the problem she'd noted earlier. "Damn it, you have to drive me."

"When we're done talking," Mac said.

"Oh," Andi told him, nodding, "trust me, we're done."

"You can't tell me that what just happened between us didn't change something."

"It changed *everything*," she said, wishing she'd suddenly sprout wings so she could just jump off his balcony and get herself home. Now. "That's the point."

"And my point is, that change doesn't have to be a bad one."

If he only knew. "Mac…"

He pulled her in close and though she was still pretty angry, she didn't fight him on it. Tipping her head back, she looked into his eyes and wished things were different. Wished she didn't love him so damn much. Wished he felt even a touch of what she felt.

"Don't say no so fast, Andi," he whispered, tucking a stray lock of her hair behind her ear. She shivered at the gentle touch and knew that something inside her was melting in spite of everything. What kind of fool did that make her?

"Wait," he said. "See." He winked. "I've still got most of the two weeks I took off left to help you set up your house. Get it in order. Let's see where we are at the end of it. Okay?"

At the end of the two weeks, they would be in the same damn place, only she'd be even more twisted up and torn over it. There was no way to win in this particular battle. When it was over they would both lose something, and she couldn't prevent that, even if it ended tonight.

So did she take the rest of those two weeks, torment herself with dreams that had no basis in reality? Or did she end it now, while she was cold and empty and sad?

"Give us the time, Andi," he urged, and caressed her cheek with the backs of his fingers. "Let's find out together where we are at the end of it."

"I know where we'll be," she said, shaking her head.

"You can't, because I don't." His gaze moved over her face and Andi felt it as she would have a touch.

"Give it a chance," he said. "Don't end it now."

Fool, she told herself. *Don't be an idiot*, her brain warned. *Step back now and make it a clean break*, her heart shouted.

But she looked up into his eyes and didn't listen to any of it.

"Okay."

Eight

Mac didn't have his phone on him and realized that it was the first time in years he'd been completely disconnected from the rest of the world. He owed Andi for that. For making him see just how attached he'd gotten to the damn thing. Now, he could go hours without even thinking about his phone, and wasn't that amazing?

As thoughts of Andi rose up in his mind, though, he forgot about his phone and wondered what she was doing. Where she was. He hadn't been able to stop thinking about her since he dropped her off at her place the night before. Who could blame him? He never would have guessed at the woman behind the cool, professional demeanor. She'd hidden that from him so well, it had to make him wonder what other secrets she had. For the first time in his life, he wanted to know more about a woman, not less. And for the first time in his life, the woman wasn't interested.

"How the hell can she not be?" he muttered, scrawling his signature across the bottom of a contract. He tossed the papers to one side and reached for the next stack.

Last night with Andi had been a revelation. He'd been with his share of women over the years, but nothing he'd ever experienced had come close to what had happened between them. Being locked inside her body had taken him higher than ever before. Her every breath, every sigh had somehow drifted within him, taking root and blossoming so richly he'd hardly been able to breathe. Touching her had awakened a tenderness in him he hadn't been aware of. Need hadn't been satisfied. If anything, it had grown, until now he felt as if he were choking with it.

He'd wanted her to stay with him last night. Another first. He didn't usually take women to his home, and on the rare occasions he had, he'd hustled them back out again as quickly as possible. But this time, it had been Andi who'd drawn a line in the sand.

Mac could admit, at least to himself, that when she'd jumped out of bed with the idea of closing things off between them, he'd felt—not panic, he assured himself— more like a sense of being rattled. He'd thought that after what they'd shared, she'd turn cuddly and, damn it, *agreeable*. Instead, she'd refused to see reason and had almost cut him off.

That had never happened before.

He didn't like it.

Pausing in his work, he tightened his grip on the sterling silver pen and stared blindly at the wall opposite, not seeing his office but the woman currently driving him around the bend.

When he dropped her off at her place, they'd agreed

to take the next day apart, to catch up on things that had to be done—but more than that, they'd both needed some time to come to grips with what had happened between them. So Mac was here, signing off on the contracts his lawyers had approved and Andi was…where?

Damn it.

He grabbed his desk phone, punched in a number and waited while it rang. When a familiar voice answered, Mac said, "Rafe. You open for lunch today?"

Mac needed to talk to another guy. A man would understand. Women were just too damned confusing.

"Yes," Rafe said. "I'm free. Is there something wrong?"

"Damned if I know," Mac muttered. "I was sort of hoping you could help me figure that out."

"Well, now I wouldn't miss lunch for anything. The diner then? About one?"

"That'll work." Mac hung up and got back to the business at hand.

Thoughts of Andi nibbled at his mind, of course. The office seemed empty without the sound of her voice or the click of her sensible black pumps on the floor. He kept expecting her to give her perfunctory knock before throwing his door open to tell him where he needed to be.

Instead, he had a neatly typed-up schedule from Laura—with no notations like *be on time* written in red ink in the margins. His office was running along and he had to admit they seemed to be managing without him fairly well.

Tim would be back next week and, meanwhile, phone calls between Laura and him were keeping everything going while Mac was gone. He didn't know how he felt about that, to be honest.

Finished signing the stack of papers, he tossed his pen

onto the desk and leaned back in his leather chair. He swiveled to look out a window at the spread of McCallum land and told himself that he should be pleased. Work was getting done. Clients were happy. Papers were being filed. It seemed his company didn't need his 24/7 dedication after all. Exactly what Andi had been trying to tell him.

So had he just been wasting his life locked away here in this building? He'd devoted himself to his job, to the exclusion of everything else only to find that the business ran just fine without him. What the hell did that say?

To him, it said that he couldn't sit here anymore. Why the hell did he agree to take this time away from Andi when all he really wanted was to be with her?

Disgusted with his own company, Mac picked up the contracts and carried them out to the main office. Dumping them all on Laura's desk, he said, "These are ready to go out."

"I'll take care of it right away," she assured him.

Mac noticed she still looked wary of him, so he made the effort to drop the brusqueness from his tone. "You're doing a great job, Laura. It's appreciated."

Surprised, she blinked up at him and a shy smile curved her mouth. "Thanks, Mr. McCallum."

He nodded. "Call me Mac. And if you've got any questions, you give Tim a call, all right?"

"I will." As he pushed open the door, he heard her call out, "Have a good day, Mac."

Not much chance of that.

"Thanks for coming out with me today, Violet."

"Are you kidding?" Vi held up several bags. "I love shopping here."

The Courtyard was just a few miles west of downtown Royal. It had begun as a ranch, then was taken over and renovated to become a bustling collection of eclectic shops. There were antiques, yarn and fabric stores, an artisan cheese maker and most Saturday mornings there was a farmer's market. You could get all the local produce you wanted, along with fresh flowers, not to mention the food stands that popped up to feed the hungry shoppers.

Since it was a long drive from Royal into the big city, having the Courtyard here was a real bonus to everyone for miles around. But as popular a spot as it was, Andi hadn't had the chance to really explore it as much as she'd wanted to. Working nonstop for Mac had kept her from doing a lot of things. But how could she regret time spent with him now that it was over?

"Anything in particular you're looking for?"

"Well, I do have a house to finally furnish," Andi said wistfully.

"Fun," Vi said. "And I'd like to stop in at the soap makers, then pop into Priceless. Raina's holding an antique rocking chair for me."

Raina Patterson Dane ran the antiques store, but she'd made it so much more by also offering craft classes in the back. Still, the furniture and wild mix of decor items had made Priceless *the* place to find different kinds of things for your house. Plus her new husband, Nolan, was opening his law office in the loft space above Priceless, so it really was a family affair.

"Sure," Andi said, turning to head over there. "I wanted to look there for the furniture, anyway."

"Good idea," Vi said as they walked side by side. "Priceless has so many nice things, I always need a truck to haul it all home when I'm finished in there. I swear every time I tell Rafe I'm going shopping, I can almost hear him thinking, *Please, not Priceless.*"

Andi didn't believe her for a minute. Vi's husband was so in love with her, he supported everything she said or did. "Rafe wants you happy."

"He really does," Vi said, and ran one hand over her belly. "And I am. Completely. God, I didn't think I'd ever get to this place, you know? Things were so muddled with Rafe for a while, I was afraid we were going to lose what we'd found together."

Andi knew just how she felt. The only difference between them was that Andi *knew* she was going to lose what was most important to her. It was just a matter of time. Less than two weeks now, to be exact.

"I'm really glad," she finally said, trying to keep that twinge of envy she felt to herself.

"Oh man." Vi came to an abrupt stop and stared at Andi. "I'm so insensitive, I should be horsewhipped. There's something wrong, isn't there? That's why the spontaneous shopping invitation today. What happened?" Her shoulders slumped and she winced. "Did Mac do something? Should I have *him* horsewhipped?"

"Thanks for the offer." Andi laughed and reached out to hug her friend. "But no, you don't have to go after your brother. I swear, Vi, I don't know what I'd do without you and Jolene."

"Well, you don't have to know, do you?" She frowned. "Speaking of Jolene, why isn't she with us on this expedition?"

Andi had called her sister first thing that morning and told her everything—about her amazing night with Mac and then how it had ended not in joy, but with a whimper. Naturally Jolene had been thrilled, then sad, then furious on her behalf. How did people live without a sister to bitch to? Since Jolene hadn't been able to join Andi and Vi today, she'd made Andi give a solemn promise to come by later with more information. "She couldn't come. Jacob had a ball game."

"That's so nice." Vi's eyes went misty as she rubbed her belly again. "We'll have ball games, too, won't we, baby?"

"What if it's a girl?"

"Well, we'll find out soon," Vi reminded her, "And if it is a girl, I'll have to say that I was the starting shortstop on my Little League team."

"I stand corrected."

"Okay, but can we do it sitting down for a minute?" Vi pointed to several cushioned iron tables and chairs positioned close to the bakery. "Maybe get a scone and some tea?"

"Great idea." Once Andi had Vi sitting down comfortably, she said, "You stay here and watch our bags. I'll get the food and drinks."

It wasn't long before Andi was carrying a tray with two iced teas and two blueberry scones back to the table. The minute she set it down, Vi snatched at a scone. "Sorry I'm so greedy, but the baby's hungry all the time."

Wistful, Andi sighed a little. She had nieces and a nephew she loved. She could watch her best friend hurrying toward motherhood. But the chances of Andi ever having a child of her own were slim to none, since the only man she wanted to father her children couldn't be less interested.

"Now that I'm sitting down—thank you for that—and

baby's getting a scone…tell me, what's got that puckered-up look on your face?"

"My what?"

"You know." Vi wrinkled her brow and pursed her lips.

"Oh fine," Andi muttered and deliberately evened out her features.

"It's Mac, isn't it?" Vi set down the scone and took a sip of tea. "No one can wrinkle a woman's forehead like my brother."

"Sad, but true." Andi took a quick look around to make sure no one was close enough to overhear. But there were only a few other people taking a break and they were seated a couple of tables over.

Shoppers wandered, a toddler whined for a toy and a busy mom pushed a stroller at a fast trot while she kept a tight grip on a five-year-old. Everything was so ordinary. So normal. But Andi's world had been knocked completely out of whack.

She looked at Vi. "I slept with him."

"Mac?" Her friend's eyes popped wide and her mouth dropped open. "You slept with my brother?"

Hunching her shoulders a little, Andi whispered, "Could you maybe not shout it loud enough to spread it through town like a brushfire?"

"Sorry, sorry." Vi winced and leaned in over the table. "This is so great, Andi. I mean really. I've hoped and hoped you two would get together and finally it's happened. Tell me everything. Well, not everything, but you know. When? Why? No, never mind why. I know why, you're nuts about him, which could just make you literally nuts, but never mind. When?"

"Last night and yes, I probably am nuts." She was

glad that Vi was so happy about the situation. Andi only wished she could be. Breaking off a tiny piece of her scone, she nibbled at it. "I don't know what I was thinking."

"If it's like what happened with Rafe and I, you weren't thinking at all." Vi sat back, took another bite of her scone. "I don't think you're *supposed* to think about something that big. You're supposed to *feel* it."

Oh, there had been lots of feeling. Sadly, it had been all on her side. "Well, fine. But I have to think now, don't I?"

Violet sighed. "Yes, being you, I guess so."

"Thanks," Andi said wryly.

"Oh, honey, I love you, but you really do think too much. Couldn't you just relax and enjoy it for a while?"

"No, because he doesn't want what I want."

"Not yet, anyway."

"Not ever, Vi." Andi had to remember that. No point in setting herself up for more crushing blows. She had to take what was left of their two weeks together and then turn her back on the past and force herself to find a future. A future that wouldn't include Mac. Damn it.

"What he wants," she said, "is to get me back into his bed and back to my job. I'm not even sure if that's the order he'd prefer it in."

"He just doesn't know what he really wants." Vi reached across the table and took Andi's hand. "It was the same with Rafe, I swear. Men can be completely clueless about this stuff. It's as if they can't admit to feeling more for a woman because it tears little chunks of their manhood off or something. But *love*, to most men, is a terrifying word. The big dummies."

"I don't know that Mac is scared of love, Vi," she said

after a moment's pause. "I just know that he doesn't feel it for me. He talked about being a great team. About how when I go back to the office, we can each have our own places and meet up for sex and nobody has to know."

"Oh, God." Vi's chin dropped to her chest. "I'm related to an idiot. It's mortifying."

Andi had to chuckle and it felt good, letting go a little of the misery crouched in the corner of her heart. Knowing Vi was on her side helped a lot. It just didn't change anything.

"I can't go back to work for him. And I've agreed to keep spending time with him until the two weeks are up, but how am I going to be able to stand it? It's not as if I can sleep with him again."

"Why the hell not?"

Andi laughed. "That's exactly what he said."

"For once, my brother was right. So why not?"

Andi took a drink of her tea to ease a suddenly desert-dry throat. "Because it'll only make it harder on me when it ends if I keep getting drawn into a fantasy that will never come true."

"You could make it true." Vi took another bite of her scone and moaned softly in appreciation.

"Fantasies, by their very definition, are just that."

"Doesn't mean you can't do something about them."

"Really?" Intrigued, Andi watched her friend's sly smile and felt only a small niggle of worry in reaction. "How?"

"Easy." Vi shrugged. "You have to dump him."

Andi blew out a pent-up breath. "Dump him? We're not together—how can I dump him?"

"You said it yourself. You spend time with him, but

you don't let him close. Do exactly what you were going to do. Don't sleep with him again. It'll drive him crazy."

Andi would like to think so, but Mac had an amazing ability to rebound from women. Why should she be any different from the legions he'd moved on from in the past?

"Think about it," Vi said. "What did Mac do when you quit your job?"

"Argued with me."

"Well, sure, but then?" She picked up her scone and gestured with it. "Mac went after you. Went to your house. Talked you into this two-week thing."

"True."

"Dump him and he'll come after you again," Violet pronounced. "I know my brother. And he won't be able to stand you walking away from him."

That did sound like Mac, Andi admitted. But coming after her because he didn't like to lose didn't mean anything, did it? That would just be him responding to a direct challenge. It wouldn't mean he cared. Briefly, she remembered how it had been between the two of them the night before and she felt a flush sweep over her in response. But letting herself be drawn into a wave of hope only to be crushed didn't sound appealing.

"I don't know," she said, shaking her head and breaking off another piece of her scone. "I'd be tricking him."

Violet gave a long, dramatic sigh. "And your point is?"

Andi laughed.

"All's fair in love and war, right?"

"He doesn't love me," Andi said.

"I wouldn't be so sure," Vi replied thoughtfully.

* * *

The Royal Diner was bustling with the usual lunch crowd, plus a handful of tourists thrown into the mix. Conversations flowed fast and furious, orders were called into the kitchen and the cook stacked finished meals on the counter, waiting for them to be picked up.

The place smelled like hamburgers and good, rich coffee and felt as comfortable as Mac's own living room. Which was why he didn't mind getting there early enough to snag a booth and people-watch until Rafe arrived.

Mac knew mostly everyone in town, really. It was nice to see Nolan and his wife, Raina, laughing together in a booth on the far side of the room. Then there were Joe Bennet and his foreman talking business over apple pie and coffee. And Sheriff Nathan Battle getting a kiss from his wife, Amanda, before taking his to-go lunch out the door with him.

Rafe came in as Nathan left, and Mac waved a hand in the air to get his friend's attention.

Sliding onto the bench seat opposite him, Rafe leaned back and said, "Thank you for the lunch invitation. I've been working since five this morning and really needed to take a break."

"Five?"

"Calls to London, Shanghai. You know how it is, dealing with international businesses."

"I do, but you know what? I've discovered something recently that you should try. Relaxing."

The other man laughed, set his phone on the table in front of him and signaled Amanda for a cup of coffee. "You are going to teach me how to relax? This is a joke, right?"

"No joke. Ironic, maybe. But not a joke." Mac glanced at his friend's phone. "You don't see me checking my phone, do you?"

Rafe frowned. "No, I do not. Where is it?"

"In the truck." Mac shrugged it off. "I'm learning to put the damn thing down. You should, too."

"Here you go, Rafe," Amanda said as she set the coffee in front of him. "What can I get you two?"

They ordered and when she moved off into the crowd again Rafe asked, "Just who is teaching you how to relax? Would it be Andrea?"

Mac nodded. "It would. Funny, but in the last few days, she's taught me a lot." *Especially last night*, he thought but didn't say. There were some things a man didn't talk about, even with his friends. What had happened between Andi and him was private and would remain that way.

"So Violet tells me. You're painting now? Repairing sinks and tile floors? Have you decided to go into the home construction business as a sideline?"

"Not exactly." Mac smiled when Amanda set his turkey sandwich in front of him and grabbed a french fry. Shaking it at Rafe, he said, "I'm helping her get her house into shape." *And stealing time with her.* "But being there with her, working alongside her, she's got me thinking."

"Please. Don't keep me waiting." Rafe took a bite of his fish sandwich and kept quiet.

"Okay. The way I see it, Andi and I are good together." He took a bite of his own sandwich, then added, "We've always worked well together and it turns out we're a great team…outside of the office, too."

Rafe lifted a dark eyebrow. "Go on."

"I want her." Three simple words that seemed to suddenly be filled with a lot more meaning than he'd expected. Yes, he wanted her back at the office, he wanted her back in his bed, but the bottom line was, he just *wanted* her. Period.

That thought was heavy enough to make him scowl down at his sandwich.

"You seem to have her," Rafe mused. "So what's the problem?"

"She's determined to back away, that's the damn problem." It irritated him to even say it. "I need to find a way to keep her."

"Do you love her?"

He jerked back. "No one said anything about love."

"Maybe you should."

Mac frowned at him. "You're feeling awful damn easy with that word. Not too long ago, it was different. You remember that?"

Rafe's eyes went dark. "Yes, all too well. I almost lost your sister to my own pride and stubborn refusal to see the truth of my own feelings. Will you let that happen to you as well, my friend? Or will you learn from my mistakes?"

"It's different," Mac insisted, grabbing a fry and popping it into his mouth. "You loved Violet."

"Well, if you do not love Andi, then let her go. Let her find a man who *will* love her as she deserves to be."

"What man?" Mac demanded, leaning over the table. "Is there some guy in town with his eye on Andi?"

Rafe blew out a laugh. "Any number of them, I should imagine. She's a lovely woman."

Scowling now, Mac snapped, "You're married to my sister, so you shouldn't be noticing things like that."

"I'm married, not dead."

"That could be arranged," Mac muttered, but Rafe only laughed.

"It seems to me that for a man who claims to not be in love, you're very territorial."

"I don't share," Mac grumbled. "Doesn't mean anything more than that."

"And so she should make herself available to you as your assistant, your mistress, your companion?"

Mac scowled again and couldn't find the appetite for more of his damn lunch. "Aren't you supposed to be on my side?"

"I am," Rafe assured him.

"Doesn't look like it from this side of the fence."

"I'm only trying to make you see that Andi deserves more than being your convenience."

"Never said she was convenient. A more argumentative woman I've never known. Except for my sister," he amended.

"I will agree that my wife is very opinionated."

Mac snorted a laugh. For all the times Rafe had made him furious over the years, for all the trouble he'd tried to stir up when he first blew into Royal, he was surely paying for it with the woman he loved. Violet had never been an easy woman, so Mac knew that Rafe's life was colorful, to say the least.

But Violet and Rafe were a team.

As he and Andi were. Or could be. If she would only see that he was right about this.

"You're walking a fine line here, Mac," Rafe said, taking a sip of his coffee. "If you step wrong, you could lose everything. I know."

Worry flickered in the back of his mind, but Mac

quashed it fast. There wasn't a damn thing Mac McCallum couldn't get once he'd made up his mind.

And his sights were set on Andi.

"I'll watch my step," he said, and picked up his sandwich again. "I know what I'm doing."

"I hope so, my friend," Rafe said with a shake of his head. "I do hope so."

Nine

Andi had never really planned to stay for so long, working for Mac.

When she started, it had seemed like a good place for her. After growing up in Royal, she'd left town, gone to college and, with her business degree, she'd headed to California. Working in LA had been exciting; living there had been less so. The crowds, the noise, the inability to look up at the sky and see more than a small square of smog-tinted blue had eventually begun wearing on her. At her core, she was a small-town girl and when she accepted that truth and moved back to Royal, things had fallen into place for her. She'd reconnected with her sister, found a fast and true friend in Violet and fallen stupidly in love with her boss.

"Okay, so not everything worked out," she muttered, setting some of her books onto the built-in shelves along one wall of her tiny living room. The house was coming together, the two weeks with Mac would soon be over and she had to do some thinking about her life.

The job with McCallum Enterprises had been good for her, though. She'd loved the energy, the rush of helping to run an international company with a great reputation. But it wasn't *hers*. Just like Mac, that company would never belong to her, and Andi wanted something of her own. To build a life and find what she was missing. To build a business from the ground up and watch it grow. She just didn't know what.

"Thank God you had tea made," Jolene said as she came into the living room carrying two tall ice-filled glasses with a small plate of cookies balanced on top of one of them. "I swear, summer's coming along too early for me."

"It's not that hot." Andi reached up to take the cookies and her glass of tea.

"Not in here, bless the air conditioning gods." Jolene eased down to the floor, maneuvering her belly as if it were a separate entity. "Oh, I should have gone shopping with you and Vi. It would have been much more relaxing, not to mention cooler. That baseball field will kill you. Blazing sun, the shouting, the crying—and that's just the parents…"

Andi laughed.

"Good," Jolene said with a brisk nod. "You can still do that."

"Of course I can. It's just, there's not a lot to laugh about right now."

"I could get Tom to go over and kick Mac's butt for you."

"No, but thanks for the thought."

Jolene shrugged. "Just as well. Tom really likes Mac."

"So do I." Andi grumbled as she bit into a cookie. "That's the problem."

"Damn it, I was so sure that once you'd had sex with the man it would either shatter your illusions or make him realize just how great you are. Numskull man."

"It's not his fault, Jolene," Andi said, taking a cookie she didn't really want and biting in, anyway. "I'm the one who fell in love."

"That's not a crime."

"No, but stupid should be."

"Honey, there aren't nearly enough jails if stupid turns out to be a crime."

"True." Taking a sip of her tea, Andi looked at her sister. "How did I live without you when I was in LA?"

"Beats hell out of me."

Andi grinned. "I was just sitting here thinking how glad I was that I moved back home. I've got you and Tom and your kids and I'll be here for the new baby's birth…"

"You bet you will. What if Tom gets called out to a fire? You're my backup."

Smiling still, Andi finished, "California just wasn't for me."

"No, but you figured that out, came home and found a job you loved. You'll do it again. As soon as you're ready."

"I think I am. Ready, I mean," Andi said as her idea solidified in her mind and settled in to stay. "But I've been doing a lot of thinking about this and I don't want a job, Jolene. I want my own business."

"Really? Great! What're you planning?"

"I'm going to be a professional organizer." It had been bumping along in her brain for a few months now and she'd toyed with it, even while she worked for Mac. She supposed that a part of her had realized that she couldn't stay at McCallum Enterprises forever, and her subconscious had been busily at work plotting her next move. She was going to organize people's homes, their businesses, heck, *garages*. She was great at finding order in chaos, so why shouldn't she make a living doing what she was so good at?

"That is the most brilliant idea you've had in years." Jolene had a wide smile on her face as she lifted her tea glass in a toast. "Honestly, I'll be your first customer. I'll expect the pregnant sister discount, of course, but you could come through and get my kids' bedrooms straightened out. Do you know I found an overlooked Easter egg in Jacob's room last week? I probably would have found it sooner, but I thought the smell coming from there was just from his discarded socks. Like usual."

Andi laughed. "Jacob's room may defeat me, but I'm willing to try."

"Then there's my kitchen and, God help you, Tom's workshop." Jolene reached out, took her sister's hand and squeezed. "It's a great idea and you'll be a huge success at it. Guaranteed."

"Thanks, I think I will, too. And God knows I've got the time to pour into it."

"But not like a workaholic again, right?" Concern shadowed Jolene's eyes briefly. "You're not going to turn into a stranger again while you bury yourself in work, right?"

"Absolutely. I want my own business," Andi said firmly, "but I want a *life*, too. And I'm going to find one, Jolene."

While her sister talked about the possibilities, Andi

thought about the night before, being in Mac's arms, the magic of the moment. A whisper of regret echoed in her heart, for all the hopes and dreams that would never be realized. Then she deliberately erased those images from her mind because it was time she started training herself to have that life she craved so much.

Without Mac.

The following day, Mac took her horseback riding.

She tried to regret agreeing to finish out the two weeks they'd originally decided on, but it wasn't easy. Because their remaining time together was really a gift to herself. When this time was up, Andi would have to walk away for her own sake, no matter what it might cost her. And in spite of what his sister might think or hope, Mac wouldn't follow her again. He didn't like losing.

These two weeks were his attempt to win her back. When that failed, Mac would move on—as he had so many times before.

Dumping him as Vi had suggested wouldn't work. And even if it would, Andi wasn't going to play games. If she had to trick Mac or trap him, he wouldn't be worth catching, would he? The heck of it was, Andi knew that if she told him the truth, admitted to loving him, it would throw him so hard, he'd walk away long before the two weeks were up. He wasn't interested in love.

But even knowing that she would be free of him if she just confessed, Andi couldn't do it. She still had her pride and damned if her last memory would be of Mac looking at her with pity shining in his eyes just before he turned away from her.

Those worries were for later. Today, they were here together, riding across open ranch land as if they were the only two people in the world. The Double M was a huge ranch, stretching out for miles. A stand of wild oaks straggled along the river and Mac led her in that direction. The sun was heating up and in another month, this ride would be downright miserable. But today was clear and just warm enough to remind you that summer was coming.

"You're thinking again," Mac said from beside her. "I can hear you from here."

"You've something against thinking?" She pulled the brim of her borrowed hat down lower over her eyes to cut the glare from the sun.

"On a day like today, while it's just us and the horses? Yeah, I do." He gave her a brief smile and nudged his horse closer to hers. "You know I didn't bring my phone with me?"

She laughed, delighted. So this time with her had changed him—if only a little. "I'm so proud."

"You should be," he said. "Without you, I'd be hunkered over in the saddle, checking stock reports, catching up with Tim and making sure Laura sent out the contracts due to be mailed today. Instead, thanks to you, I'm spending time on my ranch alongside a beautiful woman. And at the moment, I don't give two damns what's happening back at the office."

She smiled; how could she help it? The man was charming and darn near irresistible. Sadly, he knew it.

"So, are you going to show me where they set up the last water tank?"

"Interested in ranch life, are you?" The twinkle in his eye sparkled in the sunlight.

"Interested in seeing the tank I had to get road clearance approval on to bring in," she countered.

Ranchers kept huge water tanks stationed around their property to be filled by rainwater or, in times of serious drought, by water trucks brought in for that purpose. There were stock ponds, of course, natural watering holes for the animals, but they could go dry in a blistering hot Texas summer and you had to be able to refill them when necessary. The tanks were one sure way of accomplishing that. But several of them had come down during the big storm, and Mac had had to replace them. Now they were in place, only waiting to be filled before the start of summer.

Thankfully, they'd already had a good-sized storm at the beginning of the month and more were being predicted. In fact, she thought as she peered up at the sky to see gray-and-black clouds huddling together as if forming an attack strategy, it looked like another storm was headed this way so fast, Andi and Mac might get wet themselves before this ride was over.

"It's this way." He tugged on the reins and his horse moved in that direction. Nudging Apollo into a trot, Mac looked back to make sure Andi was following him. She was, and waved to him in reassurance. The gelding she rode was in no particular hurry, which was just as well. It had been a couple of years since she had been riding and she knew her muscles would be screaming by tomorrow.

Despite the heat of the sun, a brisk breeze blew, bringing the scent of the storm with it. Andi pulled her hat down hard so it wouldn't blow away and followed after Mac, determined to keep up. It was another twenty minutes to the stock pond and the water tank that stood alongside it.

"The pond looks good." She dismounted with a quiet sigh of relief.

"It's early yet," Mac said, squinting into the sun, watching a few lazy cattle meander down to the water's edge for a drink. "But yeah. Last year, the water level was only half as much at this point in the season. A couple more good storms," he said, checking out the sky, "and we'll be set. Tanks and ponds."

"It's a lot, Mac," she said softly, letting her gaze sweep across miles of grazing land. Cattle dotted the countryside, and here and there a few horses were sprinkled in as added interest. "Running your business, and the ranch, it's a lot. Do you ever want to hand the reins over to someone else? Step back from it?"

For a second, it looked as though he might give her a wink and a grin and the kind of quick, smooth answer he was best known for. But then his features evened out and he took another long look around him before turning back to her. "No. I don't. Though I'll say, if I ever had to make a choice—either the business or the ranch—the ranch would win hands down." He bent over, scooped up a handful of dirt and grass and then turned his hand over, letting it all drift to earth again. "I love this place. Every blade of grass and clod of dirt. Every stupid steer, every irritation. The worry about not enough water, too much water, calves being born, losing some to coyotes…" He stood up again and shook his head. "It's McCallum land and I guess it's in me."

She heard it in his voice, saw it in his eyes. The business he'd taken over when his parents died was something he'd built, defined, expanded because he'd needed to prove something. To his father. Himself. Maybe even the world. But this ranch was the soul of him. What kept him going, what drove him. His love for the land and the continuity of caring for it.

Her heart turned over in her chest as he looked at her, and Andi wondered how much more she could possibly love him. How could the feeling inside her keep growing, filling her up until she thought she must be glowing with it?

He tipped his head to one side, stared at her. "What is it? You've got this weird expression your face."

She smiled and walked toward him. Just when she thought she had come to grips with everything, he threw her for a loop again. Seeing him like this, standing tall and arrogant and proud on land his family had owned for generations, made her want to tell him everything. Confess her love, let him know what she thought and felt. She couldn't, though, any more than she could turn from him now and pretend she'd heard and felt nothing.

"You just…surprise me sometimes, that's all," she said, walking close enough that she could reach up and cup his cheek in her palm. Heat flowed from his body to hers and back again. "You're kind of wonderful."

Pleasure shone in his eyes. He covered her hand with his and, as their gazes locked, she felt a shift in the emotions charging around them. Passion burned just beneath the surface, a reminder that what was between them was powerful, difficult to ignore or deny.

"If I'd known it would have this effect on you," he whispered, "I'd have brought you out to the water tank before."

She laughed and shook her head. "You're also impossible."

"So it's been said." He pulled her in close until she had to tip her head back to look up at him.

"What am I doing here?" she murmured, more to herself than to him.

He took her hat off, smoothed her hair back from her face, dipped his head and whispered, "Driving me crazy."

Lightning flashed in the distance and thunder rolled toward them like an approaching army. Then he kissed her and the storm erupted around them, pelting them with rain they didn't even notice.

When the storm rushed in and lightning began to slash at the ground much closer to them, they broke apart and climbed onto the horses.

Drenched and laughing like loons, they outpaced the storm, rode up to the ranch house and turned the horses over to the stable hands. Then racing for the house, Mac and Andi ran into the kitchen and gratefully took the towels Teresa offered them.

"Couple of crazy people is what you are," she muttered, with a half smile tugging at her lips. Her short, gray-streaked brown hair hugged her head like a cap. Her lipstick was bright red and her nails were painted to match. She wore jeans, boots and a long-sleeved blue-and-white-checked shirt. "Could have been struck by lightning out in this storm. You're lucky you're just half-drowned instead."

"Thank you, Teresa," Andi said, running the towel over her hair and toeing her boots off one at a time. "We're messing up your floor. I'm so sorry."

Mac glanced behind them and saw the muddy footprints and small river of water that had followed them in. He cringed a little and added his own apology. He might own the house, but Teresa ruled it, and everyone on the ranch knew it. "We gave you more work to do, didn't we?"

Impatiently, Teresa waved that away. "Don't have

nearly enough to do around here to keep me busy, so
don't worry about that. You two go on up now and get
out of those wet clothes. I'll throw everything in the
dryer as soon as you do."

"I'll bring our clothes down in a couple minutes."
Barefoot now, Mac took Andi's hand and pulled her
along with him, though she came reluctantly. He had to
assume it was because she was embarrassed that Teresa
knew the two of them would soon be naked together.
But she'd just have to get over that or risk pneumonia.
Already, she was shivering from the effects of being
soaking wet and the air conditioning blowing through
the house. So reluctant or not, she followed after him,
down the hall, up the stairs and to his bedroom.

"Come on, get out of those wet clothes," he urged as
he stripped himself.

"You're just trying to get me out of my panties again."
Her voice trembled with cold.

"You caught on to my nefarious scheme. Make a
woman so damn cold she turns blue, then have my way
with her."

She laughed shortly. Her hands shook as she undid
buttons and then pulled off her shirt, jeans and underwear. He tried not to look because the point here was
getting her warm again, not jumping her the minute she
was vulnerable. Once they were both finished, he tossed
her his robe, then pulled on a pair of dry jeans without
bothering with boxers beneath them.

Bundling up the sodden mess of clothes, he opened
the bedroom door. "I'll just take these to Teresa and be
right back."

"Take your time. This is so humiliating," she murmured, sitting on the edge of his bed, shaking her head.

"Yeah, getting caught in a storm is a real embar-rassment." He grinned at her then bolted back down the stairs. He knew she wasn't going anywhere, but he wanted to get back to her quickly.

Teresa was waiting for him. "I'll get those dry. You take up that tray I fixed for the two of you. Get some of that hot coffee into Andi before she turns into an icicle."

"I will." Mac spotted the tray on the kitchen table and couldn't stop the smile of appreciation. There was left-over fried chicken, potato salad, a half-dozen cookies, two mugs and a small carafe of coffee.

Impulsively, he kissed her cheek and was shocked to see her blush. "You are a wonder," he said softly. "And I don't think I tell you that often enough. Thanks, Te-resa. I appreciate it."

"Well, now, you two need some warming up—and food and coffee are just one of the ways to get that done." She slid him a sly smile. "I imagine you can think of another way."

He winked at her. "Oh, one or two come to mind."

Back upstairs, he found Andi just where he'd left her. Her hair was dark and wet and she was looking a little less sure of herself, which was, he told himself, a good thing. He wanted her as off balance as he'd been lately. Damn it, all he could think about was her. From the first day of their two-week agreement, she'd been front and center in his mind. And if anything, it had only got-ten worse the more time they spent together. Her laugh haunted him, her eyes filled his dreams and the scent of her seemed to always be in the air. Andi had somehow become a part of him and he wasn't quite sure what to do about that.

Oh, he'd once thought about a future wife and children

in a vague, maybe-one-day kind of way. But that was a long time ago. Before he'd had responsibility thrust on him by his parents' deaths.

Then it had been not only the family ranch—that had been in McCallum hands for generations—and the business his father had been building, but there had also been Violet, his teenage sister he had to protect and look after. He and Vi had butted heads time and again, which was to be expected, but being brother *and* father to her had made keeping their relationship tight that much harder.

So he'd buried himself in work because at least there, he was sure of his footing. Slowly, over time, he'd lost all sense of a future because his present was packed with far too much already.

Mac's parents had been happy. He and Vi had been raised by people who loved each other and them. But when they died, it was as if Mac had shut down that loving side of himself. The part that remembered family and laughter and the ease of just being happy. He hadn't had time for happiness back then. It had all been about saving his father's company. Keeping the ranch together. Diversifying. Building on a fortune to make sure that Violet would never have to worry. He'd expanded the ranch beyond his father's dreams and he'd built a company that was larger and more successful than anyone could have imagined. And somewhere along the line, he realized, he'd lost himself.

In the past ten days or so, he'd begun to find the man he used to be. He'd laughed more, talked more and done less work than he had in ten years. But who he was now was ingrained in his soul. Wasn't it too late to go backward? To try to reclaim permanently the younger version of himself? The one that had plans beyond running a successful company? If he tried, didn't he run the risk of losing everything he'd built?

"Mac?" Andi's voice cut into his thoughts and brought him back from the meandering road his mind had taken. "You okay?"

"Yeah," he said, focusing on her and letting the rest go. For now, anyway. "Fine. Look. I bring supplies."

She smiled. "I can't imagine what Teresa's thinking right now."

"I can." He grinned and carried the tray to the table set between the two cozy chairs in front of the hearth. "She's thinking, *Look at all that mud and water. He's a lucky man to have a girl like Andrea Beaumont give him a second glance when he drags her through a thunderstorm on horseback.*"

Andi laughed as he'd meant her to.

"Come over here," he urged. "I'm gonna start a fire, get us both warmed up while we eat."

She stood up and he saw she was dwarfed by his dark red robe. The hem of it hung to well below her knees and her hands had disappeared into the sleeves. But she didn't look as pale and cold as she had before. While she took a seat, picked up one of the coffee mugs and took a sip, Mac built a fire in the hearth.

He supposed it really wasn't cold enough to warrant it. And it was completely illogical to have a fire going while the air conditioner was running. But the flames already licking at the kindling and snapping up along the stacked logs were comforting. Romantic. With a naked Andi within arm's reach, romantic was a very good thing.

"I love a fireplace," she said softly, staring at the blaze as the flickering light washed over her features. "I wish my house had one."

He took the chair beside hers, relishing the feel of the heat rushing toward him from the hearth. "Feel free to come and use mine any time you want."

"Thanks." She tipped her head to one side and smiled at him. "Maybe I will."

They ate cold chicken and talked about the town, their families, their friends, studiously avoiding all mention of what was between them. Tension coiled in the air and snapped as hungrily as the flames on wood.

By unspoken agreement, they hadn't had sex since that first time, but whenever he tried to sleep, Mac relived that night over and over again. The taste of her. The feel of her beneath his hands. The hot damp core of her that took him in and held him. Before Andi, after he'd had a woman, she retreated from his mind, as if with the need satisfied, he was content to move on to whatever— or whoever—came next.

With Andi, though, it was just the opposite. He wanted his hands on her again. Wanted to lay claim to all that she was. Wanted to hear her sighs and watch those storm-gray eyes of hers glaze over with passion then flash with completion when he took her.

Hell. He just *wanted* her. All the damn time. More than his next breath. More than anything.

"Um," she said, as if reading his mind and the quick, hungry thoughts racing through it, "we should see if our clothes are dry. Or maybe I could borrow something of yours just to get home in and—"

She was backing away. Sitting right there beside him and pulling back from him and he wasn't going to let her. Need drove him out of his chair. Want had him kneeling on the floor in front of her, staring up into gray eyes that would, he was sure, continue to haunt him for years to come.

"Or," Mac said, as he came up on his knees, "there are other options."

She took a deep breath and shook her head, making her still-damp hair swing about her face. "Mac, we shouldn't—"

"Miss a golden opportunity," he finished for her. Reaching out, he untied the robe belt at her waist, then spread the fabric apart. She shivered and her eyes went glassy as his hands skimmed over her body with sure, long strokes.

"Oh, Mac..."

She sighed and he knew he had her. Knew she wouldn't say no, wouldn't turn away from what they could find together. Running his hands up her body, he cupped her breasts and pulled gently at her rigid nipples. He loved watching that dazed expression come into her eyes. Loved the sound of her breath hitching in her lungs. Loved...

He parted her thighs, spreading her legs wide, then leaned in, covered her with his mouth and devoured her. Her quick gasp of surprise, then desperation, filled his head. Her sighs, her whimpers, her jerky movements as he pleasured her body, fed him, pushed him on. He licked, nibbled, suckled at her until she lifted her hips off the chair and threaded her fingers through his hair, holding his head to her as her cries became pleas.

She was frantic now for what he could give her and her need fueled his own. She cried out his name and the sound became a choked-off scream of release as the first explosions rocketed through her.

He continued to push, to torment her even as her body

splintered in his grasp. And before the last of the tremors shook her, he pulled her from the chair, laid her out on the rug in front of the fire and buried himself deep inside her.

The tight, damp heat of her surrounded him, and Mac paused long enough to savor the sensation of being close enough to become a part of her. He threw his head back and practically roared his satisfaction. Then she moved, arching into him, rocking her hips, urging him on.

"More, Mac," she whispered harshly. "Give me more. *Take* more of me." Her head tipped back, exposing the line of her throat, and he tucked his face into that curve, kissing her, feeling the beat of her heart in the pulse that pounded against his mouth.

His mind fogged, his heart raced. Together they rushed to completion, bodies joined in an ancient dance that felt new and wondrous. All other thoughts fled, dissolving in the wide, deep ocean of sensation they were sinking into. He felt her body tighten around his, her legs lock around his middle and even as she called his name brokenly, he joined her in the fall, giving her everything he was.

Ten

It wasn't until later, as they lay wrapped together in a blissful haze, that Mac suddenly snapped back to reality. When he realized what had just happened, he groaned, closed his eyes and muttered, "Damn it."

"What?" It came on a sigh, as if she really couldn't bring herself to care what was wrong. She slid one hand down his back and her touch felt like fire-wrapped velvet.

No way to do this an easy way. Just say it. Lifting his head, he stared down into her eyes and said, "I didn't use protection."

Well, he thought, watching her eyes flash wide with apprehension, that was dropping a lead balloon on the festivities.

"Oh, God." She covered her eyes with one hand.

He pulled away from her but didn't move far. Her skin

gleamed like fine porcelain in the firelight. Her eyes flashed and changed as emotions, like the firelit shadows, danced in them. "My fault," he said tightly. "Can't believe I did that. It's never happened before. Swear to God, you are the only woman I've ever met who could shut down my brain so completely."

She worked up a pitiful smile at that halfhearted compliment. She sat up, grabbed her blanket and drew it around her shoulders before huddling deeply into it.

"It's okay," she said firmly, as if trying to convince herself as well as him. "It was just the once. I'm sure it's fine."

Mac snorted, disgusted with himself for losing control and amused at her attempt at a positive attitude. "Yeah, I'm guessing couples have been telling each other that for centuries."

"Couples?" she repeated softly, then shook her head. "Doesn't matter. It's fine, I'm sure."

Couples. Was that what they were? For so long, they'd been colleagues. Boss and assistant. Friends. Had they worked around to where they were a couple now? When did that happen? What the hell should he do about it?

Too many things to think about when most of his blood supply was situated well below his brain. "We'll find out soon enough, won't we?" He propped his back against the closest chair, then dragged her up next to him despite her attempt to squirm away. She was stiff with tension, and he knew her mind had to be racing through every imaginable scenario and there was nothing he could do to make it easier.

He stared into the fire and tried to do some thinking of his own. The first rush of panic and self-directed fury was easing now, and Mac indulged himself in exploring a few of those future possibilities. If Andi wasn't pregnant, they could go on as they always had. Surprisingly enough, that notion wasn't as appealing as it had been even two short weeks ago.

If there was no baby and she still wanted to quit her job, he'd have to find a way to deal with that. He couldn't force her to stay if she was determined to leave. Mac frowned at the fire as Andi shifted in his grasp, probably uneasy with her thoughts. And he really couldn't blame her.

If she was pregnant, well, that opened up a whole new road. She would be carrying *his* child, so she wouldn't be walking away from him no matter what she wanted to believe.

A baby. He rubbed one hand across his face, took a deep breath and released it slowly, waiting for another wave of panic.

It didn't come.

Hell, he thought, if Andi was pregnant, she'd marry him, live here at the ranch. They'd work together, raise their kid and have great sex. The two of them would have the best of all possible worlds. That sounded pretty good to him.

The hard part would be hog-tying her until she agreed with him.

"Mac?"

"Yeah?" He tightened his hold on her in case she tried to bolt.

But she only turned her face up to his, her gray eyes stormy. "This doesn't change anything between us. It can't."

He tucked her head onto his shoulder, rested his chin on top of her head and stared into the fire blazing in the river-stone hearth. "Guess we're gonna find out about that, aren't we?"

A few days later, they still hadn't really talked about what had happened and the possible repercussions. Andi simply refused to think about it because she knew that if a part of her would really love to be pregnant with Mac's baby—it would never happen. If she were terrified at the possibility, it was almost guaranteed she'd be pregnant.

That's just the way life worked and she accepted it.

Mac, though, had been acting differently for days. She couldn't really identify what he was thinking, but she knew there was a change in him. Was it panic at the thought of perhaps being a father? Or was it something…else?

A flutter of hope tangled with anticipation in the pit of her stomach. Maybe he had come to care for her. Maybe he was looking at what the two of them had and seeing it for what it could be. Maybe.

"I bring pizza," he announced as he came in from her kitchen. He was balancing a large butcher-block cutting board that held a steaming sausage-and-mushroom pie.

All day, they'd worked on the pink room, with Mac helping the appliance delivery guy install her new black-and-chrome range. They'd tried out her new oven with a bake-it-yourself pizza she'd picked up at the market, and judging by the delicious scents wafting to her, it had worked great.

Smiling in spite of the turmoil bubbling inside her, Andi held up two glasses of dark red wine. "And I've already poured, so that's great timing."

He frowned a little as he set the pizza down on her tiny coffee table. "Maybe you shouldn't be drinking wine."

Andi sighed. "I'm not pregnant, Mac."

"We don't know that."

"Well, until we do, cheers." One glass wasn't going to hurt her or the baby if there was one. And being here with Mac, in the twilight of an early summer evening, she needed the wine.

He shrugged, served them each a slice and handed her a plate as he took a seat beside her on the floor. Andi took a bite, then waved a hand at her mouth in an attempt to cool it off.

"Yep," he said, "new oven works great. What's convection?"

"I should know that," she admitted as she huffed out a breath trying to cool the molten cheese currently burning the roof of her mouth. "But I don't."

"That makes me feel better," he admitted with a grin. Taking a sip of his wine, he looked around the living room. "We did a really good job in here, didn't we?"

"We did."

"Great team."

"Don't start."

"I'm not starting," he told her with a wink, "I'm continuing. There's a difference."

Mac being charming was hard to resist, and still, she had to. She picked up her wine for a sip.

"Andi, we've got something great." His gaze locked on to hers. "Don't walk away from it."

Sighing a little, she shook her head. "I told you, Mac, I can't keep working for you. I want a life."

"Well, so do I now." He set his glass down, then

plucked hers from her hand and set it aside, too. Taking her hands in his, he rubbed his thumbs across her knuckles while he looked deeply into her eyes. "Over the last couple of weeks, I've discovered a few things."

That flutter of hope beat a little faster in her stomach. "Such as?"

Nodding, he said, "Such as, I forgot just how good it felt to take my horse out and ride the ranch myself instead of just relying on reports from my foreman."

"I'm glad." Remembering the look on his face when he told her about what the ranch meant to him, she smiled. Maybe she had gotten through to him. At least a little.

"And," he added with a quick grin, "I learned that not answering my phone doesn't mean instant death."

Laughing, she said, "Also good."

"Mostly, though," he said, and his voice dropped to a low, throaty hush that seemed to ripple along her nerve endings, "I learned what we have."

"Mac—"

"Just wait," he said and held on to her hands when she tried to tug free. "Look, I admit, I was doing all of this to get you to come back to the office. Couldn't see how I'd run the place without you. But it's more now."

There went that flutter of hope again. "More?" She held her breath, watched his eyes.

"We're great together." He said it flatly, brooking no argument even if she'd been inclined to try. "Hell, we have *fun* together. The sex is incredible and damn it, Andi, if we can have it all, why shouldn't we?"

And the hope died.

This was only what he'd said before. Teamwork. Come

back to the office. Be his trusty sidekick. Keep separate homes. Have sex with him. Don't let anyone know.

"If it turns out you are pregnant," he was saying, and Andi warned herself to pay attention, no matter what pain it cost, "we can get married and live out at the ranch." He gave her that smile filled with charm as if that would be enough to smooth over the jagged edges of her heart. "Closer commute for both of us. And Teresa's there to take care of the baby while we're at work."

The last remaining remnants of that hope burned to a cinder and the ashes blew away.

God, she was an idiot.

Before she could tell him to leave, his phone rang. "You mind?" he asked after glancing at the readout.

"No, go ahead." It would give her another moment or two to find the right words to end this. God. How could she be so cold?

"Right… Okay, Tim… Yeah, I know you could. But I'll feel better if I meet you. Twenty minutes?" He hung up, slid the phone into his pocket and looked at Andi. "We've got to finish this later. I have to get to the office. The Brinkman deal is faltering."

Brinkman. She flipped through her mental files. "Oh. Brinkman Auto Industries."

"Right." He stood up, then leaned over and took a last bite of his now cool pizza. Still chewing, he told her, "There are a few things to be done before Hal Brinkman panics and backs out entirely."

"Why are you going in?" Sitting on the floor, she stared up at him and said, "Tim was point person on that deal. No one knows Brinkman better than he does."

"Yeah, but it's my company. Buck stops with me." He narrowed his eyes on her. "And you. Come to the office with me, Andi. You did all the prelim work on those contracts. With your mind, you remember every single detail."

Her heart actually *hurt*. "No, Mac."

Frowning, he stared at her. "What do you mean, 'no'?"

"I mean, I quit, Mac. Two weeks ago. And if that doesn't help, I quit again. This time, it's final." Mac was ready to race out the door even though this wasn't an emergency. Andi had to recognize that she simply wasn't a priority to him. Never would be.

How could he not see it? Despite everything they'd shared the past two weeks, nothing had changed. He wanted her. Back in the office. Back in his bed. And for nothing else. It hurt to accept. To realize that Mac hadn't changed. Not really. His company was still the most important thing to him.

Even now, when he was trying to finagle her back into his life, he was willing to put that conversation on hold so he could race to the office to deal with something his vice president was completely capable of handling.

"I'm done, Mac." Slowly, Andi stood up, because if she was going to stand her ground metaphorically, then she'd do it literally, too. "You're running back to the office when they don't even need you to."

"It's business," he said as if that explained everything.

"And Tim can handle it, but you won't let him. You have to be there." She shook her head sadly and looked at him as if etching this memory into her mind forever. It would help, she told herself, while she worked to get over him. "I thought your heart was really in the ranch, but I was wrong. It's in that office. In the computers and the files and the phone calls and hustle of the day. But mine's not, Mac. It's not what I want."

"What the hell *do* you want, Andi?"

She laughed quietly, sadly. "I want Easter eggs that smell like little boys' sweaty socks. I want little girls who have tea parties with their hamsters. Little League games and cheerleading practice."

He looked so confused, it broke her heart. He'd never understand so she wouldn't bother trying to explain.

"Mostly, I want love, Mac. I want to be loved like I love you."

"You—" His head jerked back as if she'd slapped him.

"Yeah," she said softly, sadly, as hope dissolved into dead dreams and left her feeling hollowed out from the inside. She'd had to say it, if only once. She didn't want his pity, but damn it, she deserved the opportunity to tell the man she loved him, even if she shouldn't. "But don't hold it against me. I'll get over it eventually."

"What the hell am I supposed to do with that?"

"If you have to ask," she said, "then I can't explain it."

"Okay." He shook his head, hard. "Leaving that aside for a second, you've known me long enough that you should understand what that company means to me. Hell, it meant a lot to you, too, once."

It had. But those days were gone. "Not as much as having a life, Mac. That means more."

"So you can just walk away? From me? From what we've had for years? What we had the last two weeks?"

"I have to," she said simply.

"You love me so much you can't get away fast enough?" He laughed shortly and there was fury and pain shining in his eyes. "What the hell kind of love is that?"

She sighed and her heart broke a little more. "The kind I can recover from. I hope."

* * *

The next two weeks were a lot less interesting than the previous ones. Mac fell back on his default settings and buried himself in work. The office. The ranch. He kept himself so damn busy he didn't have time to sleep. Because he couldn't risk dreaming.

Tim was now generally stationed at the office and working with Laura to run down new leads on failing companies that might be suitable takeover material. The Brinkman contract problems had been solved readily enough and looking back Mac could see that Andi had been right. Tim could have handled it. But the point was, this was Mac's business and his responsibility. So of course he'd had to go in. Supervise. Give his opinion and monitor the situation until it was settled. There was zero reason for him to feel guilty about doing what he had to.

So why did he?

She loved him.

A cold, tight fist squeezed his heart. Why the hell would she tell him that and then toss him out of her damn house? That was love? He rubbed at the center of his chest as if he could ease the ache that had settled in there the night he'd last walked away from Andi's house.

She loved him.

Well, if she loved him, why wasn't she *there*? You can't say you love someone and then say, *But I don't like you doing this and this. You should do that instead.* What the hell kind of love was that?

He kept remembering Andi's face, the expression in her eyes. The…disappointment he'd read there. And he didn't like it. Didn't care to remember that she'd told him to leave. That he'd never change. Hell, he had changed.

He'd asked her to come back to work for him, hadn't he? He hadn't demanded it.

Pushing up out of his chair, Mac paced the confines of his office like a tiger looking for an escape route out of his cage. That thought brought him up short. Made him frown as he looked out the window to a wide sweep of McCallum land. The office wasn't a cage. It was... what? The heart of him, as Andi had said?

"No, damned if it is," he muttered. Stalking to the window, he slapped both hands on either side of the glass and leaned toward it.

Outside, the sun was heating up. July was just around the corner and summer was settling in to stay for a while. On the ranch, they'd be moving the herd to a new pasture. The sky looked brassy and there wasn't a cloud in sight. But he didn't really care what kind of view he was staring at. "Why the hell is she being so stubborn?"

He missed her, damn it. What did sweaty Easter eggs have to do with anything?

"That's it, you're gonna snap soon. Talking to yourself." He shoved away from the window and went back to pacing. "You start answering your own questions and you're done, son."

He kicked his desk and gritted his teeth against the pain. He didn't want to miss her, but he couldn't deny that without Andi in his life, it felt as though he was missing a limb.

He'd interviewed a half dozen people for the executive assistant job and not one of them had been able to read his mind the way Andi could. Being at the office wasn't enjoyable anymore. He didn't want to be here, but he couldn't find any damn peace at his own house, either.

Every time he walked in the door, Teresa gave him a cool, disapproving look. And when he tried to sleep in his own bed, visions of Andi rose up and kept sleep at bay while his body burned. He couldn't even look at the hearth in his room without remembering those moments in the firelight with Andi. She'd changed everything on him. And now it felt as if nothing fit quite right.

The buzzer on his desk phone sounded and he glared at it. No damn peace. Three long strides had him at his desk. He hit a button and snapped, "What is it?"

"Sorry, Mac," Laura said coolly and he winced in response. "Tim's on line one."

"Fine. Thanks." His vice president was in Northern California to foster a deal on a tech company. Mac picked up, turned to look out the window again and said, "Yeah, Tim. How's it going?"

"Not good." Tim sounded hesitant—the kind of tone people used when they were about to break bad news and really wished they didn't have to. "Jackson Tully made a deal with someone else last week. We lost out, Mac. Sorry, there was nothing I could do. Tully wanted his business to stay in California."

Mac heard but was barely listening. He realized that a couple of months ago, that news would have made him furious. They'd put in a lot of time, working up strategies for the Tully takeover. The tech company was on its last legs and Mac had figured to pick it up cheap, restructure, then sell it for a profit within eighteen months. Now that plan was shot.

And he didn't care. Scrubbing one hand across the back of his neck, he acknowledged that the blown deal didn't mean anything to him. Because Andi wasn't there. She was gone so nothing else mattered.

What the hell had she done to him?

He rubbed his eyes. "It's all right, Tim. Come on home. Time to move on to something else."

"If it's okay with you," he said, "I'll stay a couple more days. Have a lead on a sinking computer company. I figure it's worth a look."

"Sure. Keep me posted."

Mac hung up, thinking that a month ago, he'd have been all over that news, eager to carve another notch in McCallum Enterprises' belt.

But what the hell did success mean when you didn't have anyone to share it with? When you didn't have the *one* person who mattered. Always before, he and Andi had celebrated every deal together, congratulated each other on the maneuvering, the planning and the final win.

But she was gone and he'd just have to get the hell over it. He wasn't going to go after her again. A man had to hang on to some of his pride, didn't he?

"I didn't know I could be this bored." Andi slumped into one of her new kitchen chairs and propped both elbows on the table. Staring at Vi, she said, "The house is painted. The new furniture's here. There's nothing left for me to *do*."

"What about starting your business?" Vi asked, reaching for an Oreo. "Isn't that on the agenda?"

"It should be," Andi mused, turning her coffee cup around and around between her palms. "But there's no hurry and I'm just not feeling real motivated, you know?"

It had been three weeks since Mac walked out of her house for the last time. July had arrived and her sister was insisting she attend the Royal Fourth of July celebration. She couldn't have felt less like being around people who would expect her to smile and mean it.

Violet sighed, dunked her cookie in her coffee and said, "Mac is being stupid."

"He's being Mac."

"That's what I said." Vi bit her cookie and muffled a groan.

Andi laughed a little, but her heart wasn't in it. Those two weeks with Mac had gone too quickly. She'd thought she was building memories, but what she'd really constructed were personalized torture devices. Whenever she closed her eyes, he was there. How was she supposed to get over him, get past this feeling, when her own subconscious was working against her?

She had to find a way because Andi knew Mac wouldn't be coming back. She'd done the unthinkable and told him no. He'd let her go and called it a lesson learned, because his pride wouldn't allow him to come for her again.

"You know," Vi spoke up again. "Mac's just as miserable as you are."

"He is?" Ridiculous how that thought cheered her up. It seemed misery did love company after all.

"That's got to make you feel a little better."

"It does." Andi got up, went to her new French-door refrigerator and got more tea to refill their glasses. "But you know, rather than the two of us being sad and gloomy apart, I'd rather we were happy. Together." She poured the tea, offered her friend more Oreos, then said, "But it's over, Vi. I can't go back to the office. I love him, so working with him every day would be a nightmare. And I can't jump back into his bed—same reason. The problem is, I haven't figured out yet how I'm supposed to live without him."

"I don't think you're going to have to," Vi said quietly.

Andi looked at her. "Why?"

Smiling, Vi said, "If there's one thing I know, it's my brother. Mac loves you, sweetie. He just hasn't figured it out yet."

"I wish I could believe that." Andi shook her head, and lifted her chin. She had to protect herself. She couldn't keep building hopes on a shaky foundation and not expect them to crash down around her. So instead of giving in to the urge to pin her dreams on Vi's words, Andi said quietly, "I can't take the chance, Vi. I can't wait and hope and keep my fingers crossed. I love Mac, but I'm not going to put my life on hold just on the chance he might wake up and realize that he loves me."

"Oh, Andi…"

"No." Taking a deep breath, Andi said, "Living without him will be the hardest thing I've ever had to do. But I've got to find a way to do it."

Eleven

Mac was working a horse in the corral when his sister found him. He was in no mood for company. Hell, hadn't he bolted from the office because he wanted to be left alone? Feeling surly, he dismounted, tossed the reins to the nearest ranch hand and crossed the dirt enclosure to where his sister waited just outside the fence.

The heat was steaming, making him even more irritable, which he wouldn't have believed possible. Snatching his hat off, he raked his fingers through his hair, then slapped the brim of the hat against his jeans to get rid of at least some of the dirt he'd managed to collect. He opened the gate, stepped through and secured it again. Only then did Mac look at his sister.

"Violet, what are you doing here?"

"It's still my home as much as yours," she reminded him.

"Bet that's news to Rafe." He tugged his hat back on. "Go home, Violet."

"Not until we have a talk," she said.

"Not in the mood."

"Too bad."

"Not a good day for this, Violet." He turned and headed for the stable, but she was right behind him, though she had to hurry her steps just to keep up.

"Pregnant here, not as fast as I used to be," she called out, and that made him stop. He couldn't risk her falling and injuring herself or the baby.

He faced her, his arms crossed over his chest, feet planted wide apart. Squinting into the sun, he glared at her. "Fine. Talk."

"What is wrong with you?" she demanded.

He gritted his teeth and sucked air in through his nose. His temper was dangerously close to erupting so he made a deliberate attempt to hold it down. "Not a damn thing except for an interfering little sister."

Poking her index finger against his chest, she asked, "Don't you see that Andi is the best thing that ever happened to you?"

Of course he saw that. Was he blind? But Andi was the one who'd ended things. "If that's all you came to talk about, this meeting is over."

Damned if he'd stand here and be lectured to by his younger sister. He had stuff to do. And he figured if he kept himself busy enough, he wouldn't have the room or the time to think about Andi.

"You're an idiot."

Mac shook his head. He'd had about enough of women lately. "Great. Thanks for stopping by. Say hi to Rafe."

"I'm not done."

"Yeah," he nearly growled. "You're done. I don't want to share my feelings, Vi. I'm not looking for a soft shoulder or a stern talking-to. You can butt the hell out because this is none of your business, understand?"

"We're *family*, you knot-head," she snapped, and leading with her prodigious belly, encroached on his personal space. "If you think you can scare me off with that nasty streak of yours, you can forget it. I'm only here because I love you."

He had already been pushed way past the edge of his control. The woman he wanted insisted she loved him, but didn't want him. His company didn't interest him. He couldn't even work up any concentration for the horses he loved. The heat was boiling his brain and his little sister dropping in to insult him was just the icing on his damn cake.

Scrubbing his hand through his hair, he muttered darkly, "Suddenly I've got women who love me giving me nothing but grief."

"That's right. Andi *loves* you. What're you going to do about it?"

He frowned at her, eyes narrowing in suspicion. "Does Rafe know you have Oreo breath?"

Vi jerked back, looked embarrassed, then shook it off and argued, "This isn't about me."

One eyebrow lifted. "So my life is up for grabs, but yours is private?"

"Yes," Vi said, lifting her chin to glare at him. "Because I'm not currently being an idiot."

Mac scowled at her. "You're not exactly endearing yourself to me."

Sighing, Violet moved in closer, gave him a hard hug and whispered, "I love you, Mac. I want you happy. So I'm asking you to try some personal growth. Fast."

He hugged her back, then released her. "It's over, Vi. Let it go."

"She's pregnant," Violet blurted out.

"What?"

"Andi. She's pregnant."

Ears ringing, heart slamming in his chest, Mac was staggered. Pregnant? Why hadn't she told him? What the hell kind of love was it that made you leave *and* hide a child? Breath caught in his chest until it felt as if he might just explode. Instantly, images, thoughts, emotions chased each other through his mind. Panic was there, naturally, along with pride, excitement, anger and a sense of satisfaction. Pregnant. Andi was carrying his child. His baby.

Mac examined exactly what he was feeling and realized the one underlying emotion that was strongest was also the most unfamiliar. Happiness. Hell, it had been so long since he'd really been completely happy, no wonder he hardly recognized it.

"Mac? You okay?"

He came up out of his thoughts like a diver breaking the water's surface. "I'm better than okay."

Giving his sister a hard kiss, he grinned at her and said, "This may never be true again, so listen up. Thank you for interfering. For sticking your nose in. For loving me."

Violet smiled up at him. "It was my pleasure."

"I know it."

"So, since you're so grateful to me, we don't have to say anything to Rafe about the cookies, right?"

He only smiled. He loved her, but his little sister could just go home and worry that she'd be ratted out. It would do her good. Leaving her there by the corral, he headed for the house. He had to change, get to town, then go see the woman who was currently driving him nuts.

Andi couldn't take boredom for long. By the following day, she had been to the Royal nursery and come home with a plan.

She had a half-dozen bags of red cedar mulch, flats of petunias and gerbera daisies and a few bags of peat moss. She didn't know much about gardening, so she also bought a book that promised to teach garden-challenged people to grow beautiful flowers. She just wanted to know enough not to kill the jewel-colored blooms.

For an hour, she worked steadily, digging holes, planting flowers, laying mulch. The sun blasted down on her, making her feel as if her blood was boiling. Didn't help that there was no breeze at all and the oaks in her yard were busily shading the area where she wasn't.

She liked knowing she was continuing to make her house beautiful. But the downside to gardening was you had too much time to think. Naturally, her thoughts kept spinning back to the man who held her heart and didn't want it.

"Way to go, Andi," she muttered, patting the dirt in around a bright red petunia. "You're doing great on the not-thinking-about-Mac thing."

Disgusted with herself, she sat back on her heels to admire her work and gave a small sigh of satisfaction. The flowers were red, white and blue, and with the red mulch it looked patriotic and fresh and beautiful. Now all she had to do was find some other chore around the house to keep her busy. Gathering up her tools and the empty bags of mulch, she stood up and wished for a moment or two that she had a pool to jump into.

Her cutoff jeans shorts were filthy, her white tank top was sticking to her skin and her ponytail was slipping free, with tendrils of hair hanging down on either side of her face. She wanted a shower, a glass of wine and maybe to lie prostrate on the cool, tiled floor of her kitchen while the air conditioner blew directly onto her.

She might have wished she was out at the ranch with Mac, maybe swimming in the pond behind the house. Skinny-dipping would have been fun on a hot summer day. But that wasn't going to happen, so she let it go on a sigh. Carrying all of her things into the garage, she heard a truck pull into her driveway. The thought of having to be polite and welcoming to a visitor right now made her tired.

Andi wanted some time alone. Time to sulk and brood and enjoy a little self-pity with her glass of cold white wine. So, if it was Vi or Jolene, she'd send them home. The two women had been tag teaming her lately, each of them taking turns to check in with Andi and make sure she wasn't lonely. Well, she *needed* a little lonely at the moment.

With her arguments ready, she came around the corner of the house and stopped dead. Mac. His huge black truck sat in the drive, sunlight glinting off the chrome. The man himself was walking toward her house, looking so good Andi wanted to bolt back into the garage and close the door after her.

She looked *hideous*. Why did he finally decide to come to her when she was hot and sweaty and covered in garden dirt? Quickly, she gathered up her hair, tightened the ponytail, checked out her reflection in the side mirror of her car and brushed spots of dirt off her cheeks. She wasn't wearing makeup because her thought that morning had been, *who needed mascara to plant flowers?* So getting rid of the dirt on her face was really the best she could do and wasn't that all kinds of sad?

She closed her eyes and took a breath. Why had he come here? Was this just another attempt to get her back to the office? Well, she thought, why else would he have come? The man didn't like to lose; Andi knew that better than most. So he'd come back to try to convince her. Again.

Steeling herself for another argument with him, Andi walked out to meet him.

He gave her that wide, slow grin when he saw her and Andi's heart jumped in response. The man would always have that effect on her, she knew. It just wasn't fair that he could score a direct hit on her heart without even trying.

"Flowers are nice," he said.

"Thanks." She tucked her hands into her shorts pockets. To resist the urge to reach for him? Probably. "What're you doing here, Mac?"

"We have to talk." His expression unreadable, Andi thought about it for a few seconds, then nodded. If this really did turn out to be a futile attempt to get her back to the office, it would be better to deal with it. To finally and at last make him see that she wasn't going back. No matter what.

"Okay, fine. Come inside, though. It's too hot out here. And I need something cold to drink."

"Should you be outside working in the heat that way?"

She tossed a quizzical glance at him over her shoulder. "The flower beds are outside, Mac. Hard to plant from the living room."

"I'm just saying, you should be more careful."

Well, that was weird. She headed down the hall toward the kitchen, with Mac right behind her. Andi went straight to the fridge and opened it, relishing the rush of cold air that swept out to greet her. "Tea? Beer?"

"No beer. I'm driving. Listen, Andi—"

"I'm going to stop you right there, Mac. If this is about the office, you can save your breath." She poured two glasses of tea and handed him one. After she took a long drink of her own, she said, "I'm not going over the same old ground again just because you can't accept no for an answer."

"It's not that." He set his tea down, then plucked her glass from her hand and set it aside, too.

The air in the room was cool, but he was standing so near to her that Andi felt the heat of him reach out for her. She'd wished to see him again, but now that he was here, it was painful to be so close to him and yet still so far away.

"Why are you here, Mac?"

He dropped both hands onto her shoulders, looked down into her eyes and said, "It's time you married me."

"What?" This was the last thing she'd expected. A proposal? Granted, not the most romantic proposal in the world, but that didn't matter so much. Demanding she marry him was very Mac after all. But the fact that he was proposing at all was so stunning, Andi felt shaken. Was it possible that he really meant it? Were her dreams about to come true?

He let go of her long enough to dip one hand into his jacket pocket and come up with a small, square ring box. He snapped open the deep red velvet to reveal a round cut diamond so big that when the sunlight caught it, the glare almost blinded her.

She slapped one hand to her chest as if she were trying to keep her heart where it belonged. Slowly, she lifted her gaze from the ring to Mac's eyes.

"Marry me, Andi," he urged, eyes bright, determination stamped on his features. "Right away. We can do it this weekend, if you want. I'll call the mayor, he'll fix us up with a license and it'll be all taken care of."

"This weekend?"

He leaned in and planted a fast, hungry kiss on her mouth. "I think that's best. Look, I don't know why you haven't told me yet, but you should know that Violet spoiled the surprise. She told me about the baby."

Andi's mind went blank. She stared at him and tried to get past the knot of emotion lodged in her throat. For a second or two, she couldn't even draw a breath. *Of course.* This was why he'd proposed to her and was insisting on a hurried wedding. It wasn't about love at all. He hadn't had an epiphany. Hadn't realized that she was what he wanted. Mac was only doing what he would consider his "duty."

"No." Andi pushed away from him and took a step backward for extra measure. "Violet lied. There's no baby. I'm not pregnant, Mac."

He looked as though someone had punched him in the stomach. "Why would she lie?"

"I don't know." Andi threw both hands up and let them fall again. Sorrow fought with anger and the sorrow won. Logically, she knew her friend, Mac's sister, had done all of this to bring the two of them together. But emotionally, she had to wonder what Vi had been thinking to play games like this with people's hearts. "She's a romantic," Andi finally said, her voice soft and tinged with a sigh. "She wants us together and probably thought that this was a sure way to make that happen. And I'm sorry but I may have to kill her."

"Get in line," he grumbled, staring down at the ring in his hand before snapping the box closed with what sounded like permanence.

Her heart aching, tears she refused to allow to fall burning her eyes, Andi whispered brokenly, "The point is, I'm not pregnant. At least I don't think so—"

His head came up and his gaze pinned her.

"—but even if it turns out I am," Andi qualified, lifting one hand for emphasis, "that doesn't mean I would marry you just because of a baby. I'm capable of raising a child on my own and I won't get married unless it's for love."

And that was never going to happen, she thought, at least not with Mac. Why was the one man she wanted also the one man she couldn't have? Spinning around, she stomped to the kitchen window, then spun back.

Furious with Violet, Andi blinked hard to keep those tears choking her at bay. For one all-too-brief moment, she'd thought that Mac had come to her because he wanted her. Instead, they were both being dragged over the coals again. And there was just no reason for it.

"Just take the diamond and go, Mac." *Please go*, she prayed silently. Before she cried.

He opened the jeweler's box, looked down at the ring, shining so brightly on its bed of red velvet, and he shook his head. "No." Shifting his gaze to her, he started toward her with long, slow steps.

Andi groaned, and naturally backed up until she hit the wall. Then she had no choice but to hold her ground and try to keep it together until he left again. *Please let that be soon.*

"I'm not going anywhere." His gaze moved over her face, her hair, her mouth, then settled on her eyes again. "When you just said there was no baby, you know what I felt?"

She huffed out a breath, then firmed her bottom lip when it trembled. "Relief?"

He shook his head. "Disappointment."

Andi blinked at him and apparently he read the surprise on her face.

"Yeah, caught me off guard, too." He laughed softly to himself. "Trust me when I say that my little sister and I are going to be having a talk about this."

"Get in line." She repeated his earlier words and he grinned.

"But," he added, moving in on her, crowding her until she couldn't draw a breath without his scent surrounding her, invading her, "it's because of Vi that I'm here. It's just the push I needed, though I doubt I'll be admitting that much to her. Being here with you, thinking about us being married and having a family, made me realize something important."

Andi swallowed hard and whispered, "What's that?"

"It wasn't a baby that had me proposing, Andi. It was *you."* He smiled, stroked her hair back from her face with the tips of his fingers. "A pregnancy gave me the excuse I thought I needed to come here again. To look at you and admit to both of us that it's you I want, Andi. You I need."

"Mac…" Thank God her back was against a wall. Otherwise, her liquefied knees just might have her slumping onto the floor.

"Not done," he said, winking. "I love you, Andi, and I'm just as surprised by that statement as I see you are."

His expression went tender, soft, as he tipped her chin up with his finger to close her mouth. "The thing is, I've counted on you being a part of my life for so long, I never noticed that you had *become* my life."

A single tear escaped and slid along her cheek. He kissed it away.

"Without you, nothing's fun anymore," he whispered, gaze roaming over her features, voice thick. "Not work. Not relaxation. Not the ranch or a damn picnic or anything. I need you, Andi, and more than that, I need you to believe me."

"Mac, I want to. I really do. More than anything." Her heart in her throat, blood rushing through her veins, she couldn't look away from those green eyes of his.

"Then do it." He cupped her face in his palms. "I'm mad at Vi, but I'm grateful to her, too. Her lie gave me the push to come here. To find my life. To do what I should have done years ago."

Confused, shaken, so touched she could hardly see through the blur of those sneaky tears in her eyes, Andi could only watch as he dropped to one knee in front of her.

"Since I'm only doing this once in my life, I'm going to do it right." He took her hand, slid the ring onto her finger and kissed it. Then looking up at her, he said, "I love you, Andrea Beaumont. Maybe I always have. I know I always will. And if you're not pregnant now, I hope you are soon. I want a houseful of kids running around the ranch."

Her free hand covering her mouth, Andi looked down at him and nodded, unable to speak past the growing knot of emotion clogging her throat.

"I'm taking that as a yes."

"Yes." Slowly, Andi sank to her knees beside him. "I love you, too, Mac. So yes, I'll marry you and have babies with you and ride horses and have picnics—"

"And sweaty Easter eggs?" he asked, his smile shining in his beautiful eyes.

Andi threw her head back and laughed. "God, yes. Sweaty Easter eggs."

"And you'll explain that to me at some point, right? Been driving me crazy trying to figure it out."

She laughed again and felt the easing of hurt and disappointment and regret as all of the negative emotions drained away leaving behind nothing but hope. And joy.

"I promise."

"Come home with me, Andi."

"I will." She looked around her shiny new kitchen and knew she'd miss it. Though Mac's ranch house was wonderful and she knew the life they would build there would be amazing, there would always be a place in her heart for this tiny house. Because it was this place that had brought her and Mac together. The hours they'd spent working on it were memories she'd never part with.

As if reading her mind, Mac whispered, "Let's keep this house. You can use it as an escape route the next time I make you mad. Then I'll always know where to find you so I can come get you and bring you home again."

How lovely to have a man know her so well and love her, anyway. Yes, there would be times they'd fight, argue, and she might storm off and come here. Where she would wait for him to come after her to take her home. *Home*. A home and a family with Mac.

"That sounds just right," she said. Then drawing her head back, she looked up at him and asked, "So, is this another rescue?"

"Yeah," he said softly, wrapping his arms tightly around her. "But this time, *you* rescued *me*."

And he kissed her to seal the promise of their future.

Epilogue

Five months later

A Christmas party at the Texas Cattleman's Club was not to be missed. It looked as though half the town of Royal was gathered to celebrate.

There were five Christmas trees, decorated with multicolored lights and ornaments gathered and collected over the years, placed around the room and at the entrance to the club. Strings of tiny white lights were draped along the walls, and the scattering of tables were covered in red and green cloths. Pine boughs jutted up from vases and lay across the tops of framed paintings, with silvery threads of tinsel hanging from them, catching the light and dazzling the eye. Christmas carols were piped through the overhead speakers and champagne flowed like water.

"You're late," Violet said, coming up to Andi for a hug.

"We're always late now." Andi rubbed her belly and gave a small, sweet smile. Turned out Violet hadn't been lying when she'd sent Mac to Andi all those months ago. Of course, she hadn't known it at the time. It had been a wild guess—although Vi liked to pretend she'd had a psychic moment of intuition. Their baby girl would be born in three months and Andi woke every morning grateful for the love in her life.

"The baby's not here yet. It's not her fault," Violet said, threading her arm through Andi's to steer her through the crowd.

"But we start talking about her and making plans and today we were painting her room," Andi admitted wryly.

"Again? I thought you were sticking with the soft peach."

"I was, but it just seemed as though it would feel hot in there in summer," Andi confessed, "so Mac's painting it that pale green it was before."

Violet laughed. "It's so good to see Mac getting all twisted up over his yet-to-be-born daughter."

"Yes," Andi said, "because Rafe is so la-di-da over your son."

Vi grinned. "I have new pictures to show you of your baby's cousin." She sighed and slapped one hand to her heart. "I swear, I never suspected you could love this much. But Rafe and I are so crazy about our baby boy, we're already talking about expanding the family."

"Good," Andi said, chuckling, "because Mac still has plans to fill every bedroom in the ranch house."

Vi blinked. "There are eight of them."

"I know." Andi sighed. "Isn't it great?"

"Hey, there you are." Mac came up behind Andi, put his arms around her and let his hands come to rest on the swell of their child. He was always touching her, touching their baby. It was as if he couldn't stand to be away from her, and Andi was loving every minute of it.

"I missed you. How you doing? Tired? You want anything?"

"Not tired," she said, "but water would be great, thank you." He kissed the side of her neck, winked at Vi, then headed for the bar.

"I'm so happy for you guys," Violet said on a sigh. "I've never seen Mac so relaxed, so...well, happy."

"I am, too." Andi took a deep breath of the pine-scented air and added, "My life is officially perfect."

She had Mac, their baby, their families and friends. Life was just *wonderful.* Looking around the room, Andi let her gaze sweep across the friends and neighbors gathered there. Case and Mellie Baxter looked amazing. She knew Case was planning on running for another term as club president, and Mellie and Andi had made an informal agreement to use their respective businesses to support each other. With Mellie's Keep N Clean, a house-sitting/cleaning business, and Andi's own Put-It-Away, they would each benefit. Andi could pick up new clients and then could recommend Keep N Clean to her customers to help their newly organized homes stay that way.

"It's pretty amazing what Mellie did for the TCC."

"Generous, for sure," Andi agreed. The TCC had decided it wanted to own the land it sat on instead of keeping the long-term lease they already had going with Mellie's family. So they'd officially made an offer for the property. Which she had promptly turned down. Then, with the agreement of her father, who was now back from rehab and doing much better, Mellie had gone ahead and made a gift of the land to the club.

So, this party was not just for Christmas, but a celebration for the Texas Cattleman's Club.

And the party was a huge success. With Christmas only two weeks away, everyone was feeling festive. Nolan and Raina Dane were laughing with the sheriff and his wife, Amanda.

Liam and Hadley Wade were married now and expecting twins, which explained why Liam was plopping Harper down into a chair in spite of her protests.

"What's the smile for?" Violet asked.

"Just thinking about all that's happened to our friends and the town in the last several months."

Nodding, Vi looked around, too. "It was crazy a lot of the time, but I think we all came through really well. Oh, look. There's Jolene and Tom!"

Tom veered off for the bar, clearly a man on a mission, and Jolene headed straight for Vi and Andi. Newly svelte, now that her fourth child and second son had been born a few months ago, Jolene looked as happy as Andi felt.

"Hi, you guys. Isn't this party amazing?" She turned her head to take in her sister. "Andi, you look gorgeous. Love the color red on you."

Andi sneaked a quick look to where Mac, Rafe and Tom were all balancing drinks and talking. "Mac likes me in red. Says it reminds him of what I wore on our first date. He surprised me with the dress this afternoon."

And then he'd taken her to bed and proved to her beyond a shadow of a doubt how beautiful he thought she was. Such a gift, she told herself, to have a man's love, to know that he felt what you did. To *know* that he would always be there for you and your children.

As if sensing her thoughts, Mac turned, looked directly at her and winked.

"Aren't our men just gorgeous?" Vi sighed a little and waved to her husband as Rafe smiled at her.

"Oh, yeah," Jolene agreed with a wink of her own for Tom.

Mac had supported her idea for a business of her own. Put-It-Away was building quickly, and Andi had as many clients as she wanted. She was picky, though, refusing to be drawn into another all-work, no-play scenario. Mac, too, had cut back on time at the office, leaving Tim more and more in charge as Mac himself concentrated on their growing family and the ranch that was the center of their lives.

"Look," Andi said, "there's Kyle and Grace Wade. They look great, don't they? Grace tells me the twins are doing so well that Maddie is quickly catching up to Maggie development-wise."

"I know. It's great." Vi nodded toward the far side of the room. "Oh, Parker Reese and Claire just came in. They're so busy planning their wedding, I've hardly seen Claire lately."

"I was sorry to hear Rafe's sister and her husband wouldn't be able to come for Christmas," Jolene said.

"Me, too," Vi murmured. "But with Nasira pregnant, Sebastian has decreed no long flights."

Jolene frowned. "Is everything all right?"

"Everything's great, but Sebastian is being as protective and proud as Mac is of our Andi. And though Nasira really wanted to be here, I think she's enjoying having Sebastian hover and take care of her."

"Well, we all like that," Jolene said, "whether we cry feminist or not."

"True." Andi turned to smile at her husband as the three men rejoined the women. Mac dropped one arm around her and pulled her into his side.

"Having a good time?"

"The best," she said, smiling up into his eyes.

"Have I mentioned lately how much I love you?"

"I believe you have but feel free to repeat yourself," Andi said, a smile twitching at her lips.

"Have Yourself a Merry Little Christmas" piped from the speakers overhead, and as his arms came around her, she knew that every Christmas from now on would be perfect.

"I think we should go home early," Mac whispered, his mouth so close to her ear that his breath brushed warmly against her skin. "Decorate the tree in our bedroom and then make love in front of the fire."

She smiled as her insides tightened. Leaning into him, she turned her head so she could look out over the crowd while enjoying this private moment.

"I think that's a wonderful idea, Mac."

He tipped her face up and gave her a quick, soft kiss. "Merry Christmas, Andi."

"Merry Christmas, Mac." She leaned into him and smiled as her heart filled with the kind of joy that would be with her forever.

* * * * *

"We shouldn't be doing this."

"Maybe." He buried his nose behind her ear and nibbled the soft skin. "Want me to stop?"

He continued to kiss her, nuzzling along her jaw to her mouth. Full lips. Soft. Sweet. Just like the woman. He deepened the kiss, waiting for her to open for him.

"Georgie?" He murmured her name against her lips.

She leaned back and stared at him, looking helpless and unsure.

"Sweet pea? What is it?"

"I've wanted this… you… I've dreamed about it… but…"

"Shh, darlin'. This is good. We're good." And it shocked him to realize he spoke the truth. This wasn't a simple seduction. He *liked* Georgie. As a person. And was just now discovering how truly sexy she was. Coming into a relationship from this direction was a revelation. "We're more than good, Georgie."

He recognized her surrender in the way her eyes softened and went unfocused, in the way her arms crept around his neck, in the way her lips sought his and her body pressed against him. "Will you stay with me tonight, Georgie? In my bed?"

* * *

The Boss and His Cowgirl
is part of the Red Dirt Royalty series:
These Oklahoma millionaires
work hard and play harder

THE BOSS AND HIS COWGIRL

BY
SILVER JAMES

All rights reserved including the right of reproduction in whole or in part in any form. This edition is published by arrangement with Harlequin Books S.A.

This is a work of fiction. Names, characters, places, locations and incidents are purely fictional and bear no relationship to any real life individuals, living or dead, or to any actual places, business establishments, locations, events or incidents. Any resemblance is entirely coincidental.

This book is sold subject to the condition that it shall not, by way of trade or otherwise, be lent, resold, hired out or otherwise circulated without the prior consent of the publisher in any form of binding or cover other than that in which it is published and without a similar condition including this condition being imposed on the subsequent purchaser.

® and ™ are trademarks owned and used by the trademark owner and/or its licensee. Trademarks marked with ® are registered with the United Kingdom Patent Office and/or the Office for Harmonisation in the Internal Market and in other countries.

First Published in Great Britain 2016
By Mills & Boon, an imprint of HarperCollins*Publishers*
1 London Bridge Street, London, SE1 9GF

© 2016 Silver James

ISBN: 978-0-263-91864-9

51-0616

Our policy is to use papers that are natural, renewable and recyclable products and made from wood grown in sustainable forests. The logging and manufacturing processes conform to the legal environmental regulations of the country of origin.

Printed and bound in Spain
by CPI, Barcelona

Silver James likes walks on the wild side and coffee. Okay. She LOVES coffee. A cowgirl at heart, she's been an army officer's wife and mum, and worked in the legal field, fire service and law enforcement. Now retired from the real world, she lives in Oklahoma, spending her days writing with the assistance of two Newfoundlands, the cat who rules them all and the characters living in her imagination.

To Jenny, Connie, Mac
and Warriors in Pink everywhere.

One

Clayton Barron owned the room—held the emotions, the very hearts and minds of his audience in the palm of his hand. He controlled them with the power of his voice and the words he uttered with such complete conviction. He was in charge, just the way he preferred it. He'd been born, bred and raised to be a US senator—and more. Now into his second term, he stood at the podium of the convention of the Western States Landowners Association in Phoenix, Arizona, and the words rolled off his tongue, his voice infused with sincerity.

Georgeanne Dreyfus, his communications director, had written and fine-tuned the speech. The phrases she'd crafted pushed all the right buttons for this audience. Just as they'd practiced at the hotel last night, he paused for a beat then raised his chin and squared his shoulders.

"I understand your frustration. My great-great-grandfather settled the Crown B Ranch long before Oklahoma achieved statehood. He worked that ranch with his own hands. He survived storms, fires, droughts and floods all so he could leave the land—our birthright—to his children and their children." He inhaled and shifted his expression to reflect a hint of arrogance. "It's time we acknowledge our family legacies. We live on the land. Work it every single day of our lives, from sunrise to dark. It's time we tell the government to back off. It's time they stop tying our hands with their arbitrary rules and regulations. It's time we take back what is ours."

The room erupted into cheers, whistles and loud applause. He basked in the crowd's admiration. After a long standing ovation, the president of the association crossed the stage to shake his hand and thank him. He glanced toward the back of the room. His chief of staff offered a dis-

creet thumbs-up. The head of Clay's personal security team
stood nearby, his restless gaze scanning the room. Time to
move through the crowd, glad-handing his way to the exit.
He had an hour to make it from downtown Phoenix out to
Scottsdale for his next engagement, a fund-raising dinner
with some of the party's biggest donors.

His gaze strayed to the indistinct figure standing just off
stage. Georgie. He didn't have to see her to picture how she
looked—straight-cut bangs, her hair scraped back from her
face and twisted up in some impossible way, black eyeglass
frames dominating her features. He'd overheard more than
one reporter comment on her sexy librarian vibe. She'd
been there in the backstage shadows the whole time, listening, and more than likely silently mouthing each word as he
spoke it. He quirked the corner of his mouth and winked at
her. Georgie had been a steady part of his team almost from
the beginning. He relied on her to put heart into his words,
to spin the press just right. She worked hard for him and he
appreciated her efforts. He was lucky to have her at his side.

He cut his eyes toward the back of the auditorium and
tilted his head—Georgie's signal to head out. As soon as he
descended the steps from the stage, Boone Tate, his chief
of staff and cousin, appeared next to him. Clay was a firm
believer in keeping it all in the family.

Boone leaned close to whisper in his ear. "Hunt says
there's a group of protesters out front. Local cops are handling them but we shouldn't linger too long."

Working a room like this came naturally to Clay. A
quick grip of hands, a few brief words, never stopping, always moving toward his goal—the exit. They reached the
convention center's lobby a few short minutes later. Outside, an exuberant crowd milled about, waiting for Clay's
appearance. A second, more sinister group pushed against
a line of local law enforcement officers.

Hunter Tate, chief of security and Boone's older brother,

arrived and steered Clay away from the wide doors. "Taking the back way out. The SUVs and local police backup will meet us at the loading dock." Flanked by the security team and led by the Phoenix Convention Center's security director, they hurried down a side hallway toward the rear of the huge building.

The group hadn't gone twenty feet when the lights went out and sparks lit up the dark. Choking smoke filled the air. The security team switched on flashlights. Hunter grabbed Clay's elbow, urging him forward.

"Wait." Clay stopped dead. "Where's Georgie?"

"On it." One of the plainclothes security guys peeled off and jogged back the way they'd come, his light bouncing in the swirling fog. He called back over his shoulder, "I'll bring her."

A few minutes later they emerged through a metal fire door. A black SUV waited in the alley between buildings. Sharp reports—too close to the sound of gunfire to be ignored—erupted nearby. The security team surrounded Clay and Boone, ran for the vehicle and pushed them into the backseat.

"No!" Clay resisted. "Georgie. We're not leaving without her." More gunshots—or firecrackers; he wasn't sure at this point—went off and then a woman's high-pitched scream scraped his nerves.

"Aw, crap." Hunter surged through the scrum of security surrounding the car, and Clay leaned around Boone to see.

Georgie lay crumpled at the bottom of the steel loading-dock steps. Police scrambled around the corner chasing a group of people wearing Guy Fawkes masks as they ran away. When Hunter grabbed Georgie, she screamed again but he hauled her to her feet and hustled her to the car. Her face was smudged with residue from the oily smoke, and her glasses looked as if they'd been sprayed with black paint. The poor girl couldn't see a thing.

Boone got out of the car but had to shout to be heard over the commotion. "Georgie, it's okay. We've got you." She visibly relaxed at the sound of his voice and let Hunter bundle her into the backseat. Boone dove in behind her as Hunter jumped into the front seat and told the driver to take off.

The SUV accelerated through the alley and they passed the cops, who had taken the protesters to the ground and were handcuffing them. Sirens wailed a shrieking duet with squealing tires as the SUV careened onto the street. Two police cars and a second SUV with Barron Security forces inside formed the motorcade as they raced away.

Georgie was wedged into the middle of the backseat between Boone and Clay, shivering uncontrollably and gulping air. Her hand flailed, found Clay's and latched on. Clay was too furious to speak. Georgie was his employee and she'd been terrorized by those sons of bitches. Her nails bit into his skin but he ignored the sharp prick. Boone removed her glasses and passed them to Hunter to clean while he took out a handkerchief and gently wiped her face. She shuddered and squeezed Clay's hand harder. He squeezed back.

Hunter twisted around in the front seat and handed the glasses back. Clay took them and gently placed them on Georgie's face. She was shaking and didn't speak. With her glasses back in place, she squinted and looked around. Boone's handkerchief was now a dirty gray so Clay retrieved the one from his back pocket and dabbed at the side of her face closest to him. He gave her hand another squeeze.

"Wh-what happened?" Georgie swallowed and Clay's gaze was drawn to her slender throat.

"Sugar, it's okay." Boone leaned in from the opposite side. "You're safe now."

She inhaled and let her breath out slowly, visibly relaxing as she did so. "The lights. And smoke. I…couldn't see. Did I fall down?" She raised her right leg and stared at her shredded nylon. "The guy with the gun? Did they get him?" She rubbed her left shoulder with her right hand since Clay still held her left.

"Gun?" Hunter's voice was sharp.

"I thought…" She inhaled and rubbed at her chest as if breathing deeply hurt. Tears glistened on her lashes and she closed her eyes. "Did I hear gunshots?"

Hunter spoke into the high-tech microphone straddling his jawline and listened before saying, "Probably firecrackers. Police didn't find any weapons."

Clay continued to wipe the smoke residue off her cheek. When she winced and jerked her head, he realized her face was bruised. "Someone hit you?" His voice was sharp and demanding.

She shook her head then pressed the heel of her free hand against her forehead. "No. I fell. A couple of times, I think. It was…dark. I couldn't see anything." Squeezing her eyes shut, she gulped in air.

Clay was afraid she'd hyperventilate. "You're okay, Georgie. Where else are you hurt?"

Georgie glanced down. Her skirt and jacket were both torn. There were runs in her hose and both knees were scraped and bleeding. Another deep breath had her clutching her side. "Ow."

"What is it?" Clay didn't recognize his own voice and regretted sounding so gruff that Georgie jerked away from him. He hadn't released the hand he held so she didn't get far.

"I'm sorry." She turned worried eyes to him then glanced away. "This is my fault. I didn't mean to make you angry."

He made an effort to soften his voice. "This isn't your fault and I'm not angry with you. I'm angry at the protesters. I'm angry because this happened to you, Georgie. Understood?" He smoothed his thumb in small circles against the back of her hand. "We're headed to the hotel so you can get cleaned up. Don't…just don't worry."

Her bottom lip quivered and she closed her eyes again. Clay cut his eyes to Hunter. The other man's expression was remote but for the regret and anger in his eyes.

"My fault. It won't happen again, Senator."

Clay nodded. Working so closely with family could blur the lines but Hunter knew his team had screwed up. He acknowledged it by using Clay's title. From the looks of things as they'd left the alley, the local authorities had the perpetrators in custody. Hunt would make sure the protesters were prosecuted.

As the SUV careened around a corner, Georgie slammed her head back against the seat and groaned. Before Clay could react, Boone had her leaning forward and was gently probing the back of her head.

"Sugar, that's a big lump you've got back there."

"Oh…uh… I think I hit a metal cabinet or something. The first time I fell. As I stood up. Maybe." She settled carefully against the back of the seat.

Boone carried on a quiet conversation over his cell phone, making arrangements for their party to arrive late at the Scottsdale fund-raiser. Without discussing it, Clay decided to leave Georgie at the hotel, along with one of the security team members. The poor girl was obviously upset, not that he blamed her. She was bruised, bloody and probably had injuries she didn't even realize she had.

Driving the wrong way, the convoy pulled into the guest exit of the Barron's Desert Crown Resort in Scottsdale. The security team wanted Clay, who was sitting behind the driver, to exit closest to the hotel's entry. The squad disembarked from their vehicle and formed a phalanx to move Clay through the lobby and onto the elevator. When his door opened, Clay stepped out and pulled Georgie out after him, refusing to relinquish her hand. He felt connected to her and protective.

A barrage of camera flashes flared and Georgie stumbled. Without thinking, Clay swept her into his arms in a princess carry. Her arms circled his neck and she buried her face against his shoulder, hiding from the cameras and shouted questions. His anger surged again but cooler heads prevailed as Boone and Hunter guided him through the lobby and onto a waiting elevator, ignoring the reporters yelling for a statement.

The express ride took them straight to the penthouse level where Clay occupied the Sonoma Suite, the hotel's equivalent of presidential lodging. He met Boone's surprised expression with quiet directions. "Go to her room and get her bags. She'll stay up here in the empty guest room."

Comprised of a living room, formal dining room, study, kitchen facilities and four bedrooms with attached baths, there was room for Clay, Boone, Hunter and now Georgie. He didn't want her alone in some random hotel room, even though every room in his family's resort was five-star. He wanted her safe and he wasn't convinced she would be out of his sight—irrational as that sounded. Without breaking stride, Clay continued into the master bedroom and straight to the massive bath. He set her on the marble vanity top without regard to the gray smudges smeared across his white Western-cut shirt. He almost smiled at the impression his turquoise bolo tie had left on Georgie's cheek. Keeping a hand on her shoulder to hold her steady, he grabbed a washcloth and wet it, squeezing out the excess water with one hand.

She remained bug-eyed, her pupils dilated, and he could almost feel her shock. Her hair, normally in a neat bun at the back of her head, was tousled and framing her pale face—and was far longer than he'd realized. With gentleness he didn't know he possessed, Clay removed her glasses and set them in the sink to be washed. He wiped her face first, rinsing the cloth before moving to her skinned knees. Her hands, clenched into tight balls on her lap, slowly relaxed.

He'd never been this…intimate with her before. They worked closely together but touching her like this? She was…Georgie. Always there when he needed a press release, a statement or a sounding board. She was efficient. Professional. And he was surprised at the curves he'd discovered when he picked her up. He realized, belatedly, that there was a very feminine woman lurking beneath her rather dowdy exterior.

Then he remembered why she was sitting on the counter in his bathroom. Anger flashed through him as hot as a grease fire. "Dammit, Georgie. This shouldn't have happened. Especially not to you."

She blinked, squinted, did her best to focus her eyes on his face. "Yeah, well." She lifted one shoulder in a shrug.

"Boone's gone to your room to get your things. Stay in here and get cleaned up. Then I want you to move into the other guest room." He tilted his head toward the door. "There's a robe on the back of the door. Okay?"

She fumbled for her glasses. He snatched them first, washed and dried them before handing them to her. Once they were back on her face, she looked more like herself, and her green eyes lost some of that shell-shocked glaze. Her nose wrinkled as she sniffed her shoulder. "Yeah, I definitely want out of these clothes. They stink like smoke."

Clay backed away. "I'll get out of here so you have some privacy."

She nodded but didn't speak so he gave her arm a little pat and steadied her as she slipped off the counter to stand on the marble floor. Once she had her balance, he backed out of the room, shutting the door firmly behind him. He almost ran over Hunter, who'd been hovering just outside.

"Dammit, Hunt. How did this happen? How did the protesters get inside?" Clay was as angry at himself as he was his security chief. Security should have watched out for her. Hell, *he* should have watched out for her. She was, ultimately, his responsibility.

Hunt made a noise that resembled a growl. "A group came through a secondary entrance in the basement and got to the main control board. Building security thinks it might have been an inside job. They're investigating."

Lightning flashed beyond the sheer curtains covering the bedroom window, followed shortly by thunder. Frowning, Hunt pulled out his cell phone, swiped the screen then punched an app icon. "I didn't know we had weather moving in tonight." He checked the forecast and radar then shrugged. "Nothing but boomers and some rain. Now, about Georgie. It won't happen again, Clay. I promise. I'll put a man on her personally."

Clay tunneled his fingers through his hair. "As soon as she's—" A massive boom rattled the window glass and seconds later, all the lights in the suite went out. A scream from inside the bathroom had both men scrambling—Hunt for light, Clay for the door handle.

Jerking the door open, Clay found Georgie kneeling on the floor, her head down, shoulders hunched. Was she gagging? Jeez, but he hated that sound. Had ever since college and drunken frat parties. He kicked the door shut in Hunter's face and bent down. Using the flashlight app on his cell, he checked her over. Clay lifted her long brown hair back from her face, though she tried to turn away. Georgie's throat worked as she swallowed hard, coughing with the effort.

To combat his very visceral reaction to what was happening, Clay recited the Gettysburg Address. Then the Preamble to the US Constitution. He figured he'd have to start on the Declaration of Independence next but Georgie finally inhaled and turned an apologetic gaze on him. He stood to retrieve another washcloth.

"I'm sorry," she murmured, not looking at him as he crouched beside her.

He wondered if her heightened color was a result of exertion or embarrassment. "It's okay—" He bit off the next word, an endearment that slipped too easily into his head. To cover, he brushed her hair back over her shoulders. Pet names didn't come as easy to him as they did Boone. The fact that one had formed on his tongue should have concerned him, but he couldn't work up the energy to worry about it at the moment. He handed her the washcloth and she wiped her mouth and face but still wouldn't look at him. It was then he realized she'd stripped down to a bra and panties—red ones. He refused to process that visual, focusing instead on the situation. "What happened? You seemed okay when I walked out."

Georgie swallowed a dry heave and wrapped her arms around her chest. "I…panicked. The dark. And the storm. I'm a tad…claustrophobic. Or something."

Clay swallowed the insane urge to laugh as his adrenaline rush faded. He bit the insides of his cheeks and when that didn't help, he bit his tongue in an aborted effort to stop the sputtering laugh that finally escaped. He immediately apologized. "It's not funny. I know. I'm sorry."

A choking sound spurted from her. She'd hidden her face in her hands so he snagged the robe from the back of the door and draped it across her shoulders and back. She slipped her arms into the sleeves and twisted her body so she could see him. Clay was surprised to see her biting her lips as if she, too, was trying to hold back her laughter. Then the robe gapped and he glimpsed the bruise on her ribs. He curled his hands into fists to keep from ripping the robe off to examine her. Those bastards had marked her with their idiotic stunt. That quelled his urge to laugh.

"You're bruised, Georgie. And you have that bump on your head. I'd like a doctor to look at you, okay?"

Her forehead furrowed in confusion before she glanced down and saw what he was talking about. "Oh. I am. Huh." Her gaze caught on his. "I was too busy being scared witless to notice, and it was dark so I couldn't see…"

She rubbed absently at her pale skin, and Clay reminded himself Georgie was in his employ and traumatized. He was not as big a jerk as his father or brothers when it came to women. He refused to be, but damn if he wasn't suddenly aware that Georgie had been hiding some very interesting attributes behind her boxy suits and thick glasses—said attributes all but staring him in the face, despite the modest cut of that red lingerie and the robe.

"I'll have the house doctor check you once the electricity—" The lights flickered, steadied and remained on. "Speaking of. Ready to get into the shower now?"

Clay stood and extended his hand to help her up. Just as she clasped his fingers, another clap of thunder shook the building and the lights extinguished. He felt her tremble and hunkered down beside her once more. "It's okay, Georgie."

He swiped his phone and when the screen lit up, he tapped the flashlight app once more. "See? We have light."

Georgie was panting again and a thin sheen of perspiration covered her face. "I'm sorry. This is stupid. I know it's stupid and irrational."

"Fear is—" The light on his phone dimmed and he glanced at the battery indicator. He flicked off the flashlight app, but the home-screen light cast a soft glow over Georgie's face. "Sorry. I'm down to the dregs of battery life. We can go outside, into the bedroom."

"No. There might be monsters under the bed."

Clay studied her face in the ghostly glow of his cell. A hint of a smile tweaked her lips. Good. This was the Georgie he knew and…liked. Yes, definitely liked. He liked

Georgie. She was his employee. He was only keeping her company in his bathroom because she'd had a traumatic day.

"I promise to slay the monsters."

"Or legislate them out of existence?"

"I can do that. I'll introduce a bill in the Senate. And then I'll take you dancing in the dark."

"Isn't that a song?"

"Springsteen."

She blinked at him, her eyes owlish behind the lenses of her glasses. "You're a fan of the Boss?"

"Hey, just because I grew up on Waylon, Willie and the boys, doesn't mean I don't have refined tastes in music."

That elicited a giggle. "Are you trying to distract me?"

"Depends. Is it working?"

"Sort of."

"Then yes." He eased down to the floor, stretching his legs out. "I'm going to take a shot in the dark here—"

"Peter Sellers!"

"I'm sorry. You didn't phrase that in the form of question." He winked at her.

"Oh, getting technical, are we? Fine. I'll take Dark for three hundred, Alex."

"Hmm. Okay." The light from his phone blinked out. Clay didn't like Georgie's quick inhalation. He tapped the phone, thinking it had just gone into sleep mode. Nothing happened. "Sorry, Georgie. I think the battery died."

"O-okay. Um…can we keep playing?"

"Sure. Dark for three hundred, right?"

"Yes."

"Ha! Got one. Michelle Pfeiffer plays the family matriarch in this—"

"What is *Dark Shadows*?"

Georgie laughed as he huffed in pretended frustration. "How did you know that?"

"Clay, your crush on Michelle Pfeiffer is not exactly a secret around the office."

"It isn't?" He did his best to sound both shocked and innocent, but damn if he didn't like the sound of his name coming from between her lips. He couldn't remember if she'd ever called him by his first name—at least not up close and personal like this.

"I'll take Dark for a thousand, Alex."

He racked his brain for an answer and when it came to him, he grinned. "Come to the dark side. We have cookies."

A sound that was a cross between a giggle and snort erupted from Georgie. "How do you even know that?"

The next thing Clay knew, Georgie was laughing—a deep belly laugh that almost lit up the dark with its happy sound. And just like that, the lights blazed, chasing the shadows away. As she dissolved into more laughter, relieved this time, he joined her. This was a side of Georgie he appreciated—her irreverent sense of humor. Working, she was reserved, thoughtful, erudite. She had a way of boiling down an issue into sound bites. She was knowledgeable and intelligent and he thought of her as his personal… His thoughts trailed off as he stared into her eyes—eyes a shade of green he was currently trying, and failing, to describe.

With a start, he realized Georgie was no longer laughing. She'd devolved into hiccuping sobs. He hated tears. The women his father married too often resorted to them, but Georgie's were real and earned. He gathered her close, stroking his palm down her back in long caresses.

"You're okay, Georgie. You're safe."

She nodded, fighting for control. "I know. I'm…" She sniffed, looked around for a tissue, then gave up and wiped her nose on the sleeve of her robe. "Sorry, boss. I'm okay. Just…nerves. I hate the dark. Hate small spaces, especially in the dark."

"Want to tell me?"

She shook her head but words tumbled out. "I was a kid. Got trapped in our old storm cellar. In the dark. Took my folks a couple of hours to find me."

He tightened his arm around her and fought the urge to kiss the top of her head. "Yeah, that would not be fun."

Georgie snuffled again so Clay reached for the roll of toilet paper and ripped off a strip. She took it and tried to discreetly wipe, then blow, her nose. Once she appeared composed, he disengaged and stood. "Why don't you stay in tonight, Georgie? You deserve a night off." When she nodded, he opened the door and edged toward it. "I'll get out so you can shower."

She nodded so he helped her up, made sure she was steady and once again retreated. He listened at the door until he heard the shower and then met Boone and Hunt in the living area of the suite. He gave his orders, grabbed clean clothes from his room and ducked into Boone's room to clean up.

Georgie was still in his bathroom when he was ready to leave for the donor dinner. Part of him wanted to stay, but the practical part, the politician he'd been born, bred and raised to be, marched out of the suite led by his chief of security and trailed by his chief of staff. Georgie would be fine. She had to be. He didn't stop to contemplate why that mattered so much.

Two

Georgie waited in the master bath huddled in her borrowed robe until all sounds diminished outside. She didn't know what to do about her ruined clothes. Wrinkling her nose didn't help dissipate the smell of smoke. She blamed her reaction on the Phobia Twins—Nycto and Claustro. When the lights had gone out in the already shadowy backstage area, she'd panicked. Like an idiot.

When the security guard found her, she'd screamed like the blonde cheerleader in a teen horror movie. She'd lost count of the times she'd fallen and scraped herself up before he arrived. Then there was that whole thing on the loading dock, in the SUV and at the hotel entrance when— She cut that thought off.

She wanted to bang her head on the nearest hard surface. Her nerves and emotions were caused by fear. Not Clay Barron holding her hand. Or carrying her. Or…nope. Clothes. She had to deal with her clothes because they reeked of smoke and stink bombs.

Checking the trash can, she found an extra folded plastic sack. She mashed the clothes into a ball and stuffed them into the bag, spinning it and tying it off. She shoved the whole thing into the trash. Georgie briefly considered digging out her bottle of spray cologne and using it to drown the odor still lingering. Considering this was Clay's bathroom, that probably wasn't a good idea. Then she thought about using his cologne—the signature scent of almond, cedar, bergamot and lemon that never failed to weaken her knees. Nope. That would not be a smart move, either.

She slipped out of the bathroom, pausing at the master bedroom door to listen. A sports program droned on the big screen TV in the living area and she saw shoulders and a head silhouetted over the back of the couch. Her embarrassment sent her scurrying, but she stopped when the guy spoke.

"You all right, Miss Dreyfus?"

"Y-yes." She didn't recognize the voice and the man didn't turn around, for which she was grateful.

"The senator and his party went to the fund-raiser. Their return ETA is midnight. Mr. Tate moved your things into the guest room next to his on the far side of the suite." He lifted his hand and gestured before continuing. "If you're hungry, I'll order room service. If there's anything else you need, just let me know. I'm Glen."

She clutched the lapels of her robe closer to her chest. Food was the last thing she wanted but she desperately wanted a Diet Coke. "Hi, Glen. Is there… I saw a kitchen. A Diet Coke, maybe?"

"I'll have one sent up, miss."

"Thanks. I'll just be in my…room."

She dashed across the open space and ducked into the bedroom the guard had pointed out. A lamp glowed next to the bed, on which the linens had been turned down. Her suitcase occupied a low bench. Checking the closet, she found her hang-up bag with her clothing inside. The case holding her personal care items had been tucked into the adjoining bath. While not nearly as opulent as the one in the master suite, it was far fancier than the bath in her previous room and was *Architectural Digest*-worthy compared to the one in her apartment back in DC. The room itself, even though it was probably the smallest bedroom in the suite, was magnificent. She needed to focus on something normal—as if brocade coverlets, silken accent rugs and needlepoint chair upholstery was normal. A hysterical giggle erupted from the back of her throat before she could stop it.

Digging through her suitcase, Georgie found her comfort

jammies—worn sweats and a long-sleeved T-shirt that said "Ways to win my heart…1. Buy me coffee 2. Make me coffee 3. Be coffee." Not that she was a caffeine addict. Much. She wondered if there was a coffeemaker in the kitchen. If she couldn't sleep—and she suspected it would be hard— she'd go look. Coffee would be a godsend.

A light tap on the bedroom door had her scrambling back into the robe. "Yes?"

"I've got your Coke, and the hotel doctor is here to see you."

"Doctor?" She'd forgotten, in the midst of her mortification, that Clay had offered to send a doctor. Georgie opened the door a crack and a kindly face with wild black eyebrows peered at her over Glen's shoulder. "Miss Dreyfus, I'm Dr. Bruce. The senator asked me to look in on you."

"Um…sure. Come in." Glen handed her a bottle of Diet Coke so cold it still had little bits of ice clinging to it.

"I'll be right out here, ma'am."

Ma'am? Ouch. She was only thirty. She pushed her glasses to the bridge of her nose and nodded, suddenly reminded of her dowdy looks. Stepping back, she opened the door wide enough for the doctor to enter.

He waved her toward the edge of the bed. "Do you mind sitting here, Ms. Dreyfus? I fear I'll need to do some prodding and poking. I hear you've had quite a day."

The snort escaped before she could stop it. "You could say that."

"Are you wearing anything under the T-shirt? Perhaps a tank or bra?"

Georgie blushed. "Oh, yeah. That would probably keep both of us from being embarrassed. Just a sec." She grabbed a spaghetti-strapped tank and dashed into the bathroom. She whipped off her sweatshirt and pulled the tank on before returning and settling on the bed once again.

She had to lift the tank so he could see her torso. Dr.

Bruce *tsked* at the bruises staining the ribs on her right side and her cheek. He *hmmed* at the knot on the back of her head. "You've got quite a collection of injuries, young lady. Are you in discomfort?"

"Only when I laugh?" She waggled her brows and the man smiled.

"Good to have a sense of humor, Ms. Dreyfus." He made sure her eyes were equal and reactive then checked her blood pressure, temperature and other vital signs before continuing. "You were lucky. You'll be sore for a few days, but the bruises will fade in a week or so." He coiled his stethoscope and dropped it into his bag before digging around in a side pocket. He pulled out a white envelope and wrote on it before retrieving a bottle of pills. He emptied six into the envelope and handed it to her. "I don't see signs of a concussion so I'm prescribing a light sleep aid. I suggest you take two tonight and then use the others as needed. Take one at bedtime over the next few nights. I'll also leave you some cold packs to help with the bruising and the bump. Once you get back to Washington, I want you to see your regular physician if you continue having trouble. Any questions?"

"No, sir. I'm good."

He patted her on the shoulder. "Get some rest, Ms. Dreyfus. That's the best thing for you."

The doctor opened the door and Glen almost fell through. Her guard was taking his duties seriously. He ushered Dr. Bruce out, shutting the door behind him. Georgie looked at the envelope and debated the pros and cons. She hated taking medicine but suspected the doctor was right. She'd replay the day's events—especially Clay's actions—on an endless loop guaranteed to keep her tossing and turning all night. Clay. She had to stop thinking of him by his first name. The senator. Her boss. The unattainable symbol of every feminine fantasy she'd had since the day she'd first walked into his campaign headquarters ten years before.

"Argh!" If her head wasn't already pounding, she might beat it against the wall. "Georgeanne Ruth Dreyfus, you are a complete and utter idiot." In self-defense, she shook two pills into her palm, twisted the top off the Diet Coke and took her medicine. Settling in bed, she snuggled into a world-class pillow.

The song "Girls Just Want to Have Fun" invaded her dream. Over and over. Georgie fumbled for her cell phone but it wasn't on the bedside table. The song stopped and she snuggled back under the covers, her brain as foggy as San Francisco Bay. She'd barely closed her eyes when the song played again. This time she threw off the covers and went hunting. She found the blasted phone in the side pocket of her messenger bag—the bag with the strap that broke yesterday when she tumbled off the loading dock, but was now perfect.

The hair prickled on the back of her neck. She didn't remember bringing it from the car last night and there was no way it could have been repaired. The phone stopped ringing, again, and she noticed the price tag still attached to the intact shoulder strap. This wasn't her bag, even though it was full of her stuff. Hers was a cheap knockoff. This one was the real deal, according to the amount listed on the tag.

Before her brain could cycle through the implications, the phone sang a third time. She answered with a snarled, "What!"

"OMG, Georgie! Are you okay? I've been so worried and then you didn't answer and where are you and are you all right, what happened—" Jennifer Antonelli, her best friend, paused to inhale.

"Slow down, Jen. How did you know something happened?"

"How did I know?" Jen's voice rose in pitch. "How did I know? Georgeanne, you're all over the morning news!"

Her stomach dropped. She found the remote control for the television and thumbed it to life. Scrolling through, she found an all-news channel. And sank to the edge of the bed, her legs no longer steady. "Oh, no. The cameras. I'm screwed."

"Georgie! What the heck happened yesterday? And were you really rescued by the senator?"

She had to put her head between her knees and breathe to keep from hyperventilating and passing out. "Dang, dang, dang," was all she could manage.

Jennifer had no such handicap. "What did it feel like? Is he as strong as he looks? I mean, gracious! He scooped you up and carried you away like…like…I don't know who! Holy cannoli, girl. Clay Barron was like Kevin Costner in that movie where he rescued Whitney Houston. Georgie? Georgie, are you listening to me?"

"Shush, Jen. I'm trying to hear the commentary on TV."

Voices droned in the background as footage played of the Tate brothers hustling her—clothes torn, knees bloody—into the rear seat of the senator's SUV. Clay looked shocked and angry as he ducked back inside to make room for her. The scene changed to their arrival at the hotel. The guards jogged up and opened the back door. Clay emerged holding her hand. Holding her hand? Georgie couldn't breathe for a minute and then, moments later when she stumbled and he swept her into his arms, she choked.

"Oh, God." Panting, she resumed her head-between-knees position.

"Georgie? Georgeanne! Speak to me. Are you okay?"

"No. I need to die. Like right now. No. I would have been better off dying last night. Oh, Mother Goose, Jen. I am *so* screwed."

"You keep saying that! What happened? Have you been holding out on me?"

"No. Oh, dang it, dang it, dang it." Georgie needed coffee. Stat. There was still liquid left in her Diet Coke bottle. She gulped it down and glanced at the clock. Five-fifteen. Arizona didn't do Daylight Savings Time so it was just after 7:00 a.m. in Washington. She rubbed her face and eyes. This was bad. *Really* bad. How many times had she dreamed of a romantic interlude with the senator? Way too often, but never played out in front of cameras. And reporters. On the national news.

Memories crowded in and she swayed. "He saw me, Jen," she whispered into the phone.

"Saw you? What do you mean?"

"In my bra and panties. I…I panicked. He… I think he held me in his lap." In full panic mode, she fled her bedroom, praying there would be a coffeemaker in the kitchen. And stationery. So she could write out her resignation letter. How in the world was she going to face Clay this morning? Sprinting through the living area, she barely noticed the bodyguard jumping to his feet. She sort of waved him back to his chair with a vague motion of her hand.

"Oh, thank you, thank you," she murmured when she spotted a Keurig machine and a display of K-Cups. "Coffee, Jen. Coffee first."

"You okay, Miss Dreyfus?" The guard watched her warily from just beyond the granite bar separating the kitchen from the dining area.

"Yeah. Yes. Coffee. I just need coffee. Sorry to have disturbed you. Um…carry on." She wanted to head-slap herself. Carry on? Seriously? Her foot tapped a jittery rhythm as the machine performed its magic. Once she had a fresh-brewed latte in her hands she could breathe again. Almost. She drained the cup in a few gulps and brewed another.

"Who are you talking to and I'm still waiting for an explanation, missy," Jen hissed through her phone.

"Shhh. I have to get back to my room."

"Back to your room? Where are you?"

"I'm in the senator's suite."

Ducking her head, she dashed back to her room and shut the door, ignoring the guard's grin as she ran past him. "Okay. I can think now. Maybe."

"How in blue blazes did the senator see you in your underwear and please tell me it was the nice stuff and not the ratty granny panties you normally wear!"

"The protesters yesterday. There were smoke bombs. And…they cut the lights, Jen. I was backstage. I fell and banged my head. Tripped on the darn stairs and fell again."

"Jiminy, girl! Are you okay?"

"I have some wicked bruises." She touched the back of her head. The lump remained but wasn't as tender. "And thank goodness, I have a hard head."

Jen's voice turned sly. "Did the senator kiss all your owies to make them better?"

"Jennifer Marie Antonelli, he did not!" Casting a worried glance at her closed door, Georgie lowered her voice. "It wasn't like that. He was holding my hand because he was being nice. And then I tripped getting out of the car because all the camera flashes blinded me. My glasses were smeary and you know how blind I am so—"

"And the man picked you up like you were a fairy-tale princess and carried you off to his castle."

"Well…sort of. They're worried about security because of the protesters so I was moved into his suite. There's lots of room. I mean serious room. Four bedrooms, five baths, all the amenities."

"You're stalling, Georgie. I don't want a travelogue. I want the down and dirty."

She inhaled and blew her breath out through puffed cheeks and pursed lips. In a resigned voice, Georgie recounted the events, ending with, "Then he left."

"Wait. You played strip Jeopardy?"

"My boss saw me in my undies and you're making up games? And what part of him holding me and…and…" She started to hyperventilate again. "OMG, Jen. I have to resign. I can't face the man."

"Breathe, Georgie. Does he have any idea how you feel?"

"You mean have I told him that I love him like crazy and have since the moment I met him? Oh, yeah, right. I definitely confessed that to him last night."

"Your sarcasm is showing. That's a good thing. It means you'll be okay. But you can't quit, Georgie. You have your dream job. Besides, if the man can't look beyond your tighty-whities and see what a jewel you are, he doesn't deserve you."

"Awww, Jen. Loyal to a fault. But they were red."

"I'm serious. You're just panicky. How many times have you had to put your head between your knees this morning?"

Laughter burst from Georgie's mouth. "Too many."

"See? I know you. Now, grab a shower. I'd tell you to put on something sexy but you don't own…wait! Red? You own red panties?"

"And a red bra."

"Are they lacy?"

"Well…um…no."

"Just as I thought. Now go put on your business suit of armor, get more coffee and do what you do best—work. Okay?"

Georgie nodded then remembered Jen couldn't see her. "Okay. You're right."

"Of course I am. I'm always right. I'm your BFF. Keep me posted. I never want to find out stuff like this from the news ever again. *Capisce*?"

"*Capisce.*"

Three

Clay stared at the press briefing folder lying front and center on his desk. He did not want to open it. He'd already seen the news coverage of yesterday's fiasco. The file would hold hard copies of clippings and photographs from print media and the internet. Georgie would have put together a digital file of clips, too, and emailed it, but she knew his preference for paper. He leaned back in his chair and swiveled so he could look out the window. A few of the more lurid headlines made him roll his eyes.

Senator Protects Aide à la *The Bodyguard*
Barron Rescues Damsel in Distress
Senator Barron—Hero in Disguise

All the articles led with a photograph of him sweeping Georgie into his arms to carry her. He leaned forward, tapping two fingers on the photo. Georgie must have been up before the Arizona sunrise to cull all the stories from the New York shows and national press and prepare them, though she evidently had gone back to bed. She'd been asleep when he returned from the fund-raising dinner last night. The night guard said she'd taken some prescribed sleeping pills and went right to bed. Her door wasn't locked so Clay had peeked in first thing this morning and she'd been curled up in a semi-fetal position under a thick pile of bedcovers. Then he'd walked into the suite's study and found his desk set up just like every other working day.

Boone rapped his knuckles against the door and sauntered in, leaning a shoulder against the doorjamb. He inclined his head toward the open file. "You've seen the headlines."

Nodding, Clay shuffled through the file, barely glancing at the various photos and clippings. "And the coverage on all the news channels. Your take?"

"You should have a nice bump in the next poll, especially in that all-important women's vote. They'll see you as heroic and dashing now. Let's face it, you're already the most eligible bachelor inside or outside the Beltway, and we all know you've got the Barron good looks." He chuckled. "Tates are more handsome, but you Barrons aren't bad."

Boone reflexively caught the pen Clay tossed at him then sobered. "In all seriousness, now you have that intangible mystique that will draw women. I'm sorry Georgie got caught in the middle, but those protesters did you a huge favor."

Clay growled under his breath. He, too, hated what had happened to Georgie. Her tears just about undid him. He couldn't deal with tears. Hadn't since— He cut off that thought, only to have it replaced by the memory of cradling Georgie in his arms—with very little between them. He'd wanted to take care of her. And maybe a little more. Doing so would have been taking advantage of a bad situation. He was not his father or his younger brothers. He could keep his libido in check.

The curves he discovered when he'd held her had been a surprise, and seeing her in that cute, if rather prim, red lingerie left no doubts. He halted that train of thought and reminded himself that Georgie was…Georgie. She dealt with the press, wrote his speeches and corralled a large portion of his staff. Boone was his right hand and she might as well be his left. Clay kept reminding himself of that. She was his employee, even if thoughts of her made him shift in his desk chair looking for a more comfortable position. Unlike his father, he didn't dip his pen in company ink.

"Is she still asleep?" Clay needed to see her, talk to her.

"Don't think so, but she's not coming out of her room."

"Have you spoken to her?"

"No."

Was Boone fidgeting? "Spit it out, cuz."

Boone stepped fully into the study and closed the door before dropping into a side chair. He put on what Clay called his "headmaster" face before asking, "What happened last night?"

"Happened?"

"Yeah. What went on between you and Georgie while I was packing up her stuff and replacing what had been ruined?"

"That's none of your business, Boone."

"It is if it affects the operation of your office. The two of you spent a lot of time in the bathroom. Alone. With the door shut."

Leaning back in the chair, Clay studied the man he trusted maybe even more than his own brothers. He weighed the pros and cons of disclosure and finally told Boone about their encounter in the bathroom.

"Ah…okay. Yeah. I can see why she's avoiding us this morning, especially given the publicity. Speaking of which, what in the world possessed you to pick her up?"

That was one question Clay hadn't asked himself. "I was right there. It just seemed…prudent."

Boone's face scrunched into a disbelieving scowl. "Prudent? Dude, there's not enough preplanning and money in the world to pay for that visual so I'm not complaining, but one of the security team could have caught her." He arched a brow. "Of course, I'm still trying to figure out why you were holding her hand in the first place."

Why had he continued to hold her hand? Clay questioned his motivation, ignoring the heat flushing his skin—color he hoped Boone didn't see. He'd held her hand because he wanted to, but he wasn't about to explain that to his cousin. "It just seemed like…" Like what? Like her hand fit in his?

Like he felt protective? Like she needed him? Him. Not Hunt. Not Boone. Not anyone but him. "Like the right thing to do. She was upset. She's a valued member of my staff."

"Oh. So you would have done the same for anyone on staff?"

Clay ignored the other man's smirking grin. "Except you. I'd let you face-plant. What are you getting at?"

"You need to be ready for the media. Georgie needs to be prepared, too. Just sayin'."

"Fine. I'll talk to her so we're on the same page. What time are we scheduled to fly back to DC?"

Boone checked his watch. "You have a meeting there at four." He appeared to be mentally checking the flight time. "We need to leave the hotel within the hour. I'll notify Hunt and Georgie."

Nodding absently, Clay continued to stare out the window. "I'll sit with Georgie on the plane so we can talk."

Unless he was in full campaign mode, he traveled light where personnel was concerned. There would be plenty of room to spread out in the jet for the flight back to DC. He could visit with Georgie with less chance of being overheard. Not that he planned to say anything the others couldn't hear; he just wanted to reassure her. Yes, definitely reassure her. That was what he wanted to do.

Georgie dodged the lead SUV while Clay had his back turned and jumped into the one carrying the luggage and extra security guards. Clay—no, she reminded herself. The senator. He was her boss. She never called him by his first name; that was reserved for her fantasies. Or nightmares, as last night had turned out to be. Call her chicken but she did not want to be in a confined space with him.

On the ride to the airport, she did her best not to think about the puzzled, almost hurt look Clay—the senator— had flashed her direction when he realized she wasn't riding with him. At the hangar, a knot of reporters were waiting on the apron. Georgie grimaced and prepared to do battle with them. This was her job, and she was very good at it, so she needed to just suck it up and get this over with. She was out of the SUV almost before it came to a complete stop. She had her game face on by the time she reached the SUV carrying Clay. One of the security guards jogged in her wake.

"The media will want a statement, Senator. I apologize we didn't have time to discuss preparing one." Yeah, because she was too much of a coward to face him even though Boone said they needed to get their story straight.

"I'll divert the reporters while you go straight to the plane. I'll have something drafted for your approval before we reach Washington." Georgie kept her voice and manner brusque. Professional. Just business as usual. Yeah, right. Nerves thrashed like piranha in a feeding frenzy in her stomach, but she asserted steely control.

The pack was already baying their questions as she plastered her patented I-got-this expression on her face and strolled off to wage a war of wits. She sauntered toward the reporters, held back by a line of uniformed police.

"Georgie! Georgie, hey, Georgie! What's up with you and the senator?"

She arched a brow and stared down her nose at the reporter. Gratified when he squirmed, she rolled her eyes at him. "Seriously, Stu? Since when did you cover the gossip beat?"

"Georgie, what's the senator's stand on that pending eminent domain case in Utah?"

Now this was a slippery slope of a different angle. "As you know, Senator Barron's family have been cattle ranchers for generations. The government coming in to deprive a landowner of his holdings is an issue that should play out in the courts, as this case is doing."

"Georgie, you and the senator sure looked cozy last night at the hotel." A female reporter surged forward, waving her microphone. "Is there something besides business between you two?"

Georgie used her oh-really? face on the reporter. "Trafficking in innuendo now, Jules?"

"The public wants to know, Georgie. Senator Barron is a very eligible bachelor. The two of you work very closely together and I have a source that says you spent the night in his suite."

Georgie forgot to breathe for a moment as she fought to school her expression. According to the Washington press corps, she had one of the best poker faces in the business. She used it now to cover her distress.

"I'm sure all of you are aware of the security breach involving the senator's appearance at the Western States Landowners Association event yesterday. Due to the protection detail's concerns, all members of the senator's immediate traveling party were relocated to the Sonoma Suite, which boasts of amenities for a large group. I'm really disappointed in you, Jules. I thought you were a political reporter. Maybe you and Stu should go to work for *Inquiring Minds*."

She pivoted to leave but one last question caught her attention.

"Yo, Georgie, so this means you aren't dating Senator Barron?"

Glancing over her shoulder, she offered the reporter—a grizzled veteran old enough to be her father—a dazzling smile. "Why, Ed? Do you want to ask me out?"

The reporters all laughed and Georgie made a mental note to send Ed a bottle of good scotch. He'd given her the perfect out and she owed him one. She glanced at the private jet waiting on the tarmac and gulped. Clay stood at the bottom of the steps, arms folded across his chest, feet braced apart. And he looked pissed.

Clay fairly vibrated with anger. Boone cleared his throat and elbowed him. "Smile, Clay. She handled it perfectly. That's why we pay her the big bucks."

"I want the names of those reporters."

"Georgie will have them."

"I don't want her to know I asked for them."

"Dammit, Clay. Take a breath, bud. This is Georgie's job and she does it damn well. Don't muck it up. She handled the situation. Subject closed." Boone angled his head so he could watch Georgie's approach and Clay's expression. "Unless… Clay, please tell me nothing happened between you two."

"Nothing happened between us."

"Well, all-righty, then."

Clay glared when Boone didn't hide his smirk quite fast enough. He ignored his cousin and focused on the woman striding toward them. The bright autumn sun bounced off her glasses. She'd done some twisty thing with her hair again and he didn't want to think too hard about why he preferred it down and loose. She stopped in front of him, her expression perfectly neutral.

"Georgie."

"Senator."

"Sit with me."

Clay noticed the slight pursing of her lips. And was that a hint of panic in her eyes? Interesting. He ushered Georgie forward and followed, his hand resting on the small of her back to steady her. He guided her to the group of seats at the front of the plane. Two pairs of seats faced each other over an inlaid wood table.

Clay guided her into the second set of seats so she'd be sitting with her back to the rest of the plane. Then he nudged her over so that she was trapped between the bulkhead and…him. He slipped her bag off her shoulder and tossed it into one of the facing seats.

"Sit, Georgie. And buckle in. We need to take off."

A few moments later the Rolls Royce engines on the Gulfstream whined to full-throated life and the plane eased onto the apron headed toward the runway. Within minutes they'd lifted off and were at cruising altitude. A vanilla latte appeared in front of her while a cup of black coffee was delivered to Clay. He waited until she took her first swallow before opening the conversation.

"You've been avoiding me. I want to know why."

Georgie grimaced and swallowed hard. He shifted in his seat so he could watch her. A surge of color stained her throat and he wondered about the reason for it. No matter what she did or said, he worried this might not end well. She couldn't stall him. He was determined to find out what was going on in her head, becoming even more curious when she curled her lips between her teeth, pursed them then chewed on them again as she evidently marshaled her thoughts.

She stared into his eyes then glanced away. "I'm a little embarrassed, Senator."

"Embarrassed." Why would the girl—woman—be embarrassed?

"Well, yes. Embarrassed." Though everyone else sat at the rear of the cabin, she dropped her voice. "Last night. In the bathroom."

"Why should you be embarrassed?"

Georgie gave him a scathing look. "Why? Oh, let's recap the situation. I trip and almost fall on my face, only my boss snatches me in mid face-plant and carries me up to his suite. Then I go into full panic mode, while wearing only my underwear, with said boss present to witness said meltdown. I end up in a puddle of tears, and then we make national news. You're right. Why in bloody blue blazes should I be embarrassed?"

Clay was a consummate politician. He knew how to camouflage his emotions. Georgie didn't realize her voice had risen in volume and that everyone on the plane, except maybe the pilots, now knew what had happened in his bathroom. With a supreme effort, he swallowed his laughter.

"Precisely. I see no reason for embarrassment."

"Argh!" She threw up her hands and almost knocked over her latte. He grabbed it and held it out as a peace offering even as she muttered, "Men!" under her breath and gripped the edge of the table.

With gentle pressure, he pried her fingers loose, placed the cup between them and curled her fingers around the porcelain mug. He studied her again as she drank.

She was his communications director. She literally put words in his mouth. His thumb traced lazy circles on the table and a part of him wished it was her skin he touched.

"There's no need to be upset, especially since I…since *we* owe you an apology." She opened her mouth to refute, but he silenced her with a finger touching her lips as he continued. "I personally promise it won't happen again. From now on, Glen will be your shadow whenever we're at a function. He'll protect you." His gaze caught and held hers. "I'm sorry, Georgie. I'm sorry I didn't take care of you."

Georgie couldn't look away from the sincerity in his gaze. She swiveled in her seat so she could face him. His expression stunned her. She'd seen him determined, angry, sad, happy, disgusted…but she'd never seen him like this. Her stomach lurched as her pulse sped up. Georgie couldn't name the emotion in his eyes with their thick, dark lashes the color of his ebony hair. In her imagination, where her fantasies lived, she described his hair in romance-novel terms—as glossy as a raven's wing. And his eyes—burnt umber, even if she didn't really know what burnt umber looked like. It sounded sexy and that term definitely fit Clay. Or cognac. Yes, that was the color. She knew what cognac looked like in a leaded glass tumbler and his eyes looked like that—smoky, swirling brown with glinting lights. Lost in his gaze, she simply took him in, letting him fill her up. The force of him edged into the empty places she'd ignored her whole life, the places where her hopes and dreams lived.

I'm in so much trouble now. Having a crush on the man was one thing, but she feared that after this trip, she'd fallen way over her head in love with her boss. She cleared her throat, dragging her gaze from his to break their connection. She managed to say one word.

"Okay."

Another emotion flickered across his expression, lightening his mood. "Okay. Good. Then we're all settled. How about some breakfast?"

Breakfast. Yes, breakfast would work to put some distance between them and let her get her fantasies back under control. "Okay."

He patted her arm. "For a woman whose job is words, you seem to have very few of them at the moment."

They were somewhere over Tennessee when Georgie fell asleep. She dreamed of Clay, of him slipping his arm over her shoulders to pull her against his side.

"Georgie?" He whispered her name.

"What?" She whispered back.

"I think I'm going to kiss you now."

She sighed, wanting to feel his lips on hers. "You think?"

"I know I want to."

"Okay."

"Okay?"

"Um…yeah. Okay." Inside the dream she wanted to bang

her head on the table. What was up with her managing to only say *okay*?

She focused on his mouth. Full lips. Firm. Hints of smile lines at the corners.

He plucked her glasses from the end of her nose and set them aside on the table. The corner of his mouth quirked as he looked at her.

"What will you taste like?" dream Clay asked. "Dessert sweet and rich? Or twenty-year-old scotch, a smoky burn in my mouth? I can't wait to find out."

He lowered his head and his lips brushed across hers. She licked her bottom lip, her tongue darting out to sample the taste of him. He moved in again, no hesitation this time. His lips fastened onto hers, sucking in her bottom lip as his teeth nipped. One hand secured the back of her head, angling it to the perfect position for his tender attack.

Normally bold in her fantasies about Clay, she now felt shy and her actions mirrored her emotions. Her hands, hesitant and timid, latched onto his leather jacket—he always wore leather in her dreams—and clung there as though her life depended on it. Emotions rushed through her and a little voice said she should run. Ignoring it, Georgie pressed into their kiss, her tongue now bold enough to dance with his—until he pulled away.

"Georgie, wake up. We're getting ready to land." Breathing hard, she opened her eyes to discover that Clay was watching her, amusement twitching his lips into a sexy grin.

"Oh, pistachios on pita. Please tell me I wasn't talking in my sleep."

Four

Clay smoothed his features into a neutral expression. He *had* heard his name on her lips several times, and the little smooching noises and puckering of her lips was both cute and…arousing. While he'd surely like to know the details, there would be a time and place to discover what Georgie dreamed about—and specifically his role in those dreams—but this wasn't it.

"Do you make a habit of talking in your sleep?" He snapped his mouth shut, shocked he'd pursued the subject.

Georgie pushed her glasses up her nose and stared at him. Her forehead crinkled and her lips pursed as she gave the question serious thought. "I…don't know, seeing as I'm usually asleep. Would you like me to set up a recorder to find out?"

She looked so serious, Clay hesitated a few seconds before laughing. He opened his mouth to say the first thing that popped into his head, but stopped as innate political instincts kicked in. Offering to watch her sleep at night was not a smart move. He relayed a stern warning to all interested body parts. Georgie was an employee and off-limits. Period.

"Would you?" He wanted to head-slap himself. And shut up. Yes, keeping his mouth shut would be a good thing right about now.

"Ah, Clay?"

Boone. Thank goodness. His cousin could always be counted on to pull his butt out of the fire. Clay turned away from Georgie and focused on his chief of staff. "What's up?"

Boone had to clear his throat before speaking and he wouldn't quite meet Clay's gaze. The words that came out were strained as he tried to stifle his laughter. "Transport is waiting at the airport. We'll head straight to the office. And you have an email from your sister-in-law."

"Cassidy?"

"Only sister-in-law I'm aware of."

"What about?"

"Thanksgiving."

"Thanksgiving?"

"Yes. As in, are we coming home for the holidays? A question also being asked repeatedly by my mother."

"I don't have time."

Boone glanced toward Georgie. "Take Georgie home with you. Make it a long working weekend. And give her time to slide home to see her dad."

"My dad?" Georgie sounded surprised. "Thanksgiving? He and his buddies go hunting in Montana every year."

Studying her for a long moment, Clay considered his next comment. "Sounds like your Thanksgivings are a lot like mine. Boone, email Cassie and tell her I'll be in touch for the details."

After Boone returned to his seat and buckled up, Clay noticed Georgie's hands were a little white-knuckled as she gripped the table. "Problem?"

"I don't like landings. Takeoffs? Not thrilled but I'm fine. Landings?" She blinked at him a few times and her bangs brushed the tops of her glasses as she wrinkled her forehead. "Yeah, not so much."

Prying one hand free, he laced his fingers through hers. "Good to know I'm not the only one." He squeezed gently. "Hold my hand to make me feel better? Boone gets all weird when I ask him to do it."

An odd little noise that was a cross between a giggle and snort burst from her and she tucked her teeth between her pressed lips to hold back the full laugh. "I can imagine."

Her green eyes flashed in the sunlight streaming through

the plane window as the pilot banked to line up on the runway. "Don't tell my constituents."

She gestured with her free hand, miming zipping her
lips, pressing them closed. "Mmm nnnllps er hhed."

"Your lips are sealed?"

Georgie nodded vigorously. "We wouldn't want the vot-
ers to know their favorite senator is a 'fraidy cat."

"Good to know I can trust you." It struck him then. He
could trust Georgie. She'd become an integral part of his
inner cadre but he'd never considered the trust he bestowed
on her as she moved into her current position. He reflected
on what he knew of her. While usually on the quiet side,
she didn't back down easily when she believed herself to
be right. And she had a wicked sense of humor, most often
directed at Boone.

A flash of jealousy zinged through him. Was there something between Boone and Georgie? Boone called her *sugar*.
All the time. Damn it. But if there was something going
on, why should Clay care?

The plane touched down and the engines whined as the
pilot applied brakes, diverting him from his thoughts.

Leaving the ground crew to deal with luggage, Clay,
Boone and Georgie headed toward his senate offices, driven
by Glen with Hunter riding shotgun. The SUV forged
through the typically heavy Washington traffic, bullying
its way from Dulles to the Russell Senate Office Building
in a drive that took almost forty-five minutes. Turning left
onto Delaware, the vehicle rolled to a smooth stop just past
the main entrance on the southwest corner of the building.

Hunt was out of the front seat and opening doors even as
his eyes roved the surroundings in a threat assessment. As
Boone stepped out first, his brother tilted his head. "Shark
at three o'clock."

Boone snorted as he helped Georgie and then Clay out.
"Parker Grace is headed this way."

"Senator! Senator Barron!"

Georgie schooled her features to keep her thoughts from leaking into her expression. A reporter for a local television station, Parker Grace scurried toward them, her four-inch heels clattering against the concrete sidewalk. With her perfectly coiffed platinum hair and inch-long eyelashes fluttering over blue eyes, the woman was always the epitome of feminine perfection. And Georgie hated her for it.

Parker's gaze flicked over her and then focused on Clay. "Senator, do you care to make a comment about your affair with a staff member?"

Sugar would have melted on the woman's tongue, but the vinegar beneath her words soured Georgie's stomach. She stepped up beside Clay, prepared to do her job, but Boone cut her off.

"Really, Parker? You get demoted to the gossip beat or something?"

The woman flushed but kept her microphone waving toward Clay. "Those pictures from Scottsdale are fairly explicit, Senator, and word has leaked out that Ms..." The reporter's gaze once again washed over Georgie and dismissed her. "Your...assistant was seen leaving your suite after spending the night there. Care to comment?"

Once again, Boone cut Georgie off and she fumed at being usurped. "Parker, Parker, Parker. Did your sources also say that I was staying in the same suite, in my capacity as the senator's chief of staff, along with his security chief, other security personnel and Ms. Dreyfus, the senator's communications director?"

Georgie couldn't remain silent any longer. "Seriously, Grace? You want to go there?"

"Most people would, Dreyfus. How wonderfully *Fifty Shades*. The mousy press secretary and the handsome, powerful senator."

Georgie laughed. "Oh, apple pie, my eye. What have

you been smoking?" Georgie gripped the woman's arm and tugged her away from the others, though the cameraman followed. Lowering her voice, she fluttered her lashes in perfect imitation of Parker. "Ooh, Senator, I'd love to get my gold-digging claws into your trust fund."

The guy with the camera huffed out a snort and rolled his eyes as Georgie stepped even closer to the reporter, her palm covering the microphone. "You want to get up and personal with me, Grace, bring it. But this vendetta you have because you threw yourself at the senator and he had the good taste to ignore you needs to stop. Don't make me go to your producers."

Arching a brow, Georgie waited. She had information Parker didn't—mainly that Barron Entertainment owned the majority shares in the station the reporter worked for. And she was fairly positive that a word to Boone would result in a phone call to Chase Barron, Barron Entertainment CEO.

"Don't threaten me, Georgeanne Dreyfus," the other woman hissed. When Georgie just continued to stare, Parker blanched. "You wouldn't dare."

"Let's get everything out in the open, Parker. When it comes to the senator, there's very little I wouldn't dare. I'm telling you unequivocally there is not, nor has there ever been anything of a romantic nature between Senator Barron and me. If you want to go fishing in that pond, be careful what bait you use. You never know what you might catch on the end of your line. Some things out there in the water bite. Hard."

Parker assessed her with a questioning eye but Georgie didn't flinch. "When did you get so tough, little girl?"

"Honey, I'm an Oklahoma cowgirl. We're born tough. And don't you forget it." Georgie offered the cameraman a sympathetic look as Parker stormed away, her ridiculous heels tap-tap-tapping on the pavement. "Yeah, good luck with that."

He snorted again and with a resigned slump of his shoulders, followed the retreating talent.

"I *am* still capable of speaking for myself, Georgie."

Startled by the voice in her ear, she whirled and almost tipped over when she bumped into Clay—who was standing inordinately close. Heat crept up her cheeks and she settled her glasses more firmly on her nose. "The last time I checked, talking to reporters is still in my job description."

"So…Parker had a thing for me, huh?"

Her mouth dropped open and she closed it, only to gape again as Boone chuckled and nudged Clay's shoulder with his. "I *told* you so." He held out his hand. "Pay up, cuz."

Georgie snapped her mouth shut again. "Wait…you made a *bet*? On what?"

While Boone tried to look innocent, she didn't fall for it. "Please don't tell me you were betting on me confronting her."

A wickedly sinful grin spread across Clay's face. "Okay. We won't tell you." He snagged her arm and headed toward the building's entrance. "But I would appreciate knowing the next time a sexy woman finds me desirable. Men need to know these things."

Sputtering, Georgie allowed Clay to tow her along beside him. Jealousy flared hot as a sparkler on the 4th of July and she stuffed it deep. As they entered the Russell's rotunda, Clay leaned down to whisper in her ear.

"And for your information, I find nothing mousy about you."

Three weeks later Clay sprawled in the desk chair in the study at the Barron family compound in Oklahoma City, feet propped on the scarred desktop. Despite his busy schedule, he'd caved to his sister-in-law's demand for a family Thanksgiving gathering. He'd insisted it was a working break and brought Georgie with him. They were currently dealing with his upcoming schedule. Georgie, all business, stood at the whiteboard ticking off a list when his nephew plowed into the room. "Uncle Clay! Aunt Cassie says time to eat. You gots to come now, 'kay?" The boy was all but bouncing out of his cowboy boots and Clay wasn't quite sure how to respond. Cord, his next younger brother, had almost died earlier in the fall. During his recovery, he'd reconnected—sort of—with his ex-girlfriend, only to discover he had a son. CJ looked like a Barron and Clay remembered when Cord and Chance had been filled with the same energy.

He'd been their caretaker during their mother's final illness and death from cancer. Their father hadn't wanted to deal with the domestic situation so he didn't. Cyrus Barron had done what he did best: abandoned his parental responsibilities. And after the accidental death of his first stepmother, Clay had also taken on the twins, Chase and Cash, when Cyrus pulled his disappearing act.

Dropping his feet to the floor, Clay pushed out of the chair and joined CJ at the door. "You heard the little man, Georgie. Aunt Cassie says it's time to eat." He ruffled the boy's hair. "Has your dad explained about the wishbone?"

CJ's eyes widened and he nodded like a bobblehead dog on the dash of a car driving down a rough road. "Yup. Uncle Cash 'n' me get to break it an' I get something cool when I win. C'mon! There's pie and hot rolls and sweet taters."

Holding the door, Clay gestured for Georgie to precede him, a part of him oddly gratified she'd agreed to come home with him for the weekend. Granted, they'd mostly been closeted in this small study since their arrival the previous day so he hadn't had much interaction with anyone besides her, but wasn't that the point? She was a buffer between him and his brothers, in much the same way that she stood between him and the press.

The meal went as family gatherings usually did in the Barron household, at least when Cyrus was absent—lots of teasing, gooey glances between Chance and his not-so-new bride as Miz Beth and Big John presided over the festivities like the surrogate parents they'd been since coming into the brothers' lives. When the time came for the wishbone pull, Cash—as the youngest brother—made a half-hearted attempt at the tradition with CJ. When the boy won, Cash pushed away from the table and strode out, angry over something.

Clay considered following his baby brother but CJ's sly wish about getting his mom and dad back together kept him in his seat as Cord stammered his way through an explanation of why that wouldn't happen. With the cleanup underway and football-watching to follow, Clay took the opportunity to slip back into the study.

Almost two hours later his father strode in. Clay glanced up at the intrusion, surprised since Chance had assured everyone that Cyrus was in Las Vegas for the duration. He sat up straighter, recognizing the set of the man's shoulders and the expression on his face.

"We need to talk." The old man glowered, anticipating he'd vacate the chair behind the desk. Clay didn't indulge him.

Irritated now more than when he'd walked in, his old man lowered himself into a less comfortable chair and didn't wait to fire the opening volley. "Get your brothers. We have family business."

Clay didn't like the derisive tone in his father's voice. "What sort of *family* business?"

"Cord and my grandson and that woman who wants to ruin them both. Now get the hell out of my chair. We'll talk more after I deal with your thickheaded brother."

Doing as he was told but dragging his feet, he went in search of his brothers. He found Cash first and received a curt nod and sneer for his trouble. "I'll round up everyone and then text Cord to meet us in the conference room," Cash informed him.

Cash's reaction and obvious previous knowledge of the situation left a bitter taste in Clay's mouth. His youngest brother had once been the most easygoing of them all—rivaling even Cord for being laid-back. He wondered what had happened to turn Cash into the man he currently was.

With reluctance, Clay headed to the conference room and sank into the chair at one end of the table. During the "family intervention" his father demanded Cord sue for full custody of CJ, and made other more personal demands about CJ's mother, Jolie. It left Clay slightly angered—at his father, at his baby brother, but proud of Cord and Chance for standing up to the old man. He should probably do the same, though a heavy sense of dread hung over him as he followed his father back into the study.

"What are your plans?"

"My plans for what?"

"The election."

"As you well know, I'm forming an exploratory committee."

"You need to declare early. Scare off the competition."

"This may not be the right cycle to run."

"Bull. You will campaign, get the party's nomination, and we'll make a successful run at the presidency."

"We," Clay said in a clipped tone, letting the pronoun hang in the emotionally charged atmosphere.

"I can't trust you not to mess it up. I'll be there every step of the way. I have some things to deal with here but I'll be in Washington next week. We'll get things started."

Despite the urge, and a certain need to do so, Clay didn't argue. A smart man picked his battles with the old man. This wasn't the time or the place.

Five

Even now, late on a snowy December day when his colleagues were preparing to flee Washington for their home districts, Clay glared at the files highlighted in the pool of stark white LED light shining on his desk. He pretended he was too busy to make it home for the holidays but in reality, he didn't want to deal with the family drama happening back in Oklahoma. The intervention at Thanksgiving involving Cord, the mother of his child and the boy himself soured Clay's stomach. As much as he'd enjoyed meeting his nephew and reconnecting with his brothers, overall, succumbing to his new sister-in-law's plea to appear for the family gathering had been an unmitigated disaster. And he still had his old man all up in his political business.

A peal of laughter floated through his half-opened office door. Georgie. She'd been the one high point in the Thanksgiving travesty. He'd all but begged her to accompany him, his excuse that she was the best speechwriter on the Hill and he had precampaign stops to make on the way back to Washington. In truth, he'd needed her there to insulate him from the dysfunction surrounding his family. Her presence and clear head kept him centered.

A male voice rumbled in the background and Georgie laughed again. A streak of jealousy twisted through him before he clamped down on his emotions. Georgie was an employee. He didn't fish in the office pond. Ever. Unlike many of his associates. He closed the file he'd been studying— the oil and gas production bill wasn't going anywhere anytime soon—and wondered who was in the reception area with her. He kept a skeleton staff during December. While Congress didn't officially break for Christmas recess until

December twenty-first, the Hill effectively ground to a stop in anticipation of the holiday weeks before.

A few moments later Boone rapped on the door and stuck his head in. "Dude, enough. We need steaks. And beer."

The Tate brothers belonged to Clay's aunt Katherine, his father's sister. While all of them carried the trademark Barron dark hair, they'd inherited their father's blue eyes, and Boone's twinkled with good humor. He stepped fully into the office and glanced over his shoulder. "I bet I can convince Georgie to come with us, since we three are the only ones still here." He waggled his brows and Clay couldn't help but chuckle at his cousin's antics.

When his stomach grumbled in agreement, Clay surrendered. As long as Boone was there to chaperone, he could keep his mind on business and not on the woman whose presence had inexplicably begun to make his breath catch and his thoughts wander to places they had no business visiting. "Are you buyin'?"

A snort of laughter was quickly followed by a shake of Boone's head. "Hell no, cuz. You're the one who makes the big bucks. We have reservations at Max's Steakhouse and we're going to miss them. Now, get your butt in gear."

The woman under discussion breezed into the room, a quiet smile on her face. She pushed the heavy black frames of her glasses up on her nose. "Did you convince him he needs beef?"

Georgie's voice did funny things to Clay—most of them centered below the belt buckle. She interacted with the press often and he'd overheard one male journalist comment that Georgie had the voice of a phone sex operator, but the rest of her didn't follow through. He'd studied Georgie following that crack and came to his own conclusion. Who knew girls in glasses looked so sexy? Thank goodness no one saw her the same way he did. He'd hate to start a fistfight.

Which was so outside the realm of his normal behavior he now second-guessed every word, thought and action where Georgie was concerned.

She'd been a fixture in his office almost since the beginning, recruited by Boone first as a campaign assistant and then as a deputy press secretary after her graduation from the University of Oklahoma's journalism school. Since that time, she'd worked her way through the ranks. After her comments regarding her own Thanksgiving and family, Clay had done a little covert checking. Her mother had been a Tulsa socialite who met and married Georgie's father in college. They'd divorced when Georgie was thirteen, after living apart most of her life. Marlena Dreyfus had hated life on the ranch. After the divorce she had moved to Dallas, and effectively ignored her daughter. George Dreyfus had raised his daughter to be a cowgirl until Georgie departed for college and then joined Clay's staff.

Putting Hunt on the trail, he learned Georgie had had one semiserious boyfriend in college, and seldom dated anyone more than a few times since coming to Washington. The idea she didn't have many men in her past pleased Clay, and he was man enough to admit that was his ego talking because he had a whole string of women peppering his past. Clay was also honest enough to admit his sudden interest was closer to stalking than infatuation. But he didn't care. Georgie was an important and trusted member of his staff. He should know these things. And finding out about her had nothing to do with the vivid dreams in which she starred, leaving him hard and wanting upon awaking. No, those dreams had nothing at all to do with his current curiosity.

"Who's driving?" Boone was shrugging into his sheepskin coat as he glared out the window into the Russell Building's inner courtyard. Snow fell thick and fast.

"Not you," Georgie teased. "I called Hunt earlier. He's

sending an SUV for us. Four-wheel drive. And he promised a driver who knows how to navigate in this stuff."

"Well, that certainly makes me feel safer." Clay jingled the keys in his coat pocket. He'd much rather drive—not that he was a control freak. Much. Georgie was smart to get a ride for them. Washingtonians and winter driving didn't mix when it came to maneuvering the streets of DC. He grabbed his topcoat from the old-fashioned coat rack in the corner while Georgie ducked out to her office to grab her own coat.

They nodded to the guard as they left the building and strode straight to the black Suburban idling next to the curb. Georgie ended up sandwiched between him and Boone in the backseat. Clay's thigh pressed against hers and he heard her breath hitch. Glancing at her, he caught the flushing of her creamy skin, obvious even in the darkness of the winter night. Interesting.

Hunt twisted around in the front to look at them. "Jeez. Did I forget my deodorant or something? Nobody fighting over who gets to ride shotgun?"

"What are you doing here?" Clay was surprised to see his chief of security in the driver's seat.

"Georgie said you were buying. At Max's. That means good beef. Hell yeah, I'm driving."

Boone laughed and jumped out, ducking into the front passenger seat a moment later. "I'll sit up here, bro, since you're such a big baby about riding all by your lonesome."

The brothers argued good-naturedly during the drive to the restaurant. Clay breathed shallowly because Georgie had barely moved into the seat vacated by Boone. She was close enough their shoulders brushed each time Hunt turned a corner. And that was so not good. Boundaries. Clay needed them. Not to mention he had plans of the romantic variety over the holiday break. A Broadway star was anticipating his presence as her escort at a variety of glittering parties in New York and Boston. Parties where the rich and powerful would be. Parties where he would make contacts to further his political aspirations and allow him to test the waters surrounding his run for the party's presidential nomination.

When they were seated in a round booth inside Max's a few minutes later, the brotherly banter continued. Clay envied his cousins. Aunt Katherine could be a domineering matriarch but she also baked cookies, was a staunch supporter of her children and loved them fiercely. He remembered his own mother as being weak and subservient to the old man. She'd loved him and his brothers in her own way, and they'd loved her. When Cyrus had married his stepmother Helen, she'd done her best to mother him, Cord and Chance, but she'd become pregnant fairly soon after the wedding and the twins kept her crazy busy. Until that fateful rainy day when a drunk driver and a blind curve had changed everything.

Georgie nudged him with her shoulder. "Penny for your thoughts?"

He scowled at her for a moment. "They aren't worth that much." Which was true. Introspection never did him any good. He tuned back in to the conversation. Boone and Hunt were going at it again, claiming each was their mother's favorite.

"My Christmas present will be the biggest." Folding his arms across his chest, Hunt smirked at Boone.

"Nuh-uh. Mine will be. Mom loves me best because I'm cutest."

Hunt snickered. "You know that's not true! That claim belongs to Deacon. Mom has always thought he was the cutest."

"That's because he's a *star*." Boone rolled his eyes as he made air quotes around the last word. "She just wants to go to the Country Music Association Awards with him."

Clay snorted, getting into the conversation. "Deke taking Aunt Katherine to the CMAs? Riiight. Not gonna happen. That boy has girls draped around him like his momma's mink stole."

Boone reached across Georgie and punched Clay's shoulder with a loose fist. "Just like someone else I know. When are you headed up to New York to see Giselle?"

After checking the calendar on his phone, Clay shrugged. "We're scheduled for a charity reception at the Plaza on the eighteenth. I'll probably fly up that morning."

The conversation paused as their waiter appeared and delivered their plates. The men all dug into their steaks and baked potatoes with gusto. Georgie was a bit daintier as she cut and chewed. The excellent medium-rare Angus beef almost melting in her mouth wasn't the only thing she chewed over.

Clay was still seeing Giselle Richards, the Tony award–winning actress from Oklahoma. That discovery shouldn't have surprised her. Except Clay seldom dated anyone for longer than a few months. Giselle had been on his horizon for almost nine. Georgie kept her eyes on her plate and worked to keep all expression off her face. Clay dated. This was a fact of life. She had absolutely no claim on him outside the office. Period. Her life was simpler that way. And her heart infinitely safer.

The men continued talking as the food disappeared from their plates.

Boone nudged her foot under the table. "Yo, Georgie, you're way too quiet."

She frowned and huffed. "Too quiet? With you three, who can get a word in edgewise?"

All three men chuckled and Hunt jostled Boone. "Ha. She's got your number, little bro."

"My number?" Boone pointed to his chest. "One." He pointed at Hunt then Clay. "Two. Three. She said, and I quote, 'With you *three*.' I think she knows us all extremely well."

Georgie glanced at her wristwatch. "Because I do, I'm going to skedaddle before this conversation deteriorates any further."

She stared at Boone as a hint to slide out of the booth so she could exit. He didn't move. She cleared her throat and Boone pointedly ignored her. Then his leg brushed across her shins. Clay jerked and stared at her. Her eyes wide, she turned her head to narrow them at Boone. "You will pay for that. Now move." She shoved at his shoulder.

Hunt slid out. "I'll take my little brother's hint. You aren't walking to the Metro. We'll drive you home."

"Good idea, bro."

A few minutes later, the tab paid, coats claimed and the valet dispatched, the four of them waited just inside the door. When the SUV pulled up, they headed out. Feeling ornery, Georgie headed around the front of the vehicle. "Shotgun!"

She caught all three men flat-footed and was ensconced in the front seat before they reacted. Hunt laughed as he climbed in behind the wheel, flashing smug looks at the other men. Georgie felt inordinately proud of herself even as she faced the thought of a confrontation with Boone. He'd been nudging Clay and her together. A lot. He needed to stop his romantic machinations immediately because… well…because!

When Hunt pulled up in front of her apartment building, Clay was out of the backseat and at her door before she could get it open. She was about to argue but he had her arm, tugging her onto the sidewalk.

"I'll walk you inside."

Six

Clay cupped Georgie's elbow with one hand while his other automatically went to the small of her back. The sidewalk was slippery. That was his excuse. She turned at the door to say good-night and he suddenly realized he didn't want her to go.

Jumping in before she could dismiss him, he said, "I'll walk you up to your apartment."

"Senator—"

"Clay."

Her lips parted slightly and he wondered if that was an invitation. Nope, he shouldn't go there. Just…

"Really, Senator, I'm fine. This is a secure building and you really don't want to hike up three flights."

And she put him right back in his place. Georgie was right, of course. He was taking off in a few days to spend the holidays with Giselle. His ironclad policy was no office shenanigans. This sudden interest in the woman who'd been under his nose for years was just…an infatuation. Or something. He curled his fingers into his palms to keep from cupping her face.

"Then I'll say good night, Georgie. See you in the office tomorrow morning."

Some emotion he couldn't quite define flickered across her expression, gone before he could capture it. He stepped back so he wouldn't do something stupid. Like kiss her while standing there on the stoop with Boone and Hunt watching from the SUV.

The lock snicked and she pushed the door open. "Good night…Senator." Georgie slipped through the opening before he could change his mind and she shut the door behind her, locking him out. He stood in the cold, his breath fogging the glass until she turned into the stairwell and disappeared from his sight. He stepped out on the sidewalk, head craned back, waiting. A few minutes later lights illuminated a set of windows on the third floor and Georgie's shadow passed across them.

The back window of the SUV slithered down and Boone leaned out. "Yo, Clay, get in the car. It's freezing."

With a reluctance he didn't quite understand, Clay settled into the front passenger seat. Silence reigned for about thirty seconds and then his cousins erupted in laughter.

"Idiots," he muttered under his breath.

"Who, us?" Boone reached between the seats to slug his shoulder. "Clay, you need to ask that girl out."

"No."

"Why not?"

"Isn't it obvious? She works for me, Boone."

"No, technically she works for me."

"And you work for me. Just…forget it. Bad idea. You're the one who pointed this out in Arizona. Besides, she doesn't—" He bit off the rest of the sentence.

"She doesn't what? Like you? Jeez, Clay. You are so freaking dense sometimes. That girl has crushed on you from the moment she walked in the door. And I only asked if you knew what you were doing in Scottsdale."

Hunt glanced over and rolled his eyes. "Huh. Are we like in junior high now?"

"Shut up, Hunt. And you, too, Boone." Clay held up his hand, cutting off their jibes. "In fact, I think I'll fly up to New York tomorrow. Hunt, make sure the plane is available and Boone, if you'll make arrangements at the Waldorf, I'd appreciate it."

Hunt looked as if he was going to say something else, but closed his mouth and grimaced before saying, "I'll instruct Cash to have a security team meet you."

"Good. I'll leave straight from home in the morning. You two can take care of the office until the winter recess."

The SUV rolled to a stop in front of Clay's Georgetown townhouse. The gray-painted brick building was almost obscured by the snow drifting down. The red brick sidewalk was completely covered. DC would be shut down by morning.

"Crap. Boone, email the staff and tell them to stay home tomorrow. There's no way the streets will be plowed. And that means I'll delay the trip to New York by a day."

"You realize you're running away, right?"

Hunt chimed in with chicken noises.

"Just do what I ordered." Clay climbed out and stomped through the snow to the wrought-iron gate protecting his small yard and entrance door. The black vehicle idled at the curb while he fought the accumulated snow to get the gate open and closed. The motion detector installed with his security system lit up the interior as he approached the door, keyed in the code and entered.

He decided to ignore the juvenile antics of his cousins. This was a matter of discretion being the better part of valor. Yes, he was tempted by Georgie but she was an employee. She was also the best speechwriter on the Hill and he was *not* going to jeopardize that relationship to pursue one of a more intimate nature.

Georgie opened her door, shoved a large, steaming mug into the hands of the woman standing there and ushered her inside. The trip up from the second floor hadn't taken her best friend long.

"Why are adult snow days not near as much fun as when we were kids and got to stay home from school?" Jen groused as she shuffled in on fuzzy house shoe–clad feet. She let loose with a huge yawn before sipping the hot chocolate in her mug. "Ooh. You put cinnamon in it."

"Of course I did. Do you want breakfast?"

"What do you have?"

Wandering into her small kitchen, Georgie checked the fridge and the cabinets. "Uhm…two boiled eggs. Instant oatmeal. And coffee."

"Put marshmallows in my next hot chocolate and we'll call it brunch." Jen settled on Georgie's couch, propped her feet on the coffee table and yawned again. "So talk to me."

Georgie topped off her coffee and curled up on the opposite end of the overstuffed couch, doing her best to seem as though she was okay. "About what?"

"Why you look so bummed out. Duh."

"I'm not bummed."

"Oh? Really? Coulda fooled me. What's up with the Oklahoma Stud?"

Blushing furiously, Georgie kicked at Jen's thigh. "Don't call him that."

"Then tell me what's going on between you two."

"Nothing." She barely avoided a sigh. "The office went to dinner last night and he walked me to the door."

"Did he kiss you?"

"Jen! Stop it! No. He did not. We don't have a…a relationship like that."

"And whose fault is that?"

Georgie stuck her fingers in her ears and sang, "La-la-la-la-la. Not listening to you."

"You know you want him, girl."

"He's my boss. And…" She pushed her glasses back to the bridge of her nose. "He's spending Christmas in New York. With Giselle Richards. And last night he told me he'd see me tomorrow…meaning today. Except he decided to leave early for New York and was going straight to the airport except…snow day."

Jen's face smoothed out and sympathy filled her gaze. "Well…that sucks."

"Yeah."

"Are they like…a thing?"

"He's been seeing her since…Valentine's Day."

"Wait. Their first date was Valentine's Day? Who does that?"

"It wasn't a date. Exactly. She was his escort for some deal at the Western Heritage Center in Oklahoma City. They went to the same high school or something."

"*Pffft*. She's got nothin' on you, Georgie."

"Says my best friend who is loyal to a fault. But have you seen her? She's a former Miss America and she won the Tony two years ago and she's gorgeous and…and…" Georgie couldn't swallow her sigh this time. "You know he's putting together an exploratory committee, right?" At Jen's nod, she continued. "Giselle is the type of woman he needs on his arm when he runs for president. She knows what to say to people. Looks amazing. Doesn't trip and fall over her own feet. Or wear glasses."

"I call BS."

"Why? She's beautiful and talented and…everything I'm not."

"And she's a total airhead. Have you ever heard her interviewed? I mean, seriously. I don't know what Senator Barron sees in her."

Georgie stared at Jen, all but gaping. "You are so not a guy. She walks by and their tongues hang out."

"Well, you're smart and funny and…and sweet and… and…"

"And nothing. I invited you over to cheer me up."

"It's too early in the morning. And there's no ice cream."

"I know. I'm a lousy hostess, which just proves my point." Georgie curled her upper lip and rolled her eyes, which made Jen laugh, as she'd intended. "At least Christmas is almost here. I'll go home. Stuff myself on Dad's turkey and dressing and drown my sorrows in giblet gravy."

"That's the spirit!"

* * *

Clay kicked back in the deep leather chair, his feet propped up on the matching ottoman. He negligently held a lead crystal glass with two fingers of scotch in one hand. Boone had decided to stay at the ranch with him while everyone else headed to downtown Oklahoma City to ring in the New Year.

"We didn't expect you for the holidays, cuz."

"Yeah. Staying in New York wasn't really an option."

"You give Giselle the boot?"

"Nope."

"She kicked you out?" Boone perked up and leaned forward. "This'll be good."

"Yeah, well." Clay lifted one shoulder in a forcibly nonchalant shrug before sipping the aged whiskey in his glass. "Not smart to forget a woman's name in the middle of things."

"You forgot Giselle's name? Oh, dude. You *are* a dog. That's what pet names are for, right?"

"Worse than that, Boone."

The other man stared at him, eyes crinkling and his mouth curling into a smirk as he figured it out. "Oh, hell, ol' son. Please don't tell me you called her by another woman's name…"

Clay did his best to maintain a poker face, but knew he'd failed the moment Boone burst out laughing. "It's not funny."

"Is, too."

"Is not."

Boone controlled his laughter but still smirked. "Whose name?" Blinking several times, the full impact hit him. "Oh, crap. Georgie."

Clay figured he looked as miserable as he felt. "How screwed up am I, Boone?"

"I don't think you're screwed up at all, man. Georgie is

a gem. Granted, she's not a supermodel, but she's got that whole sexy librarian thing, plus no one is smarter and her zingers are worth the price of admission. I mean, seriously. Why are you just now seeing what the rest of us saw from the git-go?"

"I'm a slow learner. However, I *am* seeing it now so what the hell do I do about it?"

"Simple. Ask her out."

"I can't."

"Why not? I mean, seriously, cuz, what's the problem?"

"I'd have to fire her. Which sucks because she's the best communications director on the Hill. And there's no guarantee we'd last longer than a fling. If she'd even go for it. Doesn't sound like a win-win for anybody."

"I don't follow, Clay. Why would you have to fire her? And I'm not even going into fling territory."

Draining his drink, Clay laid his head against the back of the chair and closed his eyes. "The old man, Boone. Every bit of fluff he brought into the house came from his office. The side pieces, the step-monsters he dragged in—each one younger than the previous. Well, except for Helen. She wanted to be a mom. The rest? Gold diggers, every last one."

He rubbed his fingers over his forehead, but the headache brewing behind his eyes didn't go away. "I swore I would never be him."

"So you date supermodels and actresses and pretty women who are dumber than stumps because you don't want to follow in his footsteps? I have four names for you, starting with Tammy."

Clay groaned. "Lord, that cost us a pretty penny to get rid of her, and she took the foreman with her. Thank goodness Chance made sure she signed the prenup. Besides, I wasn't referring to the quality of the women I date but where I meet them. I refuse to have an office romance."

"Then fire Georgie."

Resisting the urge to throw the now-empty glass at his cousin, Clay heaved out of the chair and went to the bar to pour another, stiffer drink. "I don't want to lose her, Boone." He tossed back the drink, barely resisting the urge to slam the glass down on the marble bar top. "I don't know what to do."

"I do. Just trust me on this."

Seven

Georgie blinked rapidly, the seldom-worn contacts irritating her eyes. She longed to take them out and stick her glasses back on. Resisting, she used drops while managing not to smear her makeup. She had to be crazy. When Boone had called with a last-minute request, she thought, *why not?* That was before she'd dressed up. Now she stood there in panic mode.

Returning to the senate offices after the holiday break had been…interesting. Boone and Hunt intimated that Clay had cut his New York trip short and spent the holidays at the family ranch north of Oklahoma City. She was curious enough to wonder if Clay had broken up with Giselle and she tried very hard to quell any internal squee moments that thought created. He was so far out of Georgie's league that…

The notes of "Girls Just Want to Have Fun" drifted in from her bedroom. She staggered on her high heels, found the impossibly small and expensive evening bag Jen had loaned her and snagged her cell phone.

"Do not have time, Jen. Go away."

"Breathe, Georgie. Things will be fine." Her best friend unleashed a sultry chuckle. "In fact, I bet he takes you back to his place for a nightcap."

"Oh, sure. Right. The man is handsome enough to be a movie star, he's a gazillionaire and he always dates the most beautiful socialites and supermodels in the world. I, on the other hand, am me. I am so totally average that the political pollsters have my type on speed dial. Men like Senator Barron do not make passes at girls who wear glasses and work in their office. One, it is a huge breach of ethics and two…have you looked at me, Jen? Yes, you're my best friend in the whole world and you love me, but let's be real. I won't ever win a beauty contest."

The buzzer sounded, alerting her that someone was at the outer door to her building, and she cut off Jen's reply. "Gotta go."

Time was up. Smoothing the formal gown, she grabbed a warm wrap and the beaded bag.

Using the same care as a tightrope walker, she managed both the apartment building's stairs and entryway without tripping on the high heels she normally avoided wearing. Her feet would kill her before the night was over but such was the price of fashion.

Boone waited beside the limo and his eyes lit up when she emerged from the door. "Dang, sugar. You clean up real nice."

His exaggerated accent made her laugh and relax. Boone always managed to walk the fine line between boss and friend. He kept up a running commentary on the way to the White House, but his words washed over her like a gentle waterfall. Since her first political job, she'd been on staff in one capacity or another. From campaign volunteer all the way up the ranks to communications director, she'd been Boone's protégé in all things political. She'd attended hometown rallies and national conventions. But this was her first state dinner. And she was slightly terrified. No. She was totally terrified.

Could she remember those long-ago cotillions where she'd learned place settings and greetings? Did she offer her hand or wait for the other person?

"Breathe, Georgie."

She gulped in air and fought the urge to put her head between her knees. The gown's tight skirt didn't leave room for that. "That's easy for you to say."

He patted her hands, which she realized were clenched on her lap. "When we arrive, your door will be opened and a military escort will offer his arm. Someone else will make sure your dress is lying correctly, whatever that means." He winked at her. "You'll enter with your escort and everything after that will just come naturally. Trust me."

"Ha. Just goes to show what you know!"

The limo turned onto Pennsylvania Avenue. Her breath caught as she focused again on the evening's events. Mainly, her escort tonight. Senator Clayton Barron. Panic choked off her breath once again and stars circled her head the way they did in the cartoons. Good thing she was the only one who could see them.

They were stopped by the guards at the gates, who checked their IDs and invitation. Moments later the big vehicle slid to a smooth stop in front of the East Doors. A man in an army dress blue uniform opened her door and handed her out, Boone tight on her heels.

He leaned closer and whispered in her ear, "Are you sure you want to do this?"

She whirled to face him. "You picked a fine time to ask me that, Boone Tate."

The sorry son of a gun laughed. At her. And winked, his devilish grin hinting that he was up to no good. She'd been well and truly set up. Narrowing her eyes, she muttered through pinched lips, "You are so going to pay for this, Boone."

"Smile, sugar. You'll thank me in the morning."

Breathing deeply, Georgie lifted her chin, but the army officer offered his arm before she could reply. A female air force officer appeared beside her and twitched the back of her dress into place. Georgie managed to murmur a "thank you" under her breath. Straightening her shoulders and lifting her chin—and wouldn't her mother be so proud of her now?—Georgie accepted her escort's arm and stepped toward the doors. She totally ignored Boone ducking back into the limo and the vehicle pulling away—and did it without hyperventilating.

The East Entrance foyer was full of people, but she saw Clay the moment she stepped inside. His head was bent in conversation with a stylish woman who looked vaguely familiar. One of Georgie's talents was remembering names and faces. After a mental file shuffle, she placed the woman—Ramona Morris, wife of Ambassador Charles Morris. The revelation settled her nerves somewhat. This might be a state dinner, but it was a working affair for the senator. Work. She could handle that.

Clay froze, his head raised, and turned to face her. His eyes widened and he looked as though he'd smacked face-first into a closed glass door. She'd never seen him appear dazed. Her heart fluttered and she flexed her free hand to keep from rubbing it down her thigh. Even though she wore elbow gloves, her palms were damp. Her eyes remained glued on the senator as he strode toward her.

His custom-tailored tux caressed his body in ways that made her jealous. Her palms itched, wanting and needing to touch him. One side of her brain berated her for the visceral reaction she had to him, reminding in the no-nonsense voice of her socialite mother that she was just an employee with no beauty to recommend her to a man as powerful as Clayton Barron. But the part of her that read romance novels and sniffled at chick flicks craved to touch him, to feel his hands on her, his lips on hers in a deep kiss. She remembered the question Boone had asked her. She had her answer now.

"Yes, Boone. I'm sure," she murmured, still mesmerized by the handsome man who stopped in front of her, his brown eyes hungry as he looked her up and down.

"Georgeanne."

"Senator." Was that her voice? She never sounded breathy. Ever.

"Tonight I'm just Clay."

Clay offered his arm and she slipped her hand under his left elbow. With his free hand, he tugged her fingers until they curled over his forearm and he could trap her hand close to his body. He inhaled deeply, filling his lungs with her scent. Vanilla, with a hint of something sweeter. He needed to acknowledge the army officer who'd escorted her inside but he really wanted to punch the guy. Which was ridiculous. He had no room in his life for jealousy, especially since the man was only doing his duty. Reining in the green monster, he nodded to the man and guided her toward the East Colonnade.

He didn't speak as he shepherded her along the windowed hallway overlooking the Kennedy Garden. As they approached the White House proper, two marines in full dress uniforms opened the doors. There was another long hall to navigate before they reached the diplomatic reception room, entrance there by special invitation only.

Clay entered the room with Georgie on his arm and didn't hide his smirk at the stir they caused. Years of practice kept his gait and demeanor smooth even as his heart raced. The strength of his reaction to her was totally unexpected. Though they'd worked together for years, sometimes rather intimately in hotel rooms, the confines of his family's business jet and his office, it wasn't until recently that he caught himself thinking about her in totally inappropriate ways.

He'd seen her in formal clothes before—campaign functions ran the gamut, but he'd never seen her look like... *this*. Red was definitely her color, but he'd decided that the moment he glimpsed her in the red bra and panties in his bathroom in Scottsdale. The vision, and the feel of her in his arms, had been the subject of many a dream during the nights since.

Her gown draped her curves, leaving enough to the

imagination—and his was active—to make him glad his tux jacket was buttoned. Heads bobbed in their direction, expressions curious, deferential or speculative, depending on the person. Georgie faltered a step and he tightened his arm against his side, trapping her arm. She found her footing and apologized in a soft mutter.

"What's wrong?" He'd been against this harebrained idea since Boone cooked it up. Granted, he'd planned on inviting Giselle to this soiree but after his incident of foot-in-mouth disease, escorting the star wasn't an option. Now he was worried about embarrassing Georgie. He valued her as an employee and didn't want to upset her. And honestly, he wanted her to have a good time. With him. As his date. Which was all kinds of messed up.

"Oh. Nothing. Clumsy feet."

She glanced up at him, her lashes fluttering, eyes glistening. Clay realized she wasn't wearing her glasses and a part of him kind of missed their black-framed heaviness on her face. She must be wearing contacts—and looked extremely uncomfortable doing so.

"Do you want to take the contacts out and put your glasses back on?"

Georgie swallowed a sigh. "Is it that obvious?"

"Only to me."

"No, I'll be fine." Her brow knit for a moment. "Why is that woman giving me the evil eye?"

With a casual twist of his head, Clay checked out the knot of people Georgie indicated by inclining her head their direction. In their midst stood a woman he knew well. Pearl Hudson, widow of the man whose seat Clay had taken in the senate, raised an eyebrow as she looked down her nose at Georgie.

And that pissed Clay off. Royally. While Mrs. Hudson was known as a Washington society maven, she was also known to be a complete snob. "Don't worry about her, Georgie. That's Pearl Hudson."

"Senator Hudson's widow?"

"That would be her. And she's notorious for creating scenes. There are a few people here I need to speak to so we'll just stay out of her way."

"Easy for you to say," Georgie muttered under her breath. "She's not cutting you into bite-size pieces with her eyes."

By the time dinner was announced, Georgie's feet were killing her. She managed to keep a smile on her face and not stumble through the receiving line. She managed protocol with the president and first lady, the secretary of state, and the Malaysian ambassador and his wife. She managed to sink halfway gracefully into the chair Clay held for her. She navigated dinner conversation and the place settings for the six-course dinner, all without incident.

After dessert, the guests were herded to the other end of the hall and into the East Room. A small orchestra from the navy occupied a dais at one end. Then the music started. Dancing. No one mentioned dancing. The Texas two-step was beyond her. How could she manage the waltz?

Clay took her hand, his fingers warm and strong as they wrapped around hers. "Relax, Georgie. This is the easy part."

No, no it wasn't. She'd flunked this part of charm school, branded with a big, fat F for Fail. Fairly certain the whites of her eyes were showing, she reluctantly followed him toward the dance floor. The president danced with the Malaysian ambassador's wife, while the first lady danced with the ambassador. After a few measures of music, others joined the twirling couples.

Stopping and facing her, Clay gathered her right hand in his left and placed his right hand against the small of her back. In time with the music, he stepped into her and she stumbled backward, her left hand automatically bracing against his shoulder. His right arm shifted and tightened, holding her close. He stepped again, this time to the side, then he stepped back, moving her with him.

"See? Not hard. One, two, three." He smiled and stepped forward again, forcing her back. "Right foot back, left foot to the side, right foot together. Left foot forward, right foot side, left foot together." He dipped his face toward her ear. "And remember to breathe, Georgie. That's important."

Was he laughing at her? She leaned back. He was smiling, and his eyes sparkled like cognac in leaded crystal, but he wasn't mocking her. She breathed. And relaxed. He moved her around the room, and at one point, he leaned close again. His breath ruffled the stray strand of her hair that had escaped her careful chignon.

"It's permissible to smile, too."

Georgie laughed—loudly enough that heads turned. She curled her lips between her teeth and bit down, fighting the urge to hide her face against Clay's starched shirt and tux jacket. When she looked up, he winked at her and twirled her out then back into his arms.

"See? Easy."

"When one is handsome and accomplished, of course it is."

"You think I'm handsome?"

She missed the next step but Clay was there to steady her. His expression portrayed genuine curiosity. Rather than the flippant answer hovering on the tip of her tongue, Georgie swallowed and considered. "Yes. You're handsome. When you walk into a room, people notice. *Women* notice." *I notice*, she wanted to yell.

"What makes me handsome?" Again, she caught a sense of curiosity rather than ego.

"High cheekbones. Strong jaw. Aristocratic nose. Your

hair is…" How could she tell him that her fingers itched to comb through his perfectly styled hair to mess it up and feel its thick, silky texture against her skin. She'd give almost anything to see him with bedhead. "Your hair is dark and luxurious. Rich. And your eyes. How do I explain about your eyes?"

She allowed a wry smile to tug at the corner of her mouth. "If I kept a diary, I'd describe them as cognac." *And burnt umber. Decadent as sweet toffee.*

"You keep a diary and I'm in it?"

Georgie's cheeks heated as he spun her away and back again.

"What else do you write about me?"

"No. No. I don't keep a diary."

"But I'd be in it if you did, right?"

The music ended and though Clay stopped dancing, he didn't release her. He studied her face through half-lidded eyes and Georgie shivered beneath his scrutiny. It was as if he peered into the darkest corners of her mind and if he struck a match, he'd see the secret room of a stalker. Pictures of him—snapshots of moments they'd shared, only without his knowledge or acknowledgment—lining the walls. His name traced over and over surrounded with hearts and flowers. She was so pathetic.

"Georgie?"

She stared up at him, horrified at the direction her thoughts had wandered. "I…uh…"

His cheeks creased as his grin widened. "I *am* in your diary."

Where was a desk when she needed one to bang her head on? "I don't keep a diary." Not now anyway. And thank goodness the darn thing was buried in the back of her closet in her room at her dad's house. The next time she was home she would burn that sucker.

A waiter passed by with a tray of crystal flutes filled

with sparkling champagne. She grabbed one and tossed it back like it was water. It didn't help. Clay relieved her of the glass and set it on an empty tray. "Don't look now but Mrs. Hudson is headed this direction. We should dance."

He didn't give Georgie a chance to catch her breath before he whirled her out on the dance floor. The music was slow, bluesy, and she just sort of melted into his arms. She couldn't help herself. She fit against him. Of course, the four-inch heels helped. And his broad shoulders. His arms curled around her, his strong hand held hers.

His lips brushed her forehead and he whispered, "I think it's time we got out of here and went back to my place."

She should say no. She should call Boone to come extricate her. She should— Georgie looked up, saw a tenderness in Clay's gaze that turned her boneless. She was in so much trouble now.

Eight

The limo slid to a smooth stop beneath the East Wing portico. The same army officer from before opened the rear door. Clay handed Georgie into the backseat and ducked to follow. Hunt would be driving and he already had his instructions.

Georgie fidgeted beside him and winced.

"Problem?"

She offered him a nose squiggle and shrug. "My feet are killing me. I don't wear high heels for a reason."

There was his opening. "Why doesn't your building have an elevator?"

"It does. But…" Her cheeks flushed. "Claustrophobia?"

Now her blush made sense because his thoughts went right back to that evening in Scottsdale, too. Red was definitely her color and he wondered if her lingerie matched her dress. He fully intended to find out.

"Ah, yes. Claustrophobia and nyctophobia all in one package, tied up with a red bow."

"Go ahead. Make fun. Must be nice to be perfect."

Clay laid his head back against the buttery-soft leather seat and offered a rumbling helping of laughter with a side order of self-deprecation. "Sweet pea, I am far from perfect. Just ask my father."

"Ha. Just goes to show he doesn't know jack."

She'd muttered but he heard what she said and hid his smile. "I'm glad you have such faith in me, Georgie."

Swiveling on the seat, she faced him. Her earnestness almost created a halo around her. "I do. We all do, Clay. Don't you get it?" She took his hand without noticing she'd done so and continued gazing into his eyes. "You care. Here." She patted his chest over his heart with her free hand. "So many don't. You do things not because they're expedient or make you look good or help out some lobby group. You do things because they're the right things to do."

Georgie's hand landed on his thigh and he barely held on to his poker face. He liked the weight and heat of her touch. A lot. She looked so earnest as she continued.

"I know people want you to run for president. I think you'd be an amazing president. I'll vote for you." Her voice trailed off and she looked down. Surprise blossomed in her expression when she realized they were holding hands. She tugged but he didn't let go.

"I hear a *but* in there, Georgie."

"The senate will miss you."

The import of her words kept him silent on the rest of the drive. The car stopped in the alley behind Clay's house. Hunt exited, checked for any possible threat, then punched the code for the secured gate next to the garage while Clay helped Georgie out.

"Come inside for a nightcap." He didn't ask, but it wasn't quite an order, either.

Georgie offered him a lopsided smile and limped beside him. He chuckled—not at her discomfort but at the twists and turns their conversation had taken. How did they get from her feet hurting to his position in the senate? He glanced back over his shoulder and dismissed Hunt with a short nod. Georgie would be staying the night.

Inside, he settled her on the couch—a piece of furniture chosen for comfort far more than design. Deep, long and covered in aged "bomber-jacket" leather, it was a couch a man could nap on during a football game or could sit on and read countless bills, feet propped on the overstuffed ottoman.

"Wine?"

"I'd prefer decaf coffee. Or a Diet Coke?"

"I can handle that." He checked the fridge. No Cokes.

Time for Plan B. Microwaves heated water, right? And somewhere in the pantry was a jar of coffee. Hopefully. Rummaging, he got lucky—a box of Starbucks single-serve tube things. Vanilla latte flavor. Georgie must have left them after one of their marathon strategy sessions. He emptied one in a coffee mug, added water and stuck it in the microwave for four minutes.

While he waited, he tugged on the ends of his black tie, unraveling the bow, and popped the first two buttons on the stiff white shirt. The microwave dinged and the water was boiling when he reached in. Maybe four minutes was a little long. He found a bigger mug, poured the boiling water in and added a splash of cold water from the tap. He stopped dead. Did Georgie use cream or sugar? Did vanilla latte need extra? He had milk, if it wasn't sour. And sugar, if he could find the sugar bowl.

"Georgie? I fixed one of your Starbucks vanilla latte things. Do you need milk or sugar?"

"Thanks, but no. It's good just the way it is, Clay."

Her voice wafted in from the living room and he breathed in relief but made a note to restock his fridge and pantry. He carried the mug out and handed it to her with a caution. "It's hot."

Dropping to the ottoman, Clay reached for Georgie's feet.

"Wait! What are you—"

He slipped off one shoe and started massaging the ball of her foot, effectively cutting her off as she let out a whimpering moan that went straight to his groin. "Want me to stop?" She whimpered again, and he chuckled. "Drink your coffee, Georgie. You did me the favor of coming to the dinner tonight at the last minute. The least I can do is rub your sore feet."

"Mmmhmmm." Her eyes closed as she relaxed against the back of the couch.

Divesting her other foot of its shoe, he rubbed them both simultaneously, using his thumbs to massage the balls of her feet. He had to stop when she almost dropped her cup. Clay snagged it and set it aside then went back to work. In moments, she was all but purring. He continued for a few minutes, stopping only when she struggled to sit up.

"Keep doing that and I'll be asleep in moments."

"Can't have that happening." He shifted, lightning-fast, from ottoman to couch, gathering her onto his lap. He teased his finger around the neckline of her dress, from one shoulder across the swells of her breasts to the other shoulder, and back again.

"Clay—"

"Georgie."

"We shouldn't be doing this."

"Maybe." He buried his nose behind her ear and nibbled the soft skin he found. "Want me to stop?"

He continued to kiss her, nuzzling along her jaw to her mouth. Full lips. Soft. Sweet. Just like the woman. He deepened the kiss, waiting for her to open for him.

"Georgie?" He murmured her name against her lips.

She leaned back and stared at him, looking helpless and unsure.

"Sweet pea? What is it?"

"I've wanted this…you… I've dreamed about it…but…"

"Shhh, darlin'. This is good. We're good." And it shocked him to realize he spoke the truth. This wasn't a simple seduction. He *liked* Georgie. As a person. And was just now discovering how truly sexy she was. Coming into a relationship from this direction was a revelation. "We're more than good, Georgie."

He recognized her surrender in the way her eyes softened and went unfocused, in the way her arms crept around his neck, in the way her lips sought his and her body pressed against him. "Will you stay with me tonight, Georgie? In my bed?"

At her sighing yes, he gathered her into his arms and stood up. She gasped and her arms clutched around his shoulders and neck. "I promise not to drop you."

Her green eyes flared with something he'd never seen there before—desire. And trust. "I never thought you would."

A soft light came on as he pushed the bedroom door open. He should thank Hunt for installing the motion sensor. Clay gently lowered Georgie to her feet. Cupping her cheeks in his palms, he kissed her. He wanted to strip her and take her right there, but his practical side poked him. Once he started making love to her, he wanted no interruptions, no distractions.

"Contacts?"

She blinked up at him, bemused and dreamy. "Oh. Um…"

"Your bag?"

"Oh. Yes." She seemed to give herself a mental shake and smiled. "Yes. Case and drops."

"If you need to…ah…" He waved toward the set of French doors on one wall. "The bathroom. I'll be right back."

"Clay?"

Something in the tone of Georgie's voice stopped him dead in his tracks. "Yeah?"

"Can you…uh, will you…unzip me?"

He turned around and schooled his features. Even in the low light, her face flamed. He wanted to be the one to strip her out of that gorgeous gown, but he could see the impracticality of that. And bless Georgie, she was always practical. "I can do that." Damn. Was that gravelly rumble his voice? He swallowed hard and returned to her.

She turned her back to him and he futzed with the hook

at the top then pulled the zipper to reveal some sort of… His brain drew a blank. Red satin and lace did that to a man. Bustier. That was the word for what she wore. Oh, yeah. He could strip her out of that. It looked like a hellava lot more fun than her dress.

"Um… Clay?"

"Mmmm?"

"I…need to…uh…you know…go?"

Embarrassed, he released her. When had his hand curled around her waist? When had his mouth dropped to kiss the nape of her neck as his other hand cupped her breast? "Yeah. Me, too." He needed to go somewhere. He did his best to focus. To the living room. That was it. To get her bag. So she could take her contacts out. He pivoted and trotted out because if he stayed, he would have watched her step out of the dress, would have followed her into the bathroom like a stray dog begging for a kind word.

When he returned, she was still in the bathroom. He knocked on the door, passed her purse through when it opened a crack and retreated to his bed. Damn but he felt awkward, like a pimple-faced kid in the backseat of his daddy's Oldsmobile. Only he'd never been that kid. Ever. Not his first time, or any of the times after. Not until now.

And that was when it hit. Tonight—Georgie. This was something more, something special. She was definitely something special and he'd been an absolute idiot and blind to boot. He stripped out of his jacket, resisted the urge to rip his shirt open, scattering the studs. Instead, he studiously removed each one. Took off his cuff links. Kicked off his boots and sat to strip off his socks. He was still sitting on the edge of the bed when Georgie stepped out.

Her legs were long and muscular, with thighs rounding into her very lovely butt. Nipped-in waist, full breasts, and… Clay dragged his gaze to her eyes—blinking owlishly at him sans glasses—and hoped to hell he wasn't drooling. He stood up, suddenly needing the extra room in his slacks. He held out a hand in silent invitation.

When she arrived, stumbling a little as she walked with one hand extended as if she was afraid of bumping into something, he gathered her against him. His hands traced up her sides, smoothed down her back. Over and over. He didn't think he'd ever be able to stop touching her. Her forehead connected with the bare skin of his chest and he forced air into his lungs. Breathing had suddenly become overrated. Her fingers clutched his shirt plackets and he felt the shiver that slid through her.

He pulled the pins and clips from her hair and tunneled his fingers through it until it framed her face. The bustier she wore was unhooked and gone with nimble flicks of his fingers, and her red panties followed with the whisper of silk against skin.

"I want you, Georgie," he murmured against her hair. She nodded, her silken hair rubbing across his lips. He twitched when she kissed his chest. "Ahhh, baby," he sighed. Scooping her into his arms, he carried her to the bed and settled her toward the center. "I've wanted this since Arizona."

She blushed and looked down, almost coy in her reaction. Then her gaze met his and Clay's pulse rate tripled. The need and want on her face were as naked as she was. He climbed on the bed, still wearing his shirt and slacks, wanting only to touch and pleasure her.

Running her hands down the hard, muscular plane of his back, Georgie found the hem of his crisply starched shirt and snuck her fingers beneath. His skin felt warm, smooth, but for the feathering of hair sprinkled across his chest, which was now gently abrading hers. His muscles flexed under her touch.

She had one too-short moment to savor the sensations

of hot skin and starched linen before he pushed up and slipped his shirt off. Capturing her wrists in one large hand, he pressed them to pillows above her head. "I get to touch you first."

She might have protested, if her brain still had the ability to form words she didn't have the breath to utter. Wide-eyed, she gazed up at him, watched his mouth curve into a predatory grin, his amber eyes looking almost feral. He simply watched her, touching her only with his breath, her hips pinned by his, her wrists still shackled.

"So pretty." His expression shifted from wonder to possessiveness. "And now mine."

Clay released her wrists but she didn't move, captured in his heated gaze. He pushed away, sat back on his knees between her legs. His gaze roamed over her, as visceral a caress as if he'd stroked his palm across her skin.

She shivered uncontrollably, not from cold, but from the heat building up inside her. He made her feel hot, crazy with need, all common sense scattered into the shadows of his bedroom. Now that she had given in to the desire, all she wanted was to touch him, to feel his weight on her, to know what he felt like buried deep inside her. Only that would satisfy her now.

Georgie didn't know where her feelings came from. This eruption of desire might stem from her long-standing crush, or it could have ignited from the look in his eyes. She ached, deep inside, needing him. Wanting him as she'd never wanted anyone else. She couldn't deny her feelings any longer.

His hand, surprisingly callused, followed the path of his gaze, stroking the curve of her cheek and down over her throat. He skimmed across her collarbone and lingered at her breasts, palm cupping her, fingers gently kneading until her breath hitched, fast and uneven. He didn't hurry, giving each breast attention, treating them to touch and tweaks until she bucked beneath him.

"Shhh, Georgie. I want to take my time." He smiled, holding her gaze a moment before the warmth and weight of his body disappeared. She heard something soft hit the floor—his slacks. Clay was back in a moment and his hand continued the journey lower. Rough fingertips teased across her belly, making her quiver and reach impatiently for him. He caught her hands, banding her wrists easily, refusing to be rushed.

He pressed on the soft curve of her belly, and she waited for embarrassed heat to flush her cheeks. She'd never had a flat, trim stomach, not like the women Clay normally dated. The feeling didn't come. How could it when he watched her, his desire so evident she could read it without her glasses. Deep appreciation shone in his eyes, and she relaxed a moment before growing bold enough to push her hips against his hand, begging for his attention.

Clay obliged, caressing from one hip to the other. His fingers curled around her curves and he squeezed gently. She closed her eyes, picturing him gripping her with both hands, thrusting into her. Where did these ideas come from? Sex before Clay had been awkward fumblings in the dark. Her mind conjured images of him spreading her legs wider, his fingers sliding into that aching space between them. Her eyes flew open as his hand did just that.

Fingertips teased her, accompanied by a low hum of male appreciation. As his fingers continued their explorations, she tensed, bracing for the moment when he reached the burning need inside her. She squeezed her eyes shut as her hips tilted upward without any prompting from her. As time, in sync with her erratic breaths, skipped to a stop, she waited for…something, the moment one of exquisite torture.

It didn't come. Instead of his sliding fingers sinking

into her, they were replaced by his breath blowing across her core. Something warm and slick brushed across her, the touch unexpected but welcome. His breath came again, stirring gently against her skin before he descended to taste her with his mouth, soft and wet and hot and sending her wits scattering.

He was going to kill her. She fisted her hands in his hair—his perfectly trimmed and styled hair—and arched against him, crying out, unable to bite back the sound. She felt his smile, her moans of pleasure urging him on. He teased her, tormenting and tasting, lapping, stroking, nibbling as if she was a feast laid out for his pleasure. She was ready to beg, plead for him to finish, to push her over the edge into the storm of pleasure he'd created deep within her. Clay had no mercy. He used his mouth shamelessly, and finally his fingers—one, followed by another—curled inside her relentlessly until she shuddered, bowing her back, feet and shoulders pressing against the bed, as she went blind from the enormity of the emotions crashing over her.

As she fell back against the soft mattress, her throat burned, raw from what? Screams?

Clay didn't wait for her to recover. He crawled up her body, a predator capturing his prey. He blocked out everything as he hovered over her, braced on his hands. He lowered his head, caught her lips with his, kissed her. Her fists released the comforter and rubbed along his lean flanks, circled his back. Her fingers dug into the taut muscles and he groaned into her mouth.

She tugged him closer, wanting his weight settled on her, wanting him buried inside her, stroking in and out. She would have crawled inside his skin if she could have, but even that wouldn't have been enough. She wanted to be part of him. Needed him to be a part of her. Then his hips lifted and he grasped her hand in his.

"Touch me, Georgie. Take me in your hand and guide me inside you."

She did as he asked, savoring the hard feel of him, a tiny part of her noticing he wore a condom. He sank inside her and her breath hitched. She'd gone a long time without a lover and never had she felt so complete, so alive, as when his body joined with hers. Clay stilled, watching her, both of them savoring the power of the moment. She wanted to look away, but she couldn't, knowing he was sinking inside her soul as easily as he had her body, stretching and filling her.

She wanted to speak, wanted to tell him how good this felt, how sexy and thrilling, how completely perfect she found this moment, but she had no ability to form the words. Instead, she just whimpered and moaned and clutched at his shoulders, lifting herself up to him.

Her fingers slid up the back of his neck, fisted in his thick, black hair. She tugged to bring his head down to hers. She wanted to taste him, fill her mouth with the flavor of him. She whimpered and Clay took mercy, claiming her mouth in a desperate kiss.

Desperate—yes, that defined how she felt. Desperation colored everything, every look, every touch, every kiss. Their bodies moved to a primitive rhythm as she reached for something less physical, something more spiritual than just a climax.

His breath, moist and heated, teased against her cheek. How was he not panting, gulping in great lungfuls of air the way she was? Tension wound tighter, then Clay shifted, changed angles, and light burst in her brain. She shattered into stardust, watching as tiny sparkles of Georgie rained down on them both.

She felt as though she needed to sweep up all that shiny glitter to save in a jar so maybe—just maybe—she could put herself back together. She felt infinite, a part of the universe, transcendent and powerful. Her vision cleared and she focused on Clay's face. His features were etched with his pleasure and she clung to him as he tensed and poured himself into her. They'd each taken and then gave back to the other pleasure a thousand times more intense.

He collapsed over her, rolling to the side and wrapping his arms around her. His sweat-sheened skin pressed against the length of her body, and the lazy strokes of his hand up and down her back made her want to arch and purr like a well-satisfied house cat. Basking in the afterglow, she concentrated on the one thing she could manage without thought—breathing. As her heart slowed, the stardust that was the essence of her settled back into the bottle made up by her skin until she once again became the woman named Georgie Dreyfus.

Her brain, like her heart, slowed its madly whirling attempt to make sense of things. A thought, not even fully formed, tapped against her consciousness. Words. She should say something, but that would mean stringing syllables together to form a coherent thought. She was too tired, too incoherent for that. Words could wait.

Everything could wait. Her world may have just gone topsy-turvy, but it would still be there in the morning, waiting to be dealt with.

At least she thought it would. With her last shred of coherence, she noted that Clay kissed her forehead and murmured something that sounded like, "Sweet dreams, love."

Nine

Georgie lay very still when she remembered where she was. Beyond the windows, the city was coming awake. Traffic. Voices. The noise of life in DC, but much closer than the sounds she normally heard from her third-floor apartment. Clay's house. Clay's room. Clay's…bed. With Clay asleep beside her.

She wanted to flail. To hyperventilate. To totally freak out as warmth at her back reminded her that she'd plunged headfirst into waters way over her head. Memories of the previous night flooded through her and she fought the temptation to get up and flee. Not just run for the hills, but escape to the farthest place on earth. Totally not practical. Plus, she'd never been a quitter. Smoothing out her breathing, she cautiously turned her head.

Clay had ended up on his back, his right arm flung above his head. She lay curled on her side, her back to him, using his biceps for a pillow. His chest—his very masculine and muscular chest with its fine feathering of dark hair—rose and fell in time with his measured breaths.

She squeezed her eyes shut. *Breathe. Just breathe*, she reminded herself. Last night had been a hundred times more wonderful than anything she'd ever dreamed. And here she was, still in Clay's bed. This had to be a good thing, right? She'd overheard Hunt and other members of the security team grousing about predawn pickup and deliveries. Georgie couldn't remember Clay spending the night with anyone but Giselle. Which meant she shouldn't make more out of this than it was. A one-night stand. An anomaly. An error in judgment… No. She refused to think that. The things they'd done last night had *not* been a mistake.

"You're thinking too loudly."

Georgie startled and flipped over to stare at Clay. His warm brown eyes appeared sleepy and amused. And there was something she couldn't quite identify lurking in his gaze—something that flushed her skin and made her want to snuggle up with him under the covers.

"I didn't mean to wake you."

His mouth quirked into a smile and she really wanted to lean up to kiss his lips. Before she could act on the urge, Clay cupped her cheek and tugged her closer. Their lips met, his nibbling hers before he swiped his tongue over them, teasing until she opened her mouth. His tongue dipped between her lips to taste her and Georgie almost choked. Mortified, she pulled away and put her hand over her mouth.

Clay stared at her, clearly confused. "Sweet pea?"

"Um…mrmingbrth."

"What?"

She ducked her head and tried not to exhale when she spoke. "Morning breath."

His eyes widened slightly and then he guffawed. "Honey, I haven't exactly brushed my teeth, either." Still laughing, Clay rolled over, pinning her to the bed and kissing her soundly. Breathless, and far more aroused than she should be, Georgie pushed against his chest—ineffectually. He held her close until her arms crept around his neck and she arched closer.

Long minutes later he raised his head. "I think we need a shower. And a toothbrush." He winked and laughed at her outraged expression before kissing her again. "C'mon. Then I'll buy you coffee."

Georgie groaned. Coffee. Up until now she hadn't necessarily believed there could be life before coffee. Clay had definitely disproved that theory. "Yes. Caffeine. I needs it, my preciousssss."

Clay insisted his shower was big enough for two, and

darn if it wasn't. That built-in bench had uses Georgie had never considered. Leaving her almost too boneless to wash her hair after making love to her, Clay stepped out while she finished. It wasn't until she was out of the shower and wearing an oversize terry-cloth robe that Georgie panicked. She peeked out the door.

"Clay?"

"Mmm?"

"I don't have any clothes here. Well…except for my formal."

He flashed a grin so wicked her knees threatened to buckle. "Damn. That's too bad, sweet pea. Guess we need to head back to bed then."

"Clay!"

"Mmm?"

She threw up her hands. "Argh!"

Laughing, he disappeared into his walk-in closet. A few moments later he reappeared wearing jeans slung low on his hips and carrying something. "You'll probably have to roll up the sweatpants, but they should fit well enough. The shirt will swamp you but with one of my jackets over it, no one will notice."

"Um, can't we just go to my place so I can change?"

He waggled his brows. "You gonna wear my robe?"

"Oh. Yeah. No."

"Get dressed, Georgie."

"Yes, boss."

She snagged her panties off the floor and ducked back into the bathroom, closing the door behind her. Sinking onto the toilet, she fought the urge to put her head between her knees. No panicking. Yes, he was her boss. Bosses dated employees all the time. But he was a *senator*. And she was a senior member of his staff and…and…

Georgie gave up when she stopped breathing. Dropping her head, she forced air into her lungs. She didn't hear the door open and didn't realize Clay was there until he was kneeling in front of her.

"Sweet pea, what's wrong?"

"I…we…can't…"

"Shhh. Yes, we can. Trust me. I've had this argument for months now. We're both adults. We're both professional." He took one of her hands in his big one and cupped her cheek with his other. "I'm going to be honest here, Georgie. I don't do commitment."

Her heart sank.

"Giselle was…convenient."

Georgie pressed her lips together so Clay couldn't see them tremble and buried her free hand in the fluffy robe for the same reason.

"You aren't."

"I'm not?"

"No. You aren't convenient at all."

"Oh." This conversation was going downhill quickly.

"I want to be honest with you, Georgie."

"Ohh…kay."

"I can't promise forever. Not right now. But I'd sure like to give this a try, see what happens. I…" He rocked back to sit on his heels and removed his palm from her cheek to rub it through his messy hair. "I want to see if maybe there's a future for us. You make me want all sorts of things. I want to take care of you. Make you smile. And I damn sure want to make love to you again."

He gave her hand a little squeeze and waited for her to respond. She just sat there, staring. He wanted to date her? Her inner fangirl squeed and bounced in excitement before her brain caught up. This was wrong on so many levels, but that didn't matter. He wanted to take care of her. To explore the feelings blossoming between them. That was the message she received from his words, from the expression on his face—a face she knew so intimately because she'd studied it, working with him to add nuance to the words she wrote for him. The man was a spectacular speaker, but this was no act. *Please*, she whispered up to the universe. *Let it be real. Let this...us...be real.*

"Okay."

He arched a brow at her. "That's not exactly the reaction I was hoping for," he replied drily.

Before she stopped to think about it, she cupped his face in her palms, leaned forward and kissed him. She focused all her feelings, all the pent-up hopes and dreams of a nerdy young woman yearning for something—someone—she never thought she'd have a chance with.

When they finally broke the breathless kiss, Clay laughed softly. "Yeah, that's more like it. Now get dressed. I need coffee."

He rose and backed out, shutting the door. Georgie found her panties and pulled them on before yanking on the sweats. She had to roll the waist of the pants after tying the drawstring as tight as she could. The thing still rode low on her generous hips, but she was pretty sure they wouldn't fall off. The long-sleeved henley covered the jerry-rigged waistline.

It wasn't until she walked out that another thought hit. "Shoes." With a disgruntled curl of her lip, she added, "I can't very well wear my heels to the local coffee shop."

"Yeah, I can see how wearing those with sweats might not go over with the fashion police."

Georgie stared at him then blinked several times. "Fashion police?"

Glancing toward the ceiling, Clay exhaled deeply. "I spent way too much time around Giselle. Then again, she wouldn't be caught dead wearing my sweats."

Georgie cringed at his words and hunched her shoulders.

"Which is stupid because I think it's sexy as hell."

Well, didn't that just perk her right up. She pressed her

lips together to keep from giggling. "Well, I spend most of my life in fashion jail but I'm revolting simply because those suckers hurt my feet."

Clay ducked out, calling over his shoulder, "Wait…"

Following him out, Georgie watched him trot downstairs and heard him rummaging around. He reappeared with a pair of rain boots in his hands.

"Aha! I thought I remembered you'd left these over here. I'll get socks for you to wear." He climbed the steps, tossed her the boots and headed into the bedroom.

She followed, her brows knit in consternation. "Are you sure these are mine? I don't remember leaving them here." In fact, she didn't remember the boots at all.

He peered at her from the closet. "Pretty sure those are yours. The only other woman who's been over here is Giselle and she wouldn't be caught dead wearing those."

Georgie's jaw dropped. "Excuse me?" She caught the pair of socks he threw with one hand. "Why wouldn't she?"

"Too practical. And they don't carry a designer label."

Clay studied her expression for a long moment then strode across the room, a second pair of socks in his hand. He dropped the socks into one of the boots and cupped his fingers over her shoulders. "Let me explain, sweet pea. Giselle is a sports car—built for speed and high maintenance. You? You're a Ford pickup, built for comfort and long distance." He kissed her before she could protest. "And trust me, this Oklahoma boy will come home to comfort every time. Now put your boots on. I want coffee and food. You wore me out last night."

He disappeared downstairs before she could process what he'd said. A truck? He compared her to a truck? And called her…comfortable. Georgie sat down on the edge of the bed and pulled on his socks. He'd been smart to give her two pairs of socks. The galoshes were made to be worn over shoes. She needed the extra padding. Clomping down the stairs, she found Clay standing by the front door, holding up a jacket. She slipped her arms into the sleeves and was surprised when he dropped a kiss on the top of her head.

"I meant that as a compliment, sweet pea." He murmured the words, slipping his arms around her waist and pulling her back against him. "Don't get bent out of shape. Yes, Giselle is beautiful in her way but when it comes down to what's important? I'm picking you."

"You are?"

"I am." He turned her, his hands rubbing up and down her arms as he gazed at her. His expression was both bemused and sincere. "You've been here right under my nose and I've been too stupid to recognize what I had. Have. Because you're here. I have you. And I want to keep you."

"You do?"

Clay threw his head back and laughed. "For a woman who makes her living with words, you've become rather… reticent."

"I have?"

He kissed her forehead, turned her toward the door and gave her a nudge. "If it makes you feel any better, I'm a bit blown away by this turn of events, too."

"You are?"

"You're repeating yourself, sweet pea."

Georgie planted her feet and twisted her head to look at him. "Clay, I need to be honest here."

His eyes shuttered but he didn't interrupt her.

"I'm…this…us…" She inhaled, held her breath and exhaled, but her hands still shook as she turned and reached out to touch his chest. "I've had a crush…"

"I know, Georgie."

"You do?"

"Well, I know now. I guess Boone saw it all along. He was just waiting for me to pull my head out and realize what a treasure you are. Professionally, yes, I knew that, but I have the feeling that—" He snapped his jaw shut and his eyes cut away from her.

"What feeling, Clay?"

"You're real, Georgie. And I find myself needing a whole lot of that—of you—in my life. Is this forever? I don't know. We've just started this—" He gestured between them with his hand. "Whatever this is. I care about you. As a friend and now as something…more. I can't make promises to you. Not yet. But damn if I don't want to give this my best shot."

Everything she'd wished for and then some was standing right here in front of her. All she had to do was acknowledge her feelings. She stretched up on her toes and placed a gentle kiss on his lips. "Me, too."

Clay exhaled on a relieved laugh. "Can we go eat now?"

Feeling lighter and happier than she had in ages, she preceded him out the door. As they exited the security gate separating his yard from the sidewalk, Georgie looked up and recoiled, stumbling backward. Clay caught her in his arms and held her steady.

"Well, well, well. Look who we have here."

Ten

They'd been ambushed by Parker Grace. With a catty smile, the reporter drawled, "Fancy meeting the two of you coming out of the senator's home the morning after you appear together at a state dinner. Lovely sweats you have on, Georgeanne, but then you've never been known for your fashion sense."

Georgie needed to remember to be careful what she wished for. She wanted to scream at the top of her lungs. Caught red-handed by the one woman who could create a maelstrom in the press and more problems for Clay's upcoming presidential bid than Georgie could shake a stick at. Her mind spun like slick tires in a mud pit. She had no response, no story spin to give the nosy reporter to make this look like something other than it was. Before her brain could engage, Clay squeezed her arm.

"Reduced to skulking now, Parker?"

The woman glared at him, a portrait of righteous indignation. "No. I just happened to be walking past."

Her excuse was flimsy and they all knew it. Georgie opened her mouth to explain away her presence, but Clay's hand gripped her shoulder. "Well, I'll make it easy for you, Parker. Georgie and I are headed to the Daily Grind for coffee and muffins. No, you aren't invited to join us. But if you hurry, you might be able to get a cameraman over there to catch two colleagues sipping coffee and stuffing blueberry muffins into our mouths."

Without waiting for a reply, Clay urged Georgie away, hand now on her back. At the end of the block, Georgie glanced over her shoulder. Parker, cell phone glued to her ear, stared after them.

"You shouldn't encourage her."

"Probably not." Clay pulled her to a stop and gazed at her. She blinked up at him owlishly. "Where are your glasses?"

She shrugged and dug the toe of her boot into the sidewalk. "I didn't have room for them in this." She pulled out the ridiculously small beaded bag Jen had loaned her.

"Can you see anything?"

"Sure." Her gaze shifted sideways. "Well, sort of. Up close anyway."

"Good. You'll have to rely on me." He didn't even try to hide the pleased grin. "Now, about Parker. It's rather fun to jerk her chain."

"She's a shark, Clay."

"Not even close. A barracuda maybe. A small one." He started walking and tugged Georgie along with him. "Are you embarrassed to be seen with me?"

Now it was her turn to stop and tug him back. "Are you serious? I'd think it was the other way around!"

He arched a brow, daring her to continue. She sputtered for a moment, flustered.

"I am serious, Georgie. I thought I'd made myself clear on this point. I want to date you."

Her face blanched and she gulped in air.

"Breathe, Georgie. I don't have a paper bag."

"Will. Not. Hyperventilate."

"Good. Look, I don't want to stress you out, but you know me. Once I make up my mind, I don't do things halfway." Her snorting giggle brought him up short.

"Clay, other than Giselle, you've never dated the same woman longer than a month."

"Well, that's true. But none of them were you."

He wanted to laugh when she sucked in a breath, beyond flustered now. Instead, he pulled her against his chest and rubbed his hands down her back. "As far as you and I are concerned, my name is officially out of the dating pool,

Georgie. At least while we are committed to this relationship. We'll take things a day at a time."

"But…the campaign. And…and…"

"And what? You are an intelligent, articulate and very sexy woman." That statement got another giggle and snort as she pushed away and glanced down at her baggy sweats. *His* baggy sweats, and didn't it just turn him on that she was wearing his clothes? Maybe he should call to have food delivered so he could take Georgie back to bed. Then his stomach rumbled. He would ensure his fridge and cabinets were stocked from now on, though, so every morning they woke up at his place, they could have breakfast in bed.

They continued walking for a couple of blocks, neither speaking. On the sidewalk outside the coffee shop, Clay halted and faced Georgie. "We'll work around things if someone discovers we have a relationship beyond work. Okay?"

Her eyes glittered as she nodded slowly. "Are you sure? I mean, plausible deniability—"

Clay silenced her with a finger over her lips. "Stop. Right there. If this leaks, I don't want to hide you, Georgie. That's not who I am." He dropped his hand and waited. This was make-or-break for him. If their relationship became common knowledge, he refused to skulk in shadows. In his position, hiding anything from the press or the public was a bad idea. Part of him wanted to throw caution to the wind, but the practical, political side counseled discretion. As Georgie had said, "Plausible deniability."

"Are you with me, Georgie?"

A smile struggled to form on her face as she squared her shoulders. "Yes, Clay."

"Good. Now I'm starved and if my brain doesn't get caffeine soon, it's going on strike." He pulled the heavy glass door open and ushered her into the softly lit shop.

Once they were seated at a table for two near the front

windows, Clay studied her, noting how she fidgeted and looked everywhere but at him. If he had less ego, he might be worried, but he had two advantages. He was a Barron and he knew Georgie. She edged toward reticence but she wasn't afraid to speak up in defense of an idea. They'd had some passionate debates over the years and to see her flustered was a real treat. This meant he'd gotten to her. He still had some reservations, despite Boone's pushing, yet sitting here with Georgie felt right.

As a rule, he considered the consequences before making a move, and this whole thing felt reckless. Yet after spending the night with Georgie, he wondered why it had taken him so long to realize what Boone had known all along. Georgie was perfect for him. Smart, politically savvy, sweet in a charmingly real way and fantastic in bed. Oh, yes, they were definitely compatible in that regard. He should have guessed given her fire when they discussed the issues.

As he watched, she pulled out her phone and read the screen. Her thumbs flew as she texted back. A stab of jealousy twisted in his gut. The ping of his own phone distracted him. He tapped the accept call button and put the phone to his ear.

"Where are you?"

"Good morning, Boone. Nice of you to call."

"Yeah, whatever. Where are you? And where's Georgie?"

"We're at the Daily Grind."

"We'll be there in a few minutes."

"Ah, no you won't."

"Hunt and I will pick you up. Please tell me Georgie isn't still wearing her gown."

"She's not. She's wearing a set of my sweats."

"Your…oh."

Silence stretched a little longer than Clay would have liked.

"So, last night…"

"Why are you calling, Boone?"

"Something's up. Besides you, I mean."

Clay groaned at his cousin's bad pun, but Boone rushed on before Clay could reply.

"Trust me. We need face time. After we pick y'all up, we'll swing by Georgie's apartment so she can change."

"What's up?"

"This is an all-hands-on-deck situation. I promise."

"Fine. See you in a few."

Clay asked the barista to change their order to go and grabbed the drink carrier and bag when she passed it over. At the table, Georgie was still madly texting. He cleared his throat to get her attention and she glanced up, looking guilty.

"Boone and Hunt are picking us up out front."

"Oh." Her head jerked, and her gaze latched onto his. "Wait. What?"

"Something's come up. C'mon."

She pushed back from the table, stood and followed him out the door. The black SUV slid to a stop at the curb about a minute later. Boone jumped out to open the back passenger door. Georgie slid in. Then Clay handed her the drinks and bag containing their muffins and climbed in. A moment later, Boone was in the front seat and Hunt pulled smoothly into traffic, despite the honking behind them.

Georgie turned to look and laughed. "Well, that was close. Parker took your advice. That was a camera crew from WTDC honking at us."

She swiveled to face the front, but the humor in her expression died as Boone stared back, worry etched on his face. Clay glanced from his cousin to Georgie and back. "Okay, cuz. We're face-to-face. What's up?"

"Cyrus."

His father's name dropped into a pool of silence and Clay's stomach clenched. "What's he done now?"

"He filed the paperwork for a PAC."

Clay wasn't too surprised, given the conversation the old man had forced on him at both Thanksgiving and Christmas. "So? It's not exactly a secret that I'll be seeking the party's nomination."

"He's hired you a—" Boone coughed into his hand. "Dream team."

Georgie leaned forward, her lips pursed and brow furrowed. "He hired handlers?"

"Yup."

Not waiting for the other shoe to drop, Clay pushed. "What else, Boone? You wouldn't be wasting your Sunday morning if there wasn't more."

"Cyrus wants to fire me and Georgie. And announce your engagement."

Georgie squeaked, her eyes wide and shocked as she pivoted in her seat to nail Clay with a look. "Our *engagement*? But…last night was our fir—"

Boone cut her off. "To Giselle."

Hunt dropped them off in front of Georgie's apartment and went in search of a parking space. Boone followed them up the stairs, which irritated Clay no end. "We don't need a chaperone."

"Yeah, I'd say that horse is already out of the barn, cuz. This isn't chaperoning, this is strategizing."

Inside her apartment, Georgie left the men in the living room while she ducked into her bedroom to change clothes. First, though, she settled her familiar black-framed glasses on her nose. Being able to see clearly was a gift. Too bad it was only her eyesight that was fixed and not her heart and brain.

Her cheeks heated at the thought of her gaffe earlier.

How could she have thought Clay would jump from a one-night stand into an engagement with her, her girlish fantasies notwithstanding?

Gathering her wits and a huge helping of intestinal fortitude, Georgie emerged to face the three men waiting for her return. Boone lounged on her couch, as if he planned to take an afternoon nap. Hunt had snagged a chair from her kitchen table and sat straddling it, his arms crossed over the back. Clay occupied her reading chair, feet propped on her ottoman. She grabbed another chair but Clay moved his feet and patted the ottoman.

"Sit here, sweet pea."

Just as she sat, her front door burst open and Jen stood there, her gaze flicking over all of them as she processed the scene. "Georgie? The senator's in your chair."

Hunt pushed up from his chair and ducked behind her best friend to shut the door, twisting the dead bolt this time.

"Jen! What are you doing here?"

"You didn't come home last night," the other woman accused. "I came down to get the juicy details." She waggled her brows.

Georgie wanted to pretend this wasn't happening. Instead, she watched Hunt extend his hand.

"Hunter Tate, Clay's director of security."

Jen glanced at Hunt, and then Georgie watched her friend's whole body react. She looked him up and down as she offered her hand. "Jennifer Antonelli. Georgie's best friend."

Her eyes cut to Boone. "Wait. Tate? Are you and Boone related?"

"Brothers."

"Holy cannoli. Are there more of you at home?"

Georgie giggled, unable to hide her amusement. "Honey, the Barrons and Tates are known for throwing sons."

"I have no clue what that means, but I think I've died

and gone to that big romancelandia buffet in the sky." She sank onto the chair Hunt had vacated, a dreamy look suffusing her face.

"It means there are five Barron brothers and..." Georgie counted on her fingers.

"Seven Tates," Boone finished for her.

Jen's mouth gaped before she screeched, "Wait. Wait! OMG! Is Deacon Tate your brother?"

Georgie pressed her lips together to keep from laughing at the look of disgust Boone and Hunt exchanged over the top of Jen's head.

"Never heard of him," Boone muttered.

She sensed Clay's silent laughter as his palm skimmed down her back. The practical angel on one shoulder cautioned her about diving into water over her head. The devil on the other side insisted she needed to take a running jump into the deep end.

Clay continued to surreptitiously pet her as he spoke up. "So what are we going to do about Cyrus?"

Eleven

Monday morning Clay arrived early at the office. He and Georgie had dodged any mention in the news cycles for Saturday and Sunday, despite Parker nosing around. He didn't expect to find his father sitting in his office.

"Who is this?" Cyrus stabbed at a blurry photo on the front page of a tabloid more likely to feature a Photoshopped picture of a Hollywood starlet and Bigfoot above the fold.

The corners of Clay's mouth curled down in a perplexed frown. "Good question."

The old man rattled the paper. "You know who it is, Clayton. You broke up with Giselle for this woman?"

"No, I can't tell who that is or when that photo was taken. And get out of my chair, Dad." When his father didn't move, Clay shrugged. "Fine. Sit there all damn day. I have work to do."

Snagging some files from his in-box, Clay pivoted and headed for the exit.

"Don't turn your back on me, Clayton."

When the desk chair squeaked, Clay turned around. "Don't order me around, especially in my own office." He pointed to one of the leather armchairs arranged in front of his antique mahogany desk. Very little occupied the desk's surface—his in-box, a telephone console, his nameplate and an antique bankers lamp with a green shade and patina-dark brass base.

Clay waited until Cyrus settled into the guest chair before he rounded his desk to sink into the worn leather seat. The files landed on the desktop. "First, I stopped seeing Giselle before Christmas, though to be precise, she broke off things with me. I won't call it a breakup as no actual relationship existed between us. She was convenient. That worked both ways."

"You need to fix it, boy. You're declaring for the presidency in a few weeks. You need a woman next to you who looks good. Giselle will make a fine first lady."

"What part of *I'm not seeing Giselle any longer* do you not understand, old man? I'm done with her."

"And I'm saying you aren't. Nobody is going to vote for a bachelor for president. Time you got with the program, boy. That doesn't include this woman." He glowered at Clay. "I know she writes your speeches. Women like her are a dime a dozen. Get her out of your system, fire her ass and then get back with Giselle."

Cyrus surged to his feet and went to the door. "I've rented space for the election team, but you need to clear out space here in your office so they can work closely with you. That woman is going to be trouble. I could see it when you brought her home. Get shed of her. My people will be ready to move into her space by the end of the week."

The door closed behind his father's back but Clay didn't move. When the door opened again, he glanced up, angry and ready to let his father know. Boone stood there, arms folded across his chest as he leaned against the doorjamb.

"So Plan A didn't work."

Clay huffed out a frustrated breath then chuckled. "Actually, it went exactly according to plan."

Friday morning dawned gray and rainy. Thursday night Clay and Boone had flown to New York for a meeting with some campaign finance bundlers. For the first time in a week, Georgie spent the night in her own bed. Alone. And she discovered she didn't like it, not one little bit. How could she have gotten so used to sleeping with Clay—she who never spent the night with anyone, not even as a kid on a sleepover?

His gentle snore, the warm solidity of his body curled around hers, the kiss he greeted her with in the morning, and if they had time, some wake-up sex. Georgie now had a whole new appreciation for wake-up sex. And shared showers. And drinking coffee sitting at the breakfast bar in Clay's kitchen.

"We are in sooo much trouble," she told her reflection in the mirror.

Racing through her morning routine, she was out the door, travel cup in her hand, and headed for the Metro well before her normal time. With fewer commuters to contend with, she arrived at the office almost an hour early. The security guard at the door greeted her with a smile as she folded her umbrella. With a wink, she passed him a vanilla chai from the coffee shop next to the Metro station, where she'd gotten a refill before walking to the building.

The door to Clay's office wasn't locked and she wondered if Evelyn, his secretary, had also come in early. None of the other staff had keys.

"Ev, it's just me."

No one answered her greeting. Moving cautiously, she headed deeper into the warren of offices. Maybe the "boys" had come back early. Ev's desk, situated just outside Clay's office, was empty and showed no signs of being recently occupied. His door was closed and locked, with no light showing beneath it. The hair on the back of her neck prickled as she crept down the hallway. Boone's office, next to Clay's, was also devoid of life. She heard a loud thump and muttered curse. The sounds came from her office, through the partially opened door. *Her* office should have been locked, too.

Georgie pulled out her phone and scrolled to the number for the senate security office. Her thumb hovered over the call button as she peeked through the door.

A man in a well-tailored business suit was pulling things

off the shelves in her bookcase. He was in his midthirties and nice-looking in a slick, Madison Avenue way. A woman, a bit older, also in an expensive black power suit, stood behind her desk emptying every personal item on her credenza into a box.

Georgie hit Call, her presence announced when she spoke into her phone. "This is Georgeanne Dreyfus. There are intruders in Senator Barron's office. I need security code red."

The couple paused and exchanged a look. Then they looked her up and down. The man's expression turned speculative while the woman dismissed her out of hand with a curled lip and a sniff.

"Why are *you* here?" the woman asked, obviously the one in charge.

"This is my office. I'll ask the questions."

"No, this is my office. You've been fired. You were supposed to be cleared out by now so I could move in."

"Fired?"

"Yes, fired. As in your services are no longer required, what with the senator running for president and all. Mr. Barron assured us that we'd have access starting today."

"*Mr.* Barron? The senator's father?"

"Is there another Mr. Barron?" The woman looked at Georgie as if she was a total idiot.

"I don't work for Mr. Barron. I work for the senator."

A male voice called from the reception area, "Miss Dreyfus?"

"Back here, officer."

Her friend from the front door and another guard appeared. "You got a problem, ma'am?"

"I do, yes. I am Sylvia Camden." The woman spoke before Georgie could. "I'm in charge of the senator's campaign. This woman has been fired. We are packing up her personal items to make sure she takes nothing of a proprietary nature with her. You will stand by until we are done so you can escort her from the premises."

Georgie felt her mouth drop open and her eyes widen at the woman's audacity.

"Ms. Dreyfus?" The guard looked uncertain now.

Punching her phone again, she called Boone, making sure the call was on speaker.

"Hey, sugar. What's up?"

"Boone, is the senator nearby?"

"Sittin' across the table from me havin' breakfast. Why?"

"Would you put me on speaker? You both need to hear this."

"Georgie?" Clay's voice washed over her and she had to remember to breathe.

"Sorry to interrupt your meal, sir, but we have a situation at the office."

"What's wrong?" His voice sharpened.

The woman strode up next to Georgie and in a strident voice announced, "Senator Barron, I'm Sylvia Camden, your campaign adviser. This woman has been fired and we're clearing out her office."

"Georgie, do you have security there?"

"Yes, two officers."

"Good. Then they can hear me. Ms. Camden does not work for me. She is to be escorted from the building and banned."

Georgie heard the anger seething in Clay's voice as he continued. "I'll say this one time, Ms. Camden. Georgie works for me. My entire staff works for me. Not my father. You, on the other hand, do work for my father. Not me. Now get out of my office and do not come back."

"Senator—" Camden attempted to cut him off, but he didn't allow it.

"Georgie, have security escort her out. I want a report

made to the capitol police for trespassing, breaking and entering, and vandalism."

Boone's voice followed on the heels of Clay's. "How'd they get in and not set off alarms?"

"The door was unlocked." Georgie eyed the woman. "How did you get a key?"

"I told you. I'm the senator's campaign advi—"

Clay's irritated voice blasted from Georgie's phone. "I don't *have* a campaign adviser, Ms. Camden. Therefore, you do not work for me."

"Sir, I work for your father."

"Georgie, make sure security retrieves any keys. And find out who gave them access."

"Yes, sir!" She shouldn't feel so gleeful but Georgie wanted to do a little Snoopy dance standing right there in the hall.

"I'll be back in Washington by early afternoon. We'll discuss this situation then."

"Yes, sir."

"Take your phone off speaker, Georgie." Clay's voice warmed and she hastened to follow his order, holding the phone to her ear and backing away from the door so the two guards could get inside.

"Yes, sir?"

"I'm sorry, sweet pea. My old man is a piece of work, as you are well aware. I'll deal with him. Inventory everything they touched. If there's so much as a smudge, he'll pay for it."

"Okay."

"Call for reservations at Max's. I'll buy you a steak then take you home and make it up to you for having to deal with the old man's crap."

"Okay."

"Bring an overnight bag, sweet pea. In fact, we need to talk about you leaving some things at my house so you don't have to run back and forth to your place when you're staying with me."

Her strangled voice choked on the word so it came out breathless. "Okay."

"I'll see you around one."

"Okay."

She hung up, dazed and feeling like an idiot. Okay? That's all she could get out of her mouth when the man she had such intense feelings for informed her that he wanted her to move some of her things into his house?

"Georgie!"

She jumped and stared at the petite woman who ruled Clay's office, his long-time secretary and administrative assistant.

"Ev?"

"Hon, I've been saying your name for nearly five minutes. You wanna tell me why security hustled those two people out of here?"

The warm, glowy feeling generated by Clay's words faded beneath the harsh reality of the past thirty minutes. "That woman and her assistant came from Mr. Barron."

"Oh, Lordy, hon. Say no more. When's the senator coming back to town?"

"This afternoon."

"Yup. Figured he'd be cutting this trip short. Did she tell you that you were fired?"

"Yes."

"That old jackass is up to his tricks again." Ev patted her shoulder. "Don't you worry, Georgie. The old coot has fired me more times than I can remember. I'll find out how they got clearance and keys."

The phone on Georgie's desk rang. "That's my cue to get to work."

Clay lathered shaving cream on his cheeks, watching Georgie through the mirror. She lay sprawled on her stomach in his bed—their bed now. He hadn't convinced her to actually move in with him, but over the last few weeks, some of her things were slowly migrating into his closet and onto the counters of the vanity in the bathroom. He *liked* having her in his house. A lot. And that was like taking a kick from a mule. There was no getting used to things, no need to make concessions to having her underfoot all the time. He preferred her with him. The nights she spent at her own place left him restless and pissed off.

He continued to feel off balance though he had a better understanding of his brothers' predicaments now. Cord and Chance both found the women who completed them. He'd never considered finding his own. Was Georgie the one? Or was this some idiotic infatuation that would cause him to crash and burn—personally and politically?

"Okay, how's this sound?" Georgie cleared her throat as he turned to face her, offering her his entire focus. "My name is Clayton Barron. Some of you are familiar with my name. By the time this election is over, the entire country will know who I am." She glanced up from her notes. "A little too arrogant?"

"Keep going."

"Okay." She coughed into her hand and pushed her glasses up to the bridge of her nose. "The Office of the President of the United States should be held by an individual who has actual solutions to change America for the better. We need to fix the things that are broken. We need to remember the principles upon which America was founded. This country needs a drastic new approach before it's too late. Change is never easy, but if we do things as they've always been done, America will stagnate even more.

"If you're sitting here tonight, it means you have questions and want answers. You're here because you care, because you want to know what I plan to do. You want to make sure I have real solutions to the problems that matter—the economy, national security, the ability of future generations to fully embrace the freedoms past generations have fought and died for. No one can truly be free without economic security. No one can truly be free when our enemies threaten our very existence."

Georgie pushed up, shifting her body so she was sitting cross-legged on the bed. "Ugh. It sucks. Totally and completely."

"It doesn't totally and completely suck."

"But it sucks." She sighed loudly, grabbed her hair and twisted it on top of her head. Jabbing her pen into the messy bun, she made a show of ripping up the top sheet of the yellow legal pad. "Maybe your father is right. Maybe you do need that team he keeps trying to shove down your throat."

She looked so thoroughly disheartened and sad he wanted to wrap her up in his arms and assure her everything would be okay. He grabbed a washcloth and wiped the shaving cream off his face so he could do just that. Joining her on the bed, he pulled the pen from her hair so it cascaded around her shoulders. He loved the silken fall of it, loved the way it played through his fingers when he kissed her, which he did at that moment.

"Love your hair down," he murmured. Leaning in, he teased her bottom lip, nipping lightly before claiming her mouth. "What's wrong, sweet pea?"

"Nothing."

"Georgie."

She sighed and leaned against his shoulder. "I hate doctors."

He furrowed his brow, trying to follow her non sequitur.

"My yearly checkup is this morning at ten," she explained.

He zeroed in on her mouth again, this time using his tongue instead of his teeth. After a long moment he put enough space between them that he could see her face. "It's just a physical, honey."

"Guys have it easy," she groused.

Only then did he understand. This wasn't just a yearly physical, this was a yearly…exam. "Oh."

Georgie nodded solemnly. "*Oh* is right."

"Want me to go with you?"

Blushing furiously, she shoved at his shoulder and scrambled away. "Ewww. No! Nada. Nyet. Nope." Then she laughed. "Thanks for the offer, but I'm a big girl and the tabloids would have a field day if they caught us together at my ob-gyn's office."

"Good point."

"I get first dibs on the shower."

"I have a better idea. Let's save water." He waggled his brows, rolled off the bed and scooped her into his arms, losing his towel along the way.

The shower was hot and steamy, which had nothing to do with the water temperature and everything to do with tongues and hands. Afterward, Clay dried Georgie off and sent her to get dressed with a pat on her very sweet, heart-shaped behind while he finally finished shaving. He had a meeting with that blasted election team so he could get them out of his hair. He didn't need or want them and he'd counted on Georgie—and Boone—to be there, to show they were a team. Still, he couldn't begrudge her the time for this appointment. He needed to take a page from his younger brothers and put his foot down where his father was concerned. He didn't need backup for that. He could handle the old man. And he would. Or else.

Twelve

Had it only been a month? Georgie peeked out the curtains of Clay's townhouse, frowning at the throng of photographers swarming the sidewalk outside his gate. She texted Hunt with the situation and received a reply that a car would pick them up in the alley behind Clay's garage.

The story had snowballed after the blurry picture of them appeared in that tabloid after the state dinner, and Parker Grace had led the charge. Talk about the poster child for Women Scorned Anonymous. Even now, Parker was camped outside with a cameraman.

Clay jogged down the stairs and cocked his head. "Georgie?"

"We have to go out the back. Hunt's bringing a car."

"I take it the herd is restless?"

She rolled her eyes. "That's an understatement." Sighing, she peeked out again and turned back to face the man who'd become her everything—and needed to become her nothing ASAP. She rubbed her fisted hand across her chest over her heart, surprised at how much the decision she'd come to this morning—after a solid week of harassment—hurt.

Clay's expression sharpened and he stepped closer, arms reaching for her. "Sweet pea?"

Despair washed over her and Georgie threw up her hands to keep him from touching her. "Listen to me, Clay. I care for you, but I care even more *about* you. I'm still your communications director, which means I'm your employee. That dang reporter outed us and look what's happened. We can't go anywhere together without getting hounded. You're the front-runner for the nomination, even without a formal declaration. You will be the next President of the United States. We can't play at being…a…a thing any longer."

"A *thing*?" Clay's voice dropped into the bass range, his displeasure evident in his tone and expression. "This is no game, Georgie, and our relationship is not a *thing*."

Her heart fluttered at his intensity. Clay Barron had a reputation on the Hill—most eligible bachelor. She'd seen the women he dated. This...*thing* between them was only a fling. It had to be. Even if walking away broke her heart.

She wasn't the right woman for him. She wasn't a star-let, supermodel or debutante. She was plain ol' Georgie Dreyfus with drab brown hair, thick glasses and muddy green eyes.

Clay grabbed her shoulders and gave her a gentle shake, the careful action totally at odds with the stormy expression on his face. "I'm not going away, Georgie. This is something real. At least to me."

His gaze searched her face, probing all the way into the place she hid her deepest secrets—especially her feelings for her boss. She swallowed and fought the urge to fall into his arms. "This won't work. *We* won't work."

Clay stared at her, his expression smoothing to that of the polished politician. "Oh...?"

He pinned her with his gaze, waiting for a reply. She blinked several times and ignored the ding on her phone. Clay didn't. He lifted her hand and removed her phone. He read the text and replied.

"Hunt's two blocks away."

"Oh. Right. Time to go."

The corners of his mouth curled up but the smile wasn't friendly. "This conversation isn't over. And we are far from done."

Before she could recoil, he had her wrapped in his arms and pressed against his chest. "I say when we're done. You got that?"

"But...why me? How can you be with someone like me?"

"Ah, sweet pea." His voice mellowed as he stroked her

back. "Why wouldn't I be? You're sweet and funny and warm. You're beautiful. And the best damn speechwriter on the Hill." His eyes twinkled as he said that last bit. "So. Are we clear, sweet pea?"

She blinked up at him. "About what?"

"About us not being done. A real thing. Yeah?"

"Oh, yeah."

"Kiss me, darlin'."

"I can do that."

"So why aren't you?"

"Oh, yeah."

Clay laughed and cupped her face so he could kiss her deeply. He only released her mouth when her phone dinged again.

"Time to go."

"Uh-huh."

Clay helped her into the backseat of the SUV then urged her to scoot over so he could join her. She didn't stop blushing until the vehicle rolled to a stop in front of the Russell Senate Office Building. A gaggle of reporters surged forward. Glen was out of the SUV before Hunt put it in Park, but he didn't open the rear door.

"Slide over, Georgie. I go out first." Clay tugged on her hand as he maneuvered in the tight space. She did as she was told without comment. "And I'll do the talking." At that, her expression cleared and her mouth opened. He took advantage and kissed her, his tongue sweeping through her open lips. With reluctance, he broke off. "Yes, you're my communications director, but in this instance, I'm doing the talking. You with me?"

"I…yes. Of course."

"Good. Now, big smile for the cameras." He winked and nodded to Hunt, who opened the driver's door and stepped out. Seconds later Glen opened the back door and Clay emerged onto the sidewalk. He met the barrage of shouted questions and whir of cameras with a smile firmly fixed in place. Then he moved away just enough to give Georgie space to come out of the SUV. He offered his arm, with elbow crooked, and she accepted his offer after a moment's hesitation. Her slim fingers slipped between his arm and side, curling over his forearm.

"So you two *are* dating, Senator!"

It wasn't a question so Clay ignored it. Glen moved to Georgie's side, protecting her from the press of reporters.

"Senator Barron, is it true you're forming an exploratory committee with an eye on the presidency?"

He flashed his patented Barron smile with its hint of dimple toward the reporter. "No. I am not forming a committee." He paused, waited two beats and his voice penetrated the shouted follow-up questions. "I've already formed it."

That statement was like throwing a two-ton boulder into a small pond. Ripples ran out in concentric circles and the crowd was shocked silent—for about ten seconds. Ten seconds that were long enough for Clay, Georgie and Glen to make it into the building. The reporters would have to go through security checks to enter, giving them time to escape into the elevator and up to Clay's office.

In the elevator, Glen kept his expression neutral as he faced the doors, his back to Clay and Georgie. Clay could feel the waves of curiosity wafting from her, but she didn't say a word. Every staffer knew the elevators and stairwells contained security cameras. The trip to the second floor was quick and as the elevator doors slid open, Glen stepped out, on guard and alert. Only after he scanned both directions in the hallway did he motion them out.

Clay and Georgie were ensconced in his office, the door shut with Ev and the rest of his staff on the other side, before Georgie spoke.

"You've already formed an exploratory committee?"

Did she sound hurt? Clay reached for her and led her to his couch. He sat down but had to tug her hand to get her to join him. "Yes."

"Oh."

Yeah, definitely hurt feelings. "Sweet pea? Look at me." When she didn't, he cupped her cheek and pressed until her head turned. "And that committee has nothing to do with those idiots my father hired. You, Boone, Hunt and a few other people I trust, including my brothers, comprise the committee."

"Me?" Her voice quivered slightly.

"Of course, you. You're my communications director." He leaned closer and dropped a soft kiss on her mouth. "And more. I trust you, Georgie. And I value your opinion. I did even before we…" He trailed off without finishing. After another gentle kiss, he added, "Before we became involved."

"Oh."

"Yeah, oh. I'm not doing anything without consulting the people I trust, and you're right there at the top, Georgeanne. Okay?"

When she smiled, her eyes lit up and Clay realized he liked being the one to put that expression on her face. Off balance at the idea, he shelved it. Things were happening too fast to stop and consider why. Later. He'd deal with his emotions later.

Thirteen

Georgie couldn't breathe and her vision was fuzzy around the edges. Pushing through the heavy glass doors of her doctor's office, she walked blindly down the street. No. No, no, no. This wasn't happening. When the nurse had called two days ago to say she needed to come in to discuss the results of one of her tests, Georgie figured it had to do with her blood sugar—her dad was diabetic—or her blood pressure. A lump in her breast had been what she least expected. Today the doctor had performed a biopsy and was sending the tissue off for further tests. She kept walking, head down, fighting tears.

"Ms. Dreyfus? Ms. Dreyfus!"

She ignored the urgent voice calling to her. She didn't know where she was going, what she was doing. This. Could. Not. Be. Happening.

"Ms. Dreyfus. Georgie!" Glen grabbed her arm and tugged her to a gentle stop. "Georgie, the car's back this way."

She looked at him and wondered for a moment who he was. Then she remembered. She nodded, numb and barely breathing. "Glen. I-I'm sorry. I-I got distracted."

"Hey, are you okay?"

"I… Yeah. I'm fine. I'm…fine."

Her bodyguard was still holding her arm as he led her back to the SUV parked at the curb. He settled her into the front passenger seat and buckled her seat belt when she made no move to do so. She watched him pass in front of the vehicle, his phone to his ear.

As they pulled up in front of the Russell Building, Hunt was waiting on the sidewalk. He opened her door and helped her out.

"Georgie? What happened?"

Finally emerging from her fog, she focused on him. "I'm fine. Really. Just. Fine."

"You don't look fine, hon. I'm gonna have Glen take you home."

She felt the blood drain from her face. "No. I…no, Hunt. Please. I'm fine. Really. I have too much to do today. I… Clay's speech for this weekend. And…stuff. Yes. I have stuff to do. Okay?"

"Okay, hon. C'mon. Let's go up to the office."

Ten minutes later Ev stood in the door of Georgie's office, arms folded across her chest, her expression one of concern. She stepped inside, closed the door and leaned against it. "Talk to me, Georgie. Whatever this is, we can fix it. You don't have to go through it alone."

Only then did Georgie manage to figure out why everyone was so freaked out. "No! Oh, spittin' sunflower seeds, no. I'm not pregnant!" She blurted out the denial.

Ev's arms relaxed and she let out an audible sigh as she crossed the patterned rug to sink into one of the chairs arranged before the desk.

Georgie soldiered on. "I…there were some…anomalies on one of my yearly tests."

Ev leaned forward, her concern evident. "Which one?"

She swallowed hard, her gaze skittering across Ev's face. "My doctor…did a biopsy today."

"Oh, honey." Ev scooted closer to the desk and reached over to clasp Georgie's hands. "It's scary, especially as young as you are. Is there a history in your family?"

Shaking her head, Georgie worked to control the tears swimming in her eyes. "No. It's so crazy. My dad's diabetic, but that's it. That's the only skeleton in my health closet."

"There's a good chance the biopsy will be benign, Georgie."

"I know. The doctor kept saying he was doing this out of

an abundance of caution. It'll be fine. Women my age…it's rare. That's what he said. And it's just a lump. That's all."

Ev squeezed her fisted hands again. "Have you told Clay?"

Panic surged through her. "No. Oh, good gravy, no. I can't tell him." Georgie twisted her hands to clasp Ev's. "You can't tell him, either. You…you know about his mother, right? About what happened to her?"

The older woman nodded. "Yes, hon. I've known Clay and the family for ages. She waited too late to get treatment for her breast cancer. His old man was a bastard about it. Clay nursed her until the end, and then raised his brothers."

"Then you understand why we can't tell him. Oh, please, Ev. He can't know. It's just a precaution. The results will come back negative and everything will be back to normal. His focus is the campaign. Not me." Her words tumbled over each other. "Okay? Promise me."

"I won't tell him. I suppose there's no need to worry him if this is a false alarm."

"Right. Exactly. You know him. He will worry. There's no need. I'm fine. Really."

The woman studied her for a long moment. "But I think you're wrong. I think he'd want to know so he can help you through this. That's the kind of man he is, Georgie."

She swallowed the saliva filling her mouth and hugged her arms around her stomach. "He's perfect, Ev. Too perfect for me. I…won't make him worry."

The day dragged interminably. Clay was on the Hill all day for a series of committee meetings and a session in the Senate chambers. By the time he arrived at her apartment to pick her up for dinner, Georgie had settled her nerves and had an unshakable poker face in place. She forced gaiety into her voice and plastered on a smile. Luckily, two other couples—supporters from home—accompanied them to dinner, and Georgie kept the focus on them and Clay. She was good at her job and she worked their guests hard to divert Clay's attention. Yet she caught his concerned looks. He knew her. Knew something was off.

After dinner and a long visit over coffee and dessert, the other couples said good-night on the sidewalk in front of the restaurant. Clay snagged her hand and tugged her along with him. "Let's walk for a bit."

She did not want to walk. She did not want to talk. Georgie had every intention of getting Clay home and in bed where she could keep him so distracted he forgot to ask her what was going on. The man was far too astute for her own good, especially now. With reluctance, she followed his lead.

"You going to talk to me?"

"'Bout what?" She feigned innocence, hoping her poker face hadn't cracked.

"Sweet pea, Hunt is family. You're family. We look after each other. What happened with the doctor today?" His voice held a hint of sharpness.

She answered quickly, without looking at him. "Nothing."

"Georgie…"

"Nothing, Clay. Just follow-ups on some tests he ran."

"Which tests?"

He was *not* going to let it go. She scrambled for an answer. "You know my dad is diabetic, right?"

"Yes."

"The doctor just wanted to confirm my results." There. Not exactly a lie, just a misdirection.

"You sure that's all?"

She controlled her expression and smiled up at him. "You know how I feel about sweets and pastry, Clay."

That brought out a deep chuckle and he squeezed her hand. "Point taken."

They walked a few blocks in companionable silence, enjoying the balmy spring night. Georgie recognized Glen leaning against the black SUV parked at the curb ahead of them.

Clay stopped and pulled her around to face him, his arms sliding around her waist. "Look at me, sweet pea." She tilted her head up. "You'd tell me if something was wrong, yeah?"

The expression on his face tugged at her heart. He was so protective and he was a "fixer." She didn't want to worry him. Ever. But especially now. "Yeah, Clay. If something was wrong, I would."

He leaned down and brushed his lips across hers. "Good. Let's go home, sweet pea. I want to make love to my woman."

Georgie's cell phone slipped from her numb fingers and she stared toward the door. For a week she'd been pretending everything was fine—convinced it would be—and she'd finally relaxed. They were gearing up for the big presentation when Clay would officially announce he was running for president. It would be a huge multimedia deal with appearances by his cousin, country music star Deacon Tate, a video presentation and the announcement speech.

But the call she'd just received slammed her world to a screeching halt. Her doctor wanted to see her ASAP. He wanted to refer her to an oncologist. And she'd asked for one in Oklahoma.

She had to go home. The ranch. Her dad. Home. She needed her roots, needed the red dirt of western Oklahoma caking her boots, the smell of hay and horses.

She called her dad. He wanted to know if Clay was coming with her. Clay. Oh, God, she couldn't tell him. She wouldn't put him through this.

"No, Daddy. It's just me comin'," she whispered and ended the call.

She typed out her resignation letter, remembered she'd have to buy a plane ticket. She so rarely flew commercial. She stayed in her office, the door closed and locked, informing her staff and Ev that she was working on Clay's speech and didn't want to be disturbed. Going online, she made a reservation to fly home. She reread her resignation, tore it up and wrote the letter ten more times before she gave up and handwrote a simple message.

Clay, we have to stop things now. We both know deep down we won't work. You deserve so much more than I can ever be. You deserve a beautiful woman by your side who will be the perfect first lady when you win. I'm sorry. I never meant to hurt you. I'll only hurt you worse if I stay. Please don't try to contact me.

She couldn't write the last three words her heart screamed she add. If she admitted how much she loved him, he'd never let her go. She didn't bother blotting the tears that smeared the ink. She sealed the letter in an envelope and wrote Clay's name on its face.

Her letter to Boone was infinitely easier.

Dear Boone,
I'm sorry. I'm quitting. Someday I'll explain. Forgive me for leaving you in the lurch.
Georgie

Georgie waited until Ev was on her break. She slipped into Clay's office and left both envelopes in the center of his desk. Back in her office, she boxed up a few of the most personal mementos. Boone would pack and ship the rest to her later if she asked. And she would. Eventually. First, she had to get out of the building, to her apartment, pack and head to the airport before 10:00 p.m. She was acutely aware of the passage of time. She had to get gone ASAP. Ev left early on Thursdays. Clay and Boone were on the Hill. She had to go now to have any chance of escaping.

Georgie closed the door to her office, but her fingers froze on the aged brass knob. She leaned her forehead against the solid wood. This place had been a huge part of her life. Her hopes. Dreams. But not anymore. Sounds of the senator's office hummed behind her. Phones rang. People chattered. Everything was so normal. Clay's office would run just fine without her. Clay would be just fine without her. In fact, he'd be better off.

"What's with the box, Georgie?"

She stiffened, heart pounding. Boone wasn't supposed to be in the office. If he was here, Clay couldn't be far behind. She had to get away. She'd fall apart if she saw Clay. Her goodbye letter, left in the center of his desk, would explain what she couldn't speak out loud to the man she loved.

"Just taking some personal effects home, Boone."

Warm fingers turned her around. "Sugar, you never could play poker with me. What's goin' on?"

Boone wasn't only her boss, he was also a friend. "I'm resigning. Going home to Oklahoma."

"You can't."

"Please don't make this harder. Clay's going to be the next president. I can't stand in his way."

"What the hell are you talkin' about?"

"My letter. It explains. He'll understand." Georgie turned to flee.

Boone stopped her. "No, he won't, Georgie. He loves you, even if he's too stubborn to admit it."

"That's impossible. We're impossible."

"You'll never know if it would work if you don't stay and fight for it."

"I can't. I'm dying."

Her words shocked him and he dropped his hand. She ran, tears streaming, heart breaking. It had to be this way.

Reaching the elevators, she stabbed the button repeatedly. Nothing. Fearing Boone would chase her down, she pivoted toward the stairwell. She managed four strides before Boone caught her arm.

"Whoa there, Georgie. You don't drop a word like *dying* into the conversation and then take off." His grip on her biceps remained gentle but firm, and he marched her toward an empty conference room. Once they were alone, he still didn't release her. "Now, what the hell is going on with you?"

"I told you. I quit."

"Because you're dying? You look pretty damn healthy to me, girl."

Her anger leached away and her shoulders drooped. "I have breast cancer, Boone. I'm going home for treatment."

Boone released her arm and slumped against the wall. "Ah, hell, sugar. How long have you known?"

"I…"

"Your appointment last week. The one Hunt said upset you."

She nodded. "I had a biopsy. The doctor called this morning to confirm."

"Does Clay know?"

She couldn't meet Boone's eyes. She was taking the coward's way out, but she couldn't face Clay, couldn't face the pity in his gaze, wouldn't survive his inevitable rejection. "No."

"You can't quit, sugar. You need the insurance."

"I…" She hadn't thought of that. Her only thought had been getting away from Clay before he told her to go away.

"And no offense, Georgie, but you're selling Clay short. You're important to him."

The door eased open behind them and the man himself

stuck his head in. "Something you two want to tell me?" He wore a wry smile, but the humor did not reach his eyes.

"That's my cue to skedaddle." Boone gave her shoulder a squeeze, took the box away from her and as he passed Clay, murmured, "Just listen, then do the right thing." He slipped through the door, closing it behind him.

"Georgie?"

She forced air into her lungs but couldn't meet his eye. "I...I quit."

"I see." His voice sounded as if it had been flash frozen.

"Boone wouldn't let me."

"Ah."

"I..." She turned away from him and dropped into the nearest chair, bending to cover her face with her hands. "You know I had a checkup a few weeks ago, Clay."

"And?"

How could one word sound so brittle? "And there was a lump." She looked up at his quick intake of breath, but he wore an expression she couldn't decipher. Her gaze dropped again. "The results from the biopsy weren't...good." More silence. She continued staring at the floor.

"Prognosis?"

"Stage three. I'm being referred to an oncologist for a lumpectomy and chemo, maybe radiation. I...want to go home, Clay. To Dad's ranch."

"Okay. Give me a few days to clear my schedule. We'll go home. Get the best oncologist in the state."

Georgie didn't want to do this, but she had no choice. She couldn't allow Clay to go with her. She was too aware of what he'd gone through with his mother. That part of his life had been glossed over in his official biography— how she'd died of breast cancer when he was a boy—but Georgie *knew* him, had overheard his interactions with his brothers and his cousins. He'd been profoundly affected by his mother's illness and death. She would not put him through it again.

"You have to stay here."

A guffaw erupted from him. She had no other way to describe the sound that blasted from his mouth. The problem was his eyes held no humor. "No."

"Clay, don't make this harder—" She pushed out of the chair.

"What part of *no* do you not understand, Georgie? You aren't leaving me."

She flattened her mouth into what she hoped was a grim line, fisted her hands on her hips and attempted to mimic her mother's best society maven voice. "Now you listen to me, Clayton Barron. You're an important man." Her right hand lifted without her conscious instruction, and her index finger pointed at him, wagging in time with each word she said. "Running for President of the United States. You don't have time to be hanging around watching me lose my hair."

Inhaling so she'd have enough breath to launch into her next argument, she never got the chance. Clay stepped into her space, cupped her cheeks in his palms and leaned down until his eyes were on the same level as hers. "Now you listen to me, Georgeanne Ruth Dreyfus."

Wait? He knew her middle name? His warm breath washed over her skin and she focused on his mouth. Full lips. Square chin. Strong jaw shadowed with a day's growth of whiskers. Which only made him look far sexier than he had a right to, given the circumstances. She wet her lips, felt her nostrils flare as his cologne wafted between them— almond, cedar, bergamot and a hint of lemon. His hands dropped to her shoulders before caressing her arms as he tugged her against him. Her head fitted against his shoulder and she relaxed against his muscular chest.

"I'm not going anywhere, Georgie. I'm staying right here next to you."

"But—" Whatever argument she intended to make fled from her brain as he captured her mouth in a soft kiss. By the time he was finished, she was breathless.

"No buts, sweet pea. I'm not going anywhere. Neither of us is."

She pushed against his chest to get a little traction and pointed her finger again. Before she could poke him with it, he captured its tip in his mouth, kissing away her defenses and defeating her offense in the process.

"Clay—"

"Georgie."

He mumbled around her finger, but his eyes twinkled and a smile curled the corners of his mouth. Dang but she loved his mouth. When he kissed her, she forgot everything. All her good intentions, all her talking points, all sense of propriety. She pulled her finger from between his lips and curled it into her palm in self-defense. With his next words, the fight left her.

"I won't let you go through this alone so you might as well stop pushing me away." He dropped a kiss on her forehead. "I'm bigger, far more stubborn, and you mean too much to me."

Georgie gave up, raising her chin to glare at him. "Fine. Just…fine." Then her breath caught as the import of his words struck her. She meant something to him?

"Wait. What?"

"You heard me. I'm here to stay."

Fourteen

Clay smoothed out the crumpled paper even though the words were branded into his memory. He knew why Georgie panicked. He knew why she wanted to run that afternoon, thinking she was doing it for him. Still, it pissed him right the hell off that she thought she needed to protect him, or that he would just walk away from her.

Not gonna happen. He wasn't his father.

A soft knock on the back door of his townhouse interrupted his reverie. He pushed off the bar stool and unlocked the door. Hunt and Boone walked in, the expressions on their faces grim.

"How's she doin'?" Boone sounded gruff, but concern radiated from him.

"She's asleep."

Hunt nodded. "Good. I have a team packing up her apartment. We'll put the furniture in storage, ship the nonessentials to her dad. Clothes and personal stuff will be delivered here."

"Clay, have you discussed this with her?" Boone's voice held a note of caution.

"No. I want her here with me. End of discussion." Damn straight he wanted her here, now that he was beginning to consider his feelings for Georgie. He couldn't think about the future. He could only think about now. Maybe tomorrow at the most. Stage three. Not stage four. Not a death sentence, but three was bad enough. He shook thoughts of his mother away. If they didn't have a lifetime, then he'd squeeze every second he could into what time they had, but he couldn't think about that future. He didn't explain. His cousins remembered, too. "What about Oklahoma City, Boone?"

"We did some scrambling, but we have the Chesapeake Energy Arena locked in. Chase's media team says no problem on the change. They're familiar with the venue for concerts and that's basically what your announcement is. Deke says he'll be there with the band. They're working on a new song for your campaign. Video people will splice it in as soon as Deke sends the audio file. The advance team will have the place filled. With Deke and the Sons of Nashville leading the way, that'll be easy." Boone's gaze flicked to the wrinkled paper on the breakfast bar, but Clay cut him off before he could comment.

"She stays with me, Boone. And I stay with her. I don't care what that damn letter says. I refuse to let her face this alone." He didn't miss the look the brothers exchanged.

"Georgie is a woman who knows her own mind, Clay."

"I'm well aware of that, Hunt."

"And you know she's like the little sister none of us had. We're all a little protective of her."

Clay glared at both men. "And I'm not?"

"Dang, ol' son," Boone murmured. "This is real."

He didn't reply. He had nothing to say.

The three of them plotted long into the night before the cousins crashed in his guest rooms. Clay slipped into his bedroom. He stood next to the bed, watching Georgie sleep, and doing his best to breathe around the knot in his chest. He was not his father. He would fight for the life of the woman he cared about. He did care, knowing that's all he was capable of. At the moment, loving her—loving anyone—seemed beyond him.

Her handwritten words had shredded his gut. She believed she wasn't good enough for him. Truth was, she was too good for him. Could he make a commitment to her? Would she refuse, thinking he asked only out of a sense of obligation and pity?

Georgie stirred, her hand reaching out to the spot where he normally slept. She might try to push him away when she was awake, but sleeping? She wanted him. He stripped quickly and slipped into bed beside her, gathering her close. She breathed a little sigh and settled against him, her head nestled on his shoulder. This is where she belonged.

He was a realist. He'd watched this damn disease ravage his mother. He'd watched her hair fall out, seen her lose weight until her skin hung off her bones, her lethargy. He'd listened to his father's cruel remarks. He was not that boy anymore. He was a man—a man who would take care of his woman. No matter what.

She'd crept into his life. He'd barely noticed her that day when she appeared in the storefront campaign headquarters during his first House run. Boone knew who she was, recognized her potential. She'd been a sweet college kid with stars in her eyes. She'd worked grueling hours with no compensation. Her smile had turned shy whenever Clay spoke to her. But he'd started to notice her. She was good at what she did. And got better with experience. She worked as his state office liaison in Oklahoma City. When Boone suggested recruiting her for the DC office, he agreed immediately.

And then she was just…there. Her smile still shy when turned his way, she always managed to fit in. She *had* become the little sister the Tate boys never had. Except he'd never looked at her like that. He wasn't sure when he first noticed she was definitely *not* a little sister, but a woman with curves and green eyes that twinkled with mischief and humor. Over the years she worked in his office, he'd come to admire her talents—as a speechwriter and in the deft way she handled the media. He also realized she hid behind her black glasses, boxy suits and messy buns.

He appreciated her talents, and as he'd reminded Boone that long-ago morning in Scottsdale, he didn't paddle in his own work pool. Until Georgie had taken the brunt of the attack by those protesters. Until she'd curled into his arms as he carried her up to his suite. Until she'd laughed and cried in the dark, sharing her fears with him.

Yeah, Georgie was his now and he would not let her go.

She moved beside him, murmuring his name.

"Shhh, darlin'. Go back to sleep."

"S'everything okay?"

"I have you in my arms, sweet pea. We're good."

He felt her smile against his chest as he dropped a kiss on the top of her head. "Sleep, Georgie. We'll deal with tomorrow when it comes. Sweet dreams."

"Love you," she mumbled, unaware of what she said.

He lay awake, thinking about her words, before finally falling asleep just as the sun rose.

Boone and Hunt were sitting at the breakfast bar drinking coffee, a laptop open between them, when Clay shuffled in. He'd left Georgie sleeping, her lashes not hiding the deep shadows under her eyes. How had he not noticed how worn out and worried she'd been? Yes, she'd hidden her concern from him, but he should have realized something was more wrong than she let on. He wouldn't make that mistake again. He poured a cup of coffee and settled on a stool across the bar from his cousins.

Boone opened the conversation, but he didn't quite meet Clay's gaze. "The office knows we won't be in today."

"What now?"

Boone swiveled the computer, but before he could hit the play button, Clay's cell phone rang, the words *Chase calling* flashing on the screen.

"You're up early," he stated with no preamble as he stabbed the speaker icon.

"Haven't been to bed yet." His younger brother was constantly in the tabloids. Head of Barron Entertainment, he flitted from Las Vegas to LA to Nashville. "But I'm not calling about me."

"Oh?"

"Yeah, I'm calling to say thanks. For once you're the headline in the grocery checkout instead of me."

Cold anger washed through him. "What are you talking about, Chase?"

"You haven't even announced yet and the media is all over you like cheese and jalapeños on nachos. But seriously, Clay, why did you break up with Giselle? She was perfect for you. I know you like strays, but Georgeanne? Though I guess it makes sense, since she works for you. You and Boone need to come up with a strategy."

Before he could respond, Boone snatched the phone. "Chase, you need to shut up."

"Boone?"

"I'm tellin' ya, cuz, shut it. Now."

Silence filled the kitchen. They heard Chase take a deep breath. "Damn. Are they really a thing?"

Boone stared at Clay. An angry tic beneath one eye and the grim line of his lips conveyed his feelings so perfectly that Boone added, "You idiot. You're damn lucky you aren't standing here where Clay can put hands on you."

"The old man is gonna blow a gasket."

"He already has."

"No, Boone. He hasn't called for an intervention. He might be pissed, but his brain hasn't exploded." A ping sounded from Chase's end and then silence. Another quick breath and then a string of cuss words dribbled from Clay's phone. "Not yet, but any minute now. Have y'all seen the latest news report?"

"Hunt and I have, but Clay hasn't."

Clay stared at Boone, his gaze shifting to Hunt before dropping to the laptop. "What?"

Boone hit Play and a video featuring a perky blonde reporter flickered on the screen, the words *Political Ploy or Play for Pity?* on a screen behind her.

"Oklahoma Senator Clayton Barron has long been Capitol Hill's most eligible bachelor. In recent months he's taken himself off the dating carousel, and his communications director, Georgeanne Dreyfus, is his constant companion. The senator broke off his long-term affair with Broadway star and fellow Oklahoman, Giselle Richards. Within days Senator Barron was seen about town with the bespectacled Dreyfus on his arm. One wonders why a man of the senator's… stature—" the female reporter stopped to waggle her brows and smirk into the camera "—would lower his standards to date his mousy employee. While known for her political savvy and ability to divert the media, Dreyfus is not the senator's typical type. We've learned from an unnamed source that Dreyfus is moving into the senator's Georgetown house. Rumors have also surfaced of numerous visits to Washington ob-gyn Dr. Mike Lane, which makes one speculate as to the reason. Another unnamed source suggests it isn't a pregnancy scare, but a medical diagnosis. Senator Barron and his party have been accused of being soft on women's issues. Is this a ploy on the part of a smart politician about to announce his campaign for the presidency? Or is a desperate woman hoping the handsome senator will take pity on her as she attempts to hitch her star to his?"

The reporter turned wide eyes to the camera, but Clay didn't listen to the rest of her drivel. He slammed the laptop shut and launched his coffee cup simultaneously. The ceramic mug hit the expensive glass-tile backsplash above the double stainless-steel sink and shattered.

Chase, voice soft and chastised, reclaimed Clay's attention. "Talk to me, Clay."

"She has breast cancer, Chase. Stage three. We're coming home next week for my announcement. I'll run my campaign from there while she undergoes treatment."

More cuss words streamed from the phone before Chase inhaled. "I'm sorry, Clay. Truly. I wouldn't wish this on anyone but especially not someone close to you."

"I care about her, Chase."

"Call Cord and Chance. They need to know. All of it. And I'm sorry for being a smart-ass."

Clay caught the relieved glance his cousins exchanged. His phone buzzed, indicating another incoming call. "Thanks, Chase. Will do." He swiped his finger to end the call and checked to see who else was on the line. Cord.

"Hey, little bro."

"Jeez, Clay, are you okay?"

"No."

"How's Georgie?"

"Scared."

"What's going on?"

Clay inhaled and then said the hateful words. "She has breast cancer."

"Ah, hell, ol' son. What's the plan?"

And this was when Clay truly appreciated his brothers. At least the next two in line. The twins sometimes swam in the jerk pool but Cord and Chance always had his back. "We're coming home next week."

"The announcement still on for Friday?"

"Yes. Boone wrangled the Peake. Deke is on board."

"We'll be there to show the colors, bud. Listen, Chance is here with me. Cassie and Jolie, too. We want to know what you need, what we can do to help."

Clay's throat clogged and his eyes burned. "You just did it, Cord. All of you."

Cord and Jolie, the mother of Cord's child, had recently married. She was an ER nurse and spoke up. "If Georgie has any questions, Clay, or needs anything at all, tell her to call me. I'll be there with her each step of the way. Tell her that, 'kay?"

"Thanks, hon. I will."

"Clay?"

He swiveled on the stool to find a disheveled Georgie standing in the doorway. Her hair was mussed, one strap of her tank hovered on the point of her shoulder ready to fall off and her cotton sleep pants rode low on her curvy hips. She blinked at Hunt and Boone, her expression confused. Her cell phone rested in the palm she stretched toward him. "Why are there movers at my apartment?"

Fifteen

Clay exchanged looks with Boone while Hunt glanced out the window.

"Clay?" Georgie's voice sounded small and a little lost.

"C'mere, sweet pea." He reached out and she moved into his arms. Glancing at her phone, he realized the call was still live. "Who're ya talking to?"

She gazed up at him, looking sleepy and confused. "Jen. She says people are in my apartment."

Hunt snatched the phone and moved away, speaking softly to Georgie's best friend. Clay kissed her forehead. "I figured you didn't want to hassle with closing down your apartment, sweetheart. Hunt arranged to have some of his crew pack up your things. We'll put your furniture in storage. Most of your personal items will get shipped to your dad. The things you need every day will come here."

Her body stiffened. "Here?"

The legs of a bar stool grated against the tile floor and Boone vacated the area, snagging his brother as he walked past.

"Yeah, baby. Here. With me. I wasn't kidding, Georgie. I'm here for the long haul. You'll stay with me when we're in DC. If I'm traveling and you don't feel up to it, you can stay with your dad in Oklahoma. I've decided to move campaign headquarters to Oklahoma City. I'll work from there while you have your treatments."

"Clay—"

"Shhh, sweet pea. We'll deal with this together."

"We will?"

"Yes." He knew she loved him and warmth spread through his chest before a chill edged in. He wished he could return her love. "C'mere." He guided her to a stool then poured coffee, nudging the mug, creamer and sugar bowl toward her, along with a spoon. He splashed more coffee in his cup while she doctored her coffee.

"What's wrong, Clay?"

He studied her face. She was awake now, and coherent. Her chin rose in a stubborn tilt. She'd survived the first blow. She'd survive what he said next. He nodded, a small acknowledgment of her strength. "Hunt will be talking to your doctor's office. Someone leaked."

Color drained from her face and she swayed on the stool. He pressed the mug into her hands. "Drink, Georgie."

"There's more." It wasn't a question.

"Yeah. Drink your coffee."

Her eyes snapped and flashed in the morning light. "I don't think I want to."

He offered a wry smile. "I know you, darlin'. The caffeine will help." He breathed easier. Georgie was back. She was still emotionally bruised and he was afraid that what he was about to share would eviscerate her, but it had to be done. Then they'd take steps to stop the bleeding.

She chugged the contents of the mug, set it down on the granite counter with a sharp *tink* of ceramic on stone. Squaring her shoulders, she nodded. "Okay. I'm ready. Show me."

He opened the laptop and hit Play. Her hand groped for his, clung, squeezed. She took her glasses off and set them aside, still listening, head bowed. His gut roiled as anger surged. When the report ended, he closed the laptop. He didn't move, unsure of how to comfort Georgie, and that left him frustrated. His instincts urged him to take her into his arms, but something held him in place. After an agonizingly long time, which was only moments according to the clock, she raised her head and put her glasses back on so she could focus on his face.

"We need to draft a statement."

"Boone will do that."

"No. We need to do it. And call a press conference." She slipped off the stool, headed to the coffeemaker and poured another cup. She returned to her seat, her expression resolute.

"You are *not* breaking up with me, Georgie."

A soft smile teased the corner of her mouth. "No, I'm not breaking up with you."

Clay leaned in and kissed her. Her knees spread to make room for him and her arms circled his chest. "Good." He whispered the word against her lips.

Georgie's cell phone rang in the other room. Boone peeked around the corner. "Not sure you want to take this one, sugar. It's CNN."

She sighed. "Let it go to voice mail. They all can." She glanced back at Clay. "When's the announcement?"

"A week from today, in Oklahoma City at The Peake."

Her lips pursed and Clay wanted to kiss them again. He could almost see the wheels turning in her head. Damn, but she turned him inside out like getting hit with a bucket of ice water followed by blazing sunshine.

Georgie pushed her glasses up. "Okay. I'll coordinate with Chase's people. We need to lock down the office here in DC. No information out, not even a *no comment*, unless it comes from you, Boone or me. Anonymous sources get cut off at the knees. For today Ev needs to put out a memo that we'll be holding a press conference Monday. There will be requests for appearances on the Tuesday morning shows. We'll see who calls after the presser. We want to answer their questions but control the supply of information."

Boone let out a soft snort followed by a chuckle. "Dang, sugar, but you make me proud."

"She's pure awesome once she gets wound up," Hunt added.

Color returned to her cheeks and a real smile curved her

lips. Warmth flooded Clay and he didn't resist the urge to kiss her this time. "Have I mentioned how much you mean to me?" He leaned back, caught the glitter of tears on her lashes. "Ah, baby."

"I'm sorry," she murmured.

Shocked, he stared at her. "For what?"

Her hand fluttered in an absentminded gesture. "For all of this."

He gripped her shoulders and gave her a gentle shake. "I'm not. Not sorry for a bit of it." That got a shocked look and a gulp. "Don't get me wrong, Georgie. What you're facing? It's killing me. I'd take it away in a heartbeat if I had the power. You'll get through this. I'll help. We'll all help."

Midday on Monday Georgie and Clay stood near the brick pad of the "Swamp Site," a spot located on the grass across the drive from the east Senate steps. A podium covered with microphones awaited them. Clay held her hand and she inhaled through her nose, exhaling through her mouth. He figured the technique was to keep her from hyperventilating. They'd worked on their statements. They were as ready as they'd ever be.

Clay gave her hand a squeeze before releasing it and stepping to the podium. "Thank you—" The high-pitched squeal of microphone feedback filled the air and people winced at the piercing noise. A sound tech ducked to the podium, fiddled with one of the microphones and slunk back into the pack of reporters and cameramen.

"Ground rules," Clay stated without preamble. "We appreciate you coming, but here's the deal. We *will* answer questions but until both Ms. Dreyfus and I have made our statements, I don't want any interruptions. We clear on that?"

Murmurs ran through the group, but no one spoke out.

"Good. First, there's been a lot of speculation about my

decisions concerning a presidential campaign. That speculation will be laid to rest this Friday, when I make an announcement in my hometown, Oklahoma City. You can check with my press office on the availability of credentials. The event will be held at Chesapeake Energy Arena. Since the OKC Thunder plays basketball there, I'm pretty sure there will be room for everyone." This elicited chuckles from the pack of reporters.

"Second, I'm here to confirm that I do have a relationship with my communications director, Georgeanne Dreyfus. We've been seeing each other exclusively for several months and haven't attempted to hide this fact. However, considering my position, innuendos and speculations have been aired freely. Now you know the truth. Yes, our relationship is serious. And that relationship is no one's business but our own."

He stretched his hand toward Georgie and she stepped closer to take it. Reeling her to his side with utmost care, he continued, "Friday morning we awoke to a report that my entire staff found offensive. That my colleagues found offensive. That my constituents found offensive." He searched the throng, found a certain reporter and met her gaze with a hard glare. He didn't smile when the people nearest her moved away, leaving her isolated. He squeezed Georgie's hand and shifted to the side, opening the microphones to her.

"As most of you know, I'm Georgeanne Dreyfus and I've been Senator Barron's communications director for the last three years. Before that I worked as his state office manager before coming to DC as his assistant press secretary and then press secretary. Most of you know me. We've talked on the phone, exchanged emails, visited in the halls of the Russell Building, at the back of Senate committee rooms and in the halls of the Capitol."

Her voice broke and Clay steeled himself to let her continue instead of taking over the microphone. All he could do was squeeze her hand to show his support. He'd wanted to be the only one speaking at this thing, but Georgie insisted she speak for herself. This was Georgie's story and she deserved to tell it.

"Thursday I received news from my doctor's office." A murmur surged through the group, but no one spoke. "I'm thirty years old and I've been diagnosed with stage three breast cancer."

Clay shifted closer to her, his arm pressed against hers as he held her hand a little tighter. She had to blink tears from her eyes and clear her throat before she could continue.

"I'm returning to my home in Oklahoma to begin treatment. This is a very difficult time for us, for Clay…for the senator and me. We would appreciate your understanding. I know he is a public figure. I know his life is a matter of a great deal of gossip and is probably infinitely entertaining. This is not funny, nor is it entertainment. This is real. It's life at its worst." She swallowed and looked at him, her gaze warm and tearstained. "I tried to quit Thursday afternoon. Senator Barron refused my resignation. Many men would have let me walk out the door, happy they dodged the bullet. Clay informed me that wasn't going to happen. He promised to walk beside me each step of the way."

She turned her head to look at the reporters. "That makes me the luckiest woman in the world."

Clay dropped her hand and pulled her into his embrace, his arms going around her as her cheek nestled against his chest. Silence enveloped the area—everyone so quiet, traffic sounds were clearly audible. There was no whir and click of cameras, no shouted questions.

Finally, one woman near the back raised her hand. Clay nodded in her direction. She had to clear her voice several times before she could get her question out. "Alexi Madison, Fox News. Our prayers to you both," she said. "Will you keep us informed of your progress? Not for the news cycle, but because we care."

He nodded, but didn't speak. A man raised his hand and Clay acknowledged him.

"David Graves, CNN. I think I can speak for all of us when I say our thoughts are with you both and we're all hoping for a swift recovery." The reporter, his expression soft, added in a gruff voice, "My wife is a survivor." When Georgie offered him a small smile in response, he continued, "I think I ask this question for everyone, Senator, given the rumors of your interest in the presidency. Will this affect your decision?"

Georgie leaned into the microphone before Clay could react. "Dave, what part of stick around for the announcement next Friday did you not understand?" This got chuckles from the group. "The senator quite clearly stated that he'll let everyone know his plans then. And no fishing for gossip in the hallways. Only four people know what he'll say and none of us will talk.

"One last question," Georgie stated as she pointed to a petite woman in the front of the group. Miriam Davis, long-time political reporter for the *Washington Post*, was known for her tough questions and bulldog devotion to digging out the truth. "Miriam?"

"Since we don't have a society reporter here, I'm just going to say this. If there's a wedding, I better have an invite."

Sixteen

They flew home Monday afternoon after the presser. Georgie's dad was at Wiley Post Airport to meet them, along with Clay's brothers, Cord and Chance, and their wives, Jolie and Cassie. After a steak dinner in the reserved back room of Cattlemen's Café, her dad kissed her cheek.

"The ranch is there when you need to come home, sweetie. You need to stay here for a while for the doctor, yeah?"

Teary-eyed, she nodded. "Can Clay and I come down this weekend? Maybe spend Saturday night?"

"Sure, baby. I'll lay in the supplies for a real ranch breakfast."

"Has Mother—" She bit off the rest of her question.

"No, Georgie. I haven't heard from her. She's in St. Tropez or someplace with that gaggle of divorcees she hangs with." His arm slipped around her shoulders as he walked her a short distance from the group. In a quiet voice, he added, "Are you sure?"

She knew exactly what he was asking. They'd shared many a conversation about Clay's romantic escapades. "I crushed on him when I was twenty, Dad. I started falling in love with him when I was twenty-five. I tripped head over heels in love with him not long after and I've stayed there ever since. Yeah, I'm sure."

"Is he?"

Georgie stretched to tiptoe so she could peek over her father's shoulders. Clay's gaze remained glued to her, his eyes warm and concerned, though his face betrayed little of his thoughts. But she knew him, knew the nuance of almost every expression. She held Clay's gaze as she replied. "I tried to run away, Dad. After I found out. I didn't want to put him through this. He wouldn't let me. He's gentle but strong and very, very stubborn. And determined to fight this battle with me."

Her lips curled into a smile she wasn't aware of until Clay returned it with one of his own. "I thought you were the only family I had, Dad." Her eyes flicked to meet his. "I was wrong. Clay is my family, too. And Boone. Hunt. Ev. Even Clay's brothers and their wives. I'm gonna be okay, Daddy. *We're* gonna be okay."

"Of course you are, Georgie. Come home Saturday. And bring your man with you."

Still on her tiptoes, she pressed a kiss to her father's weathered cheek. The man had been a rancher his entire life—working with his hands in every kind of weather southwest Oklahoma could throw at him.

Her dad dropped a kiss on her forehead. "I figure you still know the way home, girl. Call before y'all leave the city."

"I will, Daddy."

Clay approached then, offering his hand to Georgie's father. "I look forward to getting to know you better, Mr. Dreyfus."

"George, son. I figure we're gonna be stompin' around each other for a while."

When Clay's smile lit up his eyes, Georgie felt light-headed. She still couldn't believe her luck and a voice in the back of her brain urged caution. She told it to shut up and transferred from her father's embrace into Clay's.

"See you Saturday, Dad."

"We'll do burgers on the grill."

Her dad gazed at Clay for a long, tense moment, then the lines around his eyes relaxed. "Take care of my little girl, Clayton."

"Always."

An hour later Clay and his brothers were ensconced in

the media room of Clay's Heritage Hills house. Built during Oklahoma's first oil boom, the historic mansion seemed more like a museum than a home. The "boys," as Cassie referred to them, had beers and the Cardinals baseball game blaring. Cassie and Jolie had Georgie settled around the breakfast nook table, with cups of hot tea.

Jolie studied her face and Georgie forced herself to meet the other woman's gaze. Cassie and Jolie were beautiful, unlike her. Clay needed a woman like them. She pushed her glasses up her nose, breaking the staring contest. She always blinked first.

"You'll be okay," Jolie murmured, a hint of a smile transforming her expression from scrutiny to gentle concern.

"Yeah. I will."

Cassie leaned in from the other side. "What's your schedule like?"

Caught off guard, Georgie blinked at her. "My schedule?"

"Yeah. Your schedule and Clay's."

"Oh. We have to be up early to make the morning show rounds." She blanched and Jolie squeezed her hand.

"Dealing with this publicly must be hard."

"It is. But this is Clay's life. He's important." She inhaled deeply. "He'll be a fantastic president."

She didn't miss the looks the two women exchanged over her head. "What?"

"Honey, are you sure you're up to a campaign?" Cassie watched her closely.

"I don't know. It…depends."

"You know you can talk to me," Jolie interrupted. "It's been a while since I did an oncology rotation, but I can translate any medical jargon you don't understand. And Cass and I are both here for you. Miz Beth, too. You can stay with Cord and me—"

"Or Chance and me," Cass cut in.

"Whenever you have doctor appointments or treatment. I…" Jolie looked around the kitchen. "I think it would be better if you stayed with one of us instead of here alone when Clay is on the stump. I mean…oh, hon." Jolie blinked hard and swallowed. "Some of the treatments will wipe you out. You'll need someone with you."

When she could speak around the lump in her throat, Georgie's voice came out a strangled whisper. "I know. I'll… I came home so I could be with Dad. I'll stay on the ranch down at Duncan when I can't be with Clay."

"We'll drive you back and forth, then." Cassie was adamant.

"I can't ask—"

Jolie squeezed her hand. "You aren't asking. We're volunteering. We watched the press conference this morning. Good gracious. The way Clay looks at you. I've never seen him look at *anyone* that way."

"And that makes you family, Georgie. *Our* family. No way in hell you're going through this alone. *Comprende*?"

Not trusting her voice, Georgie nodded and then hugged both women. "Thank you," she whispered.

"Now, I'm thinking we girls need a spa day on Thursday to get ready for Friday's shindig. You off, Jolie?"

"Yes, ma'am. I'm off Thursday and Friday. No way am I going to miss seeing Deacon Tate on stage!"

Cassie pressed her hand to her chest and pretended to swoon. "I swear, if I'd met that man before Chance—"

"You'd do what, woman?"

Amid guilty giggles, the three women turned to face the men standing at the arched entry to the kitchen. "Chance, you know I have a major crush on your cousin."

Jolie nodded vigorously. "I second that swoon and raise you a deep feminine sigh."

The men rolled their eyes. The women laughed and pushed back from the table. Jolie and Cass hugged Geor-

gie and winked. Cass wagged a finger at Clay. "Georgie
is ours on Thursday. We're doin' the works. Mani-pedi,
facials, massage and hair. Y'all work or go play golf or
something."

This pronouncement elicited snorts from the men as
Chance wrangled Cassie, and Cord reeled Jolie to his side.
Georgie followed Clay to see them off. They stood on the
porch, hand in hand, waving as the other couples departed.
Georgie leaned against Clay and gave him a squeeze with
the arm she had looped around his waist.

"I like your family."

"Good. Because they like you, too. At least this bunch
of them."

Georgie didn't want to think about the rest of Clay's
family. She figured his father despised her and she worried about his two youngest brothers. She'd watched the
family dynamics for ten years, had seen how Mr. Barron
played his sons against each other. In fact, she couldn't believe Cyrus hadn't already intervened. She'd been amazed
when first Chance and then Cord stood up to him, threat-
ening mutiny in the face of their love for the women they
married. She glanced up at Clay and he kissed her temple,
almost as if he'd read her mind.

"We can deal with whatever gets thrown at us, Georgie. Even the old man. As long as we're together. Yeah?"

She answered without hesitation. "Yeah."

Tuesday consisted of a flurry of appearances on the net-
work morning shows, all done remotely from the various
local affiliates in Oklahoma City. Hunt chauffeured them
between each station, Clay holding her hand in the SUV,
walking with her to the studio with his arm around her
shoulders, then reclaiming her hand as they sat together for
the on-camera interviews. The afternoon brought conference calls and Skype meetings with party officials in vari-

ous states and a few of the campaign fund bundlers, and a follow-up with Chase's video people, all from the new campaign office opened on the ground floor of Barron Tower in downtown Oklahoma City. They worked late into the night, finally getting back to Clay's house around midnight.

They changed, climbed into bed and though Clay tried to hold her close, she rolled away, turning her back to him. Her brain was too busy, too filled with what-ifs she couldn't process.

Her first oncology appointment. Ten o'clock Wednesday morning couldn't come soon enough. Ten o'clock Wednesday morning could never come. Georgie lay stiff and staring at the shadowed wall of Clay's bedroom. He needed his sleep.

"Sweet pea?" He didn't sound sleepy at all.

She didn't reply. What was there to say? His finger traced down her spine, creating shivers in its wake. With a gentle grip on her shoulder, he rolled her to her back and propped up on one elbow, he gazed down at her. "Don't pull away, Georgie. Don't shut me out. Talk to me."

She almost snorted at that. Her girlfriends complained incessantly about how men never *talked*. How did she end up with the only one who did?

"I'm scared." The words, whispered as softly as a night breeze in a pine tree, hung in the air between them.

"Me, too."

She blinked at that then her eyelids shuttered half-closed as he leaned down to brush her lips with his. "You are?"

"Hell yeah, Georgie." He lay back down and snugged her against his side, so that her head was nestled against his shoulder. "I've finally realized how important you are to me, how much you mean to me." He kissed the spot on her forehead where the hair of her slight widow's peak met her skin. "How much I care about you. I don't want you to be sick. I don't want you to hurt. I want to make all that go away. But I can't."

His hand snagged hers where it lay on his abdomen, and he entwined their fingers. He brought their joined fists to his mouth and kissed the back of her hand before clutching it tight to his chest.

"It doesn't matter I'm a US senator. It doesn't matter how freaking much money I have. I can't make this go away with power or wealth. All I can do is hold you when you get scared. Sit beside you when you get sick."

Georgie embraced his words, wrapping them around her like her favorite childhood blanket. He cared, but he didn't love her. It would be enough. It had to be. She tilted her face up to his. "Make love to me, Clay."

He did. He touched her with hands so gentle they were almost reverent. He kissed her deeply, his tongue sweeping into her mouth. He fed on her like a man starved, peppering kisses along her jaw, under her chin. He nibbled along her collarbone, one hand cupping her breast with fingers both caressing and teasing. His glorious mouth paused at her other breast to nuzzle and suck until her back arched off the bed.

Clay continued his explorations, with mouth and hands trailing down her ribs, across her tummy, dipping low to the juncture of her thighs where he worked his magic. She squirmed, but he held her still. She moaned and he pressed closer to her, his tongue swirling, his fingers teasing. She cried his name as her whole body shuddered and a climax tore through her as hot and bright as a 4th of July skyrocket.

A breath later he was inside her, buried deep. Her thighs cushioned his hips, her heels hooked across the backs of his legs. He filled her, completed her. He pumped slowly, a gliding slide in and out that set her nerves on fire. This was a slow burn, hot embers growing in her middle.

"Faster," she breathed into his neck. "Harder."

"No," he murmured. "Not yet."

He loved her slow and easy, and then changed the rhythm so that she, at last, got what she craved. When he finally came, she came with him, and he inhaled her moans through his mouth as he kissed her. Still entwined, they settled softly back on earth from the high of their climaxes. "Sleep, sweet pea. Tomorrow will be what it is."

Seventeen

Wednesday morning, just after dawn, she awoke in Clay's arms, head snuggled on his shoulder. His arm was around her back, hand cupping her hip as her knee rested across his thighs. She wanted to wake up this way every morning. Life would be hectic for the next year. Hectic and scary, but she felt safe here with Clay. Strong. As though she could take on the world and win—emotions both unfamiliar and appreciated. He was right. Today would be whatever it was.

After a shared shower full of kisses and touches, they dressed and drank coffee in the kitchen, sitting close to each other. She was too keyed up to eat, knowing she'd likely toss whatever was in her stomach. Clay seemed to realize this instinctively and didn't push food on her. Instead, he suggested she do her job.

"You're still my communications director, sweet pea." He winked when he said it.

As usual, Clay was right. She threw herself into work, answering emails, returning phone calls and doing what she did best—communicating. At nine Clay came into his study and closed her laptop. "Hunt's here."

Her stomach dropped to her toes. Hunt was driving them to the University of Oklahoma medical complex to meet her oncologist, Dr. Nassad. "Hey!" she groused. "I wasn't finished with that email."

"You can finish it when we get back. C'mon, sweet pea." Clay was gentle as he pulled her from the chair.

The drive didn't take nearly long enough. Filling out the paperwork in Dr. Nassad's office should have taken days. She was done in ten minutes. Clay sat next to her in the waiting room, holding her hand. He looked calm, collected, in control. She wanted to scream and run from the room. She didn't. She sat quietly, absorbing strength from the amazing man at her side.

A nurse appeared, gave instructions. Georgie was to come with her, Clay could come back to Dr. Nassad's office to wait and the doctor would meet with both of them after the exam. They parted in the hallway as the door marked Private closed behind them.

Georgie changed into a paper gown, happy she could keep her slacks on. She only removed her blouse and bra. The nurse tapped on the door, poked her head in, nodded with a small smile and disappeared. What felt like five days later—though it was probably only five minutes—Dr. Nassad knocked and entered.

He was in his late fifties, balding and fit, with a contained energy about him that filled the atmosphere with static electricity. His handshake was no-nonsense, his words blunt. Georgie liked him immediately.

After the exam he opened her files on a rolling metal stand and studied them for a long moment. When he looked up and met her gaze, she reminded herself to breathe.

"If you wish to try to save the breast, the least invasive treatment includes chemotherapy to shrink the tumors before we try a lumpectomy. If the chemo doesn't work, we'll try radiation. I want to make the tumors as small as possible before we do the surgery." The doctor watched, waiting for her response. When she simply nodded, he continued. "If that doesn't work, or it spreads again, we need to consider a mastectomy." He had a slight accent and his eyes were kind as he explained.

The doctor glanced at her file again, and when his gaze met hers, she couldn't breathe. She knew what he would say next, and to hide from his hateful words, she hid in her memory of last night. Of Clay's hands cupping her breasts, of his mouth on her, teasing her puckered nipples. She relived the warmth shooting straight to her core, the way her body responded to his touch, the way his eyes glowed with pleasure as he touched her. Could she deprive him of that? Deprive herself?

"Ms. Dreyfus, I would recommend the mastectomy now, followed by both chemo and radiation to make sure we've caught it all. Your mammogram last year was clear. This is a particularly aggressive form of cancer. You already have a new tumor forming that was small enough it didn't show on the mammogram you took last month."

No. She didn't want to hear this, didn't want to listen. She stuck mental fingers in her ears and sang la-la-las in her head.

"Ms. Dreyfus? Georgeanne?"

She refocused her gaze on him. "Not yet." Her voice croaked the words. "Last resort. Okay?"

His lips flattened out as he pressed them together. "I don't—"

"My body, Dr. Nassad."

"Yes, it is. But I think you should discuss this with your partner. I understand losing your breasts is not an easy decision, but do you wish to gamble with your life?"

"My life, too." Anger swirled around her. Why was she acting this way? Shock? Fear? Yes, both of those. But she wasn't afraid of losing her life; she was afraid of losing Clay. Yes, he'd promised to stay by her side, but after his mother's ordeal…and the way he loved her breasts? She couldn't make that decision. Not yet. Not until every last possible cure was tried.

She stared at Dr. Nassad. "We try conservative first. And not a word about this to my partner."

The doctor's disapproval was evident in his expression and body language. "I can refer you to another—"

"No. I like you, Dr. Nassad. And I trust you, even though it seems I don't. I just know that I have to try alternatives first."

"Stubborn woman."

The smile she directed toward his scowl was wistful. "Yes, sir. I am. My way first. We'll continue to discuss the outcomes, keeping all options open. Okay?"

His scowl deepened, but he nodded. "No, not okay, but we will do as you wish." He scribbled on a prescription pad and gave her further instructions before leading her to his office. He shook hands with Clay, offered more scowls directed at Georgie and shooed them out.

Their next stop was the in-hospital pharmacy where she got the drugs making up her first round of chemo. The information sheet was ten printed pages, including six listing side effects. She took her first pill before they left the hospital complex.

By dinnertime, food was the last thing on her mind. Figured. She was part of that .2% of patients who had an immediate reaction to the drug cocktail. Clay fed her ice chips and sips of ginger ale and she worried about how long he would put up with her.

"Don't go there."

She blinked at him. "Excuse me?"

"I know you, Georgie. I recognize the panic in your eyes. Not gonna happen, sweet pea. I'm with you. No matter what. Understand?"

She stared, her vision blurred by unshed tears. "Startin' to."

"Good. Now, we're going to bed. I'm going to hold you in my arms and not only tell you how beautiful you are, but show you until you get it."

Georgie stared at Cassie and Jolie. She was an only child. She could count her close girlfriends on one hand. These two women enfolded her like they were her lifelong BFFs. She'd tried to cancel their Girls' Day Out, but they showed up at the door and wouldn't take no for an answer.

Cassie put her hands on her hips, her expression stubborn. "We're headed to JJ Nails to see Jacky and Jessica because they're the best. And Tommy gives the most amazing pedicures in the metroplex. Don't argue. You need to be pampered."

Jolie looked up from reading the medical literature. "You definitely need pampering. We'll take it easy. Plus, the massage chairs are awesome! You sit and get the works while Tommy does his magic. Then, when we have pretty feet, Jacky and Jessica take over." She offered a tentative smile. "Having acrylics will help, hon. Your nails will get brittle from the chemo drugs."

"And you'll look gorgeous tomorrow standing next to Clay on stage. I got us appointments with the top three stylists at Salon Beau Monde. Because, girl, we can't look like poor relations standing next to you!" Cassie wore a huge grin even as she eased Georgie into the passenger seat of her Highlander. Jolie climbed into the backseat as Cassie jumped into the driver's.

By lunch, with glossy, French-manicured nails and toes, Georgie felt well enough to try a light lunch of homemade noodle soup and croissants at La Baguette. The afternoon consisted of discussions about highlights, haircuts and other beauty "trauma," but by the time the girls deposited her back at Clay's, Georgie's stomach had settled and the warmth of Clay's gaze as he surveyed her from head to toe made all the hassle worth it.

"Feel up to going out for dinner?"

Invigorated, she nodded. "I do."

A little grin hovered at the corner of Clay's mouth. "I kinda like the way you say that."

Flustered, Georgie blushed as Clay leaned in to kiss the tip of her nose. "Food and then bed. Tomorrow is a long day."

* * *

Friday. Day three of her drug regime and Georgie was feeling optimistic. She'd managed a real breakfast and coffee. She'd suffered through hair and makeup. She'd acquiesced to the demands of the stylist on her outfit—a softly draped dress in a muted tangerine color that she hated until she was wearing it and her makeup had been applied. The big fight came over leaving her glasses off.

"I can't see without them."

"Doesn't matter. You don't need to see. Better yet, contacts."

She glared at the stylist and managed not to stick out her tongue as Clay arrived and ended the argument by picking up the black frames and placing them on her face, followed by a mostly chaste kiss that didn't mess up her lipstick.

By the one-hour mark until airtime, the entire family had arrived. The five Barron boys looked like fashion models in suits, starched shirts and designer ties. Every one of them wore Western boots. Jolie and Cassie also wore designer duds—Cassie in a tailored pencil skirt and jacket with slight Western touches and Jolie in a crepe wrap dress with a floaty skirt. CJ chafed at the miniature suit he'd been coerced into wearing.

The Tate brothers were just as handsome when they arrived en masse with their mother, Katherine. Deacon Tate and the Sons of Nashville had been in a separate room running through the songs they planned to play when they took the stage at the thirty-minute mark.

Cyrus held court on the opposite side of the luxurious green room and Georgie did her utmost to avoid him. An occasional chill would steal over her and she'd glance over to find his malevolent glare focused on her. She could do nothing but wait for the other shoe to drop. And it would. Cyrus was getting his way with the announcement, but sooner or later, he'd come after her. A man wearing headphones around his neck and carrying an iPad ducked into the room and asked Clay and Chase to step outside.

Jolie and Cassie were sitting with their husbands, trying to keep CJ entertained and clean as he raided the buffet laid out for the VIP guests. The governor was there, along with her entourage. Several state and US legislators were there to show support—and appear on the stage behind Clay, ready to hitch their wagons to his rising star.

A wave of nausea washed over Georgie and she headed toward the bathroom, just in case. Cyrus hijacked her before she got there.

"We need to talk," he snarled.

"No, we don't." She tried to step around him, but he cut her off.

"I'll give you five hundred thousand dollars."

Georgie rocked back and swayed, unused to the tall, skinny heels of her shoes. "Beg pardon?"

"Quit and walk away from my son. Half a million dollars."

She didn't know whether to laugh, cry or scream. "Are you serious?"

"A woman like you? It's a generous offer."

"A woman like me?" Her voice rose as adrenaline tingled all the way to her fingertips. She was vaguely aware of a flurry of movement behind her. "And what kind of woman am I?"

"You aren't worthy of Clayton. He should have stayed with Giselle. You're plain. Too plump. Those glasses are hideous. And you're just an employee. I thought I taught him better. You screw the hired help but don't move in with them. My son will be the next President of the United States and he needs a real woman at his side."

Cyrus's words felt like vicious hooks snagging into her heart and jerking. It hurt, but she was so mad, she didn't care. "Hired help? Unworthy? Real woman?" Her eyes narrowed and her mouth pursed into a snarl. She stepped into Cyrus's space and jammed her index finger into his chest, jabbing him to punctuate every point. "You listen to me, you misogynistic, dried-up old piece of manure. I've worked my butt off for your son. I've covered him with the media when you and your other sons showed up on the front pages of every tabloid in the world. I am more than *hired help* and I dang sure am *worthy* of Clay. I might not be a size three, but I don't consider some skinny model a real woman. A real woman looks like me. A real woman stands beside her man. She supports him and loves him and takes care of him." She stopped for a breath, but an arm sliding around her middle kept her from launching into part two of her tirade.

Clay hauled her up against him and she could feel his silent laughter where her back pressed against his chest. She glanced back and grew flustered when she saw his brothers standing in a half-circle behind him.

"Dang, Clay," Cord sputtered around a chuckle. "You do like 'em feisty, ol' son."

The man with the earphones stuck his head in the door. "Everyone to their places. National networks go live in five minutes."

Cyrus evidently realized they had the entire room's attention. He glared at Clay, his lips twisting into a feral snarl. "We're done here but I'm not finished with you. We'll discuss this without an audience."

It was over, for now at least. Clay entwined his fingers with hers, and then led her out toward the stage entrance. Everyone else followed. As they approached, the music of Deacon's hit song "Red Dirt Cowgirl" filled the air. The audience was singing along. The band occupied one corner of the stage, while risers covered the rest of the space. The "backdrop" people filed out while the last notes faded and the audience erupted into applause, whistles and screams.

Georgie's breath hitched. Was Cyrus right? She knew deep down she wasn't the woman Clay needed, but Clay squeezed her hand and smiled at her. "We got this, sweet pea. Yeah?"

She forced her answering smile to match his. She would not ruin this moment for him. "Yeah."

The spotlight hit them and they walked to the center of the stage while Deacon and the Sons of Nashville played the first few measures of their newest song, "Native Son," which would become Clay's campaign theme song. Clay walked to a microphone set front center stage. The audience was still going wild but calmed as the music trailed off to a soft murmur.

Clay spoke into the mic. "Hello, America. My name is Clayton Barron and I *will* be the next President of the United States."

The place erupted as music and video screens went into overdrive. Clay turned Georgie into his arms, dipped his head and kissed her, murmuring against her lips, "We're on our way, sweet pea."

Eighteen

After his speech, the music and video, after the confetti and balloons, and the cheers, life careened into the crazy zone. Clay's election team had set up a grueling schedule. He got only the weekend after his announcement with Georgie off. They went to her dad's ranch near Duncan. They ate grilled steaks and corn on the cob and charcoal baked potatoes. She slept in Clay's arms even though she shied away from doing so under her dad's roof. George just laughed and winked at Clay. And then the madness started first thing that next Monday morning.

Now, three months later, they'd been to Iowa, New Hampshire, South Carolina and more places in between. They'd appeared on morning shows, noon shows, afternoon shows from New York to Cedar Rapids to Seattle, crisscrossing the country east and west, north and south, numerous times. With many returns to the OU Medical Center for treatments. And now they were in Pittsburgh for a televised debate. His advance team was the best in the business, but Georgie remained the center of his media team. She still wrote his speeches, putting his thoughts into eloquent, heartfelt words. And the campaign process—the grueling hours, travel and constant scrutiny—was chewing her up, though it hadn't spit her out yet.

She'd grown pale, with circles under her eyes. She'd lost some weight—enough that she'd had to supplement her wardrobe to disguise that her clothes hung off her now. The doctor had changed the chemical cocktail to something far more potent. And he'd added radiation. When Clay heard her crying softly behind the bathroom door of their hotel suite, he knew the time had come.

He didn't knock, he just eased the door open. Georgie

stood staring at the hank of hair in her hand, tears streaking her ashen cheeks. "Sweet pea?"

Her green eyes met his in the mirror before dropping to her hand. "I can't do this," she whispered.

He stepped to her, wrapped his arms around her shoulders, crossing them over her chest and kissed the top of her head. "I know, love. I know. I should have sent you home sooner. Glen will fly to Oklahoma with you tomorrow. You can stay with Jolie and Cord."

She shook her head. "I want to go home, Clay. To Dad's."

"Okay, baby. Okay. That's good. Glen will be there to drive you back and forth to the city for your appointments. You can go into the campaign office when you feel up to it. The troops will love to see you."

"I'm sorry."

His eyes narrowed as he stared at their reflection. "For what?"

"For…this." She held up her hand. "For…everything."

Nothing about this situation was right. He wanted to howl in the face of the unfairness of it all. To beat his fists against the wall of gruesome reality they faced. His mother had lost her hair. His mother had turned into a shadow. And then she'd given up. He'd lost her. Cord and Chance had lost her. She'd left them alone with their father and he'd never forgiven her for that.

Clay shut down his memories and shoved steel into his spine. Georgie wasn't his mother. He'd see her through this. She wasn't a quitter. She'd fight and win. For him. For them.

"Shut up, Georgie." She blanched at his angry order. "You don't have a damn thing to apologize for." He tightened his arms and gentled his tone. "Jeez, sweet pea, you're the strongest person I know. I've watched the toll our schedule is taking on you, but I'm greedy. I want—and need— you beside me."

He inhaled and turned her in his arms so they were face-to-face. "You are beautiful and strong and intelligent and you light up my world. You don't *ever* apologize for being you, Georgie. Not to me, not to anyone. Yeah?"

A smile—an expression he hadn't seen much of lately—tugged one corner of her mouth and he bent to kiss it. "Yeah, you got it."

He kissed her again, deeper this time, with a hint of tongue teasing her lips. "Put on something comfortable, love. We're doing room service tonight."

Later, as she slept safe in his arms, Clay lay awake staring out the sheer curtains toward the Pittsburgh skyline. His phone pinged softly and he reached for it to read the text from Boone.

Plane on standby for am flight. Team set for briefing 11am. Arrive Peterson Center, U of Pitt, 6 pm. Debate goes live at 8. Georgie's tough. She'll be fine.

That last bit caused a brief smile. Clay didn't want to send her home. Not alone. Not without him. But he had to. She understood. He hit the call button on his phone and when Boone answered, he whispered instructions.

"Rearrange my schedule. I want to be in Oklahoma as much as possible and I'm damn sure going to be there whenever she has a treatment."

"Done, cuz."

And that was it. He could now settle his mind and sleep.

Two weeks later Clay was back in Oklahoma City, chafing at the delay in getting to Duncan to see Georgie. He'd arrived early that morning but the car that met him whisked him directly to Barron Tower where he was directed to the conference room for a business meeting. So here he stood.

Clay glanced at his brothers. Cord and Chance wore sympathetic expressions. Chase looked bored and Cash appeared angry, an emotion that seemed to ride his little brother harder each passing day. Their old man lounged in the chair at the far end of the table. This was new and different—and didn't bode well. Normally, Cyrus stormed in at the last minute, full of bark and belligerence.

Clay spread his feet, crossed his arms over his chest and braced for the volleys coming his way.

"What the hell, Clay?" Cash said.

He said nothing, ignoring Cash, though worry niggled at the back of his mind as he continued staring at his father. When had Cash become the old man's lap dog? Clay would have to discuss the situation with Cord and Chance when this *intervention* was over.

"You just going to stand there?" Cash pushed out of his chair and tried to intimidate him by leaning over the table. "You're weak, Clay. Weak and stupid."

"When did you learn to heel to the old man's whistle, Cash?" Chance dropped his question into the frigid silence smothering the room.

Clay still didn't acknowledge his brothers, keeping his gaze focused on his father. The tactic worked when Cyrus erupted from his chair and stalked toward him. Clay stood taller than the old man and he used that to his advantage, gazing down, expression implacable.

"You listen to me, boy. I raised you for this. I groomed you from the first breath you took to be the damn president. I hired people to take care of your announcement, to put the package together. I had your PAC organized. And what the hell did you do? Ignored everything. You spouted some idiotic nonsense that barely blipped on the polls. I'm running things, Clayton, so don't you forget it. You don't have time to be running back here like a whipped puppy. You need to be out there winnin' primary votes."

Cyrus stabbed him in the chest with his index finger and Clay fought the urge to grab it and twist.

"These are the rules. You don't fire people I hire for you. And you damn sure don't hide here at home in the middle of a campaign pantin' after that sickly, no-account woman. You're gonna be president. You better damn well act like it." Cyrus, red-faced and sputtering, jabbed him again. "You need to act like a candidate. I've hired that advance team to work the primary states for you. You should be out there pressin' the flesh, you fool. They've scheduled appearances for you every day from now until the convention. You don't have any damn time to waste on that…woman. Cut her loose. Now. We'll figure a way so it looks like she left you. That'll get you some sympathy."

Clay clenched his teeth, but didn't say anything. Was his father that crazy? Sympathy? He'd come off looking like a total jerk, not to mention that staying with Georgie was not up for debate. Loosening the fists he'd made, he didn't back away. "Here're *my* rules, old man. Don't hire people for me if you don't want them fired. I run my own campaign. I was in double digits the week after my announcement, with the package *my* team put together. I know what I'm doing."

His father cut him off. "Coulda fooled me, boy. Spendin' all your time with that woman. She's dyin', just like your mother. She's bad news and only gonna mess you up. She can't do any of her jobs—in your bed or out of it—and you're thinkin' with the wrong part of your anatomy when it comes to her." Cyrus pushed past, headed for the door. "Get rid of her, Clay. Or I will."

Disgusted, Clay headed after him, but was stopped when Cash grabbed his arm. "Don't push him on this, Clay. You won't like the consequences."

He stared at his youngest brother and his voice dropped to a menacing whisper. "Is that a threat, Cashion?" He stepped closer, until they were eye to eye. "If you, or anyone else, so much as looks at Georgie wrong—"

Cash snarled, "You're as bad as those two." He jerked

his thumb toward Cord and Chance. "Going soft over some woman. I never figured you to be this big a fool, Clay."

His fist formed and he swung before he had any conscious awareness of his action, but the forward momentum was stopped when Cord grabbed his arm and Chance pushed Cash out of range.

"Get out, Cash." Chance stared their brother down. "I don't know what bee climbed up your butt, but we're getting damn tired of it." He manhandled Cash toward the door and pushed him out. He glanced toward Chase. "You have a clue what's wrong with him?"

Chase just shook his head as Cord blew out a laugh with a wry grin. "Well, that could've been worse."

Boone appeared in the doorway and tilted his head down the corridor. "It is."

Clay stepped out in time to see Georgie disappearing into the elevator. "Did she hear?" At Boone's nod, more than a few expletives escaped. He needed to fix this.

Chance rubbed his forehead. "This is my fault. I had Glen drive Georgie up to meet you here because I thought this meeting concerned the family trust. Had no idea the old man would ambush you. Call Glen, tell him to wait so you can go after her."

Clay grabbed his phone but before he could call, Sylvia Camden appeared and snatched it.

"No time. You have to be at KWTV in twenty minutes for makeup. The interview with CBS was moved up." She tucked Clay's phone in her pocket. "She'll be fine. She's a professional. She needs some time to process. She knows how important these appearances are. Now come with me."

Boone nodded in reluctant agreement. "Glen will take her home, get her settled. You can call her later, go down tomorrow after the donor dinner tonight. You have to make this appearance, cuz. You know that."

Clay let himself be swayed. His head knew his team was

right but his heart said they were so very wrong. He cared for her. Needed her. But a part of him also admitted having her home while he was on the stump was almost a relief. That didn't make him his father. He wasn't walking away from her. She needed treatments and rest and the healing being home could bring. Things would be fine. He'd see her tomorrow, hold her in his arms and remind them both of what they meant to each other. One more day wouldn't matter. Or so he told himself.

That one more day had turned into two, and then more because the pressure of the campaign kept him away— at least that's what he'd told himself. Then he'd flown to Miami for a fund-raising dinner and Giselle was there, looking cool and elegant, and…friendly. For the paparazzi. When he saw the stories and pictures, he'd called Georgie. She didn't answer. He'd tried to call later but she'd blocked his number.

He'd finally dropped everything and come home to see her. He'd driven to her dad's ranch, found her in the barn but when he tried to kiss her hello, Georgie pulled away from him.

"Don't, Senator."

"Senator? When did we go back to being so formal, sweet pea?"

"When I realized I'm a liability and just an employee. Only I'm not even that anymore. I quit." She squared her shoulders and lifted her chin, looking at him as haughty as an English duchess. "I'm not a starry-eyed girl anymore, Senator. You remember her, right? The one who lived in your campaign office. The one who moved to DC your second term and lived on ramen noodles so she could work for you. Yeah, she's pretty much dead and gone now. So is the girl who got swept off her feet like some heroine in a romantic movie. What an idiot she was."

"Georgie—"

"Georgie what? I love you, Clay. With my whole heart. Have for ten years. I believed you. I believed *in* you. What a complete and utter fool I turned out to be. Pretty sad for someone with an IQ of a hundred and fifty-seven." She leaned against the horse she'd been brushing, her cheek resting against his arched neck as she smoothed her hand along the animal's muscled chest. "I thought we had something special. Don't get me wrong. I don't think you truly love me—you've never said the words. I'm so not your type and I'm sure not good enough to be first lady, but I thought you cared. At least a little." She sniffled and rubbed her sleeve across her nose. "You said you cared. Said you wanted to take care of me, anyway. I guess your father was right. You need a woman like Giselle. Not someone as sick as a dog who probably won't see next Christmas."

Clay didn't know what to say. This woman had always given him the words to speak. Clueless, he didn't understand why she was having a meltdown.

"Go away, Clay. You don't belong here."

He reached to touch her, but she ducked away, sliding under the horse's neck to peer at him from the other side. "Just go. I don't have the time or energy for your games, Senator."

"This isn't a game, Georgie."

She laughed, a deep, rolling burst of sound that quickly edged toward hysteria. "You're right, Senator. It's not. It's life or death. Mine. Go. You're not welcome here."

She pushed away from the horse's side and strode toward the barn's exit, leaving Clay standing flatfooted. As she slipped between the doors, she whipped off the baseball cap and the bandanna beneath it. Her once luxurious hair—the silken fall he loved to run his fingers through—was gone. Only peach fuzz remained. The potent cocktail of chemo and radiation she'd endured hoping to save her breasts had taken its toll. Just as it had with his mother.

Heat flashed through his body followed by a chill so frigid he couldn't breathe. Clay wanted to fall to his knees in the dirt and empty the contents of his stomach. Georgie didn't look back, didn't see how she'd devastated him. Instead, she marched off, head high, shoulders unbowed, her long-legged stride as graceful as a Thoroughbred racehorse's.

He watched her walk away and in that moment, Clay came to two realizations—both of which paralyzed him. He was as despicable as his old man had ever been, and he'd lost the only woman he'd ever love.

Nineteen

"So what are you going to do about it, Clay?" Cord, as always, functioned as the family's Jiminy Cricket.

Chance watched him, his expression shuttered, but anger simmered beneath his poker face. "It's been a month, Clay. She won't take calls from any of us. The girls drove down. Evidently, she was out in the barn when they got there. By the time her dad walked them down, she'd saddled up a horse and taken off. They waited all day. She didn't come back."

Clay stared at his brothers, remembering that first family intervention when everyone had ganged up on Chance, and the next when everyone but Chance had lined up against Cord. Both of his brothers had found women who loved them. Women who made them better men. In all honesty, Georgie was his touchstone. She settled him. Balanced him. Kept him centered in the crazy political storm that made up his world.

"You need to face the truth, bud," Cord chimed in.

The truth. Yes. Truth was something he'd been running from lately. He'd screwed up. Royally.

"You know who and what she is, right?" Chance's expression softened. "Because we do. She writes the words you wish you could say. She puts them in your mouth and makes not only the world believe them, but makes you believe them, too."

"She's my heart." Had he admitted that out loud? "But I'm not the man for her. I'm not good enough. Not for her." He forced down the bile burning his esophagus. "God. I don't deserve her. I…aw, hell. I didn't go after her. Not until it was too late. I ground her feelings into the dirt and then just let her walk away from me because I didn't know what to do."

Chance, ever the voice of reason—except now—gripped his shoulder. "What have you done?" His harsh voice grated in Clay's ears.

Swamped by self-loathing and helplessness, he stared at his brothers. "You saw the pictures from Miami, of Giselle kissing me?" Their expressions darkened with anger. "She was just there. For the speech. Cyrus's people set it up. Made sure of the photo op. She kissed me. I didn't kiss her back." He pushed his fingers through his hair, leaving it tousled. "And I didn't call Georgie to tell her to brace for the publicity. By the time I got around to it, she refused to talk to me, then blocked my calls."

"Dammit, Clay." Chance's curse came out as a whisper.

"That's not the worst." His brothers leaned closer. "She refused a mastectomy."

His announcement was met with silence. Chance and Cord exchanged uneasy glances before their gazes refocused on him. Chance pulled him to a chair and pushed him down to sit. A moment later they sank into their own chairs.

"Tell us."

Clay couldn't face them, despite the compassion in Chance's voice. He stared at the tips of his boots, searching for the words. Georgie. She put the words in his mouth. Always. But not this time. He inhaled and held his breath for what seemed like hours, but was only seconds. His lungs burned before he finally let the air out. He still couldn't look at them but his mouth opened and words tumbled out.

"Y'all were so little. Hell, I was only eight. One day Mom was fine and the next, it seemed like she'd faded away to nothing. The old man was never around. You know how he is. Couldn't stand to be around sickness and Mom was. Horribly, terribly sick. The doctors did a lumpectomy because the old man—" His voice broke.

Chance's expression turned harsh. "He told her she wouldn't be a woman if she had a mastectomy, right?"

Clay nodded, unable to voice the affirmative as his rage built. He swallowed around the anger and continued, his voice flat. "She tried everything. Chemo. Radiation. Homeopathic. She went to every crackpot loonytoon who hung out a sign promising a cure. She lost her hair. Her skin was paper thin and every time one of us hugged her, we left bruises."

Clay had to stop speaking, his nose and throat burning with tears he'd never been allowed to shed. Real men didn't cry, right? The gospel according to Cyrus Barron. His brothers waited as Chance placed a quiet hand on Clay's clenched fists and Cord gripped his shoulder. With their added strength, he found a way to continue.

"I brushed her hair until it all fell out. I held her head while she puked her guts up. I begged her not to die. Not to leave me alone with the old man because I swore I'd kill him." He finally glanced up but his brothers' faces swam through a wet prism. "She made me promise to take care of you two. To love you like she couldn't anymore."

"You made sure we got to say goodbye." Cord squeezed his shoulder. "I remember her getting so thin, she looked like she was fading away. And I remember the scarves she wore."

"I remember that hideous wig. Freaked me right the hell out. I thought it was some crazy animal, alive and sitting on Mom's head." Chance lifted one shoulder in a shrug as the corner of his mouth twisted into a wry slash. "Hey, I was only four."

"Man, those scarves. I bought them with my allowance. I wanted to make her smile so I bought the most colorful ones I could lay my hands on." A dry chuckle erupted before Clay could call it back. "They were god-awful."

Chance punched his shoulder lightly. "I thought they

made her look beautiful. But then anything was better than that damn wig." He shuddered—an exaggerated move meant to bring a smile to Clay's face. It worked.

But his smile faded all too soon as reality smacked him upside the head again. "When Georgie told me? I lost it. But I never let on. She needed me. She wanted to come home so we came home."

When he ran his hand through his hair again, it was shaking. "She talked to the doctor alone. I was right there but she didn't call me in for the consult. I found out later from her dad that the doctor recommended a mastectomy. She refused it. Because of me. Because of the campaign, I guess."

"What the hell, Clay?" Cord stared at him.

"She didn't say anything beyond requesting a stop at the pharmacy for her prescriptions. But I didn't push for info. I wanted her with me. Taking pills? That meant she could travel with me. I told myself that chemo's not as bad now as it was back when Mom went through it. I wanted to believe it would work. It didn't. The radiation was harder on her. I watched her get sicker, but I didn't ask. I couldn't deal with it so I built up walls and ignored what was happening. When we were in Pittsburgh, I heard her crying, walked into the bathroom…"

He couldn't say the words, scrubbing his face with the heels of his hands instead. He hated himself, well and truly. "She was holding a hunk of her hair. I sent her home alone because I had the debate." A series of raw cuss words erupted from his mouth. "I'm as big an ass as the old man. I royally screwed up and hurt the woman that is the best part of me."

"Do you love her?"

He wasn't sure which brother asked, not that it mattered. The question was on the tip of both their tongues. He didn't even think about it. "I do. Yes."

Chance pulled out his phone and dialed a number as he stood up and walked across the room. He was the master of hushed conversations. Moments later he turned around. "You need to tell her that, Clay. Boone says she had a treatment this morning. She'll be at her dad's ranch now." When Clay didn't respond, he continued. "I'll call Cassie. We'll go with you."

Staring at his younger brother, Clay wasn't sure he'd heard Chance correctly. "We?"

Cord nodded. "You don't think we'd let you do this alone, do you? Jolie and I are coming, too."

Chance hauled Clay to his feet and hugged him tightly. "Family, Clay. The Barrons might be dysfunctional as hell, but we're learning."

He couldn't speak, the lump in his throat tight and burning. Family. How in hell had his brothers figured it out when he'd been so clueless? He clung to Chance and felt Cord's arms wrap around them both.

"You were there for us, Clay, when we were growing up. You diverted the old man's attention and we owe you for that at the very least. Most of all, you're our brother and we love you. We'll get through this. All of us together."

He blinked back tears and focused on Cord's face. His brother's expression radiated determination. And compassion. What Clay said next was something he'd never voiced aloud. "I love you guys."

"You know he'll come back." Her father sounded both patient and certain. "And you need to talk to him when he does. Georgie, he wasn't with that woman. She was just there. She jumped in and kissed him for the cameras. I'm positive that's the truth." He hunkered down in front of her chair and cupped her cheeks. "You know I love you, right?" At her nod, he continued. "Don't be stubborn like your old dad, Georgie. Don't let your pride stop you from having the love of a lifetime."

Georgie pulled her shoulders up to her ears and hunched deeper into the chair. "It's not like that. He doesn't love me. I can't stand in his way. He's going to be the president. I… His father's right. I wouldn't be a good first lady." Tears gathered on her lashes and she dashed them away with the back of her hand. "I can't face him, Daddy. There's no magic wand to wave to make it all better."

"When did you stop believing in magic, baby girl?"

"When the shadows got so dark I couldn't see any longer."

"Aw, honey."

"Don't, Dad. Just…don't. The doctors say a fifty-fifty chance." A bittersweet smile formed on her face. "Today I feel half-dead."

"Don't say that, Georgeanne. Don't you give up." Her father pushed to his feet and stomped over to stare out the window. "Dang it. I hate this. I hate seein' you weak and pale. You were never sick as a kid. You'd be out there even when the winter wind was cold enough to steal your breath. I'd be out there workin', look up and there you'd be on top of ol' Lucky, movin' the cows to shelter."

He glanced at her over his shoulder. "I remember one time in particular. You came runnin' in the house, your cheeks as red as apples, laughin' and hidin' a snowball behind your back. What happened to that little girl?"

"She grew up, Daddy. Grew up and went away. Do you still love what she left behind?"

"That's a hellava thing to ask me, girl! Of course I love you. I'm your father. No matter what." He grabbed a pillow and punched it a couple of times before gently easing it behind Georgie's back. "Now, you listen to me, baby girl. You're gonna win this fight. And if you had a lick of sense in that way too smart head of yours, you'd call Clayton Barron and tell him to get his ass down here."

"No." Georgie pulled her sweater a little tighter around her shoulders. She was always cold these days. Her chair faced the window. She could see the lake where she'd learned to fish and had gone swimming with her horse on hot summer days. The afternoon sun flared just above the horizon, teasing the water with glittering fingers.

This was why she'd come home. Not to die, but to heal, surrounded by the place that *made* her. She was so scared these days. Afraid of saying goodbye to those she loved. Afraid of living the moments she had left. The look on Clay's face when she'd told him echoed in her dreams, a ghost she could neither touch nor exorcise.

Her dad dropped a kiss on her head. "Rest, baby girl. I love you."

Georgie called after him, her voice just loud enough to be heard over the clomping of his boots. "I love you, too, Daddy."

The glinting path of sunlight pulled her into the dream— the one she always reached for when the pain from the treatments got too bad.

The sun, sinking in the sky, spilled in the window and drenched Clay in shimmering gold. The light made a halo around him she knew he deserved, and he looked incredibly right mantled in the splendor. He was Oklahoma's favorite son, would be president one day soon. She admired him from afar, knowing she could never touch him, never share in the warmth of his golden glow. As she turned to walk away, he called her. And then she was in his sheltering arms, warm and safe. He dipped his head, his firm lips finding hers. She sighed, offering everything she had, everything she was, to him.

The wooden floor creaked and she startled awake. So she thought. A waking dream stood in front of her. Clay, bathed in the copper light of the setting sun. She blinked, then rubbed her eyes.

"I've missed you, sweet pea."

"Why are you here?" She shaded her eyes against the glare. Clay stood there handsome and...perfect.

Clay squatted in front of her. "I'm here because you are, Georgie."

"But...the campaign—"

"Can take place without me for a while."

"You don't mean that."

"Don't put words in my mouth, Georgie. You quit that job, remember?"

She was shocked for a moment, but caught the hint of a smile teasing the side of his mouth. Without considering the consequences, she touched his lips.

When he spoke, his breath teased her fingers. "I'm an idiot and a fool, Georgie. Can you forgive me? I've missed you more than words can say." Clay leaned closer, brushed his lips against hers. "And I love you more than life."

Unsure she'd heard correctly, she demanded, "Say that again."

"I love you, Georgie. Please forgive me. Please love me back. I won't fail you again."

"Is that a campaign promise, Senator?" Her voice was haughty and sarcastic.

"No, Georgeanne Dreyfus, that's a promise from my heart."

Twenty

Clay stayed with Georgie on the ranch, working toward redemption. He took her horseback riding when she felt strong enough. He held her cuddled on his lap in the big chair facing the wide window when she didn't. He kept her warm when her body shook with chills. He kissed her bald head and told her she was more beautiful than that Irish singer from the '80s who'd shaved her head. He told her he loved her. Every chance he got.

He talked to her, using his words, not hers. He opened his heart to her, whispering plans for the future—*their* future. He didn't mention surgery. The decision was hers. He did his best to give her hope and love, and a reason to stay with him. And he bought a ring. On a day between treatments when her color was better, when she held down breakfast, when her eyes weren't dulled with pain, he led her outside to a saddled horse.

Clay mounted, maneuvered to the edge of the porch and pulled her across the saddle in front of him. At a slow walk, they rode out and, after a short circuit of her dad's ranch, Clay guided the horse to the swath of lush grass near the lake. A picnic was set out there, arranged with the help of Cassie and Jolie, who snuck in after he and Georgie left the house. Dismounting carefully, he reached up and gathered her into a princess carry and strode to the blanket stretched across the grass.

The sun edged toward the horizon, the light soft as sunset approached. He offered her cold watermelon. He offered her cheese and crackers. He opened and poured two crystal flutes of sparkling grape juice. Then he positioned himself on one knee and took her hand.

"You know I love you, yeah?" He watched her expression, searching for a flicker of doubt. There was none when she answered.

"Yes. I know. And you know I love you, right?"

Finding he could breathe again, he nodded. "Right." He leaned forward and kissed her, a chaste brush of his lips across hers. They hadn't had sex in weeks and he didn't care. She was too fragile and that was okay. Holding her, sleeping with her in his arms, was even more satisfying than the bells and whistles of climaxes. He finally understood love, understood "for better or worse, in sickness and in health."

She sat with her back to the lake, and the sun kissed the treetops on the other side, even as it painted a gilded path across the water. Georgie was bathed in a golden aura and she'd never looked more beautiful. Holding her hand, he reached into the picnic basket and retrieved a box. With a move he'd practiced until it was flawless, he opened the jewelry box with one hand and hooked the one-carat, emerald-cut diamond solitaire with his index finger.

"I'm not waiting any longer. I want to spend the rest of our lives together. Georgeanne Ruth Dreyfus, will you marry me?"

Georgie stared, tears glittering like the sun dancing on the placid water behind her. She whispered one word and the breath he'd been holding rushed out.

"Yes."

He gathered her into his arms, kissed her with gentle lips that turned demanding, his tongue seeking hers, his hands careful, but clear in their declaration of how much he desired her.

"Thank you, sweet pea."

Clay didn't leave her often, but his numbers were falling. She fretted. Georgie believed in him, was convinced he'd be the next president. And she forced him back on the campaign trail with an argument—started by her—that left her exhausted. He didn't like being apart, scared he was missing minutes and seconds with her that he'd never get back. He shared those fears with Cord and Chance, with Boone and Hunt. He lay awake, terrified he'd get a call saying he'd missed it all.

He argued with the old man. He brooded. And he replayed Georgie's parting words over and over.

Don't you get it? This is bigger than me. Than you. Than us. This is the whole country, Clay. They need you. You can fix it. You can make it better just like you fixed my heart and made me whole.

So here he was in St. Louis, staring at his reflection in a makeup mirror. Georgie's words weren't the only ones he heard.

When it comes time for the acceptance speech at the party's convention, it better be you givin' it, boy.

His father's words remained scorched in his memory. The makeup girl babbled about his perfect hair, perfect face, perfect everything, until he wanted to growl and jerk away. He didn't need to look at the text on his phone, that message also seared into his psyche. Leave it to his sister-in-law to get right to the point.

The girl reached to comb his hair and he snagged her wrist. "Enough. You're done." She sputtered, but left him alone in the dressing room. Unable to help himself, he reread Cassie's text.

Georgie scheduled for surgery tomorrow morning. It better be you sitting beside her bed when she wakes up.

Surgery. He knew what that meant. Chemo and radiation had failed. The doctor had finally talked sense into Georgie. But she hadn't told him. He swallowed the anger. Georgie should have told him. He knew what she was doing—trying to protect him, protect the campaign. But she should have told him to come because nothing was more important than her.

Dammit, this was the last-ditch effort to save Georgie's life. She'd all but shoved him away, refused to talk to him about her treatment. Not that he could blame her. After what his old man said about her, knowing about his own experience with his mother, she had every right to be skittish, despite the fact she wore his engagement ring.

He had a speech to give—an important speech that would make or break him before the convention. But his heart wasn't in it. His heart wasn't even in the same building. It was with the woman he loved who was facing surgery without him because she was protecting his damn political career.

Clay stared out over the sea of faces, those beyond the first few rows nothing but blurry smudges in the darkened auditorium. Out of habit, he glanced into the wings but the figure he sought was no longer there because she was alone in Oklahoma facing a life-changing event. Inhaling, he continued the speech, saying the words Georgie had written for him.

"I met a man the other day, a man who served this country in three wars, a man who wasn't shy about his opinion. 'You know what I think, son?' he asked. 'No, sir, but I'd like to,' I replied. 'I'll tell ya what's wrong with the government. It's politicians. We got too many of 'em. We don't need any more of them durn politicians. What we need is more legislators. Folks who understand why they've got them fancy desks up there in the Capitol. We need smart folks workin' for the people. Not the people working for all them politicians. Here's the thing, son. Us folks out here in the vast middle of the country? We ain't got time for jawin' and fancy words. We're plain-speakin'. You gotta say what you mean and mean what you say—'"

Clay glanced down at the cards on the podium. He never used a teleprompter when Georgie wrote his speeches, as she had this one, but those last words struck him dumb. Damn but he missed her. He stared out across the audience and then glanced once more to the wings of the stage. No shadowy figure stood there mouthing the words with him. No Georgie. And there might not be a Georgie after tomorrow.

He had to breathe around the ache in his chest and he realized he'd been silent long enough that the crowd was growing restless. Clearing his throat to swallow the lump that had formed there, he continued.

"Some time ago, someone important to me was faced with a decision. She didn't consult me. She didn't ask my opinion. She made a choice and when I found out, her decision was one I didn't like. Now it's my turn to make a decision. It might be one she doesn't like, but it's the right one for me. For her. For us."

Furtive activity at the edge of the stage drew his attention. Boone stood there, hands shoved in his front pockets, watching with a slightly twisted grin on his face. It was the man and woman—the hacks hired by Cyrus to replace Georgie—who were waving frantically to get his attention. He ignored them and turned back to the audience.

"Thank you for coming and good night." Clay swiveled on his heel and headed for Boone. By the time he'd crossed the stage, Hunt was standing there, as well.

"Where to, boss?"

Clay studied his security chief for a long moment. "Where is she?"

Hunt deferred to his brother. Boone tucked his chin in a short nod of approval as he answered, "OU Med. They checked her in tonight."

"Then that's where we're going."

Thing One and Thing Two swarmed him.

"You can't!" From her.

"You didn't finish that travesty of a speech." From him.

Clay almost laughed when Hunt caught his left elbow and Boone snagged his right arm and blocked the two from reaching him. Hunt had his phone up to his ear issuing quiet orders into it. One of the organizers came puffing up.

"Senator Barron? Is there a problem, sir?" The man wasn't quite wringing his hands, unlike the Twit Twins.

"A family emergency."

"Oh. Oh! Your fiancée. Of course. I'm sorry. Is there anything I can do?"

Get out of my way for starters, Clay thought. Rather than voicing it, he smiled but kept walking. "We have it under control, thank you. Perhaps you could draft someone to fill the rest of the time set aside for my keynote?"

"Oh! Yes, yes, of course. I should do that." The man peeled away and huffed back the way they'd come.

As they reached the SUV idling at the side entrance, Clay turned to the two handlers. They'd fussed and dive-bombed him like mockingbirds with a cat in sight of their nest the whole way. "I've wanted to say this since the day you first appeared in my office. You're fired."

Clay, wearing exhaustion like a wrinkled suit, sat next to the hospital bed watching the woman he loved beyond reason. Her skin, paper-thin and translucent, felt like dry silk beneath the one finger he used to caress her arm. Georgie opened her eyes and when they widened in sleepy surprise, he smiled.

"Hello, sweet pea."

"Clay?"

"Yeah?"

"Are you really here?"

"Oh, yeah, love. I'm really here. Not going anywhere."

"But…you can't be here."

His brow knit as he stared at her. "I'm here. There's no *can't* about it."

"But…your speech."

"Given."

"You're supposed to be on your way to Denver."

"Nope. I'm supposed to be right here."

"Clay!"

"Georgie."

Color suffused her pale cheeks and the readout of her blood pressure on the machine next to her bed spiked.

"The campaign!"

"Is over."

Her mouth gaped open. She closed it. It gaped again. She breathed a shocked question. "What?"

"I'm done."

"But the polls—"

"Don't mean jack." He carefully took her hand. "I'm out, Georgie. I'm not running."

She blinked, eyes going wide. "You can't do that."

"I can and did."

"But—"

"Shush, Georgie."

"But—"

He leaned in and kissed her before she could finish speaking. He spoke against her lips. "No buts. Just listen, okay?"

When she nodded and whispered, "Okay," he straightened. "You've always been my heart, Georgie. And your words? Your words make me want to be the man you think I am. I haven't been that man lately, but I'm going to be."

"Clay—"

"Shhh. I'm talking, sweet pea." He lifted the hand he was holding and brought it to his lips for a kiss. "As president, I have eight years. *Only* eight years. I can do a lot of good, but the next person who steps in behind me can undo everything I've put into place."

He paused, gathering his thoughts. "Your words last night, they hit home and made sense. Do you remember the words you gave me to say?"

Her expression morphed into one of confusion so he quoted the words back to her. "I'll tell ya what's wrong with the government. It's politicians. We got too many of 'em. We don't need any more of them durn politicians. What we need is more legislators. Folks who understand why they've got them fancy desks up there in the Capitol. We need smart folks workin' for the people. Not the people working for all them politicians. Remember now?"

At her nod, he continued. "You're right. I don't want to be a politician. I want to be a legislator. I can't do that as president. I can by staying in the Senate. So that's what I'm doing—staying in the Senate."

His thumb brushed the tear trickling down her cheek before he kissed her. "I love you, Georgie Dreyfus, with everything I have. With everything I am. I want to make you proud."

"You do. Every day of my life, Clayton Barron. You do."

Georgie was coming home today. Clay could barely contain himself. He hated hospitals. Hated the sounds and the smells and sadness that permeated the very air. He waited outside her room while a nurse performed a final check of Georgie's vitals and changed bandages. He'd already participated in that routine, and had been schooled in all things aftercare.

Finished, the nurse slipped out, offering him a smile and an arm squeeze as she passed. "Take care of our girl," she murmured.

"Always."

He walked into the room. Georgie couldn't get dressed until the final consult with the surgeon. Jolie had packed clothes for her, but Clay had his own ideas. He set the box he'd brought in her lap as he bent to kiss her.

"Can't wait to have you home, sweet pea."

Georgie stared at the box before raising her eyes to his. "Open it, love."

Her fingers trembled, rustling the tissue paper filling the gold-foil box. Her throat worked, contracting as she swallowed. Her gaze barely lingered after colliding with his.

Clay attempted to speak, but the words came out mangled, his voice a rusty saw on metal pipe. He cleared his throat, spoke again. "Georgie? What's wrong?" His insides twisted as he second-guessed the gift. Maybe it was too soon. Or too much. Or maybe he was the world's biggest idiot. "Sweet pea?"

Her fingers again fussed with the tissue, her shoulders slumping as her chin tucked against her chest. "Why did you buy this?"

Her question was whispered from between chapped lips, and he was torn between kissing her or passing her the water glass with the bent straw. "Because I wanted you to have it."

"But it's red lingerie." She looked up, her eyes holding some emotion he wasn't sure he wanted to identify.

"You were wearing red lingerie in my bathroom in Scottsdale. And you wore red lingerie the first time we made love." He cupped her cheek in his hand. "Red is your color."

Her tears caught Clay by surprise. He settled next to her on the hospital bed, gathering her close. Brushing them away with a gentle swipe of his thumb, he kissed her forehead. "You're beautiful, Georgie, and I love seeing you in sexy lingerie."

She pushed against him ineffectually and the scarf on

her bald head slipped off. "No, I'm not. I'm not beautiful. I'm not sexy."

"Look at me, sweet pea. You will always be beautiful to me because I love you."

"Even sick?" She flicked a hand toward her bandaged chest. "Even without these?"

"You're alive. That's all that matters." He kissed her then, deep and sweet, to prove his point. That she was alive and that he loved her. Always.

Epilogue

Georgie floated down the gentle slope on her father's arm. Clay waited for her at the base of the golden path across the placid lake that led to the setting sun. His family waited with him—his cousin Boone and his brothers Cord, Chance, Chase and Cash. His nephew CJ, clutching a satin pillow with their wedding bands tied to it, stood on his right. Opposite them, her best friend and maid of honor, Jen, and her soon-to-be sisters Cassie and Jolie smiled at her.

Clay's father was notably absent. Her mother was notably not, standing on the left in her designer mother-of-the-bride dress. Ev and her husband were there, as were other friends, including Miriam Davis, the reporter from the *Washington Post*. The Tate brothers surrounded their mother. Deacon Tate stood at the back of the congregation, strumming an acoustic guitar, the song soft and romantic and perfect.

Clay stepped forward to meet her, accepted her hand when her father took it from the crook of his arm as he kissed her cheek. "I love you, baby," her dad murmured. "Take care of my little girl, Clayton."

"Always." No hesitation. No regret. The word filled with the promise of the rest of their lives. The news from her doctor, received that morning, guaranteed the future. Cancer-free. Follow-ups, but she was clear of the disease.

The ceremony was traditional. Clay's eyes were warm and moist as he said the words, "For better, for worse, in sickness and in health, to love and to cherish until death do us part."

She added her own promise to his.

When the minister pronounced them man and wife, Clay kissed her, deeply, thoroughly and with tongue before scooping her into his arms, still kissing her, much to the amusement of their audience. He didn't put her down but carried her up the hill to the backyard of her dad's house. The caterers had been busy.

Photographs. Hugs. Kisses. Well-wishes. Toasts. Cake. More toasts. And then she was in Clay's arms as Deacon and the Sons of Nashville sang Clint Black's "When I Said I Do" for their first dance. Clay held her close and moved with the music while she let the words wash over her. This wasn't the song she'd picked, but it was perfect.

Clay twirled her out and reeled her in only to bend her into a dip. He kissed her arched throat and whispered, "Are you wearing it?"

She blushed but nodded, thinking about the bridal tradition. She wore her grandmother's pearls for her something old. The blue satin ribbon garter on her right thigh got the color right. She even had a real sixpence in one of the white cowgirl boots she'd borrowed from Cassie. Clay, however, was not referring to any of those things.

"Yes," she sighed before her breath caught at the sexy glints in his eyes. Clay owned her heart.

Beneath the silk organza and lace of her full-skirted wedding gown, she wore a red satin bustier and panties—the same lingerie he'd gifted her with that day in the hospital. She hadn't worn the ensemble until she slipped into it that afternoon as she dressed for their wedding. She'd saved it for the moment he'd hold her in his arms, when he kissed her and made love to her for the first time as man and wife. This was her something new—the promise of the new life he'd given her there in her hospital room.

"Good," he murmured against her lips. "Red is definitely your color."

* * * * *

MILLS & BOON®

Desire™

PASSIONATE AND DRAMATIC LOVE STORIES

A sneak peek at next month's titles...

In stores from 2nd June 2016:

The Baby Inheritance – Maureen Child *and*
Expecting the Rancher's Child – Sara Orwig

A Little Surprise for the Boss – Elizabeth Lane *and*
Saying Yes to the Boss – Andrea Laurence

His Stolen Bride – Barbara Dunlop *and*
The Renegade Returns – Dani Wade

Available at WHSmith, Tesco, Asda, Eason, Amazon and Apple

Just can't wait?
Buy our books online a month before they hit the shops!
visit www.millsandboon.co.uk

These books are also available in eBook format!

Lynne Graham has sold 35 million books!

To settle a debt, she'll have to become his mistress…

Nikolai Drakos is determined to have his revenge against the man who destroyed his sister. So stealing his enemy's intended fiancé seems like the perfect solution! Until Nikolai discovers that woman is Ella Davies…

Read on for a tantalising excerpt from Lynne Graham's 100th book,

BOUGHT FOR THE GREEK'S REVENGE

'Mistress,' Nikolai slotted in cool as ice.

Shock had welded Ella's tongue to the roof of her mouth because he was sexually propositioning her and nothing could have prepared her for that. She wasn't drop-dead gorgeous… *he* was! Male heads didn't swivel when Ella walked down the street because she had neither the length of leg nor the curves usually deemed necessary to attract such attention. Why on earth could he be making *her* such an offer?

'But we don't even know each other,' she framed dazedly. 'You're a stranger…'

'If you live with me I won't be a stranger for long,' Nikolai pointed out with monumental calm. And the very sound of that inhuman calm and cool forced her to flip round and settle distraught eyes on his lean darkly handsome face.

'You can't be serious about this!'

'I assure you that I am deadly serious. Move in and I'll forget your family's debts.'

'But it's a *crazy* idea!' she gasped.

'It's not crazy to me,' Nikolai asserted. 'When I want anything, I go after it hard and fast.'

Her lashes dipped. Did he want her like that? Enough to track her down, buy up her father's debts, and try and buy rights to her and her body along with those debts? The very idea of that made her dizzy and plunged her brain into even greater turmoil. 'It's immoral… it's blackmail.'

'It's definitely *not* blackmail. I'm giving you the benefit of a choice you didn't have before I came through that door,' Nikolai Drakos fielded with a glittering cool. 'That choice is yours to make.'

'Like hell it is!' Ella fired back. 'It's a complete cheat of a supposed offer!'

Nikolai sent her a gleaming sideways glance. 'No the real cheat was you kissing me the way you did last year and then saying no and acting as if I had grossly insulted you,' he murmured with lethal quietness.

'You *did* insult me!' Ella flung back, her cheeks hot as fire while she wondered if her refusal that night had started off his whole chain reaction. What else could possibly be driving him?

Nikolai straightened lazily as he opened the door. 'If you take offence that easily, maybe it's just as well that the answer is no.'

Visit **www.millsandboon.co.uk/lynnegraham**
to order yours!

MILLS & BOON®

MILLS & BOON®

The One Summer Collection!

2 free books!

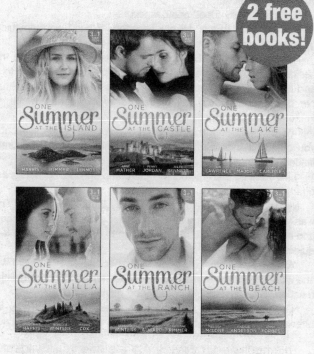

Join these heroines on a relaxing
holiday escape, where a summer fling
could turn in to so much more!

Order yours at **www.millsandboon.co.uk/onesummer**

0616_MB523_OSA

MILLS & BOON®

Mills & Boon have been at the heart of romance since 1908... and while the fashions may have changed, one thing remains the same: from pulse-pounding passion to the gentlest caress, we're always known how to bring romance alive.

Now, we're delighted to present you with these irresistible illustrations, inspired by the vintage glamour of our covers. So indulge your wildest dreams and unleash your imagination as we present the most iconic Mills & Boon moments of the last century.

Visit **www.millsandboon.co.uk/ArtofRomance** to order yours!

16_AOR

